The Hidden Road

The Hidden Road

Published by The Conrad Press Ltd. in the United Kingdom 2022

Tel: +44(0)1227 472 874
www.theconradpress.com
info@theconradpress.com

ISBN 978-1-914913-79-2

Printed and bound in Great Britain by Clays Ltd, Elcograf S.p.A

Typesetting and Cover Design by The Book Typesetters
www.thebooktypesetters.com

The Conrad Press logo was designed by Maria Priestley.

The Hidden Road

ANDREW TAMWORTH

For Martyn
Best Wishes

Andrew Tamworth

For Sue

Life isn't about finding yourself.
Life is about creating yourself.

George Bernard Shaw

Memory says 'I did that.'
Pride replies 'I could not have done that.'
Eventually memory yields.

Friedrich Nietzsche

Prologue

1982

It's stiflingly hot in here, yet I can't stop shaking. An icy dread has seized me. From the moment I stormed out of the camp it hasn't let go, creeping into every corner of my psyche: tormenting, recriminating, paralysing.

I've only been in here a few hours, but already I know every inch of it: the pitted-concrete floor; the stark strip lights; the crudely whitewashed, graffiti-plastered walls and the reinforced-steel door, pockmarked from a lifetime of angry fists and boots. On the far wall a duct oozes stagnant hot air. High up in the corner a tiny frosted window admits a measly ration of sunlight, just enough to imprint a silhouette of crossed bars onto the opposite wall.

I've barely moved since they slammed the door shut. I'm hunched over in the corner, on the steel bench that doubles as a bed, just staring at the floor, as if my eyes can burn a hole in it, as if I can somehow make this stupid mess go away. My feet are pounding some frenetic beat that I'm powerless to stop, but there's no going back from here: I've made my choices, it's too late to change them now. It's time to face up to what I've done. I knew that when I came back. Now all I can do is wait.

Sat here, I can feel the ghosts of the past all around me. How can I avoid them? They scream at me from their angry, defiant scratch marks: *Anarchy in the UK, Farnham Skins, CFC Headhunters, NF* and, the one that makes me really laugh: *Fuck off Paki's*.

The ignorant fucker who wrote that last one probably never even realised that he'd changed the whole meaning of his vile bigotry with that misplaced apostrophe.

It's not quite right though. I need to change it, but that copper took anything that could have had a point on it, right down to my belt buckle and Dad's watch. Then, I remember the stud in my left ear; my hair's long enough now that he didn't notice it.

I pause for a second to make sure no one's watching. Then, I pull it out and scratch at the wall until there's a colon after the second word. Now it reads *Fuck off: Paki's*. That's better. Now it implies that the wall belongs to Paki and that everyone *else* should fuck off.

There's not much to laugh about in here so I allow myself a moment of smug triumph. I'm with Paki; we'd get on just fine I reckon.

I wonder if Steen was ever here. He could have scratched any one of those pieces of filth. I can smell him and his mates, right in there with the stench of piss and disinfectant. I clench my fists, grit my teeth: I've been pussyfooting around this for too long. Steen got his just reward. Everything that's happened has been his fault.

Occasionally I hear noises: shouts from other cells, fists banging against doors, keys clanking, urgent footsteps pounding the concrete. Each time I hear those steps my stomach hollows out. This time they're coming for me. Each time I'm reprieved.

How long will I be cooped up like this? I panic when I think about it: this wasn't what I'd expected. Maybe they've forgotten I'm here? More likely they're trying to frighten me, while they gather up the evidence, build up their case so they can throw the book at me. Put me away for good.

Part I

UPHEAVAL

Chapter 1

The summer of '81

I wake on my mattress in the top-floor storeroom, the dawn sunlight streaming through the grimy un-curtained windows. The room is unforgiving in this light. I take in the broken, battered ceiling panels, the cobwebs that lurk in every corner, the rough floorboards and the towering racks that are crammed with misshapen cardboard boxes.

It's A-Level Results Day. That was my waking thought, before I'd even opened my eyes. Thursday the twenty-first of August: the date I've been carrying around with me all through this long hot summer, like some stupid ass with a carrot on the end of a stick. Now it's here I don't even want the bloody carrot.

I've tried to pretend that today isn't happening, but it's been niggling away at me. Judgment will be passed and I've not been able to move on until it's done. Somehow, I've conned myself into believing that the results will change everything: as if my future will suddenly become clear, a path laid out neatly in front of me, my bags all packed and ready to go.

Some of the other kids are just like that. I didn't notice at first. Then I overheard them talking about universities and the grades they needed to get in. It never occurred to me to apply to a university: nobody ever spoke to *me* about it, so why would it?

They'll be putting the results up on the board at the college at about ten. I should go up there and get them, even if all the others will be there too: gawping at the board, gawping at each other, gawping at me. They'll be oozing false sincerity with their plastic smiles and their wooden embraces.

'Fuck off,' I'll want to shout. 'You bunch of pretentious wankers.'

Instead I'll just mumble something incoherent and scuttle off. If I do go I just want to smash-and-grab my results – get in and out with no fuss, without anyone noticing.

For now, I just lie back and look around. I ought to give the place a clean at some point; maybe I'll have a chat with Ron about it later. This place has been home for over a month now and the grime and decrepitude are less important than my newfound freedom and solitude.

Ron owns the hardware shop downstairs and I've worked on and off for him for a couple of years: humping boxes up and down, serving customers, helping him with stock checks and invoices. I started out doing Saturdays, but when I finished my A levels he asked me if I wanted to do a few more days and I've taken as much as I could get.

Best of all, was the chance to stay up here. I bit his hand

off when he offered. Finally, I had my chance to move out from Estha and Jim's. I counted down the days to getting away from them: the last-of-the-foster-carers.

When I told them I'd got a job with a flat they didn't want to know any more; they just became matter-of-fact about moving out dates and fixing up meetings with the Social.

I can't say I'm missing my meetings with those scum. When we last met I just spun my social worker a yarn, telling her how calm and happy I was, pressing all her buttons. 'Shirley from the Social' I call her. Oh, I'd sussed her out all right. She nodded her head reassuringly, ticked boxes on her forms and then wished me well. That was it: with a handshake I was free.

Nobody knows that I'm here other than the Social. And Uncle Harry of course. I sent a card to his flat in Putney. He's touring with his band right now, but he'll get it soon enough.

This is *my* space and I don't want anyone else here. OK, I probably wouldn't kick Melissa out, but that's not exactly likely to happen: I doubt she even knows my name, even though we've been in the same classes for the last two years.

I'm wide-awake now. Today's not a day for lazing around in bed so I throw back the sheet and leap to my feet. Standing on the mattress and stretching my arms up I can just touch the ceiling panel with my fingertips. Rising onto my toes, I feel the resistance and then the pop as the panel starts to lift. It's a satisfying morning ritual, but, as always at this moment, I remember there are no curtains. I laugh:

the neighbours on the other side of West Street can all stare in at my hairy arse and the full glory of my morning erection. Lucky the windows are so filthy, ha-ha.

I head to the bathroom. I've decided: I will go up to the College. I'll just slip quietly in and out. Melissa might be there, so I'd better shave and wash my hair: not that she's going to notice me today for the first time, but I ought to make the effort, just in case.

First, I go to the tape deck and load up some Jam. A day like this has to start with Paul Weller. I pound the opening chords of *Going Underground* on the table and chant along. I know the lyrics off by heart and Weller always hits the spot. I saw them play live at Guildford Civic last month. What a gig that was. The place went mad when they played *Going Underground* as their encore.

I head into the bathroom and squat down in the chipped enamel bath. I fill a jug with warm water and pour it over my head, briskly lathering up some shampoo then cursing as it gets in my eyes. I pour more over my body and rub the soap all over.

Next, I'm up by the sink looking into the cheap plastic mirror that hangs precariously above it. It's got a diagonal crack that runs down my left cheek like a scar. I've got a real scar too: a couple of inches long, just over my left eyebrow. That's courtesy of Dominic Steen.

Steen's a hard-core skinhead and always hangs around with a couple of mates who are just as bad. They're racist scum: stupid, ignorant and dangerous. Steen and I were in the same foster home when I was about fourteen and he took an instant dislike to me. He's picked on me ever since, taking a demented pleasure in belittling me at every opportunity: bombarding me with insults, demanding money and cigarettes and hitting me if I don't comply. I thought I'd seen the back of him when I left school and went up to the sixth form, but then he showed up early in the first term.

I don't even know what he was doing there; he never seemed to go to any classes. I resolved not to give in to him any more and, when he first tried it on at the college, I told him where to go.

That was a big mistake. Before I'd even had the chance to defend myself he caught me with a right hook and then I was on the floor being punched and kicked. I only got off as lightly as I did because there were other people around.

I'm still haunted by the fury on his face as he lay into me, but for now I shut it out and focus on shaving. I can just about do a full beard, but I've only got a few days of growth now and it looks like bum-fluff. I fill the sink and lather up the foam on my face. Its brilliant white clashes with the black of my hair, which sits flat and streaky against my head. My cheekbones stand out like ridges against the lumpy foam, making my thin nose seem bigger and thickening and reddening my lips.

I look myself in the eyes: the grey-blue that 'Shirley from the Social' says change colour in the light. I contort my expression into a mock glare.

'What you lookin' at?' I snarl, thrusting the razor at myself in the mirror.

'Ha-ha,' my reflection replies, pirate style. 'I'm gonna carve that fluff right off, yer gobshite'.

17

Then I become focused and with slow, firm trawls, starting with my cheeks and upper jaw, I scrape off the foam, rinsing each time in the sink, as raw skin emerges beneath. I feel in control now. If I concentrate I might even get away without cutting myself. I love the slow transformation of a shave, the few moments of self-communion, like I'm noticing myself, recognising myself. It calms me, boosts me, filling me with a quiet resolve and energy.

Draining the sink, I splash my face with cold water, then slap on some of the aftershave that Uncle Harry gave me. It stings in an invigorating way.

'Seals the skin after you've shaved, Marko' he said. 'And it don't smell too poncy neither.'

I study my reflection a final time. I'm looking pale and gaunt without the stubble on my face. The gold stud in my left ear catches the light, giving some relief. I tousle my hair. I like it a bit unruly, which it does without much encouragement, but not when it juts out at funny angles over my ears and randomly straight up. I flatten and ruffle, flatten and ruffle, until its all heading in roughly the same direction.

I look down at my long neck and bony shoulders, at my chest with just the faintest definition in the pecs, at Mum's St Christopher that nestles amid a few sprouts of wiry black hair. I admire the tattoos on either arm. I've had them both done in the last year. On my right arm is Howlin' Wolf, hunched over, blowing into his harmonica; on my left is a gravestone surrounded by wild flowers, imprinted: *Mum & Dad & Charlie RIP*.

I look at it for a few seconds, my face twitching slightly.

The three of them died in a car crash a few days before my eleventh birthday. They'd been out buying me a bicycle as a surprise birthday present. Some surprise.

I haven't moved for a few seconds, but then abruptly I break myself out of my trance. I raise my fists in boxer style, as if to stay *enough pussying around*, and, after landing a couple of fake blows, I turn for the kitchen.

I put on a fresh pair of jockeys, my black jeans and my grey Joy Division T-shirt. I might put a shirt over the top before I go out. Then, I fill the kettle and put a couple of slices of toast down for my breakfast.

On the far side of the room, pushed against the wall, there's a table and a couple of chairs. As I'm waiting for the toast I change the tape, to a Bowie compilation, and clear away some of the mess from last night. I throw a couple of beer cans into the bin, empty the ashtray and tidy up some of the tapes that I'd left scattered over the table.

My harmonica, or harp as I prefer to call it, is sat where I left it. I pick it up and blow out some notes in time with Bowie's *The Jean Genie*. It was one of Uncle Harry's gifts. He always seems to come up trumps: even when he turns up a month late and I think he's forgotten about me and my birthday, but this was the best of all. Regardless of whether Bob Dylan ever played it, as he told me, it's become a part of me: usually sitting in my shirt pocket so I can pull it out in a second.

Just breathing into it, I feel like I can pour out anything: things I can't put into words, things I don't know how to deal with, things I didn't even know I was feeling. In

19

amongst them are dark, angry, dangerous thoughts; sad, lonely thoughts; sometimes, even moments of joy and elation. I launch them out into the world so they're no longer stuck inside me. And somehow, when I hear them echo back at me, they seem lighter and it all makes more sense.

Uncle Harry was Dad's younger brother. You couldn't imagine two brothers less alike, polar opposites even. Dad was an accountant, taking the train to an office every day with his newspaper and carefully wrapped sandwiches; Uncle Harry played lead guitar in a blues band, living hand-to-mouth, spending months on the road touring and then returning to beg Dad for a loan.

After the accident, Uncle Harry was my only living relative, so I went to stay with him. He managed it for a few months, largely by palming me off on a series of girlfriends, but then, just after school had finished for the summer, he sat me down and told me that he was going on a US tour with the band and that he'd arranged for some foster carers to look after me.

'I'm a rolling stone, Marko. Sorry.'

'I wanna come with you,' I shouted.

But that was never going to happen: an eleven-year-old boy on the road with four ragged bluesmen and whatever groupies they persuaded to tag along.

'I'll be back,' he said.

And he was true to his word, but they are always fleeting visits that shake me up with the excitement of his presence and his stories and then dump me back into crushing isolation. I want to hate him for it, but I can't. His visits have

been one of the few beacons of hope and belonging that I've had and I've clung to that idea with all my might.

When he was last here in March he had his guitar with him and he started playing some old blues for me. I love listening to him play. The notes and feelings he can coax out of that guitar are amazing. This time I picked up my harp and joined in. We fed off each other for ages: him leading, me following. Then he softened it, closing his eyes to hear me play, before picking up on some lick I'd blown out and taking it on into another dimension.

'That was cool, Marko. You can really play that thing,' he said afterwards. 'I'll have to get you up on the stage with the band sometime.'

I was buzzing for days after that, but then he was off again. I got a card from him in June from Chicago that just said, in his huge loopy scrawl: 'Good luck with the "A"s, Marko. I'll be around in the Fall for some Jamming!'

The card's pinned to the wall, a grainy black and white photo of Howlin' Wolf playing his harp back in the sixties, the same one that's now inked onto my right arm.

My Swiss army knife was another of his gifts. It usually sits in my right-hand jeans pocket, even if I kept it hidden from my last foster carers. They were the kind who'd have confiscated it if they'd known. It feels empowering sat in my pocket: smooth and solid and functional. Its deep red casing is the one bit of colour I allow myself, otherwise it's blacks and greys and dark khaki green.

My most prized possessions, though, are the few of Mum and Dad's things that I've kept. Dad's leather wallet sits in my left jeans' pocket. To me it still smells of him and, if I close my eyes and hold it to my nose, its rich earth-iness becomes his tobacco smoke and his aftershave and the feeling of the bristles of his moustache.

Even more of a connection, is his Omega watch. I only take off when I have to. The cool stainless steel, encircling my wrist, and the smooth movement of the second hand, never deviating, make me feel connected to his life force: as if it's still driving me; as if his blood is coursing through me.

Then there's Mum's St Christopher. I don't think I've ever taken it off, which is crazy because I don't even believe in God, but it feels cool and reassuring against my skin, as though her arms are around me, soft and comforting. When I focus on it, I can feel her presence as if she's right here beside me saying: 'Everything will be all right, Marko.'

I'd never admit this to anyone, but I still need that feeling. It's my secret shame, like I'm five years old again and still needing to hug a teddy bear. When did I last touch someone? I can't even remember. Sometimes I need that so much it hurts.

That's about the only time I can see her now, other than when I look at the photos in my box of papers. My favour-ite is the one taken of the four of us in the back garden when I was ten: the summer before the accident. Who took that picture? I wish I could remember. I don't think Uncle Harry was there so it must have been one of our neigh-bours. It's one of those photos that split into three, one large and two small, and I've cut off one of the smaller ones to keep in my wallet.

Mum's crouching down with one hand protectively on Charlie's shoulder, the other around my waist. Dad stands, slightly awkwardly behind us, pipe in his mouth as always, with a faraway look in his eyes. I always wonder where his mind went on those occasions, struggle to deal with the difference in perspective: how I viewed him then and how I see him in the picture now.

My brother Charlie must have been eight. He's beaming at the camera with crooked, gappy teeth, eyes gazing expectantly up from beneath a mass of blonde, unruly hair that bulges outwards at the ears. I always cringe that our hair is exactly the same, except Charlie's was blonde and mine black. He'd be sixteen now. I can't believe it, because he's frozen at eight in my mind: innocent and carefree, following me around, always ready to be the supporting act in my games. I was cruel to him sometimes and I hate myself for it.

I sit here in this room at night times, the bare bulb casting stark shadows, music turned up loud and reading voraciously. Sometimes I have a can and a fag going as well. I ingest them all in the same frenetic way, greedily sucking in the ale and the smoke and the words. Occasionally I stop: to contemplate something I've just read, to belch out the gas from the beer, to chant out the words to a song or blast along on the harp. Then I'll lean back on my chair and blow out a smoke ring, watching it as it drifts upwards, twisting and morphing, imagining it as the words that I've read, taking on new shapes and meanings as it merges into the world.

Then I'm off again. I read fast (newspapers, novels, poetry, politics, history, biographies, anything really) in a race to fill my mind with knowledge and understanding: burning every word into me as if I can't be whole until everything fits together.

I've got an hour before I need to start thinking about heading up to the college, so I take my time over my tea and toast. Last night I almost finished George Orwell's *Road to Wigan Pier*. I saved the last short chapter for this morning and I finish it now as I'm drinking my tea. The last line has me chuckling. 'We have nothing to lose but our aitches,' he implores: a rallying cry to the downwardly-mobile-with-a-conscience. That thought lifts my spirits. It's about being true to yourself. I'm not going to let anyone push me around or tell me what to do.

To tap into my new spikier mood I've put on *London Calling* by The Clash, but it's pushing on towards ten. I should be heading off. I'll stop in downstairs to see Ron first. He should have my pay packet ready by now. It's already warm out, but I put on an extra shirt anyway, leaving it unbuttoned, rolling it up at the sleeves and slipping my harp into the breast pocket.

Standing outside the front door, I feel a breathless pang of nerves that I hadn't expected. I look out from the top of the rusty metal steps that head down into the delivery area at the back of the shops. I can just about see the top of the college buildings from here, squat and institutional, poking out above the trees on the other side of town.

I gird myself for a second, then stomp decisively down the stairs and round the front to the shop. An old bell tinkles as I walk in through the front door. It's always cool and gloomy in here, whatever the weather outside. Dust particles hang in the sunbeams that do filter in, caught in suspended animation, as if time stands still in here. The usual tang of chemicals and metal hits the back of my throat.

Ron is standing there, in his usual spot behind the till. He's always in the same dark beige overall, covered in greasy stains, shoulders coated in dandruff and hair oil. He's been here so long that he blends into his shop, like a bird or an insect that you don't see unless you look for ages. He's surely a museum piece, I laugh, but he's been good to me and I have a grudging respect for him. A quid-an-hour cash he pays me too, with a tenner a week knocked off for letting me stay upstairs.

'Ah, young Mark. What can I do for you this morning?'

He always calls me *young Mark*, even though most people call me Marko, and he always asks me what he can do for me when I come in for my pay packet, so I play along with his game.

'Thursday's payday: remember, Mr Hicks?' Ron is old school: he likes me to call him Mr Hicks, so I oblige.

'Is it now?' he says, raising an eyebrow as usual. 'Well, let me see …'

He disappears into a backroom and returns with a packet all ready.

'Here you are, young Mark, a good five days this week. I've knocked off your rent and I've paid your NI stamp for you. Now, would you like a cuppa before you go?'

'Thanks, Mr Hicks, but I ought to get off. I'm heading up to the college to pick up my results.'

'I know. I hadn't forgotten. I wanted to wish you well, Mark. And I've been thinking. I never went to university myself, and I don't know too much about it, but I think you could do it, with all that reading you do. You've always got a job here, no matter what your grades, but don't sell yourself short. I will carry on like I've always done. I'll be very happy for you if you can go off to some fancy university and your mum and dad would have been really proud. OK, now buzz off to the college and I'll see you bright and early on Saturday. Right?'

I'm not used to this kind of fuss and I find myself starting to well up.

'Thanks, Mr Hicks,' I say, and I hold up my pay packet in mock salute. 'See you on Saturday.'

Leaving the shop, I stride round the corner into Mead Lane, away from the shops and traffic of West Street, tearing open the envelope as I go. Thirty quid in five-pound notes. I fold them into my wallet. I still had a tenner left from last week, so I'm feeling flush.

I pass the football club and head down towards the river, then cross the meadows, where people walk their dogs, and follow the footpath along the riverbank. It floods here sometimes in the winter, but it's dry and bleached now by this long, dry summer. There's barely a breath of wind and I can feel the temperature starting to rise already.

My stomach is quivering again. Half of me wants to get

up to the college fast, the other to dawdle and delay. I look around. There's not a soul in sight. A silence hangs in the air, broken only by the distant hum of traffic and some builders banging somewhere, as if the world is holding its breath with me.

I think about what Ron just said. I've got no plan for what I will do after I get my results, pass or fail. I never thought about applying to universities. My record in the first year of sixth form was so bad that they almost kicked me out: they didn't have me in mind for Oxbridge, that's for sure.

It was moving in with Estha and Jim, just after I'd done my O-Levels, that did it. I hated it there. They were just board and lodging really: with added *Rules and Regulations*. They'd printed them on laminated sheets and pinned them to every available wall: *no alcohol; no smoking; STRICTLY no drugs; dinner served at six; must be in by ten o'clock on weeknights*. On and on they went, like a prison camp. They never tried to reach out to me like some of the others had. Probably just as well really: I'd have told them to fuck off and then there'd have been trouble.

I went monosyllabic on them instead, taking refuge in my thoughts and my music and books. There were a couple of younger kids there for the last year. They were scared of me for some reason, but we just ignored each other.

Starting at the sixth-form college should have been a fresh start, but I couldn't raise myself for it. My classmates thought I was weird and gave me a wide berth. I used to have days where I didn't speak at all and I started skipping more and more classes.

I was either sat in my room or out walking. I didn't even know where I was going most of the time. I'd walk for hours in all weathers: up through Farnham Park and out the other side, into open countryside on footpaths that went nowhere. At first I didn't care whether anyone noticed, but then I started getting letters from the college. I'd failed two of my mocks and scraped an E in the third and they were threatening expulsion if my attendance didn't improve and I didn't start doing some work.

Even worse, I got called in for a *pep talk* from Shirley at the Social. The doctor put me on anti-depressants. I pretended to take them and binned them on the quiet. A battle raged inside me between fear and anger and self-loathing. I pressed them all down and sleepwalked on.

Something finally clicked in the late spring of 1980. Maybe it started with a visit from Uncle Harry towards the end of May. He took me to watch an Eric Clapton gig at Guildford Civic. Clapton comes from round here and it was a homecoming gig after he'd been on a world tour. It was a cracking night. Uncle Harry seemed to know everyone and they all took me in like I was one of their buddies: buying me beer and laughing at my jokes. I was so entranced by the music, the camaraderie and the beer that for several hours I forgot about everything. I got so drunk that I was throwing up by the end of the gig and I felt like death the next day, but it was worth it.

After a few hundred yards, I cross the little footbridge over the river to The Maltings. It was an old tannery and then a brewery before it was turned into an arts centre. They have

28

good bands playing here sometimes, but mostly it's full of old fogeys sipping tea and pretending to be arty. I head up Red Lion Lane past my favourite pub: The William Cobbett.

I have to give Mr Cobbett some credit too. He came up in our History class towards the end of the first year of A-Levels. He was an unlikely figure to spark a transformation, but something about him baited-my-hook. I went to the library and read a biography and then his famous tract *Rural Rides*. He was born and raised in Farnham, back in the eighteenth century, but what really got me was how he channelled his anger against exploitation, corruption and the plight of the rural poor. He educated himself, followed his instincts and spoke out about injustice regardless of the cost and where it took him. I was gripped: this bloke was right out there. Some of his ideas were crazy, indefensible even, but I loved his energy and his determination and his sheer bloody-mindedness. Who was to say I couldn't do the same?

I stopped skipping classes and followed the history lessons as if through his eyes. From this perspective everything became real. I imagined people being shunted from the countryside to the industrial towns and cities. How must it have felt to live through such momentous times? In amongst the acrid stench of the chimney smoke, I could smell their grief for what they'd left behind, mixed with anger and a wearied acceptance. I could feel how they must have suffered in those factories and slums and their terror at being perpetually one short step from the workhouse and a pauper's grave.

I found books about the French Revolution, the Chartists, the Tolpuddle Martyrs and the Peterloo Massacre. Then I started seeing and hearing things in my other A-level classes that I hadn't expected and finding new ways to relate to them.

I read *Jude the Obscure* by Thomas Hardy. I should have read it months before, but I was catching up. I was so absorbed by it that I turned right back to the start and read it again, fervently hoping that, this time, things would somehow turn out well for Jude and Sue, as if I could turn it around for them out of sheer force of will. Their suffering tortured me, but I empathised with Jude so strongly that I couldn't close the pages on him. He became like a trusted confidante that lived and breathed inside me.

We moved on in English to *Brighton Rock* by Graeme Greene and, for a few weeks, I became obsessed with Pinkie Brown. He merged in my mind with Jimmy Cooper in *Quadrophenia*: a film that blew my mind so much when it came out in 1979 that I went to see it three days in a row and then again at the weekend.

It sounds weird, but I spent last year getting an imaginary team together and my view of the world changed as I absorbed them: seeing things through their eyes. Yossarian from *Catch 22* and Rodion Romanovitch Roskalnikov from *Crime and Punishment* followed. Outsiders, all of them, but together we could be strong. They joined John Peel and my favourite musicians: Paul Weller, David Bowie, Joe Strummer, Ian Curtis, Bono, Bob Dylan and all the others.

I started noticing things I hadn't been aware of before.

And rather than just dismissing them with a surly shrug, as I'd done before, I tried to understand them and link them, to find patterns in them.

Towards the end of the first year at college Mr Dawson, my History teacher, asked me to stay behind after a lesson. I think I'd handed in my first assignment in more than 6 months. I was waiting for a bollocking. And I got one of a sort.

'Mr Oban, how kind of you to finally submit a piece of homework,' he said in his sarcastically formal way.

Then he paused, frowning at me, as if taking me in for the first time. He changed his tone and his voice softened.

'Where did this come from, Mark?' he asked, holding the dog-eared pages of my essay. 'I don't quite know what to say. Let's get the negative out of the way. It's too long and meandering. You wouldn't be able to get all this down in examination conditions. But on the whole I was very impressed. You've taken me by surprise, Mark. There is some excellent, incisive analysis in here and a deep and passionate knowledge of the subject matter that's way ahead of where I thought you were. If you can harness and refine that then you could do well. Keep it up, hey. I'm here if you need help or to talk.'

I think that was the longest one-to-one I'd ever had with any of my teachers. I was embarrassed more than anything. I didn't like drawing attention to myself, didn't know how to react, so I just mumbled my thanks and scuttled out as quick as I could, but that little bit of praise lifted me. It was like somebody had turned a light on and, for the first time I could remember, I saw possibility and potential ahead.

I still couldn't bring myself to mix much in class. Maybe I'd gotten too used to being the weirdo-outsider, but at least I was there and paying attention. And inside my mind was whirring with ideas.

Term was almost over by then, but I carried the momentum on over the summer. I went down to Brighton for a few days after we broke up. Ron lent me an ancient tent and I pitched it on the South Downs somewhere near town. The sea air freed my mind and I imagined Pinkie Brown and Jimmy Cooper as I traced their footsteps along the piers and seafront, drank beer and listened to bands in the pubs off the Lanes.

These thoughts remind me that there was a question in my English exam about character and place. I'd completely forgotten that. I went off on one: about Pinkie and Jimmy and Brighton; about the changing moods of the sea; about the clifftops, the narrow streets off the front and the rusting pier and about how Graham Greene and the Director of Quadrophenia had linked them all, as metaphors, to what was going on in Pinkie and Jimmy's minds. As I walk, I remember how it poured out of me so fast that my pen could barely keep up and my other hand was up in the air calling for more paper.

I was reading a book a day at times, still am, but also newspapers for the first time. I used to read Estha and Jim's *Times* when I could, but they didn't really like it particularly if I got it before them, just after it was delivered. I prefer *The Guardian* anyway, because it challenges everything and there's always an irreverent attitude between the lines that chimes with me. I read it down at the library, which has become my second home.

Politics is my other A-level, but it's only started to get real for me over the last year or so, since I started reading more and opening my eyes to what's happening in the world. It feels like the world's been going mad these last few years. How had I been so blind to it?

At times it's felt like the country, and the world, has been on the edge of a precipice: not sure whether to turn to safety or plunge into the abyss. Sometimes I see brave people like Nelson Mandela and Lech Walesa (they both went straight into my team) and they inspire me with their courage, their visions of a better future and their belief that things can change, but it's never long before reality brings me back down. There may be change in the air, but most of it doesn't feel like change for the better. It feels like everyone is being reined in and pressed down and that the world is spoiling for a fight.

With the Russians still in Afghanistan and Reagan in power in America it's only going to get worse. His words might sound soft and chummy, but you don't have to look much below the surface to understand their menace. Watching how he and Thatcher cosy up to each other makes me want to vomit.

Even here, in sleepy Farnham, the trap that Thatcher and her cronies are setting is obvious: it's sink-or-swim. The poorest and the weakest in society are being sucked under and life jackets are just some namby-pamby indulgence that will stop them from helping themselves.

Unemployment is rising by the day and the unions aren't going to take it lying down. Even as early as last spring there were riots in Bristol. This summer it's been kicking off everywhere: Brixton, Peckham, Southall, Toxteth, Moss Side, Handsworth, even Aldershot. I predicted as much in my Politics exam: said that it would be: 'the inevitable outcome of the government's economic and social policies'. I got that right, at least.

As I walk away from the river and up towards the College, I imagine a mob rampaging through Farnham looting the shops and restaurants of West Street. The houses are bigger as I head up the hill, away from the town centre, and I imagine anxious faces twitching behind their net curtains as the smoke and the noise drifts up. I'm not sure if I'm excited by that or frightened. Yeah, bring it on: it would liven things up a bit round here, that's for sure.

I've got to the end of the short lane that leads to the college. The walk's passed in a blur. I do that sometimes: get so focused on something that everything else disappears, find my mind drifting off onto a different plane, losing track of what's going on around me.

It was like that in my exams. I disappeared into a bubble, as if my chair and desk were floating in some parallel universe separate from everything and everyone else. At the end of each exam it was a surprise to find that there were a hundred or so others around me. Then I looked down at page after page of my scruffy, tightly spaced scrawl. Where had all of that come from? It felt like someone else had written it, as if I had detached from my own body for three hours.

I had no recollection of what I'd written or if any of it made any sense. I had a moment of panic when I wanted to rip my paper into shreds before anyone could read it, but, before I could, one of the invigilators had passed sweeping up my paper: just one more added to the mass of others. I looked to the front and saw Melissa's head turned sideways, laughing and joking with someone to her right. Then I upped and slipped out, anxious not to get into any postmortems.

Someone's coming down the hill towards me. I've been standing here, holding onto a railing, staring over at the college, so, quickly now, I move off towards a small group of people standing on the steps of the main building. There's twenty or thirty of them and they're all looking at a big notice board in the main entrance. That's good, I think, not too many and I can't immediately see any of the people from my classes. Heading towards them, I try to feign indifference, putting a little swagger into my stride. As I get to the board a few people melt away, allowing me to slide in easily.

A couple of guys nod their heads at me and I nod back, but I'm focusing on the board. I see a mass of names in long neat rows and it's a few seconds before I can put them into any order. The list is divided by subject. I spot English and I scan down the rows of names. I see Melissa's name first: Oakes, immediately above mine. I tilt my head back to refocus. There are two *A*s on successive lines. Below that a *D*: that must be mine. I look closer and run my finger along from my name. No, it is an *A* against my name.

That can't be right, I can't have done as well as Melissa. I keep staring at the screen, in disbelief. Then, recovering my composure, I shuffle along until I find History. An *A* again. Then Politics: another *A*. Melissa's name is above me again on each: a *B* and a *C*.

My skin has gone all tingly. Someone's playing a trick on me. I look both ways out of the corner of my eyes, expecting to find people laughing. My head swirls and all the names and letters seem to jump around on the sheet. I can't quite take this in and time seems to go again: a bit like in the exams.

I hear a voice talking to me. It's Nick Wold, who I vaguely know from History. I'm not sure I've ever spoken with him before.

'Hi, Marko. How'd you get on?'

'Oh, all right; and you?'

'Good, yeah. Got the grades; so I'm going to Leeds'

'Well done,' I say.

But he seems to have seen someone else he knows and he moves on. I stand still, looking at the board again. There are definitely three 'A's against my name. I shake my head in disbelief. Then I'm aware of a presence right next to me and I feel a soft hand on my shoulder.

I turn and look, right into Melissa's pure blue eyes. I've never been this close to her before, probably never said more than a dozen words to her. Even though her name sits right above mine on all my classes. Even though she inhabits nearly all of my fantasies.

'Marko…' she's saying. 'You got three *A*s!' And she throws her arms around me, kissing me on the cheek.

'Well done, you,' she whispers in my ear. Her soft, musky fragrance overwhelms me. I feel her lightly curled

36

blonde hair on my face, her lips against my cheek, her breasts pressed against my chest. I cling to her waist, reeling, breathless, but not wanting the moment to end.

I must have held her for a second too long because she is pulling away from me, but still looking me in the eye. I desperately hope she hasn't noticed the erection that is threatening to rip my jeans.

'So, where are you going now?' she asks, sensing my discomfort.

'Erm, I don't know, maybe up to the park?'

'No, silly,' she laughs, 'I mean which uni.'

'Oh. I don't know,' I say, 'I haven't thought about it.'

She squeezes my arm. 'Oh, you are funny. Why haven't we spoken like this before? You should go to Oxford with three 'A's. I've got my place at Exeter to read English: I can't wait.'

She's about to turn to go, but then she stops and says: 'Marko, some of us are going down to the Cobbett tonight to celebrate. You must come.'

She reaches out and gives me another peck on the cheek and, with that, she's gone.

I can't move for a while. My body is tingling with the memory of her embrace. I can still feel the warmth of her imprint and her lingering scent, as though I have absorbed her essence.

I'm clinging on to that feeling, but it's being squeezed by the presence of so many other people around me, by their inane chatter and laughter. I don't want to interact with anyone else right now. I want it to be just Melissa and me and our results on that board. I stare at it for another moment, taking in, once more, the A against my name under Politics and then I turn and head off.

I walk fast, back towards town. I'm trying not to think of anything other than the path ahead, but I'm feeling jittery, like my head's about to explode. I need space to take this in. I think I hear my name being shouted, maybe the sound of laughter. I ignore it. I keep walking, following the hill all the way down into town, then up Castle Street, before cutting through one of the alleys into Farnham Park.

Here, once I'm past the garden walls that mark the end of town, the park folds upwards to a row of trees that line the ridge and beyond that to open countryside. Only now can I let go. A surge of euphoria bursts out of me, as if I've been holding my breath for the last twenty minutes. I start to laugh uncontrollably. Anyone watching me will think I've lost the plot. For once I don't care. Three fucking *As*. And Melissa. She hugged me. Kissed me. Invited me out this evening.

'Well done, you.'

I keep replaying her voice, over and over again. I want to scream and shout. Instead I start to chant out the words to *Eton Rifles* by the Jam. Bring it on. Anything's possible from here. I've got so much adrenaline pumping I don't know what to do with it. I turn and run up the hill, fists pumping, until I'm almost at the top of the ridge and I drop to the floor, half panting, half laughing.

Slowly I start to calm. From here I'm looking down on to the town; going about its business as if nothing has changed. To my right the fortified walls of the castle stand: silently indifferent. Just below me some young kids are kicking a football around. A couple of dog walkers pass squeaking doggie-nonsense.

I need more space still, to be completely alone. Everything's changed. I've got to get used to it, try to make sense of it, work out what to do.

Jumping up, I walk, more slowly now, following a path that heads up to the top of the ridge and then along an avenue of large chestnut trees. We used to come here as a family and the memory always floods back to me. Charlie and I would collect conkers in the autumn. Dad would join in, if he wasn't reading. We'd run around kicking and throwing leaves at each other, while Mum would sit on a bench laughing and clapping at our antics. Dad called it The Champs Elysees and we would goose-step up and down shouting: 'The March of the Conkerers!'

I wish they could see me now. I wonder if they would be proud of me, or ashamed by my sad, depraved isolation.

As I carry on over the ridge, past the cricket ground and the golf course, the park turns wilder with long, unkempt grass, banks of brambles, weeds and wild flowers. Footpaths head off at random angles into woodland and across farm-land where a few cows are grazing abstractedly. I cut off onto one of the paths and find a favourite tree: an old oak.

With relief, I lower myself to the ground, the ancient timbers embracing me like a throne. I feel grounded and protected by the thick old bark. From here I can see all the way back to the ridge and the top of town beyond. I can let my guard down here. I close my eyes for a moment and breathe out a sigh. The warmth of Melissa's embrace washes over me again.

'Well done, you,' she whispers.

I feel weak suddenly, as if I'm going to cry. I imagine Mum looking at me, smiling gently, and for a moment Melissa's touch becomes indistinguishable from hers.

Then I see Dad's face puffing studiously on his pipe. 'Well done, son,' he's saying. 'We'll make a scholar of you yet.'

I open my eyes, looking out into the distance, taking back control of my emotions. There's a sturdy stick to my right, maybe a foot or so long, a few inches in diameter. I pick it up and turn it round in my hands. Then I take the Swiss Army knife from my pocket and, pulling out the main blade, start to whittle the end into a pencil-like point with long, slow strokes of the blade. The curled shavings of wood fall reassuringly into my lap and time disappears in my absorption.

Happy with my finished work, I lay the stick down to my left, the knife still unclasped to my right. I breathe deeply again. I'm no closer to knowing what to do, but something will come. Maybe I will go and see one of my tutors tomorrow, or down to the Careers Centre. Getting three As has got to be a good thing.

The sun is warm on my face. I can just hear the distant hum of noise from the town blending with the gentle rustle of leaves, the buzzing of bees, a myriad of natural noises. I look up at the sky. It's a clear blue with just a few wispy clouds sauntering along, twisting and morphing into new shapes as they drift by.

I take out my harp and breathe into it, mimicking the breeze and the procession of clouds. The notes are slow but lingering, occasionally rousing with renewed energy, into a triumphant march even, then fading to an expectant pause, as if asking a question, waiting for an unknown future to write itself. I imagine for a moment that the clouds are dancing, Pied-Piper-like, to my tune. Or am I dancing to theirs? Even better, in this moment, it feels as though everything is dancing to the *same* tune.

I put the harp back in my pocket and close my eyes, letting my mind go where it will. I'm jolted alert for a second by a scurrying sound in the undergrowth, but the noise stops. I breathe again: just a squirrel, or a bird. I rub the palms of my hands on the dry, grainy soil, trying to refocus on what I'm going to do now. The world is opening up, but all I can think about is Melissa's drinks tonight. I imagine what she'll be wearing and the smile on her face as she greets me.

Then I hear it again. First it's just a crunch. Then a ripping of the air. I try to move. Too late. I'm caught by a thunder of noise and bodies. Something hits me and I'm thrown back against the tree. Rough hands are yanking my hair and a boot is forcing down on my chest. I don't need to see who it is. A nauseous dread announces them: it's Steen and his crew.

I can't move. My ribs are being crushed as he leans into me, squeezing the air out of my lungs. I take in the white-laced, calf-length DM boot, the bleached, rolled-up jeans, the white Fred Perry and braces and the oddly shaped head that is scalped razor-sharp. His jowly face and neck are tensed with glowering contempt, his hateful eyes burning into me. I daren't look at them; they are the epicentres of his fury. Behind him I see his two goons, in identical skin-head garb, arms by their side as if primed to spring.

'So, dickhead.' he snarls. 'What's this about you getting straight fucking *A*s? Think you're fucking smart do you?'

He turns his head briefly to his mates, who jeer sarcastically with him.

'No,' I gasp 'It's just…'

'Shut the fuck up.' he shouts, spraying my face with his bile. 'And look at me when I speak to you.'

I grimace, my eyes now locked with his. Up close they are bloodshot, the whites yellowing, the pupils dark, impenetrable, but that is nothing to the hatred and rage that burns within them: it threatens to suck me in, to tear me apart.

I can't breathe. My body has gone rigid, just waiting for the first blow. I have to hold his stare; to look away would invite the start of the onslaught. I hold on for longer than he expected, but he's not fazed. He snarls at me again:

'I hear you've been working at old Ron's. You must have some fucking money, hey?' He laughs maniacally, glancing behind him, for affirmation. 'What *shall* we do?' he asks them, but he doesn't wait for an answer. 'I think we should wipe that fucking smirk off his face and relieve him of his wages. Yeah, we're the fucking taxman!'

He leans back to lap up his mates' adulation. They are roaring their approval. His boot on my chest loosens for just a second and, as I suck in some air, a surge of rage ignites from deep inside. I grab his boot and throw it out with a scream. Who's voice was that? I don't recognise it.

He's jolted backwards. This is the only chance I'm going to get; I know it with certainty. I spring to my feet, grabbing my penknife as I rise. I try to break for it, but Steen's up and lunging furiously at me. I reach out to fend him off. The knife is fused into my tensed right hand and I feel a sharp pop as the blade punctures his skin.

His body is on me. A dead weight. I can feel the bristles of his head against my face, smell the sour mix of beer and smoke on his breath. We're locked like that for an age: my right hand gripping the handle of the knife, my left hand parrying his chest. I can feel my heart beating wildly. Or is it his? Finally, I'm shoving him away with my left hand. My eyes bulge as I see his blood on the knife. Steen sees it too. There's terror in his eyes. He's staring down, clasping his side, where blood is oozing through his fingers. He staggers backwards and his mates are grabbing to catch him.

For a split second he looks up and my eyes are locked again with his. Then I run. Like a greyhound out of a trap, I burst free, smashing past them. I've just one thought in my mind now. Run. Run as fast I've ever run before.

Part II

FLIGHT

Chapter 2

Get the hell outta here

I'm running. Sprinting. Fists and knees flailing. Away from the scene of the crime. I bolt from the woods and into the open park, careering down the hill towards the town. I'm running faster than I knew I could run. My chest, my neck, my face tensed and straining. Amid the panic is a strange sense of exhilaration.

Get the hell outta here.

Around me everything is blurred, distorted, but my focus is razor sharp. People are staring at me, in alarm, giving me a wide berth. Somewhere I can sense it, but I shut them out. All I'm thinking?

Don't look back. Don't look back.

I'm hurtling down, Steen's mates snapping at my heels, towards the wall at the bottom of the hill where park turns into town. Panic surges: I'm out of control. Too fast, no brakes; I'm not going to stop. The wall at the bottom is rushing to meet me. I lean back and my feet start to slide. I'm in the air and I bounce: once, twice, back down on the grass. Somehow I land on my feet and I'm swerving at an

47

angle for one of the alleyways that runs down into town.

I'm bursting my sinews to keep ahead, bracing myself for the impact that will bring me down. Hitting the tarmac of the path, I grab onto a telegraph pole and pull myself round the corner through the gap in the wall. As I turn I snatch a look over my shoulder, expecting them to be right there. Nobody. I double take. Still nobody.

A swell of euphoria lifts me for a second then, in the same breath, drops me. The high-sided walls of the alley, just a few feet apart, are oppressive. They could cut me off at the bottom and I'd be trapped. Could I get over one of these walls? I pound on, focusing on not turning my ankle on the cobbles through the alley. And then I'm through, onto a quiet residential street.

I slide round the corner and sprint on. The houses watch me: silently, accusingly. All I can think now is that I've got to get back to the flat. Grab some stuff and then get out of town. My lungs are burning and a stitch is clawing at my gut.

Get a grip of yourself, Marko, get a grip.

I force myself on, uphill now, until I reach Castle Street: a broad avenue lined with Georgian houses that sweep grandly down into the town centre. I've got to get through it: got to appear normal.

I stop for a second looking up and down. The grandeur of the houses mock me: standing aloof, as though not wanting to be sullied by me. Deciding to avoid the busiest part of town, I hurry across the road and under the archway opposite the Nelson pub into the back alleys. It's deserted, so I keep on running, but, as I career round the corner, I almost collide with a woman in a pram.

'Watch yourself, you idiot!' she shouts after me.

I cringe, holding up a hand in apology, but she seems to have carried on and there's nobody else ahead. It's all downhill now to West Street, so I let the slope take me. As I get towards the bottom, passing along the side of Woolies, I start to slow. It's gloomy and the light pouring in from the archway at the bottom is almost blinding. I imagine a policeman stepping into the alley to block my way, or, even worse, Steen: miraculously resurrected and waiting.

Instead, I'm merging in with the traffic of West Street, as if I'm re-entering the world through a portal from some parallel universe. It's busy here. There's a constant stream of cars and the pavement is scattered with ambling shoppers. I weave between them, head down trying not to be noticed, but I'm straining and panting.

Just ahead of me I see a cash machine. I should get some more money out. Who knows when I might get another chance? I hunch over it, pushing my card in, stabbing in the numbers, burning with frustration at its dawdling formalities. It's surely going to start ringing alarm bells at any second. Behind me people are passing. I'm tensing myself for someone to spot me, for somebody to start pointing and shouting:

Grab him, there's the murderer!

Somehow the machine bleeps its assent and slides out fifty pounds. I grab it gratefully, folding the notes into my wallet. Turning around, everyone just seems to be getting on with their own business. Oblivious. As if nothing has happened.

It's too good to last. A police car is approaching. I rein myself in, slowing abruptly to a casual walk. Then, stopping, I turn towards a shop window, desperately trying to control my heaving breath. I find my shoulders lifting, as if my head can disappear into my body, as if I can make myself invisible.

I study the window display intently. I don't even know what I'm looking at. It's Mothercare. I'm staring at a display of mannequins in billowing, floral-patterned maternity dresses and cribs painted with pink flowers and smiling, blue train engines. I can't move. I feel the copper's eyes burning into my back. I'm just waiting for them to stop and get out, for the snatch of hands on my collar. But they don't. They just drive right on past, probably on their way to the scene of the crime. They're going to be looking for me any time now.

I wait for a few seconds, until I see them turning up Castle Street and then I'm off, running again. I haven't got much time. I skirt quickly past the record shop; they know me in there. I cross over just past the library and, finally, I can see Ron's shop ahead.

For a moment I think about going inside, of spilling out everything that's just happened, asking for his help. I picture him in there, straightening displays, everything quiet and orderly with its usual mix of smells: metal, paint, turps. He's just yards away, but out of reach to me now. If I went in, he'd march me straight to the Old Bill, 'to sort it all out', and I'd be in handcuffs before the afternoon was out.

No, that's not going to happen. Instead I slip round the side, into the parking lot at the back. I don't think anyone's seen me. I head as lightly up the steps as I can. I've been told before to keep the noise down: they make a hell of a clatter and I definitely don't want to be heard right now.

At the top I scrabble in my pocket for the keys. My hands are shaking. I find my penknife first. Its feeling in my hand shocks me. The last time I saw it, it was stuck between Steen's ribs. I wasn't even aware of re-clasping it or putting it back in my pocket. Was I running through the park with a bloodstained knife in my hand? What the hell have I done? I spill the keys and they almost fall through the gap in the stairs before I grab them and, forcing them into the lock, fling myself inside.

Everything is spinning now. I collapse down onto my hands and knees, my head to the floor. I'm gasping for breath, my clothes soaked with sweat. My harp slips out of my breast pocket and hits the floor with a metallic yelp.

This jolts me back to my senses. I've got no time to waste. Does Steen know that I'm living up here? He knew that I was working for Ron, so it's only a matter of time before his mates, or the police, find me here.

I jump to my feet. My mind is racing in all directions, zipping one way then another, going nowhere. I tear off my soaked shirt and T-shirt flinging it to the ground. Running to the sink I stick my head under the cold tap, jolting my mind back to some sort of clarity. I glug back a large glass of water, taking a second to breathe as it goes down. I splash water over my body, scrubbing my armpits and neck with soap, before putting on fresh clothes.

Then I remember the knife in my pocket. I pull it out

and unclasp the main blade. It's coated in dark, congealed blood. I suck in my breath at this reminder of what I have done, at the thought of Steen's life force pouring out through the wound I inflicted. Surely this hasn't really happened? I want to imagine it away, but I can't. The evidence is right there in my hand. I run the blade under the tap, scrubbing off the dried blood as quickly as I can without cutting myself, drying it on my jeans and re-clasping it.

Now I've got to get some stuff together. I've no idea where I'm going or how long I'll be gone. The police will come here: I know that. I grab my old rucksack, pull it open and lean it against the wall. I ram my sleeping bag to the bottom. Clothes: three of everything will have to do, jockeys, T-shirts, socks. It's hot out, but I'd better chuck a jumper in, an extra shirt as well. My khaki trousers. A towel: I roll it up and press it in.

Toiletries. I run to the bathroom and throw anything that comes to hand into a sponge bag: toothbrush and paste, a bar of soap, deodorant, razor, a comb. There's a pack of unopened condoms: wishful thinking when I bought them, wishful thinking now. I put them in anyway. I spin to go, then back again to grab a toilet roll.

I'm panicking again. What else? I dart over to a row of cardboard boxes that hold all my gear. One's got all my old Scout stuff. A compass: that could be useful. A billy tin with other cooking and eating stuff folded in like a puzzle: I grab it. A first-aid kit with god-knows-what inside: bung it in. A beanie hat: that won't take up much space. A torch. I've got some spare batteries somewhere. I leap up to a

52

drawer next to the sink. An unopened packet: they'll fit, great.

Other stuff in there: a box of matches, some string, clothes pegs, elastic bands, a notepad and a couple of pens; they could all be useful. Back to the box: an OS map, a cagoule that folds into its own pouch (I'll need that if we ever get any rain), a water bottle; I run to the sink to fill it up and push it into the side pocket. That'll have to do.

Shit: what about food? I run to the cupboard. There's most of a loaf of bread, a tin of beans, some soup, most of a jar of Marmite, some teabags, half a packet of biscuits. A half jar of pickle: leave that. I go the fridge. Half a pint of milk, no point in taking that, I swig it down in one. A block of cheese, some butter, a few slices of ham, a half eaten chicken pie in its foil: I throw them all in a carrier bag and into the top of the pack.

I pull the top down. I hope its not going to be too heavy. I lift it with one hand. That should be OK. I look around, squeezing my mouth and fists to contain a swelling inside me that feels like it could burst.

I've got to leave the rest: everything I've built up. I grab a box: put in my radio cassette, sweep all the cassettes in, grab handfuls of books and throw them in. Then I slide it onto the bottom shelf next to the other boxes. Jack Kerouac's 'On the Road' catches my eye: I pluck it out and slide it down the side of the pack.

Just for a moment I think about leaving a note, but I can't. That would be like a confession.

'Sorry for leaving it like this, Ron.' I mumble.

And then I'm gone.

Chapter 3

Breaking out

I hoist the pack onto my shoulders and pull the door to behind me. I'm looking at the same view as I was four hours ago, but somehow it's changed irrevocably. The town still slides down to the river, past the open spaces of the meadows; the wooded hillside still rises up on the other side, rooftops sprouting randomly; the college is still there and there are probably still students milling about comparing results and plans for the future. The light is deeper now in the full heat of the day, the sun burning down from ahigh, but it's more than that; it's the innocence and freshness and potential of this morning that has gone. It's been sucked out. Leached. The whole scene now wears a scornful leer. It's directed squarely at me. Contemptuous. Accusing. As if it's just waiting for the moment to seize me up, to punish me for what I've done.

My hands have tensed into fists. I'm not going to let that happen. If I didn't know before, now I know for sure: I've got to get out of here. I run as quietly as I can down the stairs, gripping the rails as I go. I take one last glance back up at the flat and then, with a gulp of air, I leave.

I don't want Ron to see me taking off with a pack, so I sneak round the back of the shops. I run commando style: past the delivery bays with their piled up junk, past the garage doors with their peeling paintwork and past the rusting old Cortina that's been jacked up on bricks for longer than I've been here. Coming back onto West Street, I cross quickly, before anybody I know might spot me, and duck up the alleyway on the other side. It runs past the Jolly Sailor and up towards the junior school and the art college.

The light fades. It's so narrow in here that I can touch the walls on either side. On the far wall, facing the street, someone's sprayed a big Swastika and a National Front symbol: it's bound to be Steen. My heart is pounding. Every time I turn a corner I'm expecting to bump into him.

I skirt around the outside of the school, running as fast as I can, my pack bouncing clumsily on my back. Up ahead some kids are kicking a ball around on the school playing field, their high-pitched laughter and shouting slicing through the air.

The path ends at Potter Gate and I peer out to see if anyone is coming. The space around has taken on a strange aura. Every object has a razor sharp clarity, right down to the smallest detail. I'm seeing things I'd never normally notice: a garden gate that's slightly ajar; a car parked with its sun visor down; a cat crouched under a car, its eyes fixed on me. Sounds amplify, reverberating unsteadily around me. Time has distorted. Outside the world is moving in vivid slow motion. Inside blood is pumping through my veins like it's a racetrack, my lungs demanding new air faster than I can suck it in, thoughts scrambling in and out of my head.

I force myself to focus. I've got to act normally, not draw attention to myself, I don't want anyone spotting which way I'm heading. The lane is empty, so I turn left, up towards the art college, slowing to a brisk walk. I keep my head down to avoid eye contact with the nosy parkers who are bound to be peering out of their net-curtained windows. I know just the type: prissy busybodies with nothing better to do. They'd be straight onto the police to report suspicious activity. And the police will be round here before long, that's for sure: looking out for me, making enquiries.

The art college is deserted. I pass it quickly and, jumping over a stile, join the footpath that heads diagonally up and out into open country. The space around me is a relief. I lean into the slope and march up the hill. Ten minutes ago I had no idea where I was heading, but, while I was pulling stuff out of my old Scout box, the seed of a memory planted itself. It was a three-day hike we did a few years' back following the old St Swithin's Way to Winchester. That's where I'm heading.

I know these paths well; I've walked them hundreds of times. I'm used to being invisible, I do it without trying, but today there could be police cars out looking for me. I've got to stay off the roads, make sure that nobody spots me: then I might have a chance.

They'll probably have warrants out for me before long, like the old wild-west posters: *Wanted. Dead or Alive. Mark Oban. Armed and Dangerous!*

I laugh. A surge of euphoria grabs me: Mark Oban, armed and fucking dangerous. I'm going to get out of this shithole forever; no one can stop me. I stride on up the hill, riding a wave of energy.

There's barely a cloud in the sky and the sun is beating down on me; it must be over eighty degrees. I can feel the sweat on my back already soaking through my shirt as it rubs against the pack, but that's OK. I feel good now. I've got to get a good few miles under my belt. It'll be light until eight-thirty I reckon. I can get a dozen miles away by then, maybe more, maybe even to the other side of Alton.

For now I'm still way too close to the scene of the crime. There are houses away to my left rising halfway up the hill and I'll be visible up here if anyone is looking. I walk briskly on to a staggered crossroads of paths at the end of the field. Nobody's coming in either direction so I scoot quickly up and across. The path is narrow again, heading steeply up through a thick mass of bushes and brambles and trees, with branches that arch over. I'm shielded here, but hemmed in as well. This path isn't used much, but I'm suddenly overtaken by panic at the thought of being trapped in here. What would I do? Act nonchalantly, give myself up, or fight my way out?

I give in to the surge of panic and charge up the hill, thrashing branches out of the way as I go. By the time I've made it through the trees I'm heaving for breath, my legs quivering. That was stupid. Whatever happened to not drawing attention to myself?

I stop for a minute to catch my breath taking a few deep glugs from my water bottle. There are loads of blackberries on the brambles. I pluck a big handful and stuff them greedily into my mouth. They're wonderfully refreshing, reviving me instantly. I grab a load more, filling both hands, and get going again, stuffing them in as I go.

I skirt past the edge of some stables. On the other side of the hedge I can hear whinnying and the faint sound of a voice talking to the horses. I dip in and out of a copse of trees then rise up again towards the ridge of the hill.

This is where I join the St Swithin's Way. Right to go back to the town, left, westward and away. Right to return to my old life, and all the shit that will be waiting for me, left for the unknown. It's not even a choice.

I turn left and stride on. I can't give myself the chance to change my mind; a moment's doubt could fracture me. I shut the doubts out and keep my mind on the path ahead. It's easier going now and I'm quickly into a good rhythm. For a while I almost manage to fool myself that I'm just out for an afternoon hike. I've done this many times over the summer, with the prize of a pint or two at the pub in Bentley at the end. I won't be stopping for a pint there today.

This is the western end of the old pilgrim's trail from Canterbury to Winchester. I imagine all those pilgrims treading this soil on their holy quests over the centuries and the awareness of this shared space, separated by the years, is somehow inspiring. The tune of *Onward Christian Soldiers, Marching as to War* jumps into my head. Poor deluded fools, being marched to their deaths like lemmings. I laugh sarcastically, but then my tone changes. Who's the fool now?

My thoughts spiral chaotically as I walk, but I'm making a good pace and, as I follow the path along the ridge, Farnham disappears behind me. To my left are fields of wheat, tall and straight, in massed ranks lining the hillside. It won't be long before the combines are out, scything it back to the bare earth.

I've seen nobody for the last twenty minutes and the rhythm of walking is starting to lull me into a false sense of security. Then, as I follow a dip down towards a copse, I hear something. It's the sound of a dog, no two dogs, barking. Maybe a hundred yards away on the other side of the bend. Instinctively I dart off the path and into the trees. They're thick enough with the rest of the undergrowth, that after fifty yards I can barely see the path.

I crouch down, hands on the ground, holding my breath. It's silent and conspiratorial in here, as though the trees and the earth are sharing my secret. Back on the path I can hear footsteps and the dogs growling. For a moment I think they've sniffed me out. I find myself coiled up like a spring, just waiting for them to come tearing toward me, snarling and snapping. Then I hear the muffled voice of a woman chastising them. She seems to have them back on a lead and then they're gone; their footsteps just a memory.

The tension in my chest dissolves, replaced by laughter: they were probably a pair of cutesy little lap dogs that would have licked me to death. I wait for a moment until I'm sure, finishing my blackberries and taking another glug from my bottle. Then I move on, stealthily, through the undergrowth, cutting off the corner and emerging back on the path.

The way is clear again, so I press on. From nowhere *I Fought the Law* by the Clash leaps into my mind, the jerky elation of the guitar matching my mood. It's a great song, but I've always struggled to match that with the fact that 'The Law Won'.

'It's not the result; it's the fact that you tried, Marko,' Uncle Harry would tell me.

My dad would have scoffed: 'You must respect the law, Mark. Without it we would have anarchy.'

Well, I've done what I've done. It's just me now and I'm determined that the law won't win.

I need to be careful; there's a farm just ahead. I smell it first, the pungent stench of cattle, then I hear the dejected monotone of their lowing, hanging heavily in the air. As I get closer the farm courtyard opens out. The farmer's there. I can see him, in wellies even in this dry heat.

I'm on tiptoes. I feel like I'm back in that kid's game we used to play, where you had to hide and make it back to base without being seen, but now the danger is real and I've got no base to run back to. I'm inching forwards, but his back is turned to me as he shovels feed noisily into troughs and I slip past unnoticed.

I'm on a tarmacked lane now. It's narrow with trees and high-sided hedges on either side. Ahead a series of big houses sit back from the road. They always have expensive cars parked on the driveways. One of them even has a tennis court: I can hear the sound of a ball being hit back and forth over a net. As I get closer I can just make out two women in white dresses, laughing as they scurry after returns. Just for a moment I'm transfixed, but then I remember my situation and press on.

There's a crossroads at the bottom: once I'm there I can get off the road and back onto footpaths. I hear a car approaching. I find myself stopped and leaning into the hedge, bracing myself for something, but it's on the road ahead and it speeds past in a silver blur.

At the crossroads I check both ways and, seeing it's clear, scurry across to the stile and the fields beyond. As I run, I notice the sign that sits half buried in the overgrown hedgerow: 'Hampshire' it says. I laugh as I pass: it'll have to be Hampshire coppers that feel my collar now.

Knowing that I've left Surrey has lifted a huge weight. For the first time, I'm starting to believe that I might just get away with this after all. Ahead of me are open fields all the way to Bentley and I stride though them as if walking on air, guitar chords jangling around my head, a new energy pulsing through me.

It's easy progress now. The path is pretty flat, even if there's still heat in the sun. I have the world to myself and I skirt down the sides of fields, with wheat and barley and corn growing above my head at times. It's proper countryside, with fields on either side, but also trees and overgrown hedges and wild flowers sprouting everywhere.

Occasionally, I hear the sounds of a far-off tractor and way off to my left the muted drone of the A31, but other than that I'm cushioned by the sounds of nature and, slowly, I allow myself to be lulled into a calm sense of safety.

As I get closer to Bentley, anxiety rises again. Rounding a corner, I can see the church spire, rising above the trees as if watching out for me. I stop for a minute. How the hell am I going to get through the village unnoticed? Then I remember the path that skirts around the village and soon I'm at the fork: left goes down to the main road and my usual pub, only a few hundred yards away now; right curls round the northern edge of the village.

I don't normally come this way. The path angles across an open field towards a stile in the far corner where it hits a road. I stop for a second when I get there trying to work out what to do. For a moment, I'm tempted to go cross-country, to avoid the village, but that's a stupid idea. I'd make myself even more conspicuous. I'd probably get stopped for trespassing on private property and even if I didn't I'd struggle to get through hedges between fields. I'm delaying the inevitable, I know that, I've just got to get on with it.

I take the compass from my pack and put it in my pocket. My knowledge of the paths gets hazy after Bentley, so I might have to start using it soon. It's a single-track country lane that doesn't go anyplace much and there's no sign of any cars. As I round the corner I see the thirty-limit sign and a few houses dotted ahead. I steady my pace. *Calm and relaxed*, I repeat to myself, as if I'm out for an early evening stroll without a care in the world.

The road runs straight ahead and I pass a few houses with walls and hedges that I can't see over, then a pair of cottages with perfectly tended gardens. It's only when I'm level with them that I notice an old guy crouched down, pruning his roses.

'Afternoon,' he says, hearing me pass but not turning.

I almost leap out of my skin. Somehow I manage to reply, as calmly as I can manage: 'Afternoon.'

I keep my head down; keep walking at the same pace. It seems to have been enough for him.

Ahead the road merges. As I reach it I see a pair of dog walkers, no more than fifty yards away, off towards the village. They're standing there gossiping, like they were walking in opposite directions and have stopped for a chat. I walk on the other way, casual as you like, but inside I'm churning.

Up ahead there's a sign for the village church. An image from the Scout hike, all those years ago, jumps into my mind. I was living with my first foster family, Beryl and Jeff, at the time. Jeff was the Scout leader, so I joined his troop for a while, until he got ill and couldn't do it any more.

Jeff had gone off with one of the other lads for ice creams and the rest of us waited for them in the churchyard, under the shade of some huge gnarled yew trees. I can picture us there as if it were yesterday. We all thought the place was haunted, but we soon forgot that once they returned with a load of ice lollies. They had jokes on the stick and everyone tried to eat their's fastest so they could tell their joke first.

I'm heading out of the village now, past another couple of houses hidden by high hedges, towards a rambling old cottage with a mass of flowers in the front garden. Familiar music is pulsing from an open upstairs window. It's *A Forest* by The Cure. Oh man: I love that song. It's mesmerizing. Through a window I see a woman in the kitchen busy preparing food. Is that roasting meat I can smell? Hunger pangs hit me. I'd forgotten that I haven't eaten all day. The desire to knock on that door is almost irresistible. Surely they'll be kindred spirits. I'll confess everything to them; ask for their help. Surely they would?

I feel a sudden weightlessness as I imagine being in that kid's shoes, up there in his bedroom, listening to The Cure, maybe smoking a secret spliff and wafting the smoke out the window, knowing that he's got a good meal and the company of his family to look forward to. It's Thursday evening: *Top of the Pops* will be on the telly later.

I'm starting to tremble and I curse myself for my senti-mentality. I force myself on, clenching my jaw and shoulders to keep these feelings under control, upping the pace in an effort to burn them out.

I should be feeling better now I'm through Bentley, but I'm swamped by a wave of loneliness that is sucking the energy out of me. The smell of meat from that house is still in my nostrils and my stomach is growling for food. The fields are empty, the path straight and flat: I should be marching quickly on, but instead I'm getting slower and slower, each step a bigger effort.

Finally I stop by a small copse of trees. I can see for a long way in both directions, so I tip my backpack off and sit while I rummage for the chicken pie. I wolf it down in no time and follow it with some more blackberries. I'm getting my equilibrium back slowly and I pull out my harp and blow out a few mournful notes, letting them go.

Finally, I'm able to rouse myself. I feel way better with

some food inside me and I press on, picking up the pace again. The path stretches on; the sun, ahead and then to the right, slowly starts its descent toward the horizon. The heat of the day has gone and the miles disappear beneath my boots.

Within a couple of hours I'm approaching Alton. I've walked in a kind of daze. Not much has been going on inside my head except the mantra,

Keep going. Keep going. Keep going.

An hour or so ago, as I turned a corner, a pheasant leapt out of the undergrowth, spluttering and flapping. I think I spluttered and flapped more than the pheasant. Anyone watching would have had a right laugh.

The only real scare I had was in Froyle. It's a tiny village, with a school for disabled kids and a huge old manor house that's now a fancy hotel. I came into the village round the back of an old church and no sooner had I hit the road then a car passed me and pulled up abruptly. I nearly ran back the way I'd come, but I steeled myself and kept on going. It was a Jag: all polished and gleaming. I imagined plain-clothes cops, waiting to leap out and grab me as I passed, but as I got closer I realised it was an old couple having a full-on barney. He was in a dinner jacket and was shouting and flailing his arms, while she cowered in her sequined dress. I saw the sign for the footpath not far ahead so I just kept going, holding my breath until I was off the road again, then pissing myself laughing and ploughing on with new energy.

The gloom is starting to descend now and my new worry

is how to avoid Alton. The path looks like it's drawing me into the town, so I take a farm track off to the right that follows a hedgerow steadily uphill. I've no idea where I'm going now and the track just peters out at the top of the field. I can't get through the hedge so I follow the field round, trying to find a way through, until I'm heading east again. Panic is starting to rise in me; mixing with exhaustion and a creeping despair. I'm in a labyrinth that I can't get out of and soon it's going to be pitch black.

I'm so tired and despondent that I start to think of just stopping and lying down right here, but finally I reach a gate and over it I can see a track joining another path ahead. It's heading in a better direction, curving northwards uphill and I dig in, trudging on up the hill until I'm on the edge of a ridge.

Below me a large expanse of open field folds sharply down to a lane at the bottom. I can see for miles from here. To the north and west, there are rolling hills and fields as far as I can see intersected by hedgerows and little country lanes. It's bathed in golden light, calm and pure, as though nothing bad could possibly happen in the world.

To my left I can feel the presence of Alton and I turn towards it. It's only a mile or two from here, squatting malignantly, rows of terraced houses tightly packed together, the windows like spying eyes. I see the station in the centre, surrounded by squat, grey, institutional buildings and beyond them the industrial estates straddling the A31 where cars and lorries thunder heedlessly past. I'm close enough here that I can hear them carried on the breeze.

Ahead of me, the sun is sinking. I could probably get another half an hour of walking in, maybe down into the valley and up the other side, but I'm shattered. I'm going to stop here for the night; it's as good a place as any. I turn back into the trees and they swallow me up silently.

I walk in deeper, until I'm sure that nobody can see me, and dump my pack down. It's a weird feeling, as if my body has no weight and I'm going to float off. My legs are like jelly suddenly and I crumple gratefully to the floor, leaning on my pack. I take my boots off and wiggle my toes. I'll get my sleeping bag out in a minute. Maybe I'll have some bread and cheese, but for the moment I just luxuriate in the weightlessness of the moment. The sounds of the woodland are starting to die down for the evening. Through the trees I can still see the last of the sun: turning a gradually deeper orange, infusing the few wisps of clouds around it.

The events of this crazy day are swirling around me, like birds startled by a gunshot. There's no sense or pattern in any of it. Did any of it really happen? I know it did, but lying here I can't make it real. Surely I can't have killed someone?

From nowhere another thought hits me. Right now I should be down at the Cobbett with Melissa. I'd have just arrived. They'll be sitting in the beer garden out the back, laughing and joking. I try to imagine myself there, with a beer in my hand, joining in the conversation. I try to imagine Melissa's face and to recreate the feeling of her embrace. And as my mind drifts on these thoughts, my body gives up on the day and sleep takes me.

Chapter 4

Clearing some space

It's dark in the forest. A blanket, all-consuming darkness. And there are noises everywhere. Scurrying, scratching, whispering. Infiltrating. The trees conspire: their branches writhing and clawing, reaching down for me in the darkness; their roots coiling up, seizing hold of my arms and legs, dragging me down into the earth.

An oppressive weight is pinning me to the floor. I can't move. With a creeping, icy dread I realise: it's Steen. Somehow he has found me. He's morphed so that he's half man, half tree. Now he's straddling me, pinning my arms to the floor with his branches. His face is illuminated in the darkness: white like a ghoul, eyes burning.

'You thought you could get the better of me,' he's growling.

His hands seize my throat: tightening, throttling. I struggle furiously. I'm trying to get to my penknife, but I can't find it. I can hear his voice, echoing distortedly like a badly tuned radio, but I no longer know what he's saying. The world is going out of focus, spinning and distorting. Is this how my life is going to end?

The forest floor is claiming me, sucking me in, and I'm falling into its vortex. I'm looking up through a tunnel of earth to a rectangle of white light. Above, Mum is sobbing into a white hankie. Charlie is by her side. He's crying too, because Mum his gripping his hand too tightly. Dad is standing behind them, hands on their shoulders, with furrowed brow and pursed lips.

Uncle Harry is looking lost and out of place with Ron next to him. They both look ashen and shame-faced, as if they're somehow responsible for what's happened to me.

Shirley from the Social is there too, with a whole cluster of my ex-foster parents. They're all shaking their heads and looking knowingly at one another: 'This was always going to happen,' they're saying.

Melissa is there, standing a little away from everyone else, holding hands with a bloke I don't know. They turn to each other and start to kiss passionately.

Steen and his buddies are dancing amongst them, jeering and laughing, clawing at the earth, kicking and scraping it on top of me. It's raining down on me, coarse and heavy. I screw my eyes shut, raising my arms to protect myself.

'I'm not dead.' I shout it over and over, but nobody can hear me except Steen, who just laughs louder. The weight of the earth is engulfing me, suffocating me, sealing me in for eternity.

With a great scream I lurch up. Only Steen is there now and I grab at his leg, pulling him off balance. I'm back above ground and he's coming at me with a shovel in his hand. I've found my penknife, but it's not enough. From somewhere I find a machete and I'm flailing it wildly. His mates are coming at me and I'm swinging at them too. I'm drenched in their blood and their screams and I turn and run, but there are police everywhere. They're coming from all angles, their dogs too: barking and baying for my blood.

They've got me surrounded. I start to scramble up the nearest tree. Up and up I climb, but I never seem to get to the top and the darkness only gets more intense whilst the barking and the police whistles get louder and louder. I'm clinging to the tree, but my grip is starting to weaken. I can't hold out for much longer. I'm going to fall.

I wake abruptly, panting and clawing at the earth. The first light is starting to filter through the treetops and birds are chirping raucously all around me. Where am I? What's going on? I'm disorientated, still half in the dream. I heave a sigh of relief. It was just a nightmare: everything is OK. But then the events of yesterday flood back at me. I really am here: alone, in a wood, in the middle of nowhere.

I feel dry and dirty and scratchy. Suddenly I shriek and leap to my feet. Something was biting me. I shake myself and start brushing vigorously. I'm covered in the detritus of the forest. Leaves and dirt and God knows what.

Reaching out for my pack, I pull out my water bottle. My mouth is dry, like I've been eating the dirt, and my head is pounding. I take several big gulps. Fuck, it's almost empty. I've got to get some more somehow. What an idiot, I haven't thought about even the most basic stuff. What the hell do I think I'm doing here? How can I be so stupid as to get myself in this mess?

The dream from last night hasn't quite released me from its grip. I'm struggling to work out what's real and what was in my dream, still having to persuade myself that I really am on my own in here.

I'm ravenous, I know that for sure, so I scrabble around in my pack and pull out the bag of food. I know I've got to eke out what I've got, but I'm so hungry I can't stop myself from scoffing down a load of bread and ham and cheese.

Now I'm starting to feel a bit more human, it's dawning on me that I've got to get a plan together. It's no use just running blindly: it'll only be a matter of time before I get caught. First off, I've got to get the facts straight: I stuck a knife in Steen. The thought makes me shiver, but I can't deny it. He could be dead. Seriously injured at the least. The police are going to be looking for me, probably Steen's mates too.

What if I *was* caught? I could plead self defence, but who's going to believe that? His mates were witnesses and they'll say it was an unprovoked attack. People probably saw me running away with a knife in my hand. I fled the scene.

It all shouts: *'Guilty'*.

I'm doing the right thing in getting away. I can't go back, that's for sure, so I've got to lay low for a while. Who knows for how long? Where can I go? Is there anyone who can help me? Uncle Harry would, for sure, but he's off in America with the band for at least another couple of months and I've got no way of contacting him. The cops will probably find him before I do. Anyone else would just send me straight to the police. I'm on my own with this.

But that's OK, I'm used to being on my own. I'm going to disappear and they'll never find me – like Lord Lucan.

That thought has cheered me up. I take out the OS map. Folding it out on the ground, I find Alton first and then work out pretty much exactly where I am: the wonderfully named Spollycombe Copse.

The map runs out a few miles west of here, but at least it gets me a start. I'd planned to follow the St Swithin's Way, but it goes right through Alton and then crosses to the other side of the A31. By the look of the map I can detour easily enough around Alton and, after that, a couple of footpaths head west connecting little villages. I'll have to follow them and then wing it: keep heading roughly west or southwest.

I check the compass is still in my pocket. I'm going to need that today. I look at my watch. It's just gone six and it's almost fully light now even here in the woods. If I get cracking I reckon I can get past Winchester. It took us three full days when we were kids, but we weren't exactly hacking it.

I shove the food back into the pack and reach for my boots. They were the only things I managed to take off last night before I crashed. I give them a little shake and a big spider falls out.

'That would have hurt you more than me,' I laugh, as it scurries furiously for safety.

It's a great morning to be walking. The air is clear and fresh and, for a while, the world belongs to me. Away to my left, Alton is only just starting to come to life. From my overnight stop meadowland falls steeply away to a lane at the bottom. Off to my right, at the far side of the field, I spot some deer. They're watching me intently, frozen in the moment, ears pricked, primed to take flight. It feels strange, almost empowering, to be viewed, even for a moment, as predator not prey. You've got nothing to fear from me, I want to tell them. But they remain statuesque until suddenly they're gone, as if an invisible wire has been tripped, leaping up the hill and disappearing into the woodland beyond.

A light dew on the grass sparkles in the early sunlight and I let myself run with the slope, aiming for a gate in the far corner. Straight away I have a bit of luck. Shortly after joining the lane, I pass a farmhouse and yard. It's deserted, but on the sidewall I see a tap. I dart across to it. I can't hear anything so I fill my bottle, drink as much of it as I can, refill it, then stick my head under the tap and wash my face and neck. Wow, that feels great. Within a minute I'm in and out and on my way.

The world feels different this morning. It is different. I've left my old world behind and this is a fresh start. The dew on the grass is untouched, as if it is beckoning me. I stride on, making new marks with each step.

As I walk, I start to turn plans over in my mind. I'm feeling clear headed and rational: like there'll be a solution for anything. I reckon I need to get a hundred miles or so away. If I keep going west, that's going to be Wiltshire, or Dorset, Somerset maybe. Then I need to find somewhere that I can hide out for a while, maybe for a few months, while the heat dies down; somewhere people won't spot me and somewhere I can find food and water and shelter.

I could build myself a bivouac. Jeff taught me how to do that, along with all sorts of outdoor stuff. I wonder how he and Beryl are getting on. Things might have turned out different if he hadn't had his heart attack. I wish that I hadn't been so nasty to them and that I'd listened more closely to what he taught me: I'm going to need as much of all that as I can.

All that's going to come, but I can't think about it too much for now. My first priorities are just to get to get further away without anyone spotting me. I want to be invisible, but the land stretches out around me, vast and isolated and exposed. I'm starting to feel like an alien on a hostile planet, as though I'm not meant to be here and everyone and everything is watching me. But it's not the open fields that worry me most: it's the villages. As I go through them I see hidden menace lurking in every window. I resolve that I've just got to accept it: people will see me, but they don't have to notice me.

From here on I'm just going to act natural. If I do that then people will ignore me. If anyone asks me what I'm doing, I'll tell them that I'm hiking to Winchester. I make up a story about myself as I'm going. I've just passed my 'A' levels and I'm going to university next month: to Exeter to study History. My girlfriend's going there as well. I can't wait. My parents are really proud of me. I'm just taking some time out before I go, hiking around. Some friends are waiting for me in Winchester. I keep repeating it, embellishing it, polishing it. And before long I'm almost starting to believe it myself.

Once I've got my story straight, my mood calms. Occasionally a path twists me in a direction I don't want to go, or runs out at a road which I have to follow for a while, but basically I feel like I'm heading in the right direction. I barely see anyone. Around mid-morning, I pass a postman and we exchange nods. I cross a main road, where a couple of cars whizz past. I see farmers in tractors out in the fields, but I ignore them and they ignore me.

It's good going in the morning, but slowly the heat of the day rises. For most of the time there's no shelter and the sun beats down on me mercilessly. Sweat pours off me until my clothes are sopping, yet my lips are dry and chapped, my nose peeling as it burns under the sun's spotlight. I'm so hot, yet cold where my pack presses against my T-shirt. A strange contest of heaviness and weightlessness plays out: the pack and my aching back and legs pulling down, my head like it's ready to float off into the ether.

Finally, at about one, I stop in the shade of some trees. The relief as I step out of the sun and dump my pack to the ground is immense; like I'm drunk and I'm going to fall over. I'm so thirsty that I drink nearly all of my water in one go. Then I eat a little bread and cheese, though I'm not as hungry as I thought I would be.

I could sit here forever. The grass is cool and soft beneath me and I tune in to the buzzing of the bees that blur benignly with other far-off sounds. I wipe my hands on the grass and pull my harp from my pocket. I pause, then breathe gently into it, letting it take its place in this natural melody. For a moment I'm tempted to blast it out, but I don't want to either frighten or attract. This is just a gentle merging, like I'm finding my small place in something bigger.

I don't allow myself the luxury of such complacency for long. I've got to keep cracking on, so I force myself back on my feet. It's hard going for a while, but I'm soon back into a rhythm. I find myself following the line of a field, with a high hedgerow on one side and crops towering above me on the other. It's corn and they're bursting with cobs, cloaked in their sheaths. This could be dinner.

I slide off the path, allowing myself to be swallowed up. It feels cool and mysterious in here. I cup my hands round a large cob and inhale. It's sweet and earthy. I take my pack off and load in four of the most succulent ones I can find. As an afterthought, I grab an extra one as I leave. I peel off the sheath and the threads as I walk and then bite into it. I've never eaten raw corn before, but it's really good: soft and crunchy at the same time, sweet, almost milky. It gets stuck everywhere in my teeth and I'm picking it out for the next half an hour.

It's late afternoon now, but it's still hot. My water's used up again and I'm sweating buckets, my strength draining. I feel the path drawing me southwards and I can see a town ahead of me, which I reckon must be Alresford. I'm well off the map now, but I remember that the train stops there: last stop before Winchester.

Before I can be dragged too far south, I find a path that veers off to the right and within a few minutes I'm crossing a little footbridge over a stream. It's about ten foot across, maybe more, at its widest point. I stop and look both ways:

this is beyond tempting. To the left I can see some farm buildings and the stream meanders down, presumably joining the main river in the town. Upstream, it dances down the hillside towards me through trees and reeds, sparkling in the afternoon sunshine.

I follow a rough track that heads upstream along the bank and into the trees. When I spot a shingle shoreline, I scrabble through the trees and pull off my pack. It seems to be secluded on all sides here, with a mass of reeds on the other side stopping anyone from getting close.

I pull off my boots and socks, roll my trouser legs up, and dip my feet into the water. The effect of the ice-cold water is instantaneous. Bolts of pleasure surge through me. I raise my head to the sky, my eyes clenched tight shut, my mouth forming a silent moan, as if I can suck in even more pleasure. My legs go weak on me and I feel like I'm going to subside, like a dynamited building into the water. Tension dissolves and, just for a moment, I think I'm going to cry. Instead I laugh. It's my feet: through the magnifying glass of the water they're white and pasty and distorted, as though they belong to someone else. I wiggle them and the pleasure amplifies again as the water finds its way into the crevices. Some little minnows dart around, seemingly oblivious to my arrival. Taking my cue from them my head darts off either way again to make sure I'm not being observed.

I'm alone. Stepping back to the shingle, I take off my jeans and my watch, before easing in further: tentatively, silently, feet gripping onto rocks and stones, arms out sideways like a tightrope walker. Each new piece of flesh entering the water is newly shocking and invigorating. When I'm up to my thighs, I pause for a second, scanning around me again, then, crouching down, plunge forward ducking my head under the water. I want to whoop and scream, but somehow suppressing it intensifies the effect, like it is echoing around inside me, purely for my own enjoyment.

I take a couple of strokes out into the middle and stand. It's almost up to my waist. I lean back against the current allowing it to massage my shoulders, which are sore and stiff from carrying the pack. For a few moments I just enjoy the feeling, then I pull myself back to reality. I get out and pull the soap from the bag. Back in the water I wash my T-shirt and jockeys as I'm wearing them. Then I take them off, squeeze them as dry as I can and lob them onto the bank. I'm stark-bollock-naked now, so there'd better be nobody looking: otherwise they'll have to add indecent exposure to my charge sheet.

After I've washed myself, I drape my wet clothes over a bush. There's not much sun on them, but they'll start to dry pretty quick I reckon. I go back into the water a little way and scoop up a handful, where it looks fresh and fast moving. I take a mouthful and swill it round. It tastes sweet and pure: much better than the stuff from the tap. I scoop up and drink several more handfuls then go back and fill my bottle.

Back on the bank, I desperately want to just sit some more and luxuriate in this moment: with the butterflies and dragonflies floating and swooping across the water; with the fish, tiddlers flitting nervously, the odd bigger one cruising solemnly. I could play my harp, read my book.

And a cold beer would round it off nicely.

Maybe I should call it a day right here. But no, I've got to go further; I've not even got to Winchester. I pull out a fresh pair of jockeys, T-shirt and socks from the pack and get dressed. My washed clothes are still pretty wet, but I wring as much water as I can from them, then tie them from straps on the pack and get walking again.

As I retrace my steps back through the trees, I can make someone out on the bridge ahead. I stop and crouch down, peering through the trees. They couldn't have seen me from there. I'm sure I wasn't making enough noise to have attracted attention from that distance. They stand there for what seems like an age, just gazing out into space, but eventually they head off towards the town.

That would have spooked me yesterday, but, after the swim, I'm feeling revived, back in control. At the bridge, I continue west again, making easy progress in the warmth of the early evening. I'm walking through acre after acre of farmland, gently rolling in all directions around me and bursting with corn and wheat and the brilliant yellow of mustard and rape.

Gradually, I become aware of a noise ahead of me: a steady, ominous drone. It takes me a while to suss, but it must be the M3 that heads up from Southampton, past Winchester, towards London. I'd forgotten that I've got to cross that at some point. I keep going, ignoring the problem, until at around seven the path hits a road. On either side of the road the landscape abruptly changes from open farmland to forest. It seems to go on for miles; cool and welcoming after the stark openness of the plains I've been plodding over.

The road is quiet, so I run across and into the woods. I can't see the motorway yet, but I can hear its roar, even through the trees. It must be less than a mile away. I've reached a track, which seems to run parallel with the road. I follow it, but my heart is pounding again, the hairs on my neck rising. I can see several cars parked up ahead in a clearing and a scattering of picnic tables. Then I make out the motorway. It's built up on a bank, almost like a causeway through the trees. The road I've crossed must go under it.

I'm going to stop somewhere around here for the night I decide. It's perfect, provided I stay well away from that car park. People will bring their dogs to walk here for sure. And God knows what will happen there after dark.

I head further into the trees doing a wide loop around the car park and then back towards the road. Looking up, I can clearly see the motorway, up at the top of the bank. The road passes silently beneath it, like a well-kept secret, before disappearing into the trees on the other side. All the cars are invisible, but I can just make out the tops of lorries occasionally clattering past. Where can they all be going? They've all got stories, I guess, all got family and friends that they're heading to see, warm welcomes and embraces waiting for them along with good food and drink and clean sheets to sleep on. If only they could see me here, skulking alone in the woods.

Fuck them all. I don't care what they think. I'll clear through here first thing tomorrow morning. I'll be fine on my own: that's always been the best for me. I'm going to find somewhere out of the way to kip down for the night. Maybe I can even get a little fire going and roast some of those cobs.

I walk into the woods until I find somewhere that feels right and then gratefully drop my pack. My clothes are nearly dry, but I shake them out and drape them over a branch where there's still some sunlight filtering through. The trees are dense around me, but there's enough space for me to spread out a bit. There's also a dead tree, which has keeled over at an angle. If I prop a load of branches against it, it will be a good windbreak and stop anyone from seeing me.

I sweep away an area of leaves and twigs and dust and dig out a pit for my fire, a couple of inches deep, banking up the earth around it. It's so dry that I'm not going to have any trouble starting it. Still, I'd better make sure that nobody spots it and that I don't lose control, or they'll be charging me with arson too – I'm going to be more *Wanted* than Ronnie Biggs by the end of this.

The sun has almost gone by the time I've got my fire ready to light, so I start settling myself for the night. I pull out my sleeping bag and roll it out on the bare earth close to the fire pit. I'm not going to fall asleep where I drop tonight: that was crazy last night. I pull out my towel and jumper for a pillow. Next to them I put my torch in case I need it during the night.

It's almost dark now. I pause and listen. I'm pretty sure that I can't hear anything, other than the steady roar of traffic from the motorway, maybe a couple of barking dogs away in the distance. I take a match and strike. The kindling takes almost immediately beneath the little tepee of twigs. I watch intently and add larger twigs as it takes hold. Within a few minutes I've got a good little fire going. I resist the temptation to build it bigger. I'd love to get it roaring, but this will do just fine.

I was going to boil up a couple of those sweet corn once the fire got going, but my billie tins are nowhere near big enough. I have a better idea. I take a stick and, sharpening it to a point, skewer one of the cobs with it. As I'm doing it, Steen's face leaps into my mind and I have to force myself to shut his image out.

My hunger wins out. The smell of the cob, as it sizzles and spits over the fire, is amazing, but it tastes even better: sweet and nutty. The butter has pretty much had it, it's melted and solidified so many times, but I dip the cob into the remains and cut off some slices of cheese to go with it. The cheese has gone all rubbery too, but it goes really well with the cob, all melted and sticky.

I'm still hungry, so I repeat the trick with a second cob before putting a couple more sticks onto the fire and boiling up some water in the billy tin. Some tea and a biscuit will round my meal off nicely.

Drinking my tea, I allow myself to be hypnotised by the flames, dazzled by their brilliance, drawn in from the blanket of darkness that has closed around me. It's amazing how the intensity of the light and the dark become even more extreme when placed in such close proximity. It's like they both puff themselves up, yet neither is capable of winning out against the other.

I take out my harp and blow out a long, quivering note. I let it linger, it's energy resonating in the stillness of the forest, dancing with the flames, absorbing the possibilities of the moment. And then I just sit, gazing into the fire, letting all of these thoughts and emotions sink in.

I'm tired now. Waves of fatigue roll over me and my muscles are sore and twitching from the day's exertion. The fire is almost gone, so I strip down and climb into my sleeping bag.

It's Friday night. What would I have been doing if I wasn't here? Probably just sitting in the flat, listening to music, maybe supping a beer. I lie still, looking into the embers of the fire, feeling the last of its warmth on my face.

My mind flits back to last night at The Cobbett again. This time, in my mind's eye, I'm sitting on my own in the garden at the back nursing a pint. Melissa's at the bar and it's just the two of us left. As she comes back, I slide my legs sideways to let her sit next to me. But instead of passing she shakes her head slowly and smiles, looking deeply into my eyes. She moves slowly towards me. My hands find her waist and we are kissing: softly at first, but then it becomes firm and wet and passionate. She whispers into my ear, 'I've taken off my knickers'. My cock is rock hard now and I allow it to escape from the sleeping bag, hot and pulsing. I squeeze my eyes shut. My hands have slipped up under her T-shirt. I can feel her breasts, smooth and soft, her nipples firm yet supple. She is undoing my trousers, releasing me. Taking it in both hands she slides my foreskin up and down, watching me closely. Then, kneeling on the bench either side of me, she eases me slowly inside her. I mimic her, my eyes screwed shut, gripping myself tightly. I slide my hand up and down: slowly at first as she lowers herself onto me; then more urgently as she draws me deeper inside her. In the darkness I can picture her: that look as our eyes meet. I can smell her: the musky fragrance of her perfume that fuses with her natural scent. I can taste her as we kiss. We've become one, riding to the same rhythm. She is rising and falling with increasingly reckless abandon, hair tussled, face flushed, her breathing quickening and I follow her, my fist squeezing and tensing. There's nowhere else to go, no more air to breathe, my face turns inside out and with a barely contained wail, I explode into the darkness.

Chapter 5

Living the dream

It's Wednesday morning. I've been on the run for six days, but it feels like forever. Already I can't imagine any other way of being. The land has drawn me in, swallowed me up, as if I've become part of it and it part of me. I've ploughed through it, one foot in front of the other, on and on, in a dead-eyed trance, everything blurred and dreamlike yet tangible and real.

The world has changed around me as I've gone. Like the kaleidoscope of my childhood each twist of the lens brings subtle transformations, then a dawning awareness that it has metamorphosed into something altogether different, just a distant memory of the original. Each time I turned and looked back it was as if I was seeing where I'd come for the first time: my steps erased by an invisible tide rising behind me.

I'm shattered. I must have walked over twenty miles each day, even more with all the detours and wrong turns. The pack on my back has gotten heavier with every step, dragging me down, sapping my energy until I no longer know what's keeping me going. My legs are hurting, my back is hurting, I've got blisters on my feet and shoulders, my face and lips are blistered from the sun. And I've got the shits real bad.

It's all those sweet corn and blackberries. Mix it up with a tin of baked beans and you've got the most lethal combination known to mankind. That should be funny, but it's not. I've had to scramble behind hedgerows, any cover I can find, tearing and stinging my skin on brambles and nettles. And each time it leaves me shaky and weak.

I probably should have stopped on Monday, rested up for a day or two. I found a great place to kip down on Sunday night, in some woods that sloped gently down to a lake. It must have been a mile long, a hundred yards across, curving smoothly round the trees like a boomerang.

A tiny village guarded the top of the lake where a stream fed into it, but I only had to walk for a few minutes round the bend before my only company was a load of ducks on the water. I washed my clothes and hung them up from some branches to dry in the sun. I'd love to have swum that evening, but I felt too exposed. Instead I just sat and watched the sun sink over the horizon, smudging the water with apricot and peach, infusing everything with calm, serene hope.

I've slept like the dead each night, waking abruptly with the calls of the first birds. In those moments of confusion, I've struggled to drag myself from the claws of nightmares, only to remember that the reality is just as threatening. Always there's a looming certainty that I'm being watched.

The eyes and the ears and the voices are everywhere. They are in the trees, beyond hedgerows, following behind me so I have to keep turning to confront them, in the air, below the ground, but mostly they are in my head, mercilessly invading my thoughts and dreams, twisting accusingly, tormenting and torturing me.

The cusp between night and day is the worst: that time when the sleeping and the waking fuse, becoming an alternative reality that can't be reasoned with. Unable to rest, I've upped and gone before anyone's about and before the sun got too hot. And, as I've walked briskly through the cool morning air, calmness has slowly replaced the befuddled night terrors.

Saturday and Sunday were good days. As I set off on Saturday morning I remembered that I was due to be working. An image of Ron jumped into my head. He was standing behind the counter in the shop with a worried look on his face. Or was that anger? He never gave much away, even in the flesh. I imagined him, annoyed initially that I was late, constantly checking his watch, tutting to himself. Saturday was always busy so he wouldn't have had the chance to go and bang on my door until later.

But no, it wouldn't have happened like that: the police would have got to him first. They'd have turned up at the shop on Friday morning, demanding to be let in to the flat. They'd have been swarming all over it: looking for evidence, for clues as to where I might have gone, putting all my stuff into bags. Ha: I've outfoxed them there. They'd have been trying to figure out if someone's hiding me.

They'd have been at the train station. They'd have been everywhere, but they won't have figured out that I'm a hundred miles away: hiding in a Somerset woodland.

On Saturday night I stopped just short of a village called Middle Winterslow. The next morning I felt like a thief passing through it at first light, still silent and sleeping. The Sunday papers sat unopened outside a newsagent. I was sorely tempted to nab one, but isn't it the case that criminals are usually caught for something trivial just like that?

Before long, as I crested a hill, Salisbury appeared on the horizon. I've never been there, but I recognised it from photos: the spire of the cathedral soaring above everything else. I couldn't take my eyes from it: an impervious landmark for hundreds of years, unflinching as I arced slowly around it, following a long curling ridgeway. From there I could see for miles over the city and beyond.

Leaving the city behind, Salisbury Plain opened up around me like an unfolding map. I was an insignificant speck on that bare, rolling landscape, exposed and alone. The sun beat down, baking me and everything else, but I kept on, putting Farnham further and further behind me, and with that came a sense of freedom and being in control of my own destiny.

It's the last two days that have really ground me down. At times I've felt like a zombie, stumbling along on some God forsaken mission, no longer knowing where I was, where I was going, or what the point of it all was. Nightmarish thoughts have plagued me, night and day; paranoid delusions seizing me until I was struggling to tell the difference between reality and the tricks my mind and body were playing.

Somehow I kept going. I grasped the compass in my hand, forcing everything out of my head other than the need to follow that needle southwestward. Occasionally something jolted me back with a surge of adrenaline. Late on Tuesday morning, I found myself being drawn north and into a village. It was too late by the time I worked out what was happening: there were footsteps behind me. I had no alternative but to keep going. I started reciting my story again about going to university, to try to calm my panic, but it was all starting to get confused in my mind.

After the space of the country paths, I was suddenly hemmed in by stone walls and houses, all hewn from the same grey rock. I hurried on, past a graveyard with an austere church looming beyond. Why is it that I always seem to be welcomed into a village by its graveyard? I thought I could make out voices coming from it.

'Greetings from the departed! Creeping into our village like a ghoul? We don't want your sort here.'

I came round a corner and, abruptly, I was on the main street of the small market town of Mere. It was busier then anywhere I'd been since Farnham, with pubs and shops and people everywhere. I froze for a moment. Surely everyone would be pointing at me:

'That's the lad who's been on the news, quick, call the police'.

But they didn't. They were just going about their business normally. Two old boys sat between a war memorial and a clock tower, puffing on their pipes and chewing the cud. An old woman passed, hunched over and pushing a wicker shopping trolley. Another woman in a similar pose pushed a pram, cooing at her baby as she walked. There was a Spa, a chemist, a hairdresser, a butcher, a baker, a zebra crossing, a Chinese takeaway.

I had a sudden craving for egg-fried rice and some sweet-and-sour pork balls. In that moment, I'd have given anything to just pretend that everything was normal, to walk in and order it up, to find somewhere quiet to sit and then scoff the lot straight out of their foil trays, not giving a toss about the sticky sauce dribbling down my chin.

Then I took a risk. To my left was a footpath sign for The Monarch's Way. I'd been following it all day, and much of the day before, so I knew it was heading in the right direction. Instead I went straight on, towards the main road, towards a petrol station. It was the toilet, that's what did it. My stomach was griping again and the thought of a sit-down loo trumped everything. It was dirty and it stank, but the relief was immense.

I washed myself and refilled my water bottle from the tap. I reckoned that I'd probably been spotted anyway, so I went into the shop. I picked up a small loaf of bread, some ham and cheese and a packet of crisps and took them to the till. The guy wasn't much older than me and looked bored to hell.

'You alright, mate?' he asked, with a broad drawl.

Then, some quick thinking on my part: 'Yeah, I'm hitching up to London,' I replied, deliberately giving a false steer.

'Hope you won't wait too long. Getting hot out there,' he replied, tapping the prices into his till.

'Cheers, mate.'

'See ya.'

And with that, I was gone. I don't think he even looked up.

I don't remember much about the rest of the day. I stopped an hour or so out of Mere, once I was sure nobody had followed me, for a cheese and ham sandwich with crisps. That was good. I love putting crisps into a sandwich. It felt like I was eating proper food again.

Other than that I just walked, or stumbled, not seeing a soul. By dusk, I was absolutely knackered and needed to stop, but I couldn't get it out of my mind that someone must have reported me in Mere and that the police would be tracking me. Everywhere felt too exposed so I kept going until it was virtually dark. Then I had to make do with a grassy bank by the side of an old stonewall.

I'd completely lost track of where I was. Away to the north I could hear the roar of the A303 and in the distance the sky glowed from the streetlights of some unknown town. I'm normally pretty good at place names. When I was younger I used to stare for ages at maps, taking in the names and how they fitted together. On Tuesday night I was too tired to care: I just slept where I dropped.

The next morning, yesterday, I woke with a start from feverish dreams. It wasn't just the light that had woken me. A load of cows had come over to investigate, surrounding me with their sonorous lowing. They'd infiltrated my dreams, become bovine agents-of-the-law, herding me off to an Orwellian penal colony. One of them was licking the dew off my sleeping bag, prodding me awake. I leapt back, shouting and shooing at it. They backed off a few yards, then held their ground, staring back at me with a mix of boredom and recrimination.

Groggy and barely rested, I forced myself up. I couldn't exactly hang around with the cows, or risk the farmer turning up to find out what was going on. I crossed a stream soon after starting and I was able to wash myself and fill my bottle.

Finding water has been a constant worry. Each day has seemed hotter than the last and, as I've marched on, the sweat has poured off me. I've tried to ration my water, but it always seems to be running low. It probably hasn't helped my stomach, drinking water from streams. God knows what goes into them from upstream: *Dorset stream water – gently filtered through a rotting sheep's carcass!*

The drudge of the previous day continued, plodding on, head down, with the occasional emergency race for cover to evacuate my bowels. Late in the afternoon two military jets, one right after the other, appeared from nowhere, roaring low overhead. The shock was enough to knock me to the ground. I lay there for minutes unable to move, until finally I rolled myself over, drank some water and recovered my resolve.

The planes had landed not far ahead and soon the path reached a tall barbed-wire fence. On the other side were the runways and buildings of RNAS Yeovilton. I could see the two jets, taxiing slowly towards some hangars on the far side. If this was the RAF base, then Yeovil could only be a few miles further. As I walked, getting past it started to become my finishing line.

My body was screaming to stop, but the thought of an end kept me going. If I could get past Yeovil, I reckoned I'd have gone far enough for the moment and then I could rest up for a while. I passed it in a big loop to the north, the A303, which I'd more or less been walking parallel with since my stop at the petrol station, never far to my right.

The A303's always had exciting connotations for me: images of journeys to Cornwall for holidays, Stonehenge and Glastonbury. It's felt rather less glamorous this past couple of days, that distant roar constantly in the background, but at least it's given me a direction.

In the early evening the path curled back to the south. I came over a ridge and found myself looking down into the bowl of a valley. After hours of trekking over dry farmland it was balm to my spirit, the evening sunlight bathing the valley in a golden sheen. Below me, on the valley floor, stone houses clustered around a church tower and lush pastures were dotted with sheep and wildflowers. Framing it all was woodland that rolled down from the hillsides, becoming a darker, richer, enigmatic green, its shadows slowly encroaching, shielding the secrets held within. The heat of the day was finally dissipating, the sky fading into a cool blue with just a few wisps of white cloud. I imagined a pub down there in the village with a garden where I could sit and sup on a pint of cider. Down there, I knew instinctively, was the place for me to stop.

And this is where I am: up on the far slopes of the valley, a mile or so on from the village of Montacute. Last night I came down the slopes of the valley with renewed vigour, skirting round the edge of the village, following a footpath along the tree line half way up from the valley floor. The woods were all fenced off, but I found a stile and headed uphill, gratefully allowing the trees to close around me.

Part III

ISOLATION

Chapter 6

Montacute or bust

It was nearly dark by the time I stopped last night. I was so tired that I fell into my sleeping bag on the first clear bit of ground I could find and was asleep within seconds. This morning I woke floundering in the terrified confusion that has become the norm. Then I remembered my decision to stop here awhile and my panic became a surge of relief: today I wouldn't have to hoist that pack; today I wouldn't have to force myself onto unknown paths and roads; today I wouldn't have to drag my aching limbs and blistered feet any further.

For a few moments I relived that excitement I used to get when I woke on the first day of a holiday, after a long journey: an impatient curiosity to see how everything looks in the fresh light of day, mixed with that thrilling prospect of discovery and a fresh canvas on which to leave my mark.

I luxuriated in that feeling, trying vainly to eke it out, but, like the stones that were digging into my back, I couldn't ignore reality for long. Instead of seeing potential in my new surroundings, suddenly all I could think about was staying hidden and the unseen dangers that surely lurked everywhere. The hard truths of my situation came down on me, layer after heavy layer: I was almost out of water again and the only food I had left was the last few scraps from the petrol station and a couple of sweetcorn. I didn't even want to think about the prospect of running out of toilet roll.

My mind raced on, adding one problem after another. I needed to find myself a place to sleep. What happened if it rained? Not if, when. This long, hot summer was going to break soon enough, and then I'd get a proper soaking if I had no shelter. How long could I hide here for? What was I going to do with myself? Sit and wait? Sit and wait for what?

Weariness coursed through me. Thank God I didn't have to hike on any further. Today, I decided, I was just going to take it easy, get to know my surroundings, get my shit together.

I sat up and looked around, taking in my new surroundings for the first time. This woodland felt old. Chaotic. Dense. Trees rose high above me, the canopy thick enough to dim the light long after the sun had risen. Some of them must be hundreds of years old. I've always imagined how wonderful it must be to be rooted so firmly to such familiar ground, how much they must have seen and how they must laugh at the vain trivialities of human lives.

In the semi-darkness of the woodland, everything seemed to be fighting for space. Anything that could deal with the dimness joined the fray, seizing any space, reaching up and clinging to the trunks of the trees, their tendrils coiling and grasping. If I sat there long enough they would surely tangle around me, binding my limbs, slowly but surely imprisoning me.

Then I listened. Sounds emerged everywhere: the urgent twittering of birds flitting about, right there, but impossible to pinpoint; secret scurrying and scratching, urgent, close, but never quite identifiable; the buzzing of insects; the movement of branches and leaves in the air and far off in the background the familiar sounds of cattle and sheep.

I felt a hundred eyes watching me, weighing me up, conspiring against me, but as I sat, focusing in on each noise, order slowly emerged from the chaos. Noises became less urgent, patterns revealing themselves, the threat slowly diminishing. Birds continued to call out all around me, but I started to understand it: they were alarm calls, mating calls, dinner calls, information calls, calls of laughter and calls just for the sheer joy of calling. I'd get my harp out later and see if I could join in with them – a little nature-jam. For the moment, it was like I'd been assessed, then accepted, then admitted: the jungle-vine and jury passing its verdict.

I looked downhill and out towards the valley beyond. The trees were so dense I could barely make it out through the gloom. I decided to leave my stuff where it was, while I went to suss out the lay of the land.

Worrying that I would never find my gear again, I looked around for landmarks: a tree that forked halfway up like a wishbone, two big oak trees about ten paces apart, clawed branches that seemed to reach out to each other. Then I set off, counting a hundred and twelve paces before I reached the fence. There I carved an *M* on a fence post, to remind myself where I had to turn in.

I looked down into the valley below. It felt different from the night before. In the morning sunshine, everything was clearer, fresher, and more distinct. To the left, the houses of Montacute huddled together, dominated by a church tower on one side and to the other, standing a little aloof, the turrets of a grand old manor house. From where I was standing, pasture folded down to the valley floor and then back up again to more woodland on the other side. Away to my right, the land slipped gently away to a dense, seemingly impenetrable, thicket.

Beyond, hills rolled away into the far distance. An old stone house sat in splendid isolation, incongruous amid the wild surrounding nature, its manicured square of lawn with multi-coloured flowers fenced neatly off from the encroaching fields, as if to emphasise it's difference, it's sep-arateness, it's superiority. Have they done that to keep nature out, or humanity in, I wondered.

At the bottom of the field, randomly scattered sheep grazed, but they were about the only sign of life. I tuned into their bleating, one responding to the other, a random cascade of tremulous monotones. They've got to be the dumbest animals out there, even if those cows from the night before last would have to run them close. Then I had to laugh: who was I to call *them* dumb animals?

I followed the tree line away from the village. At the

bottom I rose up to cross a narrow lane that ran back towards Montacute. I hadn't noticed it earlier, but from there the land opened up at a right angle, exposing a whole new valley floor shaped just like the last. Again it was framed by woodland on either side, but this felt even more secluded.

As I carried on I spotted what looked like a water hole on the valley floor. There was nobody in sight, so I trotted down. A couple of sheep bleated peevishly at me as I approached, then hurried away at the last moment.

The ground around it was trodden into dust by a thousand hooves. It looked like I'd be sharing my water with a whole bunch of sheep and cows. It didn't look that appealing either: kind of stagnant and partially covered in a green sludge, even if there were some bubbles rippling the water on the far side. I scooped up a handful of water from close to what appeared to be the source, sniffed it and took a couple of sips. It tasted OK, but I wasn't sure: it would have to be my water of last resort if I couldn't find anything else. If I boiled it up, it would be fine I reckoned.

I stood and took a three-sixty view around. From the valley floor I got a different perspective. To the south, it sloped gradually away from me to some trees at the bottom. I could just make out the top of another house on the other side – maybe the farmhouse for this land?

The western side looked like the most promising. It sloped quite steeply up to a large area of woodland, which was fenced off, just like where I was last night. The trees were thick enough that, from the valley floor, you couldn't see more than a few yards in. I took off up the slope towards a gate and stile that led into the woods.

I knew right away that this was going to be the spot for me. These woods are a little less dense then last night's, but still thick enough to keep me hidden, and they go on for much further then I initially thought, spreading out over the ridge of the hill and beyond. Even better, I heard the sound of water and traced it to a little stream that runs down the far side of the hill, almost becoming a mini-waterfall in places. I doused myself all over with the water and then drank and drank. It tasted beautiful: cool and sweet and reviving.

I didn't need to see any more. I turned and retraced my steps to get my stuff and here I find myself. I've got a great little spot. When I got back with my pack, I went over the ridge of the hill and found that the woods ran on as far as I could see in all directions. The stream runs down the steepest part of the hill, forming a gully, but a couple of hundred yards from there is a flatter shelf of land, hidden away by a thick cluster of trees and bushes.

A small tree has lurched over in a storm, but it only went over half way and it now leans at a forty-five degree angle, trunk wedged between the branches of its neighbour, half its roots exposed to the world, but somehow still growing. It will be a perfect base for a bivouac.

The ground is thick with vegetation, but it's not too bad here. I reckon I can clear it without too much trouble and there'll be enough space to make a fire pit. Most important someone would have to get really close to spot me and there are no obvious signs of paths or people walking through. Yes, this will do just fine and even with my griping stomach, my spirits are rising.

Chapter 7

Pinch, punch, first of the month

'*P inch, punch, first of the month – and no returns.*'
Charlie and I always used to do that. We got really competitive with it, even though Charlie used to forget, so I would win pretty much every time. Even when he remembered the night before, and told me he was going to be first this time, he'd nearly always forgotten by morning. And it was always really funny; except when I punched him too hard, then he'd start crying and run off to Mum.

Today is Tuesday the first of September and I pinch-punched myself. I laughed, as I always do, but there's no fun in it really, it's just one of those things that I cling to as a link to the past, that takes me right back to that time, to the warmth of being part of something, of not being alone. I can still picture the changes in Charlie's expressions when I got him: from surprise, to annoyance to determination; his bottom lip and chin jutting out defiantly.

'I'm gonna win next time,' he'd shout.

And I'd laugh. 'No, you won't.'

'Yes, I will.'

Once, he tried *'Pinch, punch, second of the month.'* He must have been carrying that thought around with him all day and night. Another month, he was so determined that I woke up with him sitting on my bed and he got me before I'd even fully opened my eyes. He was so pleased with himself that I just had to laugh. He was running round like a champion all day.

I've been thinking about Charlie and Mum and Dad a lot this week. It's like they've been guiding me, filling the silences and the emptiness. I've always struggled to deal with their ghosts. One moment I'm battling to keep their memories alive, inking them forever onto my arm, clinging to the few of their things that I have left, the next I'm trying to shut them out. One moment I want them back so much it hurts, the next I'm screaming at them to *fuck off and leave me alone.*

This week I've accepted their presence, not tried to change them, just listened to them, allowed them to be. It's a new feeling: light and easy and reassuring.

If I close my eyes, I can see them. Mum is smiling at me. There's a calm, golden light emanating from her and she's gently whispering:

'It'll all be OK, Mark. You'll see.'

Dad is taking his pipe out of his mouth and saying to me:

'Chin up Marko: keep strong and don't let the buggers get you down!'

That was always his advice, straight out of the Winston Churchill quotation book. And Charlie is just being

Charlie. Running around, turning everything into a game, collecting sticks for me, finding new little hiding places, smiling and laughing.

I've always fantasised about what life would have been like if they were still around. What it comes down to, mostly, is me telling them things and them listening: Dad nodding with murmurs of approval; Mum beaming, laughing in all the right places and Charlie rapt, looking up at me admiringly.

Sometimes some small part of me even believes that, if I focus hard enough, it will become real, but even then I can only hold onto it for a few moments until something tears inside and I'm yanked back to reality, cursing myself for my naivety. Somehow, sat here in these woods, I've been able to let their words and images appear and to accept them gratefully.

On that first afternoon, once I'd chosen my new base, I set about building a bivouac. I'd done this once with Jeff in the Scouts and, not for the last time this week, I wished that I'd listened to him more closely. All I could remember was his lispy voice that turned into a slight stammer when he got stressed.

'Pack the bwanches clothely together boys,' he'd shout. 'That's it, juth like that.'

Some of the kids used to take the piss out of him behind his back and it always came as a surprise how much that annoyed me. Eventually they used to cut me out of their jokes: I suppose they must have thought I would rat on them.

I struggled on with the bivouac, trying vainly to remember what Jeff had said, but anyone watching me would have had a right old laugh. First I was trying to carry too much and couldn't see where I was going, getting caught in branches, tripping over things, cursing at anything and everything. Then, when I'd finally got most of one side in place, I pressed down on it, trying to get it nice and tight, and some of the branches snapped, sending me crashing through a big hole of my own creation, scratching and cutting myself in the process.

It was early evening by the time I'd got the basic frame up. For the first time in a week I had a roof over my head and a wave of exhilaration lifted me as I crawled in for the first time, lying on my back to look up at my handiwork. I laid all my stuff out at the low end and there was still plenty of room to stretch out my sleeping bag. I could sit up easily enough and, at the open end, it was almost high enough to stand. Looking up I could still see gaps between the branches, but it didn't feel like it was going to collapse on me anytime soon and it there was no rain in sight. It would do for the moment.

My mind had turned to getting a fire going later, so I set about clearing some space of undergrowth. I could have done with some shears and a shovel to get rid of it, but all I had was my penknife and some improvised sticks so I just kicked at it, cut as much of it as I could with the blade on my penknife and finally got down on my hands and knees and ripped it out. That was hard work: my hands were cut to pieces by the time I'd finished, but I got enough out so that there was space for a small fire.

It felt great sleeping under the bivouac that first night. I was warm from the fire I'd got going and then, once the embers had almost died down, I crawled into the close darkness of my new cocoon. Even if I didn't have enough food in my belly, and even if my hands were stinging and sore, I still went to sleep feeling snug and secure, galvanised by the belief that I could turn my hand to anything if I needed to.

The next morning I woke ravenous, my stomach growling me back to reality. A rising panic gripped me as I remembered that I'd roasted the last sweetcorn on the fire last night. I had nothing left to eat. Finding something had to be my top priority, so I took a couple of plastic bags from my pack and set off deeper into the woods to start my search.

It's weird how everything changes through experience: transforming from the blurry unknown to the intimately familiar. Now, just a week later, I have this whole area mapped in my mind. I know what is over the next ridge. I know the little dip where someone once strung a rope from the great branch that reaches over it. I know the great redwood tree that is the largest around. I know how far the woods extend and what lies beyond. But then, at the start, uncertainty bathed everything in a darker hue: mysterious, malevolent and fearful.

I scrambled through dense undergrowth for an age until, eventually, I found the faintest of paths. This in turn led to other paths, veering off in random directions, twisting back on themselves, widening and then petering out.

The tree canopy above me was still thick, but everywhere I was starting to feel the bells of this hot summer ringing their last orders. There was something in the light that was becoming less intense; in the leaves that had once been bright and fresh but were now slowly losing their lustre and in the wilting ferns, their fringes an inching grey-brown, as their life-forces were sucked from them, slowly but inexorably.

I had a sudden premonition of the autumn and winter that surely lay ahead, of the chill winds and rains that would strip this place, leaving each tree and creature exposed and alone to fend for itself. I saw myself amongst it, lying naked and wretched, clinging to life. It was a mere shiver, like the first sneeze of a cold that has yet to take hold, but from that moment a small seed of foreboding was germinating deep inside me.

Ahead, the woods rolled onwards, but to my left I could now see a tree line with bright sunshine filtering in from beyond. I moved towards a patch of sunlight where a mass of brambles was filled with blackberries and filled my mouth greedily. These wouldn't be here for much longer so I plucked a few handfuls more into one of my bags.

Through the tree line I could see the land falling away to another village: what I now know to be Norton-sub-Hamdon. It's barely a hundred houses, spilling down the hillside to a cluster at the bottom of the hill around a church steeple. Beyond its rooftops the land is much flatter and from here I can see for miles across farmland, picking out more hamlets and villages here and there and, in the far distance, the A303 forging on southwestwards.

Sometimes I sit for ages gazing out at that view, but on Thursday morning all I could think about was how starving I was and where my next food was going to come from. Looking down the hill into the village, I could make out trees laden with fruit, what looked like allotments and, from some source I couldn't identify, the raucous clucking of chickens.

In the fields, many of the crops had already been harvested. I'd seen the farmers out in their great combine harvesters in the least few days. Here and there some had already started to burn the stubble, ready for sowing next year's crop. I could see one combine out, even this early, making its stately progress up and down, dust trailing in its wake.

Other than that one farmer there was no sign of anyone else stirring yet, so I crept down the hill towards the hedgerow that bordered the edge of the village. On the other side were some of the fruit trees I'd spotted from the top. There I had my first bit of luck of the day. A couple of trees brimming with apples were within easy reach and the hedge was thin enough for me to reach through and pluck half a dozen.

This was going to be a regular stomping ground for me. On the lower slopes around the village I've found orchards full of fruit this week: apples, pears, plums, cherries. I've gorged myself on them, unable to resist, even knowing the inevitable consequence once they start to ferment in my growling stomach.

I thought the apples might have been sour, but they

weren't, they were perfect, crisp and sweet. I ate two of them, crouched down behind the hedge, and put the other four into a bag. Then I turned my attention to trying to find some more corn. They'd become my staple and I desperately wanted to get more before they'd all been harvested.

I walked for miles looking. The temperature rose quickly and it was more humid then it had been, like there was a storm coming, so I was soon sweating heavily and my head pounding. My energy was sapping with each step, especially after a couple of emergency toilet stops had taken their toll. I followed footpaths all around, my hopes rising each time I passed a hedgerow, only to be dashed on the hard soil of another ploughed field.

I was despondent and on the edge of giving up, but finally, just as I was starting to turn back towards base, I came across a field bursting with cobs. My spirit soared, as if I was greeting a long-lost friend, and I filled one of my bags with a whole load of them.

As if that wasn't enough good fortune for one day, on the way back came my big break. I'd have missed it if I'd found a way of getting past the village without following the lane for a while. I didn't want to be clocked then: not only was I a fugitive on the run, but I was carrying a whole load of pilfered corn and apples. Just before the village, I passed the allotments on my left. And there, resting on the wall, were a whole load of veggies neatly laid out in cardboard boxes. Even better: some eggs. Next to them was a little box with a sign:

'Honesty Box: all proceeds to SSHWI.'

In that moment, I couldn't have cared less what SSHWI was. I quickly grabbed a courgette, some carrots, a couple of onions, a big handful of potatoes and four eggs. I scrabbled in my pockets for some change and put three ten pence pieces and some coppers into the box. Then I hurried away, my bags laden with food, shaking with excitement. All I had on my mind was that I was going to have some proper food to eat that night. I nearly ran up the hill on the way back, my energy miraculously restored, fantasising about the omelette I was going to make myself later.

And what an omelette I cooked up. I got a little fire going and fried up some coarsely chopped onion and courgette. Then I cracked in two eggs and some corn from one of the cobs for good measure. It stuck to my pan and turned out more like scrambled egg then an omelette, but the smell still had me dribbling into the fire in anticipation and it tasted amazing. I'd have loved a beer to wash it down, but I made do with a brew of tea instead.

Then I pulled out my harp and played some feisty licks, really giving it some for the first time since Farnham. Normally I play along to something on the tape deck, but it's great sometimes to just play random stuff as it comes to me and see where it goes. I started off with Bowie's Jean Genie and that somehow morphed into some funky Motown riffs and then LA Woman by The Doors.

I imagined Jim Morrison sat across the fire drawling out the lyrics with me. That would have been cracking. But this was OK too: just me and my fire and my harp and a bellyful of good food. I picked up Jack Kerouac and read a few pages. Dean Moriarty and Jim Morrison, they'd be fine fireside companions. Three ghosts by the fire: one dead, one imagined and one disappeared.

Maybe I'd tell them my story. Or maybe I'd say nothing. Maybe I'd just sit and listen to their banter and their stories, play some harp; the musical accompaniment to their verbal jousting. Whatever we did, by the end of the night we'd be best buddies.

What would they have to say about my situation, if I did tell them? I can't even figure it out for myself. I keep trying to ignore it, press it down, but like a Jack-in-the-Box it just pops up again. Except it's not Jack that pops up with his shiny, smiley face, but Steen, scowling at me, his eyes burning accusingly into me.

Early the next morning I woke abruptly with a new image of him in my mind. It was a moment that I'd forgotten, from when I first got to know him. It was when I was in Montgomery House for a few months, back in seventy-eight, so I must have been fourteen going on fifteen. I'd been creeping up the stairs, quietly, trying not to attract any attention. As I got onto the landing, I saw that the door to his room was open and he was sat on his bed, leant over and staring into space.

It was only a split-second, but in that moment it was like a window had opened into him that he'd never exposed before. Through it I saw pain and sadness and self-doubt. I saw loneliness, I saw vulnerability, even a little naivety, but most of all I saw a desperate craving. I recognised it instantly, because it felt just like my own: a craving for approval and a craving to be loved and to belong.

Seeing it in him was shocking. I couldn't believe that he harboured the same feelings as I did, that he was suppressing them just like I was. It was only the mask that was different. His was designed to scare, to warn off trespassers. Mine was more of a cloak of invisibility. That unmasked image stayed with me for a long time; somehow it was even more terrifying than the mask itself.

At the top of the stairs I was frozen to that spot: unable to move, unable to pull my eyes away from him. A floorboard must have creaked or something, because he suddenly looked up and the moment was shattered. His guard snapped shut again, back to his usual cocktail of hate and fury. Before I could move he launched himself at me, pinning me against the wall. I still remember how his breath stank of beer and stale cigarettes.

'What you fucking staring at?' he yelled. 'Think you're something special huh? Think you're the only one who's lost something? At least your folks wanted you. My old dear pissed off before I even knew her. Fuck knows who the old man was. You sort yourself out round here, 'coz no one else will. Now fuck off and leave me alone, before I kick ten types of shit out of you.'

He turned and stomped back into his room, slamming the door behind him. I was left cowering, breathless against the wall, rubbing my face with my sleeve, trying to clear off the spit he'd sprayed and the tears that were threatening to burst.

All I have in my mind now is that fraction of a second when I saw the real Steen. Who knows how he might have turned out if life had dealt him a different hand, because stripped of the bile and the angry sneer he'd been a frightened little boy, just like me.

I'm tormented by guilt. How could I have done this? Am I really a murderer? Whatever he'd done, he surely didn't deserve a knife stuck in his gut. It happened less than two weeks ago, but already it feels like a different age, something that happened to someone like me, but not actually me. It's become hazy, taken on a life of its own.

It did happen, though, I can't deny it. I heard the pop as the blade punctured him, felt it tearing through flesh, saw the terror in his eyes as he clutched his wound, smelt the blood and later cleaned it off the blade as it congealed, dark and sticky and crusty.

Those images feel like they've branded themselves indelibly into me, yet at some other level my brain can't accept that version of events. It wants to build a better one: one that is more palatable, a version that will pass the finger of blame away from me: justify it, sweep it under the carpet, get rid of it. Only then can I make sense of what happened, accept it as part of me and who I am.

I've got this weird fracturing between my conscious and subconscious. I know what has happened, but when I try and think about it I feel like it's going to engulf me and I go round in circles of self-recrimination, becoming my own pitiless judge and jury. And all the time, in the background, my mind is whirring away on a different trajectory altogether, one that I seem to have no control over, one that will reach its own conclusion regardless.

I woke up a couple of days after this with the image of

Steen lunging at me again. There was no longer any vulnerability in those eyes, just savage intent. I knew, in that moment, that I'd had to protect myself and I did it in the only way that I could. It was suddenly clear to me that it wasn't my fault after all. Why had I been beating myself up, when I just did what anyone would do? I leapt up with the feeling of a weight lifted from me. It wasn't long though, before the doubts started to creep back. Yes, I had to defend myself, but stabbing him? I shivered again at the horror of what I've done. I don't even know if he's dead or alive.

On Friday morning it rained: the first time in about two weeks. I could feel it coming all through the morning. I'd scrumped a few more apples and sat looking out over Norton. I could smell it first: that harsh, dry, dustiness replaced by something softer and richer. Then I felt the humidity: rising in my skin and squeezing at my temples. I watched the clouds bubbling up in the west, as if they were being conjured. I was hypnotized by it for a while, but then abruptly realised that I should head back to the camp and do some work on the bivouac to prepare it.

Earlier, I'd pulled out yards of overgrown ivy, which I reckoned I could use as twine. When I got back I lashed it around the branches as they overlapped on the roof. I should have been doing this before when I first put the branches down: now I was struggling to reach all the joins. It was too late to start all over again so I just did a rough old job: it made it a bit stronger at least. Then I cut a load of ferns and layered them on top of the roof, pressing them down and hoping they wouldn't blow off with the first gust.

I felt the wind starting to pick up, bringing a sweet scent of rain in the air. Then I suddenly thought about firewood. I ran off, returning with armfuls of kindling, dumping them under my roof to keep them dry. The wind lifted a notch, swirling and churning, and then down it came, sudden and loud, with large, heavy drops crashing through the trees, obliterating the silence that had been gathering.

I made it back with a final bundle of logs just as it started to come down. I fell panting to the dry earth beneath my roof, half cursing, half laughing. I watched it for a while, then, on a whim, stripped off down to my jockeys and jumped outside, stretching my arms out wide to welcome the cleansing rain.

I raised my face to the sky to catch drops in my mouth, whooping with the exhilaration as the raindrops pounded me. The rain was warm, but refreshing at the same time, my skin tingling. I tasted it on my tongue: sweet, then tangy as it mixed with the salt from my skin. I closed my eyes and felt the dirt and grime of the past week being washed away.

Finally, a loud clap of thunder startled me from my reverie and I dived back under cover. Then I was happy to just sit and watch as the rain drummed down, listening to the soundtrack of the storm, sucking and blowing out some notes from my harp and inhaling that beautiful, rich, earthy smell of summer rain on parched earth.

It only rained for an hour or so and, amazingly, barely a

drop made it through my makeshift roof. A few of the ferns had blown off, but I soon replaced those and over the next week I've kept adding more foliage, until it looks like some misshapen creature from the swamp.

There were more showers over the following days, but mostly the warm, sunny weather has continued, so each day I've kept on exploring all around and settling myself. The camp's getting pretty domesticated now – I've even rigged myself a short clothesline. Best of all, the eggs seemed to bind me up a bit and I got a few days of ceasefire from the war waging in my belly.

I head down to the allotments most days. I've found a way I can circle round Norton and spy on it from a spot in the woods where I can't be seen. It's less than a hundred yards away, looking down on it from the side of the hill, so I can see everyone coming in and out and what they're up to. There are a handful of them that seem to go down there, mostly old folk. At the weekends the place is full of them and I reckon they spend as much of their time gossiping and drinking tea as actually doing any work.

On Saturday a woman came down with a load of eggs in cartons. I could see her offering them around. They were obviously being polite, holding their hands up as if to say '*no, thanks,*' then changing their mind and taking a couple, '*since she insisted.*' I was cursing. I reckon she'd have left any spares on the wall like before, but they all got taken. That seemed to put them all into bartering mode:

'Would you like some of my runner beans?' Someone seemed to be saying.

'Ooh, yes please, but you must have some of my potatoes. I'll go and dig some out for you.'

It's a decent spot, my spy nest over the allotment, so I'm happy to just sit there and bide my time while all this goes on. There's a tree I lean against and from there I can see through the branches, down to the lane at the bottom of the hill and over the hedge to the patchwork strips of the allotments and its assortment of little sheds and homemade scarecrows.

I take Jack Kerouac with me for company. I'd read the whole book within a few days, but that's OK, I just went back to the start and read it again. I'm a bit too close to play my harp: they might hear me if I get carried away and play too hard, so I just make up little tunes and play them in my head.

Eventually, I always have the place to myself and usually someone's left some veggies over. Then I nip down and help myself to what's there and leave a few pence in the tin. I've had more potatoes, onions, carrots, runner beans, courgettes, some tomatoes and a couple of times some eggs, which always gets me really excited. This place has been my lifesaver.

By Monday, I'm almost out of change. I don't want them to think there's someone thieving, because then they might stop leaving stuff out, or worse, put someone on watch, so I folded up a pound note and stuffed it in the tin. At least I was now in credit.

After the rain on Friday and Saturday the land came alive again, sucking up the water gratefully. The water gushed down my stream with renewed vigour and the grass, which had wilted to a parched-straw colour, reclaimed its vibrant green.

Then, on Sunday afternoon, returning from the allotment, I spotted some mushrooms in the field by the edge of the woods. I was sure they hadn't been there in the morning. They'd come out of nowhere, huge things, shouting out their presence to the world. I'm wary of eating anything poisonous, but I was pretty sure they were field mushrooms, so I cut a few to try. They cooked up really well and I've been eating them pretty much every night since.

I reckon the farmer will harvest the sweetcorn anytime now, so I've been building a stash of them. Once they've finished, I've decided that my next staple is going to be sweet chestnuts. I can see them swelling in their prickly pouches on the trees. When I can get my hands on them, I'll gather up a load and roast them on the fire. A few of them fell after the rain on Friday and Saturday, but there's not much in them. They're biding their time and I try to do the same, but food is constantly on my mind and I'm pretty much ravenous all the time.

I fantasise about a big Sunday roast with all the trimmings, the plate piled high and swimming in gravy, or that Chinese takeaway on the way here. Instead I make do with the meagre rations I can get my hands on and by the end of the week I'm starting to get used to it and rejoicing in the occasional egg and potato.

Other than the camp, the stream is my most important place. I go down there first thing each morning to fill up my water bottle and to wash. It's only a few feet across at its widest and no more than a couple of feet deep, but it runs down the hill pretty quick, especially after it's rained.

I kneel on the bank and dunk my head right in, the ice-cold water zinging me to life. I don't like washing my hair with soap, but I've done it a couple of times, when it was starting to feel really greasy and dirty. It's just as I well I don't have a mirror because I must be looking a right state by now.

Then there's my beard. I've not grown it this long before and I'm constantly running my fingers through it, scratching and pulling at it, as if it doesn't belong to me.

It's hard to keep clean in here. I've washed all my clothes at least a couple of times, scrubbing them with soap in the stream and then hanging them up from my new clothesline. Even with all that, I still feel grubby and itchy all the time and sore from all the cuts and scratches and stings and bites. I'm paranoid that they're going to get infected, but luckily there was a bottle of TCP and some plasters in my first-aid kit. I only threw it in my pack as an afterthought, but I'm glad I did.

However much I'm getting used to being here, I still can't get rid of that ominous feeling that I'm being watched. I feel most exposed when I'm down by the stream. With the noise of the water it would be easy not to hear someone creeping up, so I'm extra vigilant when I'm there. I must look like one of those little birds that I watch, doing everything with rapid jerky movements, constantly looking up at the slightest noise.

I'm probably just being paranoid, because I've only seen people in here a couple of times, both dog walkers and I'm pretty sure they've not seen me. They mostly seem to stick to the paths that follow the valley, or skirt along and across the treeline.

I understand this place better now that I've been here a week. These woods are basically a ribbon of trees that curl along the hilltop and it's upper slopes. On the northern side there's a couple of old quarries that don't look like they've been worked for years and beyond that the land falls away to flat farmland for as far as I can see. Most of the buildings in the villages round here seem to have been made of stone from the quarry. It's a golden colour, making them look like gingerbread houses when I look down on them.

There might not be people, but there's plenty of life. Not just the birds and the insects either, or the squirrels, always darting about, hanging from branches like Spiderman. I've seen foxes, deer and a couple of badgers too.

At dusk, as I'm lighting my fire, the bats come out. They swoop around and through the trees like the Red Arrows, somehow avoiding all obstacles. I lose them for a moment then pick up their dark shapes again in the gaps in the trees. It's mesmerising, sitting here watching them, especially once the fire is going and it's almost completely dark.

My favourite, of all the creatures in here, is the hedgehog. I first saw him at the end of last week, scurrying through the undergrowth. He's my new neighbour and buddy now. I call him Spike, because as soon as he sussed that I'd seen him he rolled into a spiky ball, as if preparing himself for my imminent attack. I crouched on all fours, barely breathing, watching and waiting to see what he'd do next.

'Hey, I'm not going to hurt you, buddy,' I cooed.

Finally, he started to unfurl, his pointy little face and ears tentatively emerging. Underneath his spiky exterior he was soft and furry and vulnerable. I saw this for no more than a split second because then he was off, darting for the safety of cover.

I pretty much know where his nest is now and he's the first thing I look out for each morning when I head down towards the stream. He'll often be scurrying back across the hill to his nest from his nocturnal ramblings.

'Morning, Spike,' I always call out. 'You dirty stop out. Did'ya get lucky...? No, me neither.'

I'm not holding my breath for a reply, but he doesn't do his *rolling-up-in-a-ball* trick when he sees me anymore, so I reckon he must recognise me now. Whatever, it's the closest I get to a conversation each day, so I look forward to our little banter. I usually see him at night as well, when I'm sat by the fire. I always hear him first, rooting around in the undergrowth, digging up worms or slugs, or whatever his favourites are. I keep looking in the direction of his scrabblings and eventually I spot his eyes reflecting back the flames of the fire.

'Ha, gotcha, you can't hide from me, Spike!'

We watch each other for a few minutes before he's off again. I can still sense he's around though, so I play him something on the harp. I reckon Spike's got to be a punk, so I play stuff like *Hangin' Around* or *No More Heroes* by the

Stranglers. I'd love to feed him, but I reckon he knows how to survive in here better than I do. I take inspiration from him: if he can survive in here, so can I.

It's not just Spike out there. I don't often see many of the other creatures, but I can hear them. I'm starting to recognise their noises, getting to know where they go and when they like to come out. Funny, they're just like me: wary of humans. When they first notice me they freeze, all evidence of their presence vanishing, no doubt watching me, sniffing me, weighing me up; but if I sit still for long enough, they eventually resume their business, even in daylight. They've taken me in and concluded that I'm not a threat to them.

At night, the woods come alive to an altogether different tune. My roof protects me, but it entombs me as well. Most nights now I struggle to get off to sleep and I find myself lying there, sleeping bag wedged right up to my chin, my body rigid with fearful anticipation.

Inside, the darkness is total. In that void of light my other senses amplify to maximum volume, as if to take the place of my eyes. In the first week or so after my escape I was so exhausted each night that I must have slept through it all, oblivious to the drama unfolding around me, but now I hear and feel and smell everything, the noises and vibrations and scents of the hunters and the hunted. The woods buzz with insects. The hoots of owls echo ominously all around. Foxes and badgers and who knows what scurry past, seemingly close enough to reach out and touch.

Then there are the blood-curdling screeches. Are they the dread-filled squeals of the hunted as they realise their fate, or the victory cries of the hunters, pouncing and swooping for their kill? In the darkness, my imagination fills in the gaps. I picture the adrenaline-fuelled terror of the chase: little creatures bursting every sinew to escape; the thud of impact; the explosion of feathers; the savage tussle of talons and claws and teeth and then the sickening silence as life is extinguished and the victor savours it's spoils.

In those dark moments I convince myself that something is going to come in here, something with a taste for human flesh. It's watching me, breathing in my fear, just waiting until I drift into sleep before it pounces. So I lie, tense and waiting. Sometimes I grip a stick as a weapon to ward off any intruders, but finally I succumb, drifting into sleep, with the soundtrack and narrative of the forest blurring seamlessly into my dreams.

There, I once again become the hunted. I'm hunted by the police, by Steen and his skinhead mates, by farmers armed with pitchforks, by rabid dogs howling for my blood. I'm running and I'm hiding, but they keep coming, until I wake up feverish, screaming and flailing, trying to remember where I am and how I got here.

Often in the mornings I'll find the remnants of these nocturnal fights: skeletons stripped of flesh, feathers or fur strewn chaotically, as if their lives had never happened, nor mattered. In the golden early light it's hard to believe the battleground it becomes once darkness descends. The mornings are when I make this place my own. The birds celebrate with me, always the same cacophonous cocktail of joy, as if they can't quite believe that they've survived another night and the sun has risen again.

I've got my favourite spots to sit now: spots where I can see out, but not be seen. The best times are early morning and early evening. In the morning I look eastwards, as the rising sun breathes life into Montacute, and in the evening I watch the sun finish its journey dipping down over Norton and the fields beyond.

I stay there until the light has almost gone. That's my cue to go and light my fire for the evening, to wait for the bats to start their show, for Spike to poke his head out and then for the resumption of the nocturnal battles of my subconscious.

Getting the fire going each night is my moment of triumph, my moment of wizardry. It's like I've released a pure and powerful and cleansing force, a force of which I am master. Here, I feel safe, as though the light from the flames will protect me from anything.

Once I've cooked and eaten my food and brewed up some tea I just sit, gazing into the flames, letting my mind drift where it will. There's something hypnotic about losing myself in their infinite flickering patterns, letting thoughts and memories and feelings brew up, like clouds in the sky, from some secret place deep within me.

All the people who have been part of my life come to visit me here, as if they have some, yet unknown, message to deliver. I can see their faces in the flames, hear them talking, feel their presence as if they were sat right here with me. I imagine that I've found my way to America and I'm touring with Uncle Harry, playing gigs together, just the two of us. We're like Dean Moriarty and Sal Paradise in 'On the Road'. The place names spin past me: New York, Chicago, Denver, San Francisco, Los Angeles, New Orleans. Everything is possible and new adventures wait over every horizon.

I try to bring Melissa here too, but it's getting harder. She'd come and sit here with me and we'd talk about anything and everything: about music and books and politics, about the world that's waiting for us to explore and about how *small-time* Farnham is. And sex, of course, we'd talk openly about it, no holds barred, about what turns us on and turns us off. I'd serenade her on my harp and she'd listen rapt, as we gazed into each other's eyes, the light from the fire dancing in her eyes. I try hard to believe in this fantasy, but I just can't get it to stick.

She'll be getting ready to head off to university in Exeter by now. She'll probably be driving right past here in a week or so, with her parents, all her possessions loaded into the boot of their car. She won't have given me a second thought. Why would she? She might have wondered why I didn't show up at The Cobbett on results day, but more likely she forgot she even asked me.

She must have heard that I stabbed Steen; it might even have become the *Scandal of the Summer* in Farnham. I try to believe that I've become a hero to her, but the reality is it probably just reconfirmed her impression of what a loser I am. No, with each day that passes, it's getting harder to keep anything of Farnham alive and the certainty rises that there's nothing there for me to go back to now.

It's not just Farnham that's disappearing, it's the whole outside world. My world is shrinking into this island of woods and the pastoral shoreline that surrounds it. Each morning the sun rises on one side and each evening it sets on the other. As I watch its slow arc each day, these woods feel more and more like the centre of the universe, as though it's the sun that rotates around *them*. No wonder folk used to think that the world was flat.

In my universe, nothing now exists outside of here. Everything else has been suspended. All those dramatic news stories that had captivated me, what felt like the tide of history, the backdrop to my life, have dissolved into irrelevance, an alternative reality that no longer exists.

Are they still going on? The inner-city riots, the IRA hunger strikes, mass unemployment, the war in Afghanistan, the threat of nuclear Armageddon: none of that exists in here. It's just me and Spike and the rest of my woodland co-residents: getting by, from one day to the next.

All told, I reckoned I'd been doing pretty well holding things together, focusing on what had to be done to get myself safe and secure. Then, yesterday morning, I had my first crash to earth.

I was sitting just inside the tree line looking down into the valley towards Montacute. The old farmer was coming back along the valley floor on his funny quad-bike thing, as he does every morning. I guess he goes up and down checking on his animals.

It always makes me laugh, because for some reason it reminds of that scene from *The Great Escape*: the one where Steve McQueen sits astride his Triumph, figuring out his last chance of jumping the fence and escaping the Nazis. Except he looked cool, where the farmer doesn't: he looks more Wurzel Gummidge and the bike more like a mobility scooter.

Yesterday morning, as he came up the valley, he stopped to speak with an old woman who was coming the other way with a couple of dogs. They obviously knew each other. The dogs came running up to him and he cut the engine, leaning over to pat them briskly, ruffing up their collars. She caught up and said something to him. They both laughed, freely, easily, and continued chatting for a few minutes, as if they were resuming a conversation they'd only just interrupted. Then she turned and, with a parting gesture, started to walk away. The dogs lingered for a moment, enjoying the attention.

'Come on, girls.' I heard her shout.

The dogs turned to scamper after her and the farmer restarted his bike resuming his progress along the valley.

That's when I found I was crying. Not just crying, but sobbing. I was sobbing for all those easy, friendly chats that I've missed over the years: with Mum, with Dad, with my brother, with all of the friends that I've lost or never had. I was sobbing for how totally alone I felt in that moment. And I was sobbing at the sudden certainty that I would never again experience the warmth and comfort of such friendships. I had no defence to it: the emotion just poured out of me, my body jerking, my head buried in my hands, my knees scrunched up to my chin.

What I really wanted, more than anything, was a hug from my mum: warm, consoling, forgiving. But this real-isation only served to swell the shame that was swamping me. I pictured the whole world looking down at me laughing:

'Look at that fucking loser, sitting all on his own in the woods, jealous of Wurzel Gummidge and Molly Sugden, crying for his mum: he'll be sucking his thumb next!'

After a few minutes like this, I slowly started to pull myself together. Like I always do. Once, when I was about fifteen, I punched a hole in my bedroom door. I can't even remember what caused it exactly. It was after I'd got out of the children's home and moved in with Sarah and Jock, a Scottish couple who had no kids of their own.

Things should have got better for me after that, because it was terrible in the home and I don't think I could have lasted much longer. There were some really messed up kids, of all ages, in there; the ones that would never find a foster home or get adopted; their last stop before borstal.

Steen was just one of them, but he went to the same school as me and he'd got his claws into me. If anything, the fact that I'd got a foster home made it worse. He was picking on me at every chance and I was missing lunch most days, because he'd stolen my lunch money.

At my new home I liked Sarah, but Jock was a macho man, wanting to lay down the law all the time. One evening he tore into me about something, probably about what I was doing with my money, which just pushed me over the edge. I ran into my room and locked the door. I stood there for a minute or so, straining to hold back the tears, listening to them arguing about whatever had just happened.

I got this weird feeling like I was in a washing machine. Then I lost it. I turned and screamed and punched the door. It could have been Steen or Jock, but the door got it instead. It couldn't have been that thick, because my fist went straight through it. I was left there, white as a sheet, with my body in my room and my arm dangling through the hole into the corridor. I was expecting Jock to go berserk, but he must have sensed something.

He just said: 'Come on, son, open the door and we'll clear this up. We can fix it up at the weekend.'

So, that weekend, I got a crash course in carpentry and plastering. We repaired the door and nothing more was said about it, although they decided to move back to Scotland the following summer, just after I'd done my 'O' Levels and I was on my way to Estha and Jim: the last of the foster carers.

Sat here in my wood, thoughts like this keep rearing up, like demons coming back to haunt me. It's like I'm replaying my life, trying to make sense of it, so that I can move on. But right now the future feels like it's just going to be me and these trees and the fear and the paranoia and the loneliness that grips me relentlessly.

Chapter 8

Darkening days

I seem to have entered some sort of time warp here in these woods. Time has stopped moving like it used to. Instead, it twists and loops and drags and slips, as if the order of the minutes and the hours and the days has been shuffled, so they no longer connect the way they used to. Somehow, despite all these tricks, it keeps on moving forward. I only know for sure that it does because the date on my watch has clicked on by another number each morning. Otherwise each day and night blurs and merges, as does my waking and dreaming and my conscious and subconscious, so that it becomes hard to tell the difference between reality and the swirling stories and images in my mind.

I've started writing the days in my notebook. I'm not sure it really matters what day it is, if it's a Wednesday or a Sunday. I don't have any need for those markers in here, no schedule that I have to keep to, no appointments that I have to make, but somehow that makes it even more important. Knowing what day of the week it is has become my last finger-hold on reality, or at least on my old reality, my way of continuing to believe that this is all only temporary. I write a few words for each day: nothing profound, I've not got enough pages in it for that, but just so I can look back and see that the days really have passed.

For Thursday 20th August, I wrote: 'It was self-defence, I didn't mean to stab him. Steen and his two accomplices were trying to beat me up and rob me. They've done it before. This time, by chance, I had my penknife with me and I reacted purely to protect myself.'

I felt better having written that down, but that wasn't what prompted me. A seed of angst had been niggling away at the back of my mind for days. What if I died in here? There would be nobody to tell my story, so everyone would think I'd killed him in cold blood.

That would be my epitaph: 'Mark Oban. Murderer.'

I thought about all the people I'd learned about in History. If they hadn't told their own story, then someone else would have told it for them, maybe even someone who hated them, someone who would pervert everything about them, everything they stood for, turning them into a different person altogether, unrecognisable from the reality of what they knew themselves to be.

Imagine if Robin Hood's story had been written by the Sherriff of Nottingham. They'd have turned him into a violent bandit, into someone who was fuelled by greed rather than a desire to feed the poor, who wanted to destroy rather than protect, a menace to society rather than a seeker of truth and justice and respect.

Not that I'm comparing myself to Robin Hood: I'm just

some small-town loser who hasn't even made it to first base, but I still can't bear the thought of people thinking of me in such a monstrous way.

When I think like this, it makes me want to get out of here right away, to go back and tell the truth, to keep telling it until they believe me. The thought sends shivers of excitement through me, but reality brings me back to earth with a thud. Nobody would believe me. It's way too late for that. And the harsher truth is that I'm paralysed by fear. All I've been able to do is to run and to hide. This brazen admission fills me with self-hatred. I'm a snivelling, fucking coward. There, I've said it. So, I write these few words each day instead. It's a start I suppose, a reminder of the truth, and one day I *will* shout it out loud so that every-one will hear it, believe it and understand it.

For now, all I can focus on is self-preservation. I've got no plan other than to stay in here, stay alive and bide my time until something comes to me. Some days disappear in a whirl of activity; others just drag, refusing to move on. One day turns into the next and repeats itself. Farnham seems like a lifetime ago, a distant memory, as if nothing that happened there really happened at all or, if it did, it happened to someone else.

My moods follow the same pattern. Little things like getting hold of some eggs, or catching the right note on my harp, can lift me to breathless peaks of exhilaration, but then, before I've even managed to get used to that feeling, something can dump me back into a dark hole of self-pity and desperation.

Sometimes it feels as if these woods are absorbing me, sucking me in bit by bit. It's happening so slowly that I can't even see it, but it *is* happening, each day I can feel it, I'm just not sure if that's a good thing or a bad thing.

The longer I spend in here the more I'm tuning into its rhythms and melodies and tempos. I've become aware of things I'd never noticed before. They were obvious things at first: light, noise, movement, scents and textures. Then they became subtler: ebbs and flows, inhalations and exhalations, changes in mood and atmosphere and a creeping awareness of how everything in here fits together, like pieces in a jigsaw puzzle, into a much bigger picture.

This wood is communicating with me in ways I've never experienced before: I'm feeling the messages with senses I didn't even know I had, becoming aware without even knowing how I became aware. I'm starting to see it now: these woods are one big, living, breathing entity. No single organism makes any sense on its own, but put them together and everything becomes clear.

I spotted an ant. When I looked closer there were loads and loads of them, scurrying frantically around in all directions. It was dizzying to watch, utter chaos, until I noticed that they were all following a trail that *they* had worn, charging back and forwards on their own super-highway. Some of them were carrying things, all sorts of things: bits of leaf, bark from a tree, dead insects. A big group of them were carrying a whole fly many times bigger then any one of them, hauling it up a slope, some of them lifting, some of them pulling, some of them pushing. I kept watching them until I found where they were taking it, to their great subterranean nests, and finally I got their place in this whole ecosystem: the rag and bone men of the woods.

Then I laughed, because I reckoned Spike was having a good few mouthfuls of them each night as well.

Sometimes I just sit and look at something until I see it in a way I've never appreciated before. I notice the bark on a tree, how it forms a mosaic with infinite patterns of deeply etched rivulets. I notice new branches sprouting from a spot on the trunk that seems random at first, until I sense that it's the only place from which it could have sprouted, as it reaches for the sun. I notice the leaves, fanning out into their pre-ordained shapes, ridged with the most delicate veins that seem to be drinking the sunshine, drawing the energy back into its core.

To really understand the tree, I have to close my eyes and feel it: press the palms of my hands and my face and my chest against its trunk, feel its cool, calm energy, feel my own heartbeat echoing back at me. I've got my favourite trees all over these woods now, each of them with their own characteristics and energies.

The great redwood: a loner, like me, the only one of its kind in here, so broad that I can't get close to embracing it, driving straight up and beyond all the others. It's not changing for anything; it'll be here when everything else has gone.

My favourite old oak is solid and rooted deeply to its spot, its thick, sinuous arms raised like an ogre trying to roar, but there's no threat, it just feels calm and safe and knowing, as if it has seen and understands everything.

Then there's the silver birch sapling: taller than me, but

still slender enough for me to grasp with my hands. It sways with the breeze, but as I hold it I can feel a vital pulse of energy and potential. I close my eyes and hold onto it when I find I'm losing the ability to believe that there's a future: something that seems to be happening more and more often.

The weather in the first couple of weeks of September was glorious. The few heavy downpours at the end of August broke the back of the heat and gave me my best days in these woods.

The woods change after it rains: it smells different, it sounds different, it looks different, as though nature has cleansed itself, reinvented and reinvigorated itself, becoming fresher, but at the same time earthier, more alive. The water keeps on filtering through, even way after the rain has stopped, dripping off branches and leaves as they're stirred in the breeze, running down trunks and stalks, pooling together and merging joyously into the streams and springs.

The mornings and evenings became cooler with a light crispness, like biting into one of my apples. During the days, the sun shone, but the intense heat of August had gone from it. The farmer on the other side of Norton still hadn't harvested his corn, so I kept on helping myself to them. By the middle of September it seemed like the last field of crops around that hadn't been brought in.

Mushrooms kept springing up in the fields and I kept cutting them out and frying them up on my fire each night. Lulled by a burgeoning understanding of my new home, those benign days felt like a new start and for a while I really started to believe that I could make it work.

It was too good to last. Over the second half of September, the weather has turned ugly. A big storm tore in on Saturday afternoon. The skies became dark and heavy with clouds and I watched as the front rolled in from the southwest.

The wood held its breath, but the rain still surprised me with the abrupt ferocity of its arrival: one moment silence, the next a cacophony as the rain crashed through the canopy. This wasn't one of those summer downpours I'd enjoyed after my first week. There was no relief in this. It just kept on coming down, barely stopping for two days, and the wind came with it, howling and tearing through the treetops.

I'd done everything I could to strengthen my shelter, but I felt like it was going to be torn apart. All I could do was sit tight beneath my makeshift roof, putting myself at the mercy of the storm, waiting for it to pass. I felt like I was inside a sandcastle disintegrating under the force of the incoming tide, each wave wreaking new havoc, but somehow it remained standing.

The storm cleared through sometime during the second night. As its fury abated I'd finally given in to sleep and I woke, bewildered, to a fresh clear day. It was like I'd been given a new lifeline and, despite my exhaustion, I leapt up and out with renewed energy, my spirits revived. Even my bivouac wasn't too badly damaged and I was able to patch it up again pretty easily.

Even better the storm had started to bring down some of those sweet chestnuts that I'd been eyeing on the branches. They were scattered everywhere, clamped tightly on the ground like electric-green sea urchins. Over the last few days they've started to open, tentatively at first, their dark skins poking shyly from their prickly casings, then wide open and topped up with new falls.

I always wonder whether Spike is able to get his nose into them. I bet he can. He was almost the first thing I saw the morning after the storm. He must have hunkered down as well.

I called out to him: 'Hey, Spike, I bet your nest was drier than mine! You must be as hungry me, huh?'

There was one dry day after the storm and then the rain set in again. It hasn't been as heavy as before, but it's gone on for days and the temperature has fallen with it. I've been going stir-crazy sat under the bivouac for hour after hour. I haven't even got anything to read. I've gone through Kerouac four times; once more and I'll be able to recite it word for word.

Each time there's a break in the rain I make a break for it. If it's dry for long enough, I go all the way down to the allotments, but they haven't been there much and they're leaving fewer and fewer veggies out.

Alternatively I go out picking chestnuts. I've got two carrier bags filled now and, in the afternoons, I sit and cut crosses into them. Jeff always told us that if we put them on the fire without cutting the skins they'd explode. I remember one of the kids sneaked a whole one on, just to

138

test his theory out, and after a few minutes it popped, leaping off the grill tray and onto some kids lap. I've never seen anyone move so fast. He yelped and squawked, flapping his arms like a turkey on heat. The rest of us just pissed ourselves laughing. That was funny, even if Jeff wasn't so amused.

It's a relief when memories like that jump back in my head, lightening my mood for a few minutes, reminding me that there were times when my life was normal. I try hard to hold onto those thoughts, but it's getting harder.

The rains have made everything slippery and muddy and I've lost count of the number of times I've gone over: always the same, feet up in the air and ending flat on my arse. I would laugh, but each time I get caked in that thick, sticky mud which gets everywhere.

I washed it off at first, but after a while I've stopped bothering. I'm getting used to it, or just accepting it, like those poor cows down in the field below. This must have been what it was like to be in a trench in the war: everything smells and tastes rotten and I sit here ravenous and shivering, huddled up in my sleeping bag and waiting.

The best antidote is to get a fire going. The warmth and the light of the flames are nourishment, banishing the darkness and the cold and the damp for precious moments, but I've only been able to get one lit once in the last four days, so I can't even have a hot mug of tea to warm me up.

I keep looking out, hoping there'll be some respite, but it just goes on and on. I've put a load of leaves into the fire pit, to stop it filling with water, and kept as much dry firewood as I can under the bivouac so I'm ready to go when it does stop, but right now that feels like never.

Worse then that, my provisions are running out fast. I've used up the last of my matches, so I have to use my cigarette lighter to get the fire going. The batteries for my torch have gone. My loo roll ran out way back. That's become the grimmest ritual of the day: scraping a hole somewhere away from the camp for a shit, then having to clean myself with leaves afterwards. I don't think I'll ever get used to that, it always leaves me feeling weak and nauseous and shaky.

I still try and wash myself in the stream each morning, but that's becoming an ordeal as well, as the mornings grow steadily colder. After dousing myself in that icy water, I'm shaking like a miserable dog and it takes me ages to warm up again. I'm almost out of toothpaste and then, this morning, I dropped my last tiny bit of soap into the stream.

I know I stink and look like shit, but I reckon I could cope with that if it wasn't for the constant, gnawing hunger. I've always been on the skinny side, but now I'm getting seriously scrawny. My clothes are hanging off me and I've had to pull my belt in another notch to keep my trousers up.

I'd looked forward to those chestnuts, but they've been pretty miserable fodder: all the effort of preparing each one for a single measly, mushy mouthful that's gone in a second. They're not too bad if I can roast them on the fire, but now I'm just eating them raw, just for the feeling of chewing something. The mushrooms and the corn are a bit better and anything from the allotments, but I can't rely on that. I'm even down to my last few tea bags: not that I can use them, unless I can get a fire going again.

I'm trying desperately not to face up to the obvious, but below the surface it's nagging away at me all the time: it's not even the end of September and already life's getting tough. How am I going to cope when winter really hits? It's only going to get colder and wetter and darker. I think back to that premonition on my first morning, of me lying here barely alive. The vision keeps coming back at me, raw and vivid, making me shiver each time it appears, unthinkable yet inescapable. Am I going to just sit here and wait for it?

Chapter 9

Caution to the wind

It's Wednesday, the final day of September, and I've woken with a plan. I'll go into Yeovil and stock up with provisions. It'll be a risk, that's for sure, people might have seen my face on the news, but I can't see any alternative: I can't survive in here for much longer with what little I've got left. Maybe Yeovil is big enough that people won't notice a stranger. And even if they do, surely I'm yesterday's news by now.

I wonder what the photo they've put out of me looks like and where they got it. The last one I remember having taken was when I was sixteen, before my 'O' Levels. Everyone had theirs done and parents had the chance to buy them. I don't know why they bothered taking mine: nobody was going to buy it. I bet it doesn't look anything like me now.

It's nearly six weeks since the stabbing: that's six week's growth on my face; six week's grime caked into my skin, hair and clothes and six week's worth of news that would have taken over people's attention. Yeah, they'll have forgotten my little story by now. As long as I act natural and don't draw attention to myself, I'll be fine. The weather is dry as well and the winds have stilled. It's time to go for it, before I lose my bottle.

Once I've made the decision to go, I start getting excited by the prospect. My mind races off in all sorts of directions: I could have a Chinese take-away, maybe a pint of beer in a pub. I rein myself in, remembering my situation, and start to plan the trip more carefully: it's got to be like a military raiding party, in and out quick.

First off, I know that I must look a right state. I need to clean myself up. I head down to the stream and, emboldened by the day ahead, dunk myself in the icy water, doing the best job I can I can without any soap. Then I put on the least dirty and ragged of my clothes: that doesn't say much; they're all dirty and ragged. Next I empty my backpack into my sleeping bag and hide it in a thicket a few yards away from the bivouac. It must be at least four or five miles each way to get into Yeovil so I'll be gone most of the day and I don't want anyone stumbling on my camp and nicking my gear.

Once I've made a list of things I need, I head off, before I have a chance to talk myself out of it. My pack is light on my back with nothing in it other than a water bottle, so walking is much easier then when I was on the way here from Farnham. I set off towards Montacute, then cut down narrow little country lanes and footpaths to avoid the couple of villages that lie between here and Yeovil.

There's a spring in my stride and I find myself singing and pounding a drumbeat with my fists as I go. I can't seem to help myself. Whatever happened to not drawing attention to myself?

I quieten and focus instead on rebuilding the story about starting at Exeter University next week: I'm out for some last-minute shopping before heading off. Having this story gives me confidence and I march purposefully on until after about an hour of walking I come to a road heading due East towards the town.

My body tenses at the sight, everything inside me is screaming to turn right back around, to run back for the cover of the woods. Cars are thundering past in both directions, their vibrations shaking me each time, and for a few moments I stand there frozen to the spot, unable to move. Then there's a gap in the traffic and without thinking I find myself running across the road.

I'm drawn into a housing estate that sits between the main road and the edge of town. After my absorption into the woods for the past weeks, it feels weird coming back into a town, a strange mix of the alien and the familiar, as if from a previous life. Most of all, it seems sterile: smooth tarmacked pavements; a road with neat, straight white lines splitting it in two; concrete streetlights arching above in symmetrical rows; ranks of identical modern houses, their curtained windows staring blindly out, each one with a few, measly square yards of front garden, no more than a shaved patch of grass, parted by a straight concrete path. It's hard to imagine that there are lives going on behind each anonymous door.

I can't see anyone, but it feels like I'm being watched from everywhere: from every window, from every car, from around every corner. It's not cold, but suddenly I'm shivering. I keep walking, ignoring the pounding of my heart, forcing myself to breathe and to keep my eyes fixed dead ahead.

I walk past a crematorium where a hearse and a procession of cars are drawing in, a couple of pubs and a bookies yet to open for their lunchtime punters, a small local shop, its windows covered with hand-written signs, and an industrial estate with what looks like an airfield on the other side.

I carry on down the hill towards the town centre; the street lined by old terraces with tiny doors that open straight onto the street. A couple of buses pass in either direction. One of them stops at a zebra crossing. I see all the older folk coming in for their shopping, sat in neat and orderly rows, but right in the middle of them is a punk with black leather jacket, chewing gum furiously, his green hair spiking out from a sea of grey.

Shops and offices are now replacing houses and, finally, I turn a corner and there I am, right in the main shopping street. Here are all the names I know: Woolworths, Boots, Smiths; others I don't. The street is filled with people, coming at me from all directions and that wall of panic hits me again. I'm trying to focus on all of them at the same time, to suss out if any of them has clocked me, but all I can see is danger everywhere My head is spinning, like a mad dog chasing its tail, my hands reaching out, as if I'll fall if I can't grab onto something.

A bench appears and I drop into it gratefully, breathing heavily. A searing need to get the hell out of there has its claws in me, but it's too late for that. I inhale deeply, trying to get the world back into focus, trying to think about the job in hand.

I'm looking for a supermarket and maybe a hardware shop. I run through in my mind again the list of things that I need. I'm just getting myself together again in the bubble I've created when I become aware of a bloke sitting down next to me. I smell him rather than see him: a rank odour of piss and damp, sweat and rotting gums, sour alcohol and stale tobacco that makes my eyes water. God, I hope I don't reek like that. I keep looking dead ahead and then, just as I've resolved to get up and go, he speaks, or rather slurs:

'Hey, mate, have yer got a light please?'

I find myself tensing. I want to ignore him, to get up and go, but instead I nod and, pulling the lighter from my pocket, flick a flame for him. He leans over, grasping my wrist with a coarse, shaky hand. He's got half of a miserable looking rollie in his mouth, which he sucks on with deep concentration. His body jerks with a violent rasping cough, which doubles him up, until the spasm subsides and he sits in stunned silence for a moment, the fag held between his stained, swollen fingers.

'Thanks, buddy,' he wheezes.

For a split second my eyes are locked to his, to their watery, bloodshot yellow, submerged in a puffy weather-beaten face and a mass of dirty, unkempt hair. I find myself drawn to them as if to an abyss, an abyss into which he's fallen, where he's now trapped in some hellish underworld, a slave to a body he's forced to lug around like an unwanted ball and chain. In there somewhere, though, I can sense just the faintest flicker of humanity, of a previous life that must have been entirely different to this one.

How has he got to this point? What has gone so wrong, to drag him this low? Why has nobody helped him? I'm trapped between pity and terror for this poor bloke who looks like he's clinging to life by the slenderest of threads. He takes another draw on his fag. Then, as if remembering something important, he hunches over and whispers conspiratorially to me:

'You want some hash, mate? I can get it for you.'

'No thanks, mate'

'Hey, it's good shit. Some weed? Acid? Speed?'

I can feel myself recoiling. I've got to get away from here. 'No thanks, mate. I gotta go.'

I rise to leave. He looks defeated, but then he grabs my arm.

'Could you spare some change, mate, for a cuppa.'

I just want to get away, but instinctively I find myself fumbling in my pocket. Then I remember that I've got no change left.

'Sorry, mate,' I mumble. 'I haven't got any money'.

'No worries, mate, God bless yer'. He slumps back into the bench and I leave, as calmly as I can manage, my heart pounding, my face burning.

Ahead of me I've spotted a Fine Fare supermarket. I visualise a tunnel and set off through it, head down, shutting everything else out. I'm convinced for a moment that he's going to follow me, but I can't feel his presence behind me and I keep going. Did he pick on me because I look like

147

him? He asked me for money, so maybe not, but seeing how far someone can fall has spooked me. Is that the direction I am heading?

As I walk the prospect of falling zooms up and grabs me. My legs feel like jelly and the pavement has become wafer-thin, as if I'm going to be sucked through it at any moment. A stomach-churning awareness hits me: that if I start to fall there is nothing to stop me. I'm clinging on by my fingernails, nothing beneath me but the fathomless darkness of the abyss. The same abyss that I just saw in his eyes.

From somewhere comes a surge of determination. I resolve, in that moment, never to give in, not while there's an ounce of breath left in my body. This resolution empowers me and I press on with renewed vigour, forcing those negative thoughts out of my mind, focusing in on the supermarket ahead. Just beyond it I see a hardware shop and decide to go there first.

Inside it's quiet: calm and still as a church. I breathe it in. It smells familiar, like being back in old Ron's shop, with that reassuring cocktail of odours: paint, turps, cardboard, metal. I put my hand into a box of steel bolts and run them through my fingers. How I wish I was back there and that none of this shit had happened.

I can't afford to linger, so I go briskly about my business. I find a small trowel, then a grill tray of about the right size to put over my fire pit, a big box of matches, some batteries for my torch and a small thermos flask. I imagine making tea at night and still having some piping hot for the morning. Then I spot a picnic blanket. That wasn't on my list, but it's reduced so I grab it.

I've been putting off whether to buy a gas camping stove. I don't want to give up on my fire each night, but it's been getting harder and harder to get it lit. Then I spot a bunch of them, reduced by half, so I take one: I don't have to give up on my fires; this is just a back up. Even better, when I get to the counter, it turns out it comes with a free refill.

The guy at the counter is probably about the same age as Ron, but more wiry, with little glasses and a moustache. He's looking at me oddly, peering at me over the top of his glasses. I pretend to ignore it and busy myself with loading my backpack, but the grill tray's almost too big to get in and I can feel myself flushing as I struggle with it.

Eventually, he tuts: 'Here, let me help you with that, son,' he says coming round from the counter. 'You open the bag and I'll shove it in. There you go.'

He's looking at me with something more like concern now. 'Are you alright, son? You look like you haven't had a square meal in a month.'

'Yeah, I'm fine thanks. I'm going off to university next week and I'm camping until I start, until I get my grant cheque.'

My heart is pounding as I tell him my fabricated story and suddenly I feel like Pinocchio, lying to try and create a more palatable version of myself. Is it my imagination, or is my voice quavering? He's surely going to see right through this bullshit.

'Ah, you're a student are you? You should have said. We have a ten per cent discount for students. Have you got a card or anything?'

Now I'm getting worried. He's fishing to get my name. 'Er, no… I haven't started yet. I guess they'll give me one when I get there.'

This is getting utterly preposterous. I'm digging a deeper and deeper hole for myself. I'm right on the edge of 'fessing up and telling him the whole story's made up, but then he shrugs:

'OK. Well not a problem.' He walks back around the counter and, re-opening the till, gives me a few more coins back. 'We'll take that on trust, hey. Which university are you going to?'

'Exeter.' I replied. 'I'm going to read History.'

'Oh, good university. Well, good luck, son, see you again some time.'

'Thanks. Bye.' And I walk out, calm and slow, but inside I'm spinning. I've got no idea what's just happened, whether he believed my fantasy or not, but I've got all the stuff I wanted and I've even got some more change now. Maybe I will get that guy a cup of tea after all.

The supermarket's entirely different. A cold wave of air hits me as I walk in, its high ceilings and bleached white lighting and floors leaving nowhere to hide. It's filled with people, milling around with trolleys, each in their own little bubble.

A security guard watches me as I walk in. He's a great meat-head of a guy dressed in quasi-military style to give him an air of authority: black trousers, a dark blue, crested jumper with gold epaulettes, which he fills like one of their own-brand sausages, and a large peaked cap wedged onto a severe crew-cut head. I see him straighten up as soon as I walk in. As I pick up a basket and walk up the first aisle I can feel his eyes following me. He doesn't even bother to hide his suspicion.

I feel like I'm shrivelling under his scrutiny, acutely aware of every movement I'm making, as if I'm watching myself. I'm glad that I made that list of the things I wanted and I pull it out of my pocket now to give myself something to focus on. Then I move quickly, putting things in my basket and ticking them off my list. I don't want to linger around here any longer than I have to: that will just make me look even more suspicious.

I've decided not to get too much fresh meat, because it might attract foxes and rats, or fresh fruit and veg because I'm still hoping to get more from the allotments and in the fields around. So I get a small pack of ham, a loaf of bread, some cheese and a carton of milk, but other than that I go for tins. I've decided that I'll ration them out: only open them when I can't get anything else. That way I can make them last for ages and I won't have to come back here anytime soon.

I've picked up a load of tins of soup, sardines, tuna, corned beef, baked beans, some Bovril. On a whim I throw in a big bag of peanuts and a pack of digestives. I'm salivating like mad with all this food around, my stomach squealing like a spoiled child. I want to cram everything into my mouth at once and gorge on it: chunks of roasting meat, burgers, pizzas, pies, biscuits, ice cream. Instead, I step calmly amongst the throng of mothers with babies, the doddering old couples and the office workers out for their lunch breaks, dodging the trollies and pretending that this is my Wednesday routine.

I finish up in the toiletries section, reloading with soap and toothpaste and shampoo. And, most importantly, toilet paper. I can't believe I'm fantasising about a clean porcelain bowl and a roll of soft white bog roll. People have been giving me a wide berth all the way round and as I pick up a bar of soap I catch someone looking at me as if to say: 'Yeah, mate, perhaps you should be using it.'

At the till, I have to stand in a queue for what seems like an eternity. I stand and stare down at my basket, studiously avoiding any eye contact. Then I begin a battle of wills with the sweet counter. I'm determined to win, but at the last second I succumb to a Mars Bar: it's only ten pence and by the time I get to the front, I've convinced myself that it's the best ten pence I'll ever spend.

The cashier is bored out of her mind. She barely acknowledges me, just bashing the prices into the till, and for once I'm grateful for the anonymity. The security guard is still watching me though. I'm trying not to look in his direction, but I can feel his eyes burning into me from over by the exit, so I very slowly and carefully put everything into carrier bags and then load them into my pack where he can see it.

I pay up, then lift my pack onto my shoulders and walk towards the exit as calmly as I can manage, eyes straight ahead. *Meathead* is standing at the exit, arms crossed. I pretend to ignore him, if I play it cool maybe he'll just let me pass, but as I get almost level, he thrusts out an arm to block my path.

'Can I see what you've got in your bag please…Sir?'

It's the way he says *Sir* that riles me the most. He spits it out with contempt, with a malicious, cutting irony, that says: *'I have power over you'* and *'You're not worthy of cleaning the shit off my shoe.'*

One half of me wants to bolt for it, the other to come up with some smart quip that will put him in his place. Instead I just groan and, hauling my pack off, open it up for him. My eyes are darting everywhere: I can't stop them. I can feel people watching me, recoiling, pulling their children away, as if I'm infested with some sort of contagious moral depravity.

An impulse surges from somewhere: to reach out to them with clawed hands and a bulging-eyed grimace, to belt out a pantomime-villain cackle, just to see the terror on their faces. They're labelling me as some sort of vile, shoplifting, lout; I can just feel it. Well, I know better. I've paid for every one of the groceries in my bag. But it's worse than that, much worse, I've got another man's blood on my hands and that will never wash off.

So I just stand here, silently accepting the ignominy of this wanker rifling through my bags, burning with rage and humiliation, but most of all with the certainty that, at any moment, a policeman will come along to see what's going on. Has someone recognised me? Is this just a ruse to delay me, while they wait for the police to arrive?

As he goes through each carrier bag, checking each item against my receipt, I became more and more convinced that this is the end. I should never have come into town. It was a crazy thing to do. My heart is beating wildly again.

Events are unfolding in slow motion. I can hear every little noise and I'm searching through them for the sound of sirens. Every muscle in my body is tensed; primed for action. What should I do? Leave my stuff here and run? Could I outrun them? I'm visualising the direction that I would take, swerving round the people leaving the shop, then back along the high street and up the hill towards the woods.

Then I hear his voice again: 'Thank you, Sir, you can go.'

There's no apology in his tone, just the same oozing contempt. The best I can manage in response is to blank him, pretending my pack is light as a feather as I sling it over my shoulder and march out of the shop without looking back. The truth is I'm so relieved to get out of that supermarket, that I couldn't care less about saving my dignity, or scoring points over him. I just want to get the hell out of there, back to the calm, anonymous, solitude of my woods.

Retracing my steps, I spot the old tramp from earlier. He's slumped in the doorway of an empty shop with a little cardboard sign that reads:

Hungry & Homeless. Please Help.

I've got some change now, but I pull out a pound note and press it into his hand.

'Thanks, mate. God bless,' he croaks.

He shows no signs of recognising me. I guess that he's retreated back into the sanctuary of his inner world: like Spike rolling up into his ball. Or me heading back to the woods. We're all hiding from something, I guess.

Heading up and out of the town centre I start picking up the scent of roasting meat. It smells dizzyingly good and my empty belly screams a mutinous chorus. It comes from a kebab shop halfway up the hill and I'm powerless to resist.

Inside are two tall, lean guys, one shaving slices from a huge slab of skewered-meat with a murderous looking blade as it rotates slowly around the grill, the other chopping up salad. I order a large shish kebab and sit on the edge of a chair, sucking in the aroma of the roasting meat, as my insides melt in tortured anticipation.

I'm so hungry that I think for a second about scoffing it right here, but the need to get away trumps my hunger pangs. They swaddle it in paper for me and I leave clutching it to my stomach beneath my cagoule.

Twenty minutes later and I'm out of town, crossing the main road and heading back out into open fields. Finally, I can breathe again. I stride fast, across the first field and over a stile into the next until I find a quiet spot hidden from view.

I can't get into the food quickly enough. Leant against a rough stone wall, I tear into it: ripping at the meat and chewing frenziedly. It's so good that I have to screw my eyes tightly shut, engulfing myself in the tastes and the smells and the sheer joy of biting and chewing: thick juicy chunks of lamb; fresh, crunchy salad; sweet, spicy, tangy sauce. The whole thing is falling apart as I eat, but I don't care. In this moment, the only thing that exists in the world is the kebab and I bury my face into it and scoff. Pieces of meat fell to the ground. I don't care. I just grab them up and stuff them back in.

When I've finished, I just sit there groaning with pleasure, savouring the memory, savouring that feeling of a full belly that I'd all but forgotten. I'm covered with the remnants of the meal: on my hands, on my face, on my clothes, great dollops of sauce and fat spilled everywhere. I suck on each finger in turn, lick my lips; I don't want to waste any of it. If I could purr, I think I would.

Some notes for the harp jump into my head, but I'm too bloated to move. Then, from nowhere, I start laughing, a great belly laugh, like I haven't had for an age. I'm laughing at the audacity, bordering on lunacy, of my escapade. How the hell have I pulled it off? I'm laughing at that wanker in the supermarket, so filled with his own self-importance; at that bloke in the hardware shop, buying my story about Exeter and even giving me a student discount; but most of all I'm laughing at the sheer joy of this moment, of being alive and free and with a bellyful of food.

My laughter subsides and my thoughts turn to the tramp. I hope he's scraped enough money together to get himself a decent feed, that he's sitting somewhere right now with his hands warming around a mug of hot tea, nursing a full belly just like me. I wish that I could have sat with him and found out his story, but most of all, I just hope that he's going to be OK and that somehow he'll find a way to get his shit together.

I sit here for ages after I've finished eating just letting my thoughts drift. I don't want to give up on this moment. God knows there have been precious few of them.

Halfway back I pay the price for my excess. As I walk, the food starts to repeat on me, my stomach grumbling and gurgling and griping. Then, almost without warning, I'm throwing up in the hedgerow. It spews out of me with volcanic force, before I've even had the chance to drop my pack. The heat of the sauce stings the back my throat, its oiliness making me even queasier. I stagger on a few yards, but then a second wave hits me. I must have chucked up virtually the whole thing by now. I'm on my knees, doubled up and retching, spitting out nothing but mucus.

To add insult to injury, something sharp in my pack is digging into my back. I yank it off and drop it to the ground beside me. I'm shaking with the trauma and it takes all of my focus to undo my pack and pull out my water bottle. The nausea and the rancid burning in my throat are all-consuming. It tastes familiar, blurring with my own self-disgust, as if it's been lurking in some dark corner and has now thrust itself, stark and exposed, back into the spotlight. How dare I laugh and smile and fill my belly with tasty food, as if I'm something special.

I rinse and swill my mouth, spitting it out, then repeating, desperately trying to get rid of the taste. All that's left of my meal is a queasy vacuum in the pit of my stomach. This feels familiar too. It's the feeling of emptiness and exposure, of loneliness and vulnerability, all the feelings that I have spent my life trying to ignore, disguise and suppress. Now here it is. Undeniable. Uncontestable. Great steaming piles of vomit: the semi-digested evidence of my wretchedness.

A memory of the last time I was sick hits me. It was at

the Clapton gig in Guildford with Uncle Harry and his friends. Back then it had been almost funny.

'You been praying to the 'great God of the toilet pan'?' someone had teased.

You'll be alright, Marko, get a pint of water down yer,' Uncle Harry had said, wrapping his arm around me, ruffling my hair.

The banter had carried on and I was part of it. This is different. There's nothing more abject then throwing up on your own, with nobody there to put their arm around you. The adrenaline from the day has long gone and I feel like I've been scoured bare. I press my forehead down into the turf, clinging onto some tufts of grass as if they are my last grasp on this world.

I remember being sick when I was little and my mum always being there. I want her back desperately right now, to release me from this great void that's engulfing me, threatening to suck me in deeper and deeper until I implode.

Somehow I make it back. The pack's a dead weight on my back and every step has been tortuous, but somehow I've got here. As I enter the woods again I feel a surge of relief. It's like a homecoming of sorts, the trees forming a protective cloak as they close around me. I can hide again in here, lick my wounds, knowing that nobody's watching. But how am I going to deal with this emptiness that stalks me night and day?

Back at the camp I just lie on the earth, flat on my back,

feeling the last warmth of the afternoon sun. I look up at the branches of the trees as they sway gently in the light breeze. The earth seems to move with them, as if I'm lying on the deck of a ship. Slowly I feel my equilibrium returning, until I find enough energy to prop myself up on my elbows. I scan my surroundings again, looking at them as if for the first time. This is my new reality now: just me and the silent indifference of the forest. It's less threatening than those watchful, judging eyes that stalked me in Yeovil. I close my eyes and breathe in the cool, still air. I can hear it talking to me: telling me not to worry; telling me that everything is one; telling me that I am who I am and that there is a place for me here.

It's evening and I've got a good fire going, the flames rekindling me with the nourishment of their warmth and light. Earlier I dug the fire pit a little deeper with my new trowel and I've got the new grill tray resting over the fire with a couple of pieces of bread toasting and some slices of cheese on top.

I find I'm chuckling to myself, as I sit there watching the cheese melt and bubble. What a day it's been. I can't quite make sense of it all, how I've been lifted and dropped so many times in such a short space of time, so I just have to laugh. It's my new toys as well, and, combined with the thought of all that food in my pack, a warm glow of contentedness that I haven't felt for a long time washes over me.

I don't feel like too much to eat so I make do with the cheese on toast followed by a cup of tea with a biscuit, and these rid me of the last rancid stains of earlier. Then I reach for my harp and, closing my eyes, blow out some sounds to fill the silence of the woods. I'm playing them for the tramp and the shopkeeper in the hardware store and, just to show there's no hard feelings, for the guard in the supermarket. As I blow I feel a single note bringing us all together. It's a long, extended note that starts sad and lonely and powerless, but then, from somewhere, picks up energy and momentum and transforms itself into hope.

Traumatic as it had been, that trip into town gave me a new lease of life. All the dark, toxic negativity that I'd been fermenting lifted like an autumn mist, replaced by something new: something calmer and lighter. And, for a while at least, I stopped blaming myself for everything, accepting my situation for what it was.

For the first week of October the weather mirrored my mood. The mornings were cool but clear and it pretty much stayed dry all week. The trees were rich with reds and golds and everything felt bountiful: I gorged myself with fruit from the fields and gardens around Norton and Montacute; I cut mushrooms by the handfuls and I even got some eggs and veggies from the allotments. I barely touched the food I'd bought in Yeovil. Except for that Mars bar of course: that was a moment of sheer heaven, on the morning after my return.

The other things I'd bought made the biggest difference. Digging a hole with my new trowel, a fresh toilet roll beside me, made my morning bowel movements almost tolerable: no more scratching at the earth with my fingernails, no more smearing myself clean with cold, slimy leaves. And then there were all the new toiletries. After brushing my teeth, shampooing my hair and cleaning myself with a virgin bar of soap I felt like a new man.

In the dry days of that week, I collected loads of wood and piled it up under my bivouac, alongside bags of chestnuts, apples, plums, corn cobs and vegetables of various types until there was barely room for myself in there.

My reprieve only lasted for a week. Then the rains arrived again and, from that day on, it's barely let up. As October has worn on, it's got steadily colder and wetter. Even when the sun does come out, it's rising later and setting earlier, giving less and less respite from the cold nights. At some point the clocks must have gone back, but my fingers are too numb to fiddle with my watch and, anyway, who cares what the right time is; it hardly matters in here.

The claws of winter are relentlessly tightening their grip. The leaves on the trees were the harbingers: their green zest draining from them; curling, streaking yellow then blood-red, before, powerless to resist their destinies, they finally deserted their sinking ship, drifting defeated to the woodland floor. With each burst of rain, each gust of wind, more leaves come down, as if they'll never stop. The woods are different now and I feel indivisible from those trees: exposed and abandoned.

My supply of dry wood is almost gone, so even when I can get a fire going, I have to ration the wood. That little gas stove I bought has been my saviour. I heat soup up on it, huddling up close to get some warmth and cupping my hands around the little flame. I boil water on it as well and make tea for my thermos. I'm so cold when I wake each morning that the knowledge of that hot cup of tea left in the flask is the only thing that gets me going.

My food supplies are running seriously low again. The farmer has long since harvested the corn and the last of the fruit's gone from the trees, but unless it's absolutely throwing it down I still go down to the allotments each day. Often there's nothing there, but occasionally there's some potatoes, carrots, onions or some funny squash like things that are edible once I've cut through their rock like skin.

I've been trying to ration the food, but still all I've got left now is a can of soup and a tin of sardines. The prospect of having to drag myself back to Yeovil fills me with dread. I wouldn't get so lucky again; they'd be looking out for me next time. That security guard at the supermarket would surely call the police as soon as he spotted me.

Anyway, I'm getting used to being hungry; it's the cold and the wet that are my enemies now. I just can't get warm. Thank fuck I bought that blanket in the hardware shop. I sit in my sleeping bag with the blanket wrapped tightly around me and even then I can't stop shivering. I keep thinking of things I should have bought, like another jumper or a coat from a charity shop. The cold reaches up from the ground, down from the sky and, somehow, from inside my bones; there's no escaping it.

After the cold and the hunger, boredom comes next. Why didn't I buy something else to read? It was on my list, but I freaked a bit after my run-in with *meathead* in the supermarket and just needed to get out. I've found myself reading every word on the back of the tins of soup and stew, just for something to occupy my mind for a minute or two.

Mostly, I just stare out at the trees, letting my thoughts swirl. Sometimes I find I'm counting the leaves that are left on the branches. They're almost bare now and I can see clear through to the sky above. At night, if there's no cloud, I can see the stars through the bare branches. Then, the next morning, the leaves on the ground are iced silver and crunch beneath my feet.

I've tried to make up games for myself. For a while I lined up the empty tins and threw stones at them, but I can't be bothered with that any more, it's too much effort scurrying round for stones just to throw them away in a couple of minutes. Instead I line the tins up to catch rain-water, to use for brushing my teeth or boiling vegetables, so I don't have to scramble down to the stream so often.

Half of the cans have gone now. It's foxes I reckon; they come and scavenge whenever I'm out. Maybe they can still smell the food that was in them, or maybe they just like the shiny surfaces, but I'm pretty sure it's foxes. They've been in my bivouac as well. Sometimes when I get back from the allotments I can smell them and some of my stuff looks like it's been scattered around. I count up my stash of food and I'm sure some of it's missing. A couple of times I pretended to go off to the allotments then doubled back and hid somewhere, but I just ended up crouched there for hours and nothing happened.

The birds are always flitting round and over, twittering out their messages. They're the spies of these woods: that's what I've sussed out. Sometimes I think they've got it in for me, they're just watching, waiting for a moment of weakness. Who knows what else is lurking in here.

Spike's my only ally. He's out there each night, keeping his ear to the ground for me. When I see him in the mornings, or hear him scurrying around at night, I know that everything's fine. I can tell his scurrying noises now: they're different to the others, gentler, more good-natured. He pauses when he comes past, almost like he's stopping for a chat. I know he's not judging me, so I can tell him things: I've told him where I came from; how shit life was after the car crash; all about Uncle Harry; that Steen was a right bastard, but that, in spite everything he did to me, he still hadn't deserved to die.

My diary entry for Wednesday 28th October has just three words:

'Found Spike dead.'

That was a bad day. A bad, bad day. It sounds pathetic that I could get so upset by finding a dead hedgehog, but I lost the plot for a while. He'd become my little buddy. I saw him most days, scurrying off somewhere, full of energy and determination. He was an inspiration, something for me to latch onto. He never moped around giving into anger and self-pity; he just got on with the business of surviving.

Then on that Wednesday morning, I found his limp, useless body, torn and ripped apart like some discarded old rag. All that mischievous energy that had propelled him. Gone. As if he had never existed.

I wouldn't believe it at first, as if my refusal could stop reality. I almost missed him as I walked past, first thing in the morning on the way to the stream. Something caught my eye and I had to do a double take. Then a terrible recognition sucked the air out of me. I fell to my knees, dumbstruck, staring at his remains in shocked silence, slowly taking them in, re-assembling him in my mind. I couldn't move for several minutes, as shock became denial, became anger, became a gut-wrenching sense of abandonment.

I pleaded with some God that I don't believe in: 'Please, please, please, don't let it be Spike,' but I knew it was no good.

Suddenly, I was eleven years old again, on the afternoon I was told that Mum and Dad and Charlie weren't coming home. Ever. Back then I couldn't take it in, couldn't believe what I was being told. It was just too big for me to comprehend.

Spike might only have been a hedgehog, but the godforsaken sense of desolation took me right back to that day. Over seven years on and I felt even more alone than I was then, my life stripped back to nothing. My body collapsed in half, my head buried between my knees, and I sobbed, my body jerking, my fists beating the ground. I didn't even care if anyone was watching. I don't have any armour like Spike, but what good had that done him?

For the rest of that day I just lolloped about the camp. I couldn't bring myself to do anything, even to go the allotments. After a couple of hours of staring blankly into space, I decided that I needed to give him some sort of burial. I dug a small hole and rolled what was left of him in, piling the earth over and patting it down into a small mound. Then I lashed two sticks into a cross, carved his name into it and pressed it into the ground to mark the spot.

I didn't know what to do next, so I sat there quietly for a while and then started playing on my harp. I thought he'd have liked that. It turned out like something between *The Last Post* and *Love Will Tear Us Apart* by Joy Division. Even as I played, the irony of that wasn't escaping me. Whatever it was that tore Spike apart, it certainly wasn't Love.

By the end of the day, I roused myself just enough to make a small fire, but even that was a struggle and I turned in early for the night, lying awake under my bivouac, listening hatefully to all the noises, each one potentially his killer.

It's the last day of October. Halloween. I've dragged myself through these last couple of days. Without Spike, everything's changed. I keep telling myself that he was only a hedgehog, but the mood of the forest has changed. I've got twitchy, jumping with every noise, seeing danger everywhere and I've barely slept the last two nights.

Now the weather's turning ugly again, matching my mood. I can feel a storm brewing: in the ominous silence that's consuming the woods; in the dark foreboding sky that feels like night even at midday and in the air that's starting to toss the branches and fill the air with swirling leaves.

I've been lying, listless, just staring up at the roof, but now I rise, forcing myself to work on strengthening my shelter. I tighten some of the ivy lashings, press the branches together where they feel loose, dig the bases into the earth to give them more strength, add more ferns and leaves and dirt to cover the outside. I'm not even sure why I'm doing it. My brain feels disconnected from my body, as if it's someone else's hands that are doing all of this, but I just keep on going

The rain is coming down now, the wind picking up with it. A branch comes down from somewhere above hitting the ground just a couple of yards away from me. It's enough to burst me from my trance:

'Come on,' I scream, 'Give it your best shot, piss down on me, see if I fucking care.'

The sound of my own voice is weird, like it belongs to someone else. The words echo round, but now they are drowned out by the sound of the rain and the wind. I'm standing there, shaking, fists clenched by my side, as if I'm ready to fight someone, but the only things moving are the wind and the rain and already I'm soaked through.

Finally, I dive for the cover of my bivouac. Soon the rain is coming down so hard that the noise obliterates everything. With it the wind is revving up, tearing through the branches, my roof quaking under the onslaught. I've never known anything like this. I sit and look out at the power of the storm, awestruck. The trees are turning into great monsters, their branches writhing and thrashing dementedly, casting off anything that is loose. Wind and water seem to be coming from all angles in great, frenzied squalls.

As night falls, the winds lift up another gear, ferocious, berserk, as if it's sucking a demonic intensity from the darkness. It's beginning to sink in; how dangerous this is. My whole shelter is shaking: even the main trunk, on which everything is resting, is heaving and creaking. Outside there's a great crack and then a crash that builds toward a crescendo, like it's coming for me. I fling myself flat to the floor, waiting for an impact that doesn't come. It must have been a tree that's come down and come down close.

The first serious cracks in my fortifications have started to appear. I shine the torch and see that at least the front couple of roof branches have been ripped off. I can just about make out the trunk that forms my roof: it's still wedged into the tree in front, but this is swaying ominously in the onslaught and my roof is rattling like a runaway ghost train.

Then there's another loud crack. One of the roof branches snaps, whipping my left arm. I yelp, stung by the shock as much as the pain. I can't move. I lie, shaking and breathless, waiting for the end. The rest of the wall is holding for the moment and slowly I slide my right hand up my arm. My shirt and jumper are torn and I can feel the warmth of my own blood beneath. I'm properly scared now, but all I can do is cower while the storm screams relentlessly on around me.

I've lost all track of time, but at some point in the night, the wind starts to die down. I don't believe it to start with, but then I tentatively raise myself and, pulling the torch from my pocket, start to survey the damage. It looks like more of the front branches of the bivouac have been torn away. There are gaping holes in each side and some branches are bowing inwards perilously, like they're going to cave in imminently.

I become aware of my arm, which is now throbbing. It looks ugly in the torchlight: a gash about three inches long, like an arrow scything into the tattoo of my family's gravestone. I squeeze the flesh around it: it's tender, but at least I don't think it's broken. I find a T-shirt and tie it around the wound, wincing as I tighten. There's not much more I can do right now; just make sure it doesn't bleed too much.

Now I poke my head outside. It's pitch black, but I hold the torch in my mouth and start trying to straighten and reattach a couple of the branches. I'm not making much headway, because the rain and the wind have already started to pick up again.

I do as much as I can then duck back under cover. It was a false reprieve. I flash the torch around me, trying to work out what to do. My heart is pounding. Should I try and make a break for it? Is there anything more I can do to shore up my shelter? I can feel the rain coming in through the sides already.

Before I can work anything out, there's another crash directly above me. Once again I fling myself to the ground. I thought that really was it, but it could only been a small branch, because the roof has held. It's too late to do anything now, so I just slide down into the lowest part of the bivouac, as far from the opening as I can. Then I curl into a ball, knees to chin, sleeping bag wrapped tight around me, my rucksack over my head. And I wait for the worst.

I don't think I sleep a wink. This is the night that won't end. The storm has raged on, relentless in its fury, and all I've been able to do is to lie here, rigid, waiting for the final devastating crash that will bring my life to an end, put me out of my misery.

What will it sound like when it comes? Where will it hit me? Will there be pain? Will it happen quickly? I've died a thousand times already. Will it be the next one? It's so dark that I can see nothing, but I can picture every gust of wind, seeking me out to rip me from my hideaway and smash me down into the earth. Every tree is a battering ram ready to pound me, every branch a spear waiting to skewer me, every piece of my bivouac just waiting for the signal to engulf me, to entomb me in my final resting place.

I'm going to be buried alive here, side by side with Spike, joined together with him in our final resting places. No one will find me here. My body will just lie, right here, until it rots, food for the residents of this wood. They'll tear at my flesh until there's nothing left of me but my bones. No one will miss me. I'm going to die a miserable, lonely, virgin. Untouched. Untouchable. I came from nothing, I've done nothing and I'm ending as nothing.

In this darkness, the howling of the wind sounds like all of the hounds of hell have been unleashed and are coming to hunt me down, to rip me apart. There are voices in the wind too. They are angry: Steen is screaming at me, exulting in his revenge; other kids from school are shouting insults; policemen, teachers, Ron at the hardware shop, all firing accusations at me for what I've done, for what I've not done, for letting them down. I hear Melissa's voice in there, angry with me for standing her up. She's calling me a weirdo and a loser: did I really think I was good enough for her?

Each accusation is a stinging blow, but beneath them, I start to notice the faintest of whispers. I could barely hear them to start with, they were so quiet, but now I've tuned into them I realise that they are soft words. Words of love and encouragement.

I hear Uncle Harry first. He's playing a riff on his guitar for me.

'Come on, Marko,' he's saying. 'You can get through this. You can't sing the blues unless you've suffered, hey. When you get through this, we can play together. It'll be great.'

Then I hear my Mum and Dad and Charlie. They're all talking at once. Dad's voice is quiet, but strong: 'You can do this, Marko. You're stronger than you know. We're proud of you, son.'

Charlie is just singing my name over and over and clapping his hands: 'Marko, Marko, Marko...' as if he's cheering me on in a game.

Softest and warmest of all is Mum: 'We love you, Mark. You're not alone. You're the most wonderful son we could ever have hoped for. Everything is going to be fine. You'll see.'

Tears are starting to pour out of me, but I'm clinging to these words, as if they are my very life. They seem to be coming from the St Christopher sat against my chest and I find I'm clutching it with one hand, eyes screwed tightly shut, focusing in on the words, shutting everything else out. There's a glowing light coming from them that feels like it could banish the deepest darkness, if only I can hold onto them.

In this moment, I know that Mum and Dad and Charlie may be dead, but their spirits are alive inside me for as long as I chose to keep them there. Outside the ferocity of the storm is unrelenting, as though the world around me is tearing itself to pieces, but I am no longer part of it.

My shelter is collapsing, burying me branch by branch, roughly pinning me to the earth, but all I can hear are these words, all I can feel is their warmth and their light. I've submitted myself completely into the hands of my fate. If this is where my journey ends then I am ready for it: ready to accept whatever comes my way.

Slowly, I become aware that the glowing light radiating from Mum's words is actually sunlight. The enraged voices of the storm have dissolved and her words have transformed into bird song, the sweetest I have ever heard. A surge of elation swells with the certainty that all the pain is over and soon I will see my family again.

I don't know how long I've lain here indulging in this fantasy, but now the world is coming back into focus, my mind and my body reconvening. My next thoughts are confused. I'm completely cocooned by my sleeping bag, but I can feel a rough weight above me. For an instant, I think I'm dead again, that I've been buried alive, like one of my nightmares realised, but then the horrors of last night's storm flood back.

I'm covered in sticks and branches. Very gingerly, I start to dislodge them until I'm able to slide out to the side, where the walls of my bivouac used to be.

Sitting up, I survey the carnage around me. It's barely recognisable, as though I'm looking at this place for the first time. Several trees are down, crushing whatever had been in their path; others have been partially uprooted and now lurch drunkenly against one another; bushes have been ripped out of the ground and branches and other flotsam and jetsam spewed out by the storm lie everywhere.

Even as I take all this in, what I'm feeling most is the stillness. After the manic fury of last night's storm it is now utterly still, as though nothing is brave enough to move, even to breathe, in case it returns.

Sound has a different quality. With less to absorb and deflect them, noises seem to float in the air for a second before dissolving into the sky, like I'm in a house that has lost its roof. Maybe that's why the birds sound so different, their song lifting on the breeze and drifting upwards.

With all of the branches and leaves that have come down, the sunlight now pours through, lighting up all those places that were perpetually in shade. I feel exposed suddenly, like I've had all of my hair cut off and can't get used to the feeling.

I look more closely at where I've spent the last hours. The tree that formed the ridge of my roof has somehow survived, still wedged between the branches of the next tree. These two trees have saved me. I've been huddled under a trunk, right up against the roots that must have been partially uprooted in a previous storm: after that they must have burrowed further underground, clinging even

173

more tenaciously to life. Hidden behind this root wall, I was in the lee of the worst of the wind; protected from much of the carnage it had hurled my way.

There's nothing much left of my little camp. My bivouac is all but gone, beyond a few branches at its base. I can't even make out my fire pit any more; it must have been scooped out and filled in by the storm. My clothesline has gone, bar a short piece of string, dangling limply from a tree just ahead of me.

I suddenly worry about all the other creatures I've been sharing this space with. Maybe some of them have perished. Maybe, like me, their nests have been destroyed. I can't believe I've been so lucky. I'm covered in cuts and bruises, but nothing serious. The forest is traumatised, I can sense it, and like me it's licking its wounds, trying to take on board this new reality and figure how to make the first tentative steps to recovery.

How can I recover from this? I've no idea. I don't know where to start, or even if I've got the strength to do it, but I've got to try.

My boots. Where are my boots?

A little jolt of panic jerks me back. I took them off last night, like I always do, but I can't see them. I turn and start sifting through some of the branches, until eventually I find them squashed into the mud and filled with water. Most of the rest of my stuff is still in my backpack, which I clung to during the night. It's also soaked, as is my sleeping bag, but I can't think of anything I've lost just yet.

My first priority, I decide, is to get myself cleaned up. All my cuts and scrapes are starting to sting and throb and I'm covered in dirt. I'm thirsty too, really thirsty, and my water bottle is empty. I've still got a few apples left, so I eat one of them as I gather the stuff I need from my pack.

It's slower progress than normal, getting to the stream. I find I'm limping, new cuts and bruises revealing themselves as they rub against my clothes. I know the way blindfolded, but so many of my landmarks are gone, or changed, or shed in a new light that I'm getting disoriented.

I realise that I'm looking for Spike and I find myself welling up. I try to bring back the voices that protected me last night, but they're gone. I can't seem to conjure them back, no matter how hard I focus. I have to stop for a second. The air has gone all wavy around me and for a second I think I'm going to fall. There was a small silver birch tree right here, but I find I'm groping for air. I look down and see its roots upturned, its trunk reaching down the hillside.

I turn slowly, scanning the new landscape around me. A new feeling is crystallising. It's been there since I woke this morning, but I'm only now becoming aware of it. Last night, I communed with the spirits of my parents and my brother: they were right there with me and their presence gave me the strength to endure, but this morning has brought a new understanding and acceptance.

I stand completely still, letting these new thoughts seed themselves. In a physical sense they are gone, there's no point in denying that, but somehow I don't think I've properly accepted that before.

In the same instant, I know that there's no point trying to blame anyone for it, least of all myself. All these years I've pointed fingers of blame, mostly at myself, as if that will bring them back, but suddenly everything has become clear: I can't change it, it's just how it is.

A new feeling is replacing these dark old thoughts. It's the knowledge that I've kept their spirits alive: they've left an imprint deep inside me, a flame that will never go out so long as there is life in my body.

I pull out my wallet and look at their photo: the four of us, frozen in time. I'm crying again. I'm crying, I know, because I'm letting them go, accepting that they've gone and that it's just me now. I'm the survivor. I have to live my life, without them. I put the photo back into my wallet and, bowing my head and closing my eyes, I whisper:

'Rest in Peace Mum. Rest in Peace Dad. Rest in Peace Charlie.'

The stream, when I get there, is gushing, filled with new vitality. That's the awesome thing about nature: what kills one thing gives life to another; for everything that is weakened, or depleted, something else is strengthened or replenished. Here is harmony amid chaos, brutality within beauty, an unsentimental natural order that can't be disputed.

The unfairness fills me with rage for a moment: it sounds like some sort of extreme Thatcherite ideology, where the strong get stronger and the weak are left to rot. But no, that's not how it works. If nature is to exist in balance, the exact opposite must be true: everything must contribute and nothing can dominate, because the success of the whole is what matters. No such thing as Society? Well, this whole woodland is a Society, everything working together for the benefit of the whole.

Already, I can feel these woods recovering all around me, coming back into balance, taking stock of, and accepting, this new equilibrium. I'm dumbstruck that I have somehow survived the shake-out. How did that happen, when I am so undeserving? What is my contribution? Where is my place in the new order? I still feel like an intruder in here, as though I am staying in someone else's home. Where do I go from here? Can I really start again and rebuild? Can I really see out the winter in here?

Thoughts are swirling around my head, crystal clear one second, confused the next, but somehow they are galvanising and I feel a new resolve arising. If I can get through this, then I can get through anything. If I am still here, living and breathing, then there must be a purpose for me. Maybe I don't know it yet, but I will find it and like these trees around me, I will emerge stronger.

There's no sign of anyone. It's been ages since I had a full wash, but I ignore the chill in the air to strip off and then slide down to the edge of the stream. First off I drink, cupping the water in my hands and slurping greedily. Next, I splash my face, before dipping my whole head in, yelping from the cold shock. Then, bracing myself, I ladle water all over my body. It tingles with an almost masochistic pleasure. I do all this as fast as possible, then grab my towel and, kneeling naked, shivering and scrawny, vigorously rub myself dry.

I'm so cold that my cock has shrunk to the size of a chipolata and my bollocks seem to have gone into hiding altogether. I must look a wretched specimen, all skin and bone after more than two months hiding in here. My hair feels lank and greasy, my face spotty with an itchy, scraggly, half-beard and my body covered in cuts and scratches, bites and bruises.

The wound on my arm is the worst. I rinse it with water, rubbing some soap into it. It stings to fuck, but it's not as bad as I thought last night. It looks like there's a lightning bolt coming out of my family's gravestone. Maybe I should get it inked in, make it part of the tattoo. The rest aren't too bad, just superficial scratches and bruises really. I can't believe that I got off so lightly.

Once I've brushed my teeth I stand and reach up the bank for my jockeys. As I'm bending over to put them on, I hear something. I whirl around, almost tripping over them as I do. Then I freeze, rooted to the spot, because standing there on the other bank, no more than ten yards away from me is a bloke. He's just standing there, arms folded, watching me intently.

Part IV

FELLOWSHIP

Chapter 10

A new dawn

I stand, stock-still, for what feels like an age. I seem to have stopped breathing. My eyes are locked to his. My first, crazed, thought is that this is Jesus Christ. Maybe I have died in the storm after all. It's the eyes: they're a bright, piercing blue, filled with a calm intensity. It feels like they're boring deep inside me, weighing me up, reaching into my most secret places and I'm powerless to resist. It's the rest of him as well: the sandy, shoulder-length hair that juts out at angles in thick braids; the wispy beard, a shade darker than the hair on his head; the tall, lean, body, that stands easily upright and his clothes, which are not much more than rags, but somehow look regal on him.

A smile slowly spreads on his face and the spell is broken. I look down and realise that I've only half pulled up my jockeys and my tackle is hanging out unceremoniously. I hastily pull them up, then reach for my T-shirt, my heart pounding as I try vainly to shut out the fact that he's watching my every move. For an instant I think of running, but as if he's reading my thoughts he calls out to me:

'Whoa, no need to be in such a rush, matey. Get some clothes on at least!'

He leaps the stream in one easy stride and, ambling over, picks up my jeans from the bank and throws them down to me.

'Thanks,' I say and quickly pull them on. I look up and he throws the rest of my clothes down, the grin on his face getting bigger by the second. As I'm dressing, he looks up and calls out through cupped hands:

'Jade, Freddie… I've found him.' Looking back, he sees my startled expression. 'Hey, chill-out, man. We were worried about you. Is all. After that fuckin' storm, we thought we should check you were still alive. Just being neighbourly, right?'

His voice is deep and slow, with a slight West Country burr and the same mix of calm and wildness as his appearance.

He laughs: 'That was some fuckin' storm, wannit?'

I just nod. I open my mouth to speak, but no words will come out.

'Ha, you thought you'd kept yourself hidden in here, huh? Matey, you can't keep anything secret around here. The locals have been watching you – even been leaving food out for you by the allotments I hear. They're most grateful to you for your contributions to their WI. Not sure I'd be encouraging all that shite though: jam and fuckin' Jerusalem, for breakfast, lunch and dinner.

'Old Barry, the farmer, thought you were one of our mates. He was over the minute we got back from The Fayres. Anyway, we thought we ought to come over and see for ourselves. Thought you might be Phil the Ferret – ain't seen him for nearly a year now.'

He looks up again and I can hear voices and movement from the top of the hill.

'That'll be Jade and Freddie,' he says, beckoning them over.

I'm feeling more and more trapped, like a noose is tightening around me. My brain is scrambling, trying to make sense of what is happening. Sensing my unease he lowers himself gently to the ground, dangling his feet over the edge of the bank. He looks over towards Jade and Freddie, who are still a way off, then leans in towards me conspiratorially:

'Seriously though, matey. Are you OK? You look like shite. That's a nasty looking cut on your arm.'

I'm finding it hard to speak, but I manage to grunt: 'Yeah, thanks, I'm fine.'

Up close like this he smells of wood smoke and tobacco and coffee. The wind and the sun have worn his skin, but I reckon he must be in his late twenties, at least. He's got several studs in his left ear, a cross in his right and, now I can see, another stud just below his lip. I can just make out what looks like a Celtic Cross tattooed on his chest and some others on his arms: one that looks like a CND logo; a Sun God of some sort and some hieroglyphics that I can't make out.

He looks at me, encouraging me to elaborate, and I find myself talking, without even knowing what I'm saying. Somehow he seems to draw the words out of me.

'My bivouac came down on me in the night. That was

183

pretty freaky…I gotta rebuild it I guess.'

My voice sounds strange, but he nods gravely, as if I've said something really profound, then we both look up as his friends approach.

I can hear Jade, jangling, from twenty yards away. She's wearing a really cool tie-dyed dress, with a whole load of bangles and necklaces, that are causing all the jangling, a beaten up pair of DMs and an even older, khaki army-surplus coat over which a mass of blonde, braided hair falls.

She's looking down at her footing, but as she realises we've seen her she looks up. In that moment her eyes catch mine. They are a pale, mesmerising green that reel me in, even before she's with us. I've never seen anyone quite like her. I'm under her spell in an instant, powerless to resist, until a big grin illuminates her face, releasing me. She lowers her head and walks the last few paces down to join us.

I barely notice Freddie. He's walking a pace behind Jade, a mass of jet-black hair and denim. He looks like one of the Freak Brothers. Maybe that's why they call him Freddie. My eyes are stuck on Jade, though. I'm just glad I've got my clothes back on.

They're here now and regarding me with bemused expressions.

'Not the Ferret then,' says Freddie.

'Ha, how rude, we haven't even introduced ourselves,' he says, turning back to me. 'I'm Jake, this is Jade and Freddie…'

I nod, with panic rising, knowing I've got to introduce myself.

'I'm Bill.' I blurt out.

Jake raises an eyebrow, tilting his head back suspiciously.

'Bill Cobbett,' I continue, knowing even as I'm saying it that it sounds laughable and that I'm digging a hole for myself.

'Bill Cobbett?' laughs Freddie. 'Looks more like Bilbo Baggins to me. No...not Bilbo Baggins, more like Gollum. Have you got a ring there, my preciousss?' he lisps, crouching over and swinging his arms.

I hate being the butt of the joke, even when I've asked for it like this, and I can feel my face flushing and my fists clenching. If I had Gollum's ring, I would most certainly slip it on right now, make myself disappear, but all I can do is stand here, rooted to the spot, my eyes darting between them, trying to figure out if it's not too late to scarper.

I'm fully dressed again: I could burst out of here and run, head west again until I find somewhere new to hide. These guys have no idea who I am and I'd never see them again.

Jake comes to my rescue: 'Don't worry, matey, you don't have to tell us your real name just yet. You picked a good'un though: William Cobbett Esquire on a latter day *Rural Ride*, only a hundred and fifty years after his alleged passing – rumours of his death were clearly much exaggerated!'

'Are you on the run?' asks Jade, eyes widening. There's a pause: 'You are, aren't you!' She claps her hands, squealing with delight.

'Whoa, whoa,' says Jake, making calming gestures with his palms and looking at his friends. 'Let's not overload him with questions; he's in a bad way... look at him, the poor bastard. He was out here on his own in that storm last night. His shelter's collapsed on him and he looks like he hasn't eaten in a month.'

He turns and looks at me for a few seconds, taking me in again and then smiling: 'Hey, whatever you've done, whoever you're hiding from, it'll take a lot to shock us. So don't worry, we're not about to dob you into the local plod.'

Jade's been watching me closely and now she looks up at Jake and says: 'Hey, why doesn't he come and stay with us for a while. If the big, bad wolf has blown his house down he'll need somewhere to kip. Stella and Ruth aren't coming back from Greenham anytime soon, he could use the ambulance.' She turns and looks me right in the eye: 'Bilbo, why don't you come and stay with us for a bit? You'd love it.'

Things are moving way too quick for me now and the intensity of the spotlight being shone on me is paralysing. Jade seems to be looking at me like some kind of pitiful, stray dog that she wants to take in. Am I to just stand here, mute, waiting for them to decide what to do with me? I feel like a paper bag that's been filled by a gust of wind, lifted way off the ground, giddy and swirling out of control, at the mercy of the wind. There's something about these people though: I've never come across anyone like them before. The way they look and talk and behave is intoxicating. Maybe I should just go with the flow, things can't get worse than they already are, can they?

Jake is looking at Freddie. He shrugs. 'I don't care.

Whatever. Have you got any spliff?' he asks, looking at me.

'No, I'm running out of everything.' I reply. 'I've got some food still.'

'What'ya got?' asks Jake, smiling again.

'I've got a load of apples and cobs and chestnuts. Oh and some veg from the allotments. And some mushrooms.'

'Magic ones?' asks Freddie, suddenly getting interested.

'You fuckin' trip-head, Freddie. Give the poor kid a break.' Then he looks at me: 'That sounds good. Frank could put those in his veggie curry.' He pauses for a moment: 'Look, why don't you come down with us for a cuppa and something to eat, meet some of the other guys. You look like you could do with a good feed and we can take care of those cuts of yours. You're gonna have to tell us your real name first though, none of this Bill Cobbett bollocks!'

'My name's Mark,' I say, before I've even thought about it. 'People call me Marko.'

'Marko? That's more like it. Marko it is!'

'Still prefer Bilbo,' says Freddie.

'Come on, Marko, you come with us,' says Jade.

I feel my destiny being sucked along by these people and, right now, I don't seem to have the strength to do anything other than go with it. Those words just came out of my mouth and I'm rapidly committing myself to going with them. What if I don't want to go though? What if I just stay here on my own? I'd be OK. I could rebuild my bivouac. I could get a fire going tonight, sit by it with some sizzling cobs and a cup of tea, blow some tunes out on my harp. But I know I'm deluding myself. The terror of last night leaps back into my mind, the roaring of the wind and the world caving in on me. I imagine myself in here as winter starts to bite, cold and wet and hungry, just like my premonition.

They're all looking at me now and I'm filled with a sudden need for the warmth of company, to be part of something that's not just me and my own inner voice, to fill this lonely void that's consumed me for as long as I can remember.

'Yeah, let's go.' I say.

Chapter 11

Base camp

I trail back up the hill, with Jake, Jade and Freddie following. This route that's become so familiar to me feels different now, after the storm and with company. Behind me, I can hear Jade jangling and Freddie huffing and wheezing. Jake, by contrast, is almost silent, picking his way nimbly through bushes and branches as if they're not there. No wonder I didn't hear him approach just now. I look round to check he's still there. He's right behind me and I jump.

He laughs: 'So, this is where you've been hiding out, Marko?'

'Just over there.' I point.

I remember picking the space because nobody could see it unless they were right on it. It's even more hidden now. We crouch under some low-hanging branches that have sheared in the storm and then we're in what's left of my camp. Jake and I stand there, waiting for Jade and Freddie to catch up. I see him scanning the scene slowly, nodding his head, as he takes it in.

I try to see it for the first time, as if through his eyes. It's a mess, literally as if a bomb's been dropped on it. The birch tree that was my ridgepole is still there, but now it's surrounded by a mass of snapped and broken branches. I scraped a load of them away this morning, so now they're mostly in two ragged heaps. Between them is my scratched and torn sleeping bag, folded in half, with my backpack sat on top of it. I can just about make out where my fire pit was and the remnant of my limply dangling washing line, but that's about it.

'How long you been here?' he asks.

I have to think about it for a moment: 'I got here toward the end of August, so…'

'Wow. Over two months. You done well to hold it together, man,' he says, shaking his head. Then he laughs again, lightening the tone: 'Your bivouacking skills could do with some work though.'

I laugh too. It's a warm, conspiratorial laugh. He's laughing with me, not at me, and it feels like he understands what I've been through. Have I done well? It doesn't feel like it. I'm alive, that's about all I can say.

It's more than that, though. I've had to dig deep. I've had to find strength from somewhere, from places I didn't know existed in me: strength to keep it going each minute and each hour of each day; strength to find food and water and shelter; strength to stop myself from being overwhelmed by all the accusing inner voices that have haunted me night and day and the strength to forgive myself and accept what has happened.

I don't know how, but I've found that strength. I've

teetered on the edge at times, but yes, I *have* held it together. And despite everything, I've got this new feeling building inside: a feeling of quiet confidence, an acceptance of who I am, a readiness to let the past go and to build a new future.

Right here, in this moment, I feel like I'm on a different edge: it's the edge that separates me from the rest of the world. This thought hits me with a vertiginous force, because suddenly I know that I can't continue my journey on my own. I've got to take this leap of faith, let the light in, expose myself to it and be ready for whatever comes my way.

I smile: 'Thanks, Jake. I guess I wasn't expecting any visitors.'

Jade and Freddie are with us now. Jade comes up and puts an arm around me:

'Oh, Marko, is this where you've been sleeping?'

'Yeah. It was OK until last night. The storm just tore it all up.'

'Holy shit! You were under there last night? You're lucky to be alive, mate,' says Freddie, slowly shaking his head.

I just nod and we all stand there for a few seconds, heads bowed, as if we're standing at someone's grave.

'Hey, we should get back,' says Jake. 'We've still got a load of clearing up ourselves, there's trees and branches down everywhere.'

I step gingerly over to the remains of my shelter and roll my sleeping bag up and into its bag. Everything else is pretty much in the pack already: I guess I've been in a perpetual state of readiness to flee ever since I've been here. I sling my backpack over my shoulders, and then pause for a second to look around me one last time. My eyes stop on the marker for Spike's grave that still stands defiantly.

'See ya later, Spike,' I whisper under my breath and then, turning before I risk getting emotional, I march off with my new friends.

We seem to be heading down towards the southern corner of my wood. Other than my trip into Yeovil, I've spent most of my time on the western side, looking towards Norton, or in the east towards Montacute. The woods stretch on for quite a way to the south, so I guess that's why I've not often gone too far in this direction.

'So, where do you all live?' I ask them, as we walk.

It feels weird walking along, with no idea of where we're going, my fate for the moment out of my hands. They look at each other and laugh.

'Oh, not far from here,' Jake replies. 'We're camped out on the old track between Norton and Odcombe. You'll see soon enough, so let's not spoil the surprise, hey?

'There's a few things you should know before we get there. We live a bit off the grid. Not quite as off the grid as you've been, but off the grid nonetheless. The most important thing for us is that we're a community and we all live together collectively.

'There's no strict rules, we don't need any of that fascist bollocks, but everyone is expected to contribute. It's all about tolerance and respect for each other and our environment, about creating a space where we can be the best we can be. And it works, because everyone believes in it.

'Most people sleep walk through their lives, Marko, while a few greedy bastards at the top suck everything out of them: their minds, their bodies, their spirits, until they're nothing but hollow, compliant, alienated shells. Well, we ain't falling for that, we see through it. We live life how *we* want to live it.'

'That's what it's all about,' says Jade. 'Being true to your mind and your body and your spirit. Freeing yourself. Living to your potential. Finding your place in the Cosmos and going with that flow.'

I stay quiet for as they speak. I don't want to make myself look like a fool, so I just listen, trying to work out who these guys are. They seem like a bunch of hippies, but hippies have only ever been on the edge of my radar, more cartoon figures to lampoon then real people.

I've never met people quite like them before, that's for sure. All the stuff they're saying isn't quite making sense yet. A lot of it resonates and sounds exotic, exciting even, but Jade's lost me when she talks about *finding your place in the Cosmos*. For the moment I will take her advice and *go with the flow.*

We come out of the woods and then skirt along the edge of a field where a bunch of cows are grazing. I haven't been any further than this, so I'm into new territory as the path curls around and then starts to descend. At the far side the field gives way to more trees and the path cuts down a steep bank between them.

'What's your star sign, Marko?' Jade is asking me

'Um, I don't know...'

She laughs. 'Well when's your birthday?'

'Oh. The twenty-first of March'

'Ah, well you're an Aries then, right on the cusp of Pisces. Born on the very first day of the Zodiac. Wow. I'll have to do your chart.'

'Great, thanks'. I've no idea what that is, but best to be polite I guess.

We have to go in single file now and the path down is slippery, so we descend in silence, Jake at the front, Freddie at the back. At the bottom, the path comes out onto a narrow little lane, full of rain-filled potholes and scattered with branches and other detritus from the storm. To the right the lane heads back into Norton, I've sussed that, but we go left past a farm, with a big house surrounded by out-buildings.

'That's Barry's gaff,' says Freddie, seeing me looking at it. 'Barry the farmer. A bit of a grumpy old bloke, but he's basically sound.'

'Barry? Oh he's a sweetheart,' says Jade.

'He has to be,' says Jake. 'He knows we've got friends in high places! That's why he lets us use the field for a peppercorn rent, gives us the odd rabbit, or pheasant. Anyway, we look after the place for him.'

I just let this banter go back and forth over my head. It all feels surreal to me right now: enigmatic, mysterious, full of possibility, but terrifying at the same time; rather like the wood when I first arrived back in August. I wonder what it will look like once the mists start to clear. Will it feel like a new home with new like-minded friends, a new way of living and seeing the world, or am I walking into a baited trap that will destroy me? My stomach is hollowing again and my muscles tensing, as Jake pulls open a wide, six-bar gate and we walk into their camp.

I feel like I'm walking into a circus troop. On my left, just in from the hedge, is a solid-looking outbuilding. Radiating away from it, in a horseshoe, is a ramshackle medley of old vehicles: a couple of caravans, one of which appears to be held up on bricks; an old ambulance that could be mine; a trio of Combie vans in varying stages of decrepitude; something that was probably an ice cream van in a previous life; a minibus that looks like it might still run and, dominating everything, a larger bus with a tarpaulin extension held up on wooden struts.

A little away from the big bus is a great fire pit, surrounded by a load of seats which look like they must have been stripped out of the bus and half a tree that has been carved into a bench shape. The ground is heavily trodden down here and partially covered with wood chippings.

All of the vehicles have been spray-painted with the most amazing images: on one of the vans there's a rainbow surrounded by meadows and waterfalls; on the ambulance the St George's Cross has been incorporated into a shield held by a knight who is fending off a grotesque dragon with a face that looks like Maggie Thatcher and the large bus has a huge CND logo with murals of what looks like Jimmi Hendrix and other guitarists.

Freddy sees me looking at it and a big grin comes over his face.

'That's the Magic Bus. You'll love it. It's where we all hang out when the weather's bad. Anything and everything goes on in there.'

Jake and Jade are already walking on past the fire pit. They turn and beckon me to follow them. I see now that there's steam coming out from under the tarpaulin. They're walking over to an older guy who's stirring a great cauldron that's sitting on a rusted old oil drum.

I follow them over. As I do the most wonderful aroma coming from the cauldron engulfs me. My stomach starts to gurgle, as if the smells have flicked a switch, and I feel like I'm going to swoon. It's all I can do to stop myself from sticking my head straight in.

'Frank, this is Marko. We found him up in the woods, out towards Hamdon Hill. Been through a rough time, ain't you, Marko?' Jake pauses to look at me, then carries on: 'We thought he might stay with us for a while. Have you got enough in there for one more?'

Frank carries on with his stirring, as if he hasn't heard Jake. He's a big guy: not as tall as Jake, but stocky, built like a bull, with thick, strong looking forearms that are covered in faded tattoos. He must be forty, I reckon, at least: his beard and collar length hair are dark, but flecked with bits of ginger and grey and his face is pockmarked and worn.

His opinion clearly matters, because Jake and Jade are both standing in quiet, almost nervous, anticipation and I find myself holding my breath with them.

Eventually he stops, takes a taste from the pot, then, without looking up, asks: 'You hungry, Marko?'

'I'm ravenous.' I reply. 'That smells delicious.'

He looks up, taking me in with one glance, and just nods his head.

'See you later then, Marko.'

'I've got some food in my pack. Would you like it?' I blurt out.

'Oh, Marko, sort that out later, hey?' says Jade. 'There should be some hot water left. I bet it's a long time since you had a shower.'

'You've got a shower? Oh my God, yeah…'

'Let's go then, I'll show you the way.'

'You gonna soap his back for him?' laughs Jake

I can feel I'm flushing and everyone is laughing, including Freddie who has been lingering just away from us.

The shower is in the outbuilding I saw as we came in: a couple of cubicles, with a wash-hand basin on either side. There's a mirror above one of the basins and I catch a glimpse of myself as we come in. I didn't recognise my own reflection for a second, but we're past it before I can take a longer look.

Jade leaves me and I strip off and get in the shower. The water's hot and instantly I'm in heaven: I just stand under it, wallowing in the glorious feeling of it pouring over me. Then I scrub myself, from tip to toe, two months worth of dirt and grime pealing off me like a caterpillar sloughing. My skin stings from the soap getting in my cuts and scratches, but I don't care: right now I'd happily stay in here for the rest of my life.

Finally, I can feel the water starting to cool so, reluctantly, I get out. I wrap my towel around me and go to the basin with the mirror. It's all steamed up, so I reach over and smear it away tentatively with my hand. I find that I'm holding my breath, fearful suddenly at what I will find reflected back.

For a few seconds, the face revealed beneath the steam seems alien. Who is this hairy freak staring back at me? Surely it's not me. It's been nearly three months since I've seen my own face and it's like I have to re-introduce myself. Of all the things that define you, it's your own image that you think of first, but now here I am, changed almost beyond recognition.

It was the same with my voice when I talked with Jake and Jade and Freddie earlier. I was hearing myself speak, but it sounded as if it came from someone else. In my isolation I've become detached from my own image and my own voice. I've retreated so deep inside that I've ceased to have a use for them, defining myself solely by my inner voice and my memories and external observations.

I keep staring. My face is covered in a scraggly beard. I've been running my fingers through it and scratching it almost constantly these past weeks, but seeing it is still a shock: as if it doesn't belong to me, as if it's one of those pretend, comedy beards that someone's stuck on.

My hair's grown too. I used to keep it shortish: not like the Rude Boys and Skinheads, but shortish nevertheless. It must have needed cutting even before I left, because it's really long now, curling at the ends, covering my ears and encroaching on my face to merge with the beard. I look like a garden that's been abandoned, left untended, so that everything's gone wild, all the plants and weeds growing into each other and jostling for space.

My skin's in a terrible state: burnt by the sun and wind;

covered with spots and scratches and bites. I feel a flush of embarrassment at Jade seeing me like this.

I keep staring. I'm seeing the differences, but there's something that I can't yet define. The eyes looking back at me are mine, but something has changed. They're blood-shot, with deep shadows under them, almost like I've been in a fight and they've both been blackened. I guess I've barely slept the last couple of nights. I've lost so much weight, that even my cheekbones have become more prominent. I look like a bloody ghoul.

Slowly, as I keep looking, the real changes start to come into focus. I sense them because they chime with what I've been feeling inside, but haven't acknowledged before. There's a new hardness staring back at me. Behind it I can see fear and anger, suspicion and sadness, but there's determination too and a quiet watchfulness and awareness.

From nowhere, I start to laugh: I look like someone you wouldn't want to mess with. The mirror is steaming up again, so I give it another wipe. Maybe there's just a little hope in those eyes too, maybe even the start of an accept-ance of who I am and what has happened to me.

My mood is starting to lighten; I'm even feeling an excitement I haven't known for ages at the thought of getting to know these guys. Maybe I can make some friends here; maybe things are about to make a turn for the better and maybe I can finally put all the shit from Farnham behind me.

I start to run my fingers through my hair, trying to make myself look a bit less wild. I start messing around, pouting at myself and blowing myself a kiss, flexing the muscles on my arms and chest and shoulders, which seem to have hardened with all the physical exertions of the past couple of months.

Then, from behind me, I hear laughter. I spin round, clutching tightly onto the towel that I've almost dropped. Jade is leaning against the door, with a big grin on her face.

'Come on pretty boy, enough preening, Frank's curry will be ready soon and I wanna take a look at that cut for you. Get yourself dressed and I'll see you over by the fire circle.'

She gives me a little wink and turns away, giggling to herself.

I just stand there for a minute, clinging onto the basin. When I'm sure she's gone, I grab my head in my hands and curse myself under my breath: 'Fuckin' idiot! She's gonna think you're a complete twat. What a wanker!'

I'm feeling shaky again. Maybe it's still not too late to disappear?

No, don't be stupid, pull yourself together.

I finish off as quickly as I can, put on my clothes and head back outside.

There are a few more people around now: a man and a woman talking with Frank, a bloke walking away to one of the vans and another walking towards the fire pit with an armful of logs. I see Jade over at the far side by the ambulance beckoning me and I hurry over, head down, my pack slung over my shoulder.

'Marko, you can stay in here,' she says. 'It was Sheila and Ruth's, but they've stayed at Greenham. You know about the Peace Camp?'

'Uh, no…'

'There's an American Air Force base there and Thatcher's invited Reagan to put his Cruise, bloody missiles there. There's a big demo in London at the weekend to protest about it, but at Greenham itself dozens of women, mostly from Wales, but others as well, are camping on the Common outside the base.

We all stayed there for a couple of weeks in September. They've got a great vibe going on. Ruth's Welsh and knows a few of the other women, so she and Sheila decided to stay. Anyway, dump your gear in there, take your shirt off and I'll put a dressing on that cut.'

At the back of the ambulance, facing away from the camp, the double doors open outwards to reveal a large mattress. I take my shirt off and sit bare-chested on the edge, tense with cold and embarrassment. Jade senses my discomfort. She kneels at my feet with a big box full of first-aid stuff and looks up at me:

She puts on a mock-serious tone. 'This is going to hurt, Marko. Are you man enough?'

I play along with it laughing and flexing my biceps again. 'Do you think you'll be able to save my arm, Doc?'

'It'll be touch and go, but we'll see what we can do…'

She leans over, taking the inside of my arm in one hand, running her fingers over the cut with the other. Up close like this her heady mix of scents overwhelms me.

I close my eyes. There's the same soap that I've just used, which smells like honey and mint and all sorts of other things that I can't name. Then there's that same mix of wood smoke and tobacco that I got from Jake earlier.

Beneath all of that is something intoxicating, what feels like her essence, her natural scent. It's a dangerous smell. I can feel myself starting to get aroused, my cock starting to swell. I'm trying to rein myself in, focus my thoughts away from her presence so close to me.

I can sense that she's looking at the tattoo on my arm and that thought brings me back. I know I have to say something and I'm tensing up again.

'They all died when I was younger,' I say. 'I got the tattoo done to commemorate them.'

She's stroking the tattoo now and she looks up at me. 'Oh, Marko. I'm sorry. How old were you?'

'I was eleven, going on twelve. They were in a car accident. Ancient history now.'

I'm trying to speak casually, but I can feel that I'm stumbling over the words. My voice sounds strained, almost cracking. I'm not used to talking about this.

'You poor thing. That must have been awful for you.'

She's still looking up at me with a gentle frown. I can feel the weight of my emotion building and swelling in my face and neck and shoulders. My lips are starting to quiver and I force them together, squeezing my face, clenching my fists trying to keep it in.

She gets up and sits on the mattress right next to me. 'It's OK, Marko. Whatever you've been going through, you're safe now.'

She rests a hand on my shoulder.

Even that light weight is enough to burst the wall of my dam. Something between a moan and a snort bursts out of me, and then the tears are uncorked. I'm desperately trying to restrain them, but I feel her hand squeeze my shoulder and then they are gushing out of me uncontrollably, my body heaving under the force of what I've unleashed.

I fold over with my head in my hands, as if I can hide myself somehow from the shame. I feel like I'm falling from a great height with nothing to stop me. Then, abruptly, I stop, as if the water from the dam has all escaped. I'm seized by acute embarrassment again and, in panic, I jolt upright, rubbing the tears out of my eyes.

'I'm sorry. I'm sorry.' I plead with Jade.

'What are you sorry for?' she asks, her arm still around my shoulder. 'You blokes, emotionally repressed every bloody one of you! If the emotion's there you've got to let it out, or it will fester, dark and malignant, consuming you until that's all that's left. I'm glad you can cry in front of me, Marko: that's the sign of a real man.'

She leans over to the box and breaks off a load of tissue. 'Here, give your nose a blow. You'll feel much better. I always do after a good cry. Right, now let's deal with these cuts of yours.'

I blow my nose as she fiddles in the box. She's right, I do feel better: lighter somehow, unburdened, a dark, dense fog dispersed as if by the morning sun. I've made a complete prat of myself in front of Jade, twice in the space of about fifteen minutes, but rather than use that against me, she's reacted as if it's completely normal and she likes me all the more for it.

She's got a bottle of disinfectant in her hand now and she soaks it in some cotton wool and starts to dab it on my cuts, starting with my arm. It stings, but I've got some self-respect left, so I pretend that it's nothing. Jade laughs, seeing that I'm restraining my reaction.

I'm feeling braver now, so I ask her: 'How long have you been living here?'

'Oh, this'll be my second winter,' she replies, putting some cotton wool with some antiseptic on the wound and fixing it with a load of tape. It now obscures half of my tattoo. 'I met some of the guys at festivals when I was still at university and I used to travel round with them sometimes. Then last summer I caught up with them again at the Stonehenge Festival and I thought I'd just stick with them. It's such a natural way of living. Beats getting caught up in the Rat Race, that's for sure; there was no way I was going to swallow that bullshit. The whole world wants to live like this, Marko, they're just too repressed and oppressed to know it.

'The people have changed a bit, but Frank and Jake are still here and Abi and Travis – you haven't met them yet have you? They're lovely. Abi's just told everyone that she'll be having a baby next Spring – she'll be our first mother!

'Freddie's like me: this'll be his second winter The only other guys you haven't met yet are Rick and Pete. They're both really cool; they've come and gone a few times, but I reckon they'll stay for the winter this year. There's always people coming and going, some people like to go back to London, or Bristol, or wherever during the winter. Rick's a great guitarist; he's the one that keeps our band together really.'

'Wow – you've got a band?'

'Yeah. We're called AlienNation – one word, with a

capital *N* in the middle. Sometimes we call ourselves The Enlightenment, depends on how we're feeling. We played at some of the festivals this year and we do the odd pub gig round here.

'Jake and I kinda split the vocals. Frank's pretty decent on a bass guitar, or any guitar really, and Freddie and Pete thump away on their bongos. You play anything Marko?'

'My Uncle Harry's a Blues guitarist and he taught me a few chords, but the harp's my main thing.'

'The harmonica you mean, or have you managed to get a stringed harp in that pack of yours?'

I laugh. 'Yeah, the harmonica. I couldn't fit the stringed one in.'

'I know, I was only teasing. I saw the tattoo on your other arm. Is that you?'

'No, no, that's Howlin' Wolf. I'd love to play like him, but I give it a blow anyway.'

'Well, you'll have to have an audition for the band later. Some harp in our mix would be great. Right, that's you patched up. Frank will be serving his curry up anytime soon, so I'm going to go and help him. Why don't you come over in a few minutes?'

'Thanks, Jade. I'll see you there.'

With Jade gone, I lean back on the bed for a few seconds taking in my new surroundings. After all these weeks in the woods it's weird to be sitting inside an enclosed, man-made space. It's the stillness, that's what feels so strange. As soon as Jade had left and shut the doors behind her it hit me: as though I'm suspended in a lifeless vacuum, with just a few particles of dust floating listlessly in the sun's spotlight that angles through the window.

I'm not sure if this sense of containment is comforting or claustrophobic. Maybe it's the imprint of Sheila and Ruth that I'm feeling? They were here and now they're not. I've never met them, yet here I am: lying where they lay, looking at the same walls, inhabiting their space, their posters still stuck to the walls.

There are all sorts of images mixed up artfully: publicity materials for novels by Emily Bronte, Angela Carter and Virginia Woolf; a poster of the Stonehenge Free Festival for last year and a load of abstract images and photos.

The one I like the most is a blown up photo of Janis Joplin on stage. I can feel the passion in it, as if I was right up there on stage: her head is thrown back, her wild hair billowing behind her, her bared arms and shoulders coiled with tension, a cascade of necklaces leaping about her neck and breasts in suspended animation, her eyes squeezed tightly shut as the words explode from somewhere deep inside. The sense of exhilaration and abandonment sucks me in and I find my cock swelling again as I imagine her breasts straining against her top.

I lie back on the bed, letting the image wash over me. It's a big double mattress wedged into one corner. It's amazing to be on a bed again. It's soft and firm at the same time, embracing me.

An image of Sheila and Ruth slides into my mind without warning: they're lying here at night, kissing and writhing, naked against each other. It feels shameful, letting these thoughts into my mind, like I'm invading their space, but I can't seem to help it and the more I chastise myself the more erotic it becomes. My eyes are getting heavy, my body fighting a battle between lust and fatigue, but, just as I'm slipping into sleep, I'm interrupted by a booming voice from outside.

'Grub's up. Grub's up.' Frank is shouting.

I lurch back to consciousness, scrambling myself upright and flinging my legs over the side of the bed. Somebody's watching me, I'm convinced of it. I spin my head around, but it's still just me. Eyes closed, I breathe out, slowly deflating. I'm trying to think of excuses for staying right here, but I know that I've got to go and join them all for lunch.

Suddenly I'm shivering and I realise that I'm gripping the edge of the mattress, as if I'm clinging to it for dear life. An image leaps into my head: I'm ten years old and I've climbed to the top diving board at the swimming baths. I can't climb back down, but I can't make myself jump either. I remember how I stood up there for ages, seized by terror, until I felt a surge of bravado and, taking a running jump, I leapt into the void. Outside I hear voices and before I can dwell on it any more I jump up and, pulling on a T-shirt and jumper, make for the door.

Over by the Magic Bus everyone's gathering around the oil drum and a trestle table. It's laden down with plates and cutlery, a couple of big loaves of bread and some jars filled with what look like pickles. Jake and Freddie are standing there, talking under their breaths, chuckling and taking sidelong glances in my direction as they do.

What are they talking about? Are they laughing at me? Are they plotting something?

I'm trying to act naturally, but it's like I've forgotten how to walk. I can feel everyone's eyes burning into me, weighing me up, trying to suss me out. I'm going to have to speak in a minute, but I feel like my mouth has dried out and my tongue is filling my mouth like a swollen foot that won't come out of it's boot. I want to disappear again, but my hunger and a determination not to fail drive me forward. The food smells amazing, rich and spicy, and my stomach is gurgling like mad in anticipation.

Jake sees me coming and, stepping away from Freddie, shouts out:

'Listen up, folks: this is Marko. He's the bloke Old Barry was talking about. Definitely not the Ferret, but he's going to stay with us for a while. Go easy on him, hey, he's been hiding out in the woods for a couple of months and he almost got buried alive in the storm last night!'

There's a murmur of greetings. I can't quite make them out, other than Frank who shouts out: 'Come on, Marko, come and get some grub.'

They're all looking even more closely at me now. I don't quite know what to say or do, so I just nod gratefully at Frank and pick up a plate from the table. He spoons on some rice and a load of the curry and then Jake leans over with a big hunk of bread.

'Go on get that down you, matey. You'll feel way better,' and he claps a hand on my shoulder.

I just about manage to thank them, lingering awkwardly for a second until I spot a space next to Freddie. He's already tucking in and I slide in next to him. He nods at me and then, finishing a mouthful, says:

'Cleaned yourself up a bit, hey? You're looking almost human again; not like that creature from the swamp we found earlier!'

He laughs at his own joke and I laugh with him. Everyone seems to be focusing on eating rather than talking and I'm grateful for that. The food is delicious: hot and spicy and nutty. I'm trying not to wolf it down too fast, after my experience in Yeovil, but that takes some doing: I'm so hungry I just want to cram it all in at once, devour it and head back for more.

It looks like everyone is here now and there's a comfortable hubbub of cutlery on plates, eating noises and everyone talking at once in little groups. I notice Abi, sat opposite me, on the other side of the fire pit. She's got straight-black hair, with hints of henna, that's pulled back from her face and tied in a ponytail. She seems to be almost glowing. Maybe that's just her personality, or maybe it's because she's pregnant.

She's listening to the guy sitting next to her, who I guess must be Travis. Her eyes are bright and friendly, as if she's excited by the conversation. Then she notices me looking at her. I'm embarrassed for a split second, until I see that she's smiling at me in a warm and welcoming way, so I smile back and carry on eating.

That tiny exchange, combined with the food in my belly, has melted my anxiety for the moment and I continue eating with a grin still on my face. I'm starting to feel a warm glow that I haven't felt for a long time. Part of me's still wary that this is all a bit too good to be true, but I can't help but feel a tingling of anticipation, a rising hope that maybe, by chance, I find myself amongst kindred spirits.

I look around at the group. The conversation is moving now, to more of a group discussion about what needs to be done this afternoon. There's a togetherness about them and, instinctively, I want to be part of it. I decide, right here in this moment, that I'm going to give it a shot. Keep my wits about me, but give it my best shot.

This afternoon, I threw myself into working and making myself useful. After we'd finished lunch, the first thing I did was to get all the food from my pack and take it to Frank. There wasn't a whole lot (a tin of sardines, a couple of onions, some carrots and green beans from the allotment and a few manky mushrooms and chestnuts), but he seemed to be pleased. He was particularly impressed with the mushrooms and wanted to know where I'd found them.

He nodded his head as I described where I got them: 'That makes sense, the perfect spot. I go out foraging early most mornings – you'll have to come with me Marko. Freddie comes sometimes, occasionally one of the others. This is a good time of year for them and they're bountiful in the fields and woodlands around here if you know what you're looking for – Field Mushrooms and Parasols like yours, Boletus, Chicken-of-the-Woods, Beefsteak. They're all good for eating and we fry them up for breakfast. And then there's the magic Psilocybin – go easy on those Marko. Have you done magic mushrooms before?'

'Err, no. I've heard about them, but I've never tried.'

'Well, they're wonderful things Marko, in moderation. They can open your psyche up to the universe, shine a light on parts of your mind you never even knew existed. Just think about all the great music and literature that's been animated by their ministrations. But if you overdo it, they'll scramble your brain, tip you into a pit of paranoia that you'll struggle to get out of. We make a little tea out of them once in a while, but you've got to make sure your head's in a good place first and just have a wee cup of diluted tea when you first try it.'

I'd been wary of Frank after my first exchange with him. He hadn't said much, but I'd sensed from Jake and Jade that they were a bit in awe of him, almost that they needed his permission to do anything. Sat on my own with him after lunch, he opened up and I got the feeling, like I some-times did with Uncle Harry, that here was someone who had seen the world, who knew about everything, and could do almost anything he turned his hand to.

There was something more to Frank too. He was a big, stocky guy, with leathered hands and face and he exuded a quiet strength. I already knew that, when he spoke, he had something to say and it was going to be something import-ant, something I should listen to. He spoke quietly, but with the occasional extravagant flourish and with a Scot-tish accent that had, no doubt, been eroded by years of living away, but all that just added to the spell that his words cast.

He rolled up a joint as we spoke. I was amazed at how nimble his thick fingers were: neatly flaking off fine crumbs of hash into the tobacco, working the paper delicately between his thumbs and forefingers until it was tightly impacted, sealing it as if he was zipping his mouth along a harp, inserting a little cardboard roach that fitted perfectly like a master carpenter and finally twisting the end with a theatrical flourish.

He seemed to do all this in just a few fluid movements and then lit it, inhaling deeply and exhaling a long stream of sweet-smelling smoke like a dragon from both nostrils. He took a second, deep drag before reaching over to me with the joint. Then, as if changing his mind, he paused, holding it aloft and said:

'You seem like a good lad, Marko, but you've clearly been through some heavy stuff. Take your time to get your shit together. Nobody here's going to put pressure on you, as long as you pull your weight. Och – Jade and Abi will probably try and mother you and wheedle stuff out of you, but they're good sorts. You'll be fine.'

Only when he'd made his point did he reach over to me with the joint. I took it, an abrupt awareness hitting me that I'd somehow been weighed-up and judged. I'd hardly said anything, but somehow he'd surreptitiously been sussing me out. Not for the first, or last, time today I felt like I was sitting there naked, everyone looking right into me, my darkest, most shameful secrets exposed for all to see. I shuddered for a moment with embarrassment, but then thought: *So what? They've looked at me at my lowest ebb and they still seem to be opening their arms out.*

I took the joint and our eyes locked for a second.

I nodded my head: 'Thanks, Frank. And thanks for your

welcome, I really appreciate it.'

Looking at the joint I smiled, trying to lighten the tone: 'This is my first smoke for a couple of months.'

I took a short, tentative drag, then, thankful that I hadn't spluttered and coughed, a second deeper one, before passing it back to him. Fuck, it was strong: I felt almost instantly lightheaded, even with just a couple of tokes.

Frank smiled back: 'Right, Marko, we'd better get this show back on the road. There's a lot of clearing up still to be done after last night's tempest.'

It's early evening now. The sun has sunk behind the Magic Bus and there's a fire going, courtesy of Jake and Freddie. It's way bigger than the ones I used to light up in the woods. They were timid little things that spluttered apologetically, not wanting to be seen. This is a shouting-out-loud fire, big enough for everyone to sit around and be warmed by, and it crackles and sparks, sending its embers dancing up into the night sky.

Rick is perched on one of the log benches, strumming on a guitar. He looks just like Jim Morrison sat there, with a mass of unruly hair and broody eyes that hint at hidden depths. Jade was right: he can play that guitar, even just hearing him strumming I can tell that, the way he changes chord seamlessly and the easy rhythm he keeps.

He's playing some Neil Young and Jade is dancing and singing along: 'You *were*... like a Hurricane,' and everyone laughs along, last night's storm, or tempest as Frank called it, finally fading into folklore.

I've been working all afternoon, helping cut up a tree

that had fallen on the far side of the field. One of the branches came down on Abi and Travis' caravan. It's a big old tree; they'd have been flattened if there'd been a direct hit, but, luckily, the hedge took the main force.

Rick and Pete were off helping Barry the farmer, but the rest of us spent the afternoon there: Jake and Frank taking turns with a saw, Freddie and I sharing an axe, then all of us carrying armfuls of logs and branches over to a storage area where the wood is stacked in big piles to season it. That's what I could have done with up in the woods, a place to stack and dry the wood, to stop my fires spluttering and smoking like they did.

By the end of the afternoon there was nothing left of the tree but a stub of half uprooted trunk and an indent in the hedge that had broken its fall. We were in fine spirits and these were lifted even more when Rick and Pete arrived back, just as the sun was setting, Pete carrying a brace of pheasants and Rick a pair of rabbits already skinned.

'Look what Old Barry's given us!' Rick shouted.

'These boys'll need to be hung for another couple of days,' said Pete holding his pheasants up triumphantly, 'but the rabbits are good straight away.'

As it happened, Jade and I had already started working on stewing up some lentils to mix up with the remains of Frank's veggie curry, but the rabbit would be good for tomorrow.

Best of all, I'm now standing here with a glass of home-brewed ale. They make their own beer and cider here. Round the back of the shower block there's an old cider press and some buckets filled with evil looking swamp water and some wooden barrels where the ale is nicely fermenting. It tastes great and I'm already rocking by the time I'm into my second one.

The lively mood carries on through dinner: everyone talking animatedly as they eat and the beer and cider flowing. After we've eaten and cleared away, a contented calm descends on us for a while.

Later, as if on some hidden signal that only they know, Jake, Freddie, Pete and Travis take up their bongo drums and get a little rhythm going. Jake starts it with a simple little beat: slowly, slowly, like a murmur. The others pick it up one-by-one, each adding a new layer, stealthily building up the momentum, until it starts to take on a life of its own: urgent, compelling and humming with energy.

My body tingles with the vibrations. I can feel the rhythm seeping deep into me, mimicking my own heartbeat, as if it's connecting me with something I haven't experienced before: with all these people around the fire, yes, but with something more elemental too, like the wind and the trees and the energy from the earth.

As the rhythm builds, more sounds are joining: Jade's got a tambourine, which she's shaking and tapping; Rick has picked up the beat and is teasing in some chords on his guitar; voices are humming and hands clapping; everything blending as if it has all just been waiting for this moment to come together. As I sit, absorbing the energy, I feel myself being drawn into a fuzzy, cosy, contented trance.

The rhythm lifts and lulls, lifts and lulls, rising to another level with each cycle. I look up and see Jade dancing: her body lithe, entwining with the pulse of the music, as she swirls the tambourine in orbiting arcs, her braided hair flailing in her wake. Her skin shines, translucent, with little beads of perspiration and those brilliant, green eyes are sparkling in the firelight with a demonic intensity.

I watch, entranced. Maybe she senses it, because she lifts her dancing up another gear, her bare feet rooted to the earth, hips gyrating, arms raised, swirling frantically like a tree in a storm. Now it feels as though the rhythm is coming from her, reflecting her life-force, so that where she goes it follows, faster and faster, until, with a final flourish, she slows and the rhythm stills with her, becoming calm like water emerging from a rapids. With this, she seems to return to her body, as if she had been possessed. Seeing me watching, her face is transformed by a flicker of recognition.

She stops and, with a big smile on her face, shouts out as if nothing had just happened: 'Hey, listen up guys, I've just remembered: Marko told me he plays the harp!' Then she looks at me and whispers: 'Have you got it?'

'Yeah…come on, Marko,' everyone takes up.

'Marko, what can you play?'

'Play us something, Marko!'

I'm jolted out of my reverie. For a moment I freeze. It feels like I've forgotten how to breathe. I don't know if I can remember how to do it. Jake's sat next to me and I feel his hand on my shoulder, squeezing reassuringly.

'Go on, play us something, Marko,' he whispers in my ear. 'Nobody's judging you. You'll be fine.'

I look up and see that everyone's watching me. I reach

into my pocket and pull out my harp, holding it up with a sheepish grin. Everyone cheers. They're on my side, I think, I've got to give it a go.

I inhale deeply and, lifting the harp to my mouth, squeeze out a long, single note, letting it fade, then lift, then waiver at the end. I hear a few murmurs around, which sound appreciative. I'm agonizing about what to play, until I remember I've got Jim Morrison opposite: it has to be the Doors.

I remember playing alone by the fire up in the woods and I close my eyes and imagine myself back there. I breathe out the first few notes of *LA Women*: softly, with a slow tempo, almost as if they're just for me. The notes are soothing, uplifting, filling me with the courage to press on. I fire out another single, louder note, then raise the tempo, jazzing it up, cupping my hands to vibrate the sound, mimicking the funky guitar riffs.

To my left I hear Jade starting to swish her tambourine. Freddie's picked up a beat and I hear him rapping lightly on his drum. I keep it going, looping the licks, and I hear Rick chiming in. Pete's joined in with Freddie and Rick is starting to take over, driving it along with his guitar. I follow him: blowing soft, then hard to embellish his chords. The sound is building and blending and I allow myself to be swept away by the exhilaration, to go where it goes, to express myself in ways I hadn't thought possible. Suddenly, I'm not a lone voice anymore and I realise that my voice sounds so much better when it's combined with all these other voices.

I look up and see Jake is on his feet. He winks at me and

then, raising his arms slows the tempo with a calming gesture, before starting to growl out:

'Get your mojo raasing...raasing, raasing....raasing, raasing.'

Slowly and softly at first, then lifting his arms upward to raise the tempo, faster and faster, louder and louder, whipping the beat and the guitar and my harp into a frenzy until, with Jake conducting, we hit the climax and we all stop in one last wall of noise.

Everyone's laughing and cheering now and then they're rising and clapping me on the back. Even Frank is joining in:

'You've got a real feel for that harp, Marko. You can't teach that, you've got to feel the music. You'll have to play in the band. Your sound adds something, that's for sure.'

I sit there, beaming, my feet jigging up and down on the ground. My head feels like it's going to explode. I want to play some more, but I want to talk to everyone as well.

The mood is slowly calming now. Rick is strumming quietly and Freddie is building a monster spliff on his lap. He must be using a dozen Rizzlas and when it's finished it looks like an ice cream cone, tight at the base and then splaying out.

I find myself telling Frank and Rick about Uncle Harry and his band. Frank reckons he might have seen them play somewhere back in the mid-seventies. I've had a couple of tokes on Freddie's spliff and everything's starting to blur and spin.

'It looks like the Eiffel Tower turned upside down,' I tell

him. Then after a few seconds pause: 'Not that I've ever seen the Eiffel Tower.'

When I add that, Jake almost snorts out his cider. That get's me going too, and once I've started I can't stop, until I'm laughing so hard I think I'm going to wet myself. Rick starts playing *Chanson D'Amour* and singing it in an exaggerated French accent and within a few seconds everyone's laughing. Every time he raises and eyebrow and sings 'Ra-ta-da-da-da,' it's like reigniting the flames. I don't think I've laughed so much. Ever.

There are only a few of us left now. Abi and Travis must have slipped away at some point. Frank's not here any more either, or Pete. The world has shrunk in around the fire: just embers now, with one big log that flickers and spits occasionally. Freddie has his head down rolling another joint: his face shining in the firelight, the rest of him blurring into the darkness. Jade's telling a story, about living in a squat when she was at university in Norwich.

It's a clear night and I'm leaning back, looking at the stars. They seem to be really close and I imagine that I'm swimming in them as they move across the sky. I don't know how long I've been watching them for, but after a while I realise that I'm lying on my back on the ground, my legs up in the air and resting on the log bench. I must have slipped off. I hear laughter and voices, as if from far away, with my name being mentioned, but I can't quite manage to reply. I just lie here and watch the stars, giggling quietly to myself.

Chapter 12

Feet under the table

I wake nauseous, disoriented and busting for a piss. Where am I? I dreamt I was in a coffin. There's a mattress beneath me, walls and a roof and an artificial stillness in the air that feels wrong. The air is stained by sour beer and smoke, the same combination that has infiltrated my skin and my eyes and my mouth, tainting everything with its rancid aftermath. It comes back to me: I'm not in a coffin, I'm in an ambulance.

I lie, flat on my back, squinting up at the roof, as the events of yesterday slowly seep back into my consciousness. Each time a new memory flashes into my mind I wince, my body quivering with shameful denial. They come at me one-by-one: Jake finding me, naked, down by the stream; telling them that my name was Bill Cobbett; Jade catching me prancing around in front of the mirror; crying like a baby in front of her and my pathetic food offering to Frank. Surely these things didn't happen.

Next come the events of last night. I remember the beer and the music, the laughter and the warmth of the company, the rhythm of the drums and that great fire, its flames leaping unashamedly into the night sky. It was a cracking night. Or was it? Doubt hits me like a punch in the gut. What did I say? What did I do? I made a complete twat of myself again; I know it. Everything's hazy, confused, in my morning fug. I try to piece it back together. I played a load of harp; I remember that. They all told me how good I was, but they were just saying it, patronising me. They were probably all sniggering behind their backs.

I talked way too much as well, letting the beer and the dope take over. I remember bigging up Uncle Harry and his band. God knows what else I spilled the beans about. Whatever happened to playing my cards close to my chest?

Even worse than that: how did I get back here? Nightmarish images creep over me like an icy shadow. At some point I was lying on my back, staring up at the stars. How long was I lying there for? I remember thinking the stars were so close that I could reach up and pluck them, a vague awareness of muffled sounds of laughter and voices, then sometime later Jake's head peering down at me, all distorted, as if I was seeing him through a fish-eye lens. I remember arms pulling me up, but refusing their help and staggering off in the wrong direction. Oh God, I think I tried to get into the wrong van, until Jake and Freddie steered me back in the right direction.

Waves of nausea have started to consume me. I groan and roll over, trying vainly to make reality disappear, but of all the symptoms my bursting bladder triumphs. I find my water bottle, empty, by the side of the bed and piss gratefully into it.

I lay there for ages that first morning, battling those feelings. Eventually I started to hear voices outside and knew that I just had to get up and get on with it. I needn't have worried, of course, I got a bit of ribbing from Freddie and Jake, but it was just light-hearted banter really. I decided to knuckle down and make myself as useful as possible, so I volunteered for as many jobs as I could and went about them with gusto.

On Wednesday, only my third full day, I woke with a fever and a sore throat. I forced myself up and tried to pretend that everything was fine, but Abi wasn't fooled: I saw her looking at me as I tried to eat some breakfast. Then she walked up to me and put icy hands onto my forehead.

'Marko, you're burning up! You need to get back to bed. Look at you, you're all puffy.'

Frank was looking sternly over by then. 'She's right, Marko. You look like shite. Get back to bed, we'll sort you out, don't worry. Drink lots of water mind, you gotta sweat it out.'

I filled my water bottle and trudged back to my ambulance. They were right, I was feeling awful, aching all over, my throat so sore I could barely swallow. Even the act of trying to get up had taken it out of me. Almost as soon as I was back in my sleeping bag the fever grabbed me and within half an hour I was drenched with sweat, my head throbbing and my throat raw. I drifted in and out of delirious sleep until, at some point that morning, Frank and Jade came in. I thought I was dreaming them at first, but then I felt Frank's fingers gripping my jaw, twisting it one way then the other.

'Open your mouth wide, Marko,' he demanded.

I complied. There was a moment's silence, then: 'Och, he's got fucking tonsillitis. Look at that Jade.'

I saw Jade peering over his shoulder.

'Oh my God. Look at them, they're all blotchy. You poor darling, your throat must be really sore!'

I just nodded my head, pitifully. I wanted Jade nursing me more than anything. For a moment, even the thought of it started making me feel a little better.

'Right,' said Frank, looking at me. 'You need to stay where you are for a few days, rest up, keep hydrated. Your immune system must be compromised after your sojourn in the woods. You'll feel like shite for a couple of days, but you'll be fine. We'll make up some herbal teas for you and some mushroom soup.'

'Ha – Frank's solution for everything: herbal tea and mushrooms!' laughed Jade.

I tried to laugh with her, but nothing came out. Jade took over, producing a thermometer. I felt like I was ten years old again, tucked up in bed with a thermometer under my tongue. I watched as she pulled out some crystals and hung them in two corners of the van, telling me that they would help to build healing energy.

Frank stood for a moment, grinning, and then, with a wink in my direction, started backing out.

'I hope you feel better soon, Marko. I will leave you to Jade's crystalline panaceas!'

Jade paused for a moment until he had gone. Then, sitting back on the edge of the mattress, she held out a collection of stones.

'Which one do you like, Marko? Which one draws you?'

I looked at her, puzzled for a second, before picking a smooth, shiny grey stone.

'Ah, that's hematite. Good choice. It's a stone for protection. It absorbs negative energy and transforms it with positive vibes.'

She closed my hand around it.

'How does it feel?'

'It feels smooth … cooling.' I said at last. That was true, but I was enjoying the feeling of her hand on mine even more.

'Good,' she smiled. 'Well hold onto it and let its energy bind with yours.'

The last few days have passed in a feverish haze. Jade seems to have taken on the role of my carer: coming in to mop my face and neck and bearing Frank's concoctions: foul herbal teas and mushroom soup which tasted amazing, even if each swallow was a torture.

'Frank's big into his medicinal herbs and his mushrooms,' she said. 'He goes out for them nearly every morning. I tease him about it, but really there's a lot in it. The bloody pharmaceutical companies don't want us curing ourselves though, so it all get's suppressed.'

Abi came as well, apologising that she hadn't been before. 'I'm expecting a child next Spring, Marko, and I was frightened of catching something, but Frank and Jade told me that tonsillitis isn't infectious.'

I mouthed her a thank you and she sat for a while, helping me drink some tea and telling me about their plans for their child. I struggled to take it in, but it was nice of her to come and sit with me.

Even Freddie came, carrying a couple of books: Remarque's *All Quiet on the Western Front* and *Our Man in Havana* by Graham Greene.

'These'll cheer you up, Marko. Two of my faves.'

I was overwhelmed by their kindness. I'd only just met them and here they were feeding me and nursing me and offering me their hands of friendship. I lay there, in my weakened state, unworthy, but gratefully accepting their charity. I'm not sure I knew what it meant to feel humbled before, but that's what I felt.

Time has become distorted again lying here. It drags, interminably, then I doze and a couple of hours disappear in a groggy chunk. I turn Jade's stone round and round in my hand, its cool, smooth surface reassuring, but, still, thoughts whirl around uncontrollably: people and places confusing themselves, my guilty conscience digging and stirring up events accusingly.

In my delirium, I became convinced that I was still up in the woods, in my bivouac, surrounded by a forest fire that was drawing closer and closer from all sides until I was clinging to a small patch of land, immersed in a sea of flames. I knew that I had to get out of there, to run for my life, but my body was so weak I couldn't lift myself.

I woke with a start, panting, sweat pouring off me. I reached for my bottle and drank and drank, then poured water over my head, as if I was dousing the flames. Time had slipped again as I slept and the sun had set. It was dark and I could hear music outside. I came back to reality, with a surge of relief, remembering that it would probably be Rick, Pete, Freddie and Travis, maybe Frank as well, maybe Jade dancing with her tambourine. I was safe and, for once, no longer on my own.

I've stayed in the caravan for more than three days. The worst of the fever had broken by Friday night, but I still felt washed-out. Today's Saturday and the camp is eerily quiet. Most of the others have gone up to London for the CND March. There've been buses going from all over Somerset apparently and only Abi and Freddie have stayed behind.

I was going to try and get up, but then Freddie arrived with a bowl of rabbit stew for lunch. It has to be one of the most delicious things I've ever eaten. We tried to have a game of chess afterwards, but I couldn't quite focus on it, so we just sat and chatted for a while.

He's much more open when it's just the two of us and, as we talked, I could tell that he's actually really intelligent. He's even got a degree in Physics, from Birmingham University. I guess he must feel overawed by some of the others, Jake in particular, so he just plays the clown. As he talked I found myself wondering what he's hiding from, here in this camp, floating in a constant cloud of dope behind that big bushy beard. I suppose that, in some shape or form, we must all be hiding from something, or running from something.

It's Sunday morning. I've got up and had a shower, which has made me feel a whole lot better. I step tentatively outside, my legs still feeling a little wobbly. It's cold and grey and the place is deserted. I wonder for a moment if

226

they're all still up in London. Maybe the demo kicked off and they got arrested. Then I see smoke coming from a chimney on top of the Magic Bus and voices coming from inside.

I amble over, but stop as I get to the door. Nobody's seen me. Just for a second I think about heading back to the ambulance, maybe even clearing out altogether, before anyone can notice, but I push open the doors and climb up and on before my jitters can take a hold. I don't know what reaction to expect: half of me is waiting for them to look up and say: 'Who the fuck are you?'

Instead it feels almost like a homecoming. The warmth from the stove feels nourishing to my bones and the heady mix of smells draws me in, but it's the welcome that really melts me. As soon as they see me a big cheer rises up. Everyone's back from London now apart from Rick, who stayed up there with a girl he met on the march.

Jade's leaning over in the corner, where there are a couple of boxes of LPs and rows of books lined up on some make-shift shelves. Her face lights up when she sees me, and she leaps up to give me a hug.

'Marko, you're looking so much better. Let's have a look at those tonsils.'

I stretch my arms out and open my mouth wide, as if I'm singing an aria in an opera and she peers in.

'Hmm, still a bit swollen I think, but much better. Come and have some coffee and some toast.'

She puts on *Tapestry* by Carole King, which I've not heard before, but it's mellow, heartfelt music, perfect for the moment. I sit down and now they're all talking at once, asking me how I'm feeling and telling me to take it easy. I don't need too much encouragement: fresh coffee has been brewed, toast is browning on a grill, mushrooms frying in a pan and Frank and Freddie have been down into the village to get some Sunday papers.

The coffee smells great and tastes better: thick and strong, with milk and sugar. The mood on the bus is lively and I find I'm smiling so hard my face is hurting. The guys who got back from London late last night are still buzzing from being at the demo and Abi, Freddie and I want to hear all about it. Frank holds up photos from the front pages of the papers showing hordes of people streaming up Piccadilly, arms raised with placards and banners. There were more than a quarter of a million people apparently.

'And not just a bunch of hippies either, there were all sorts of folk,' Jade says. 'I got talking to the squarest two dudes you've ever seen. One of them worked in insurance, the other one did something *really* boring. I said to him: "You can't insure Nuclear Armageddon." And he said: "I know. That's why we're here." The whole thing was such a great vibe.'

It took them over four hours to walk from the start to Hyde Park, so they missed Tony Benn and Joan Ruddock and all the other speeches, but the atmosphere and solidarity was the important thing. Frank reckons that it had a similar feel to the anti-Vietnam marches of the late sixties, even if this was bigger, probably the biggest demonstration ever held in this country.

'But there's an important difference,' he says. 'Back then we weren't even in the war and Harold Wilson was in

228

power. Now I wasn't always his biggest fan, but at least he was prepared to stand up to the Yanks. Thatcher's an altogether different sort. She's contemptuous of all the types who were there yesterday. We're the scum of the earth as far as she's concerned. She's after all the nice, middle-class families, with their box houses and driveways and two-point-four kids. She'll turn the tables, so that those folk are more scared of us then they are of those Yankee missiles.'

'You're not wrong, Frank, she's a devious, warmongering bitch,' says Jake.

'Succinctly put as always, Jake.'

Jade chimes in again with her more optimistic tone: 'Yeah, but guys, you can't ignore the energy of that march. It was even bigger in West Germany apparently. That energy will build momentum, until it's so big that everyone will feel it. Then change will happen. Look at the opinion polls out today. Thatcher's history, she'll be out at the next election.'

While they're speaking, Freddie has picked up one of the placards they brought back with them and is waving it up and down. It's deep red with a black mushroom cloud in the background and a bold white slogan saying: 'Fall Out with Thatcher.'

I'd love to join the debate, but, for the moment, I'm happy just listening. As soon as a piece of paper is free I grab it and spend the rest of the morning devouring the news.

It feels weird coming back to news from the outside world after all this time. I used to read *The Guardian* every day, sometimes *The Times* as well. I thought I would have missed it, all of those news storylines suspended without resolution in mid-air, but the reality is I've barely even thought about it.

I've been so focused on my own issues, that what was happening in the world became irrelevant to me. I'd been transfixed by the drama of the IRA Hunger Strike, but how could I think about that when I was constantly ravenous and worrying about where *my* next feed was going to come from? And how could I even conceive of riots on the streets of cities hundreds of miles away, when I was hiding out in the woods, rarely seeing another human being from one day to the next? My world shrank in on itself, until all that was left was a self-constructed bubble for one.

Reading all the stories now, nothing quite seems real: all the photos and descriptions from yesterday's demo, the latest opinion polls which put the Tories back in third place, a General Election in Belgium.

For some reason it reminds me of the time when I went back to my old school: most of the teachers were still there, but the kids were different, everything seemed smaller, less relevant, and I couldn't reconcile my memories with how it looked to me with my older eyes.

Crises that had seemed so important, have resolved, or changed, or disappeared. New stories have appeared from nowhere and it's like I'm coming into the middle of a conversation, where I missed how it started. There's an article about the future direction of the IRA now that the Hunger Strike has ended. The Hunger Strike has ended? How did that happen? It had seemed unresolvable. There's an article about Hosni Mubarak, the new President of Egypt. I hadn't even heard that Sadat had been assassinated. But then why would I? The sound of the gunshots was never going to carry that far.

It's my first time on board the Magic Bus and Freddie was right, I loved it from the moment I stepped through the door. Inside, they've pretty much stripped out all the seats, to create an open space in the centre. At the far end there's an old, wood-burning Aga with a discoloured, scratched, cream frame and a jet-black hob. A hole has been carved in the roof and a flue fed through to extract the wood smoke. Freddie tells me that, as soon as it's too cold to sit outside, this is kept going continuously, from first thing in the morning to last thing at night.

'If you're on your own, don't let it go out, Marko, or you'll piss everyone off and be down on your hands and knees re-lighting it.'

It's used to heat the bus, cook meals and there always seems to be a kettle on the hob boiling for a brew.

Between the door and the Aga, is a roughly hewn, oak table, thick and solid and big enough for us all to sit down and eat. It's scorched and stained with burns and spills and faded ring-marks from all of the hot mugs that have sat there, but this just adds to the character, like it's telling its own story, a silent witness to events and to all the people who have sat around it.

Anyone who comes here is asked to carve their name into it. They told me that about half an hour ago and ever since I've been studying it carefully. I've found them all there: Jade, with a big loopy *J* and an elegant, elongated *d*;

Jake, scored with strong, confident strokes; Frank, with heavy, old-fashioned letters, like they used on old newspaper mastheads; Freddie with two capitalised *D*s turned into mischievous-looking eyes with thick eyebrows and a spiral of smoke trailing from the *i*. Abi, Travis, Rick and Pete are there too and dozens of other names that I will probably never know.

Eventually, I pluck up the courage and find a space for my name next to Jade's. I take out my penknife and carve it as stylishly as I can, but even before I've finished I realise it looks timid and insignificant, almost apologetic, amongst all those other names.

I wish I could erase it and do it better, but it's too late for that. There are some things in life that you only get one chance at. It's done: the mark of one moment in time that will define me forever, whether I like it or not. I've branded myself irrevocably into this place now and I find myself wondering what people in the future will think when they look down and see my name carved there.

I'm sat now at one of the old bus seats that's been moved and re-bolted to the floor with its back to the window. There's a few of these, plus a load of other chairs, randomly positioned about the bus. They're scattered with cushions and covered with a collage of different fabrics and colours.

The ceiling has been plastered with posters of gigs and festivals (Stonehenge, Glastonbury, Avebury, Windsor Free Fayre, The Stones, Pink Floyd, Hawkwind, The Velvet Underground, The Clash, Cat Stevens, Bob Dylan, Joan Baez, Neil Young – on and on, a who's who of musical subculture from the last twenty years), overlapping each other so that there's not an inch of uncovered space.

Hanging from the ceiling are a load of mobiles made from scrap metal and embellished with crystals, stained glass, feathers and all sorts of other materials. They catch and reflect the light and tinkle melodically when there's a breeze. I sense Jade's involvement, but it seems that nearly everyone's involved to some extent. Frank's got a little soldering workshop set up in the ice cream van and Jake, Freddie and Travis are also pretty handy at that sort of thing. They've sold a load of them at festivals and to local hippie shops in the last couple of years, along with handmade jewellery and clothes.

The only original seats that have been left unmoved are for the driver at the front and the bench seat at the back. That's reserved for overnight visitors, or for Freddie to crash on when he's too stoned to make it back to his bed.

The floor is covered in a hodgepodge of old rugs and carpets. Frank brought one of them back from a trip to Afghanistan in the late sixties apparently. Some of them are pretty threadbare and most of them are stained, or burnt from fag butts, but they give the bus a warm, illicit feel, transforming it into an opulent, Aladdin's Cave.

I've only been here for a couple of hours, but already I sense that there must be a ton of dope smoked in here. The air is filled with a haze of smoke that lingers lazily until occasionally someone opens the door or a window and the cloud slowly dissipates, sending smoke signals out into the world.

It's Tuesday afternoon and I've been working all morning

chopping up wood and preparing lunch. Everything is cleared away and I'm sat on the Magic Bus, just me, reading one of the books that Freddie gave me. It's a calm, untroubled moment of the sort I haven't known for a long time. The air is still, as if time has paused to yawn and stretch before ambling comfortably on again. I allow myself to relax into it, losing myself in the story of Wormold and his drawings of vacuum cleaners masquerading as nuclear missile silos.

I look up and see Jake and Frank coming towards me. Immediately, I sense something ominous in their bearing. There's a sudden chill in the air and my eyes dart between them, trying to work out what's happening.

'You don't mind if we join you, do you, Marko?' Jake asks.

'No...of course not.'

I find I'm scrambling myself into a more upright posture, almost as if I was still at school and the headmaster has walked into the room unexpectedly.

'So, how you getting on, Marko?' he continues.

'Yeah, good thanks. Reading one of Freddie's books,' I say, lifting it up for them to see.

'No, I meant how are you settling in here? You've been here pretty much a week now, haven't you?'

'Oh...I'm settling in great thanks. Everyone's been so nice to me, particularly when I was ill.'

'Good,' says Frank, taking over. 'You're a decent lad, Marko, and we reckon you fit in just fine too. Now, we pride ourselves on our hospitality, particularly when someone's in trouble like you seem to be, but I won't beat around the bush – if you want to stay here longer term, then you're gonna need to pay your way.'

He paused for a few seconds and my breath paused with him, just waiting for some terrible punchline. 'You know what day it is on Thursday, Marko?' he continues.

'Uh..no.'

'It's Giro Day. We all go into Yeovil once a fortnight to sign on and cash our Giros. Twenty-two pounds fifty a week is the miserable pittance that's doled out and everyone puts twenty quid a fortnight of that into a kitty. We use it to buy all the food and diesel and anything else we need to keep the camp and the vans going.

'We can just about get by on that, as long as we top it up a bit here and there, like selling the stuff we make at the Fayres in the summer, but that's all we've agreed really: that everyone coughs up a tenner a week. If we're feeling flush, we might buy a little stash of communal weed, but we try and keep something back, in case an engine blows up or something.'

They're both watching me now. I'm dumbstruck, staring at the floor, desperate to avoid eye contact while I try to get my mind straight. I can't possibly go and sign on. I might just as well walk into the police station and hand myself in. But I can't just sponge off these guys either. It wouldn't be fair: I can see that now. I've not really thought about where the money came from. I guess I've been deluding myself that if I'm nice to everyone and do as many jobs as I can, then somehow everything will be fine.

The image of my old Politics teacher jumps into my mind: 'There's no such thing as a free lunch,' he always used to say, laughing smugly at how clever he was being. My mind is spinning, trying to work out what to say and do. How can I explain to them why I can't go and sign on? Can I tell them the truth? Throw myself on their mercy? Maybe I could just do more than my share of the jobs around the camp and they will put in for me? No, that's not going to work. I'll still have to explain why I can't sign on and who would have enough spare to put in for me anyway?

This moment was always going to come. I've been lulling myself into a false sense of security. Maybe I should just say thanks for all the hospitality and leave. But where would I go? Now I've started to settle myself here, the thought of going back into those woods, all alone, as winter sets in, fills me with terror.

Frank and Jake are sitting there, quietly watching me stew. I can feel their eyes, burning holes in me, but I just can't think what to say or do. Eventually, I hear Jake speak:

'Look, Marko, we're not blind and we're not stupid. We've sussed out that you're in some sort of shit and that signing on could be a problem for you, but we need to get round this somehow, we can't subsidise you indefinitely.' He turns to Frank. 'Am I right?'

'Yeah…right.' There's another big silence. I'm staring at the ground and I can feel that my hands are starting to shake.

Frank's talking again now: 'Look, Marko, whatever has happened to you is burning you up. You can keep it to yourself if you want son, we're not ones to pry, but maybe you need to get it off your chest, hey? We're not exactly agents of the establishment here.'

Jake nods his head. 'As I said before, Marko, we're not easy to shock and we ain't about to dob you in to the local Plod, but you can't keep on tearing yourself apart like this and you've got to find a way to live in the real world.'

I've got my head in my hands now, my fingers pulling at the roots of my hair, my face screwed up tight, as if I'm about to implode. Then, abruptly, I look up and it spills out:

'I stabbed someone.'

There's another long silence. The loudest silence I've ever heard.

Then I continue, the words suddenly pouring out of me: 'There's a bunch of skinheads where I used to live. They always used to pick on me. Back in August they caught me on my own up in the park: three of them. They must have known I'd just got paid for the week.

'The main-man, Steen, a right fuckin' bastard, had me pinned to a tree. They were going to kick shit out of me, take my money. Somehow I managed to knock him off balance. I tried to run, but he came right at me again. For some reason my penknife was in my hand. I'd been carving a stick. It just happened. I felt it go in. Right in his gut. Pop. Blood everywhere. I saw his eyes for a split second before he fell, clutching his belly. Then I just ran…'

There was another long pause, until Frank finished off my sentence, almost under his breath: '…And you've been running ever since.'

'Yeah…'

I'm shaking now. It's the first time I've said these words out loud and it's like I'm right back there: Steen's blood on my hands; the shock in his eyes and the terror engulfing me as I turned and fled.

From the front of the bus, there's a noise. Freddie is walking on.

'Hey guys, got to be tea time, who wants a ...' He stops in his tracks, realising that something's going on and I see Frank out of the corner of my eye, waving him away.

There's silence again, which is broken by Jake:

'Fucking Nazi scum. Sounds like he had it coming...'

Frank is calmer: 'OK, Marko, you've got that off your chest. From what I'm hearing it sounds like self-defence, but I'm not sure I'd trust the Old Bill to see it the same way, particularly now you've fled the scene and not looked back. Anyways, as Jake said, we're not about to turn you in, that's for sure.'

'Too fucking right!' Jake's looking at me now, with a mix of awe and astonishment. 'You done well to stand up to them, that's what I say.'

I'm still staring at the ground, but I feel him clapping me on the shoulder.

'Right,' says Frank. 'Let's get that brew going and we'll work out a plan. How about that, Marko?'

I just about manage to nod my head and I hear Jake getting up to make the tea. I'm feeling lightheaded now, a weight gone from my shoulders, but it's being replaced by a new worry. Have I done the right thing telling them? I don't think I've ever opened up about anything like this before. I'm shivering suddenly, despite the heat coming from the Aga and I can't do anything but sit there, staring straight ahead.

Jake returns with tea for us all.

'Here you go, Marko, get that down you. It'll warm you up.'

Frank's been sitting there stroking his beard.

'OK, Marko. First thing's first. If you want to stay here with us, you're welcome. I suggest that we keep this between the three of us for the moment, but no one here is going to tip the police off. No one can blame you for what you did, but at least now we can understand what you were doing hiding out in the woods all that time and why you can't sign on. You probably haven't got any ID either, have you?'

I shake my head.

'Now, we've got to work out how you can stay and still make a contribution. We had a good summer, so there's still some cash in the kitty, but it can run down really quick if we're not careful.'

I sit up abruptly.

'I've just remembered: I've got some money! I'd just got paid and I took out some more, before I left town. So I've got enough for five or six weeks at least I reckon.'

'Well that's a start at least, but it'll soon run out. We've got some gigs coming up ain't we Jake?'

'Yeah, a week on Friday at the Prince of Wales on Ham Hill. That normally clears us a fiver each and a couple of beers, but it could be more. Word got round on the way to and from the demo, so I reckon we'll get a good turn out. There'll be more coming up, as we get closer to Christmas. Can you play that harp with us, Marko? You can hide in the shadows where no one will spot you!'

He's laughing now.

'Yeah – I'd love to!' I've suddenly got a smile on my face again, allowing myself to be drawn along by their plans.

'Good. And we do some busking once in a while as well. Leading up to Christmas is always good. We go into Yeovil, or Taunton, or over to Sherborne or Wells sometimes. That could make you a few quid. I'll ask Barry if he needs anything done. He's a bit of an old scrooge, but you never know.'

Jake adds: 'You could help us with some of our mobiles and our woodcarvings as well. If we can sell some of those to the shops in Sherborne and Yeovil before Christmas, we could have some dosh to divvy up.'

'Right, there we go,' says Frank. 'Sounds like we can keep you solvent up to the end of the year at least, hey, Marko?'

Chapter 13

Light in the darkness, darkness in the light

It's the last day of 1981. We've got a New Year's bash going on here tonight. We're expecting a hundred people to show up and we've been building up a great big bonfire all day. The last of the snow has finally gone and it looks like it will be dry enough to keep a fire going. Jake and Jade went out this morning and filled up with diesel for the generator, so we'll be able to crank up the music again.

I'm perched on one of the log benches in front of the Magic Bus, with a brew in my hands to keep me warm. Freddie, Rick and Pete are with me. We've been building the bonfire non-stop for the last few hours, dragging up branches from all around and piling them on until it's as tall as me, a great beacon that will burn for hours.

It's starting to get cold, now that we've stopped working, and the sun has all but sunk, so we've all got beanie huts pulled down over our ears and are clutching our mugs with both hands, letting the steam warm our faces. The cold isn't dampening our spirits though; this is positively tropical compared with what we've been through these past weeks.

'There'll be lots of chicks coming tonight, lads,' Rick's whispering, conspiratorially. He's got an eye for the women and, with his Jim Morrison looks and his easy confidence, he never seems to have to try too hard.

'Sabrina from the Nelson says she's coming. She's not working tonight and she's asked some of her mates too. Fill your boots hey – we might even get Freddie laid!'

We all laugh with him. Then he looks up and winks at me.

'Maybe even you too, Marko!'

I laugh along, feigning nonchalance. It's a sore point, but it's just a bit of banter and I'm looking forward to tonight too much to let it dampen my spirits. I keep my virginity a close secret, but I think they know: you can't hide anything here.

Jade's walking past and she shakes her head wearily: 'What a bunch of cocks,' she sneers. 'Nearly 1982 and you're still treating women like sex objects. Sexism is dead. Long live the Sexists!'

We all go quiet for a moment, hunched sheepishly over our mugs of tea, until Jade's out of sight. Then Rick and Pete burst with laughter, as if they've been holding their breath, and Freddie and I can't help but join in. We all know she's right, of course, but I think Rick just likes winding her up anyway.

I feel a glowing warmth that doesn't just come from the tea. It comes from the easy companionship and an unfamiliar sense of a future that I can look forward to. How has this happened? Just a few months ago I was riven by self-hatred and the certainty that I would never know these feelings again.

I can't believe that I've been here for two months already. I can't believe that 1981 is finally coming to a close. Everything's been turned upside down so many times this year that nothing feels real any more. Sat here in this warm bubble, it's as if all the shit that has happened has not happened at all, or has happened to someone else and I've just been watching from the sidelines. But, no matter how much I want to, I can't pretend it away. I've got the scars to prove it.

How everything has changed. Right up until that fateful day in August, I was drifting along like a ghost afraid of his own shadow. I thought I was just minding my own business, but I can see it now. It was like I was living a parallel life with everyone else: sharing the same spaces, but never interacting with them in any real way. It must have been inevitable that something like my run-in with Steen and his mates would happen. Maybe Steen was the only one who could really see me. Maybe he was always going to be the one who would rip me out of my somnolence.

I shiver even thinking about it. I hit rock bottom so many times, over the next couple of months, I don't know how I kept going. Each pit in which I was mired seemed ever deeper, darker and more desolate than the last, pressing me down into depths from which it felt impossible to return. Yet here I am. Sometimes I have to think hard to remember where that is exactly and how I got here, but here I am.

For the first time in years I'm starting to feel at home, amongst kindred spirits who seem to like me for who I am, even when I reveal the dirty secrets that I'd thought made me untouchable. Everyone seems to know about Steen and the stabbing now. It just seeped out, like everything does round here, until it was an open secret.

Along the way, the story seems to have taken on a life of its own: instead of a cowardly act of desperation, I knifed a racist thug, standing up to a gang of skinheads who were terrorising the town. It's even given me a little respect and credibility. Instead of someone who runs away from their fears, I've become someone who stands up for what they believe in; someone who isn't to be messed with.

With that burden lifting, I'm starting to grow again, like a tree that has been hacked back, almost to the ground, then unexpectedly finds new shoots emerging. I'm learning new things every day, just like I used to, regaining a sense that good things are possible.

I find myself thinking back to when I was a child, before my parents and brother died. I'd almost forgotten, but I used to have friends. Other kids used to like me and we'd play together without any thoughts of betrayal, or rejection, or being hurt. I used to be one of the cool kids. I used to make people laugh.

All of that was beaten out of me by one hammer blow after another: the death of my family, Uncle Harry buggering off, the dangerous isolation of children's homes, the false dawns of foster carers and the violent anarchy of secondary school. Everything after that was about building layers of armour, of perfecting the art of invisibility, but now here I am with a bunch of folk who specialise in disappearing too, each of them with their own reasons for not wanting to be part of the mainstream, each of them finding strength and inspiration from the friendship of the others.

I get up early most mornings and head out foraging with Frank. Freddie or Pete come along sometimes as well, but more often than not it's just the two of us, especially if the weather's bad, or they've had a heavy session the night before. When I was on my own up in the woods, it was a matter of necessity and I was always looking at things, wondering if I could eat them. I was ravenous all the time back then, which I'm not now, but the memory of it still seems real.

Now, my appetite for knowledge is back. I want to know about everything: to understand its essence, what it can be used for and how it fits into the world. I love spending time with Frank. He's a walking encyclopaedia and, particularly when it's just the two of us, he tells stories about everything, which I soak up like a shrivelled plant being watered.

Not just the botanical stuff, but stories about his past as well. He was a welder on the shipyards on the Clyde in the early sixties, which was where he started learning how to do things with his hands.

'That was hard graft, Marko,' he told me. 'The toughest apprenticeship you could ever have. They were hard bastards on those yards…but they knew how to live and they always stuck together.'

His travel stories are what I love the most and, as we walk, I ask questions to get him to open up. As soon as he'd saved up some money, he quit the yards and went down to London with a mate. They bought an old van, which they did up and then took off. They had almost nothing with them, other than a few sheets of LSD tabs and a bunch of other stuff they thought they could sell on the way.

They were trailblazers on the hippy trail. Even the names of the places set my imagination alight: Istanbul, Aleppo, Baghdad, Tehran, Tashkent, Samarkand, Herat, Kabul, Kandahar, Lahore, Amritsar, Dharamsala, Agra, Benares, Kathmandu. Typical Frank: he tells his stories deadpan, with ironic understatement mixed in with the odd mischievous, theatrical flourish. They are stories that take my breath away, leaving me with the impression that not only is every word true, but that he's only telling me the half of it. There were run-ins with the police and local criminals, detours with hitch-hikers, an audience with the Dalai Lama, drug smuggling, risky trade deals, car and motorbike crashes, breakdowns in the desert, serious illness and forever he seemed to live on the edge with no more than a few quid in his pocket.

I'm always left with the feeling that my troubles are minor, surmountable molehills that can easily be traversed. Maybe, in his round-about way, that's what he's trying to tell me, but he has a way of conveying it so that I feel empowered, rather than belittled, swept up by a sense that anything is possible and no challenge too difficult to overcome.

We walk for miles: up and around the woods where I'd been hiding out, in the fields around Norton and Odcombe, up towards Montacute and the remains of what used to be the medieval village of Whitcombe. He has his favourite places where he knows to find a specific mushroom, herb, or weed, right down to a particular tree, or a little dip in the ground. When he's squatted down examining something, he goes into a zone, as if nothing else exists in the world in that moment, other than him and what he's looking at. I stand silently beside him, watching and waiting for him to resurface.

The first time we went out, he had me digging up dandelions, roots and all. I thought it was a wind-up, like at Scouts when the older lads would send a new kid up to the hardware shop to buy some elbow grease, but when we got back we chopped up the roots and roasted them in the Aga, then pounded them until we got a powder and brewed up a thick black sludge that tasted just like coffee. Then we put the leaves and flowers into our salads, with all the other weeds we'd picked up, and I was gobsmacked by how good it tasted.

Right up to the end of November we were finding things. We came back with bagfuls of Bitter Cress, Chickweed, Hedge Mustard and Pennywort that were all good to go into our salads with the dandelions. We'll be walking along, him telling a story, and then he'll abruptly stop, stooping to expose a hidden weed.

'Cardamine Hirsuta, Marko…more commonly known as Hairy Bitter Cress. Here taste.'

He loves to use the Latin name for things. He asked me if I'd studied Latin or Greek and even though I told him I hadn't he still uses it. I thought he was showing off at first, as if he wanted to demonstrate his superiority to me, but now I think he does it out of a simple sense of wonderment and the enjoyment of connecting things into a learned order.

We nearly always come back with loads of mushrooms as well. I'm starting to get the eye for spotting some of them now, like the Boletus, with their dark, chestnut caps and lighter, foam like under-belly, or Wood Ears that we find clinging to the sides of fallen tree trunks. We slice them up and lay them out to dry when we get back and add them to soups and stuff. We've got jars full of them now. The guys back at the camp prefer it when we get back with mushrooms that we can use straight away, like Oysters, Field Mushrooms and Chanterelles. We chop them up and throw them in with the eggs to make omelettes.

Frank saves his greatest reverence for the Liberty Cap, which is the most common type of magic mushroom, or Psilocybin to give it Frank's favoured Greek name. They're tiny little things with thin stems and pale conical caps. So unassuming to look at, for all the fervour they rouse. I've stayed off them up to now, largely because Frank told me to be wary, but also because I've seen some of the others on them and they always seem to go really weird after they've had a brew. I might try a cup tonight, though, just to see this bad old year out.

Back at the camp, there's a great collection of books. They're stacked up, dozens of them, on the Magic Bus. It felt rather pitiful adding my solitary, dog-eared copy of *On the Road* to the library.

Jake laughed at me, but Frank came to my aid: 'Ignore him, Marko. If you've only got one book, then make sure it's a good'un. And that's a good'un.'

It sounded like just the kind of thing my Uncle Harry would say. They're quite alike; I reckon they'd get on really well. At Frank's recommendation, I started with Robert Pirsig's *Zen and The Art of Motorcycle Maintenance* ('that would be my one book' he'd said). It was so profound, that as soon as I'd finished, I went right back to the beginning and read it again.

I could see Frank all the way through it, the way he connects with everything he does. When he does something he seems to live and breathe it, focusing on it exclusively, until he understands its essence and can fulfil it perfectly. I resolved to do the same: to live in the moment, to build my understanding of the world and to put *Quality* into everything I do.

I resumed my reading, like I used to back above the shop, devouring the words as fast as I could suck them in, losing myself in them for hour after hour. They've got great stuff here, by writers I've never read before: Albert Camus, Jean-Paul Sartre, Franz Kafka, Milan Kundera, Gabriel Garcia Marquez, Ernest Hemingway, Hunter S Thompson, William Burroughs, Philip Roth, VS Naipul and many others.

I'd never thought about it before, but Jade's first question was why I was only reading male authors. I don't think it had even occurred to me, so under her direction I added Doris Lessing, Sylvia Plath, Virginia Woolf, Iris Murdoch and Simone de Beauvoir to my pile.

I was so ignorant of the female perspective on anything that these books were a revelation to me. I never said this to Jade, but in my mind it's like I've attached to women the status of forbidden fruit. I've mythologised them to such an extent that they've become terrifying and unknowable to me, touchable only in my fantasies, the gatekeepers to a secret garden to which I would never be admitted.

Now it's like I've been allowed into their inner world, to wander freely in the minds of these feminist thinkers and to see how different everything looks when you turn a hundred and eighty degrees, and light bulbs have been flashing in my mind with every word I've read.

This new perspective has made me think about how we react to something that's important, yet incomprehensible or challenging to our preconceptions. How easy it is to take fright and, when that happens, to become evasive, making elaborate detours to avoid facing up to a fearful unknown or, worse, to suppress or destroy, casting out poisonous seeds of ignorance to justify and propagate our childish terrors.

Well, it's becoming clearer to me now that there's a third way and that's to shine a light into the darkness, to illuminate, to get to the root of our fears and our troubled relationships with them, to embrace the truth and to open ourselves to it, no matter how difficult.

The biggest difference between being here and back in Farnham is about way more than just my choice of reading material. There, I was a phantom watching on from the sidelines of life. Sure, I was reading voraciously, taking in information from wherever I could get it, but only now can I see that I was growing like an isolated tree on a wind-beaten headland: stunted, lopsided, clinging precariously to the face of the earth.

I couldn't see it then. How could I? It took all of my strength just to survive, rooted as I was in such hostile soil. Only now am I starting to understand that nothing can flourish for long in isolation. I'm getting it because I can feel how different it is to be part of something. I can feel those old anxieties of ridicule and attack starting to melt away, like sherbet on my tongue.

Other than the odd put-down from Jake, people have responded really well when I've made contributions and gradually I've become more confident about expressing myself. There are still things that I hold back and I still feel those old knots in my stomach, when I even think about speaking up on something, but I can feel cogs moving, rearranging themselves, like I'm rebuilding myself from the inside out.

Here, everyone's got ideas and opinions and things that they know, or are good at. But nobody keeps these things to themselves. They share them and bounce them off each other all the time and new and unexpected things emerge from it, like when we're jamming and someone comes up with a new rhythm and someone else adds a riff, or a melody and before we know it, something new and unique, with its own energy and momentum, has emerged.

I've been learning new skills too: woodcarving, metal soldering, glass staining…and expanding my cooking skills beyond omelettes and opening cans. We always eat well here and the daily ritual of sharing food and drink together has been a revelation to me. I always used to eat alone, shovelling it down as fast as I could, taking no joy in it.

Here, it's the big thing that draws everyone together. We prepare the food together and we sit and eat it together, savouring it leisurely, and everything else, the conversation and the music and the laughter, all follows on from that.

Top of my learning wish list was the guitar. Uncle Harry showed me some chords, but he was never around long enough for me to properly get into it and, of course, I never had my own guitar. Rick's got two, an electric and an acoustic, and Frank's got an old four-string bass guitar. Rick doesn't like leaving either of his out of his sight, but he's usually fine with us playing them together.

He's a bit cocky, Rick, but he's been happy to show me some chords and to sit and strum with me and nothing much seems to faze him. It's more difficult than I expected, but I've got the basic chords now and getting to the point where I can join them together for a simple tune. My fingertips were really sore for a while, but the others just laughed and told me I had to play through it, until they hardened up and formed callouses, and they were pretty much right.

Most afternoons, or sometimes after dinner, we seem to have a little jamming session and practice a couple of numbers for the band. After our little jam on my first night, they brought *LA Woman* into the set list and that's going really well now. Those are the moments that I enjoy the most, even if there are times when Jake is starting to rile me.

It's Rick and Frank who really hold the band together, but Jake always has to be in charge: because he's the *front man*, even though he can't really play any instruments. He struts around at times like he's Mick fucking Jagger or something.

He's always putting his arm round me, ruffling my hair, making some smart-aleck remark. Worse than that: it feels like he sees right through me, reading my mind, just like he did on that first day when he caught me with my pants down, up by the stream.

One afternoon he saw me watching Jade, before I even knew I was doing it myself. He put an arm round me, squeezing my shoulder, and whispered in my ear: 'Out of your league, matey,' then carried on with what he was doing, as if nothing had been said.

I feel increasingly on edge when he's around. He has that knack of making me feel small and inadequate, no matter what I do. Maybe it's because I know he's with Jade every night and that drives me mad with envy. They're always talking about *free love*, but he still acts as if he possesses her. I don't know why she goes along with it.

It's true. I have been spending a lot of time with Jade. Maybe that's why he seems to have this need to undermine me at every opportunity. Every time he does it, I think I'm going to come up with some clever riposte, but he's too subtle and I'm too clumsy, so I end up just sitting there burning with mute humiliation.

Instead, I revel in the attention that Jade gives me. I don't know why she's so interested in me, but she seems to have taken me on as her project. Maybe it's because she senses the power she has over me, or the effect it has on Jake.

I wish it was lust that I stir up in her, but it's probably some fucked up maternal instinct. I suppose I'd take that, if it keeps me as the centre of her attentions. Whatever it is, she has a way of teasing me, like a cat playing with a mouse. I rise to the bait every time. I'm just too dumb, or spellbound, to do anything other than go along with it.

One afternoon, not long after I'd arrived, she found me on my own, reading on the Magic Bus. She breezed on and, coming up behind me, wrapped her arms around me, her chin resting on my head. I could feel her breasts pressing against the back of my neck and my cock spiked instantly to attention.

'Hey, Marko, what'ya reading?' she asked.

She knew what I was reading, because she'd given it to me the day before, but I held it up anyway: *The Mandarins* by Simone de Beauvoir. I tried vainly to act nonchalantly, as if this was just a friendly, platonic hug she was giving, which I'm sure it probably was, as far as she was concerned.

'Just started it,' I told her. 'I'm hooked already. The dynamic of the relationship between Henri and Paula is really interesting.'

I hoped that I was sounding sophisticated, so that we could keep the conversation, but especially the embrace, going.

'Ha – maybe we'll make a feminist of you yet, hey?' she replied, then pulled away to tell me why she'd really come: 'I promised I'd do your birth chart for you, Marko, but I've been thinking about it, and I thought I'd read your Tarot instead.' She looked at me, with that way she has, that sucks the breath out of me. 'Are you game?' she said, raising an eyebrow.

I spluttered my assent, as I usually do when she looks at me like that, and she came and sat to my right, close enough that our knees were touching and my head refilled with her scent. I shuffled in under the table, casually placing my hands across my lap to hide the bulge of my erection.

She had taken out a jet-black, silk cloth and was gently laying it across the table. Inside the cloth was a huge old deck of cards, almost as big as the span of my hand. They were worn, through much use, but wonderfully exotic, a rich blue, embossed with inter-woven golden symbols. She gave them to me to hold, as she spread the cloth. I watched, mesmerised by her fingers as they caressed the silk, teasing out the creases to reveal a grid of silver-marked boxes. They are lithe and sensuous, those fingers, as if there is an energy resonating from them. Sometimes, I imagine them grasping my cock, sliding up and down, as she holds me in her gaze.

Each finger has a ring. They are silver, inscribed with mystical symbols and Celtic engravings, or inlaid with jade, jet, and other stones and crystals. Her wrists are also encircled: by a tangle of bracelets and beads and tied fabrics. I noticed then that the tattoos on her wrists matched the symbols on the back of the deck of cards: on one wrist a five pointed star perching in an open chalice, on the other a lit torch, or maybe a wand, crossing with a double-sided sword.

'Close your eyes for a few seconds and feel the cards, Marko,' she said. 'Let your mind go. I want you to allow a question or a theme to come to you, something that's at the core of where your head is right now and where your life is going.'

We sat in silence for a while. All I could think of to start with was my stiffy and hoping that she hadn't noticed, or that if she had, the next thing I would feel would be her pulling open my jeans and releasing it.

Eventually, I managed to clear those thoughts and started to think about my position here in the group and whether these people were to be my salvation, or my ruination. In those first couple of weeks I'd been yo-yoing between wanting to share my innermost feelings and that breathless terror of exposure; between a desire to become properly accepted as one of them and an urgent need to backtrack and withdraw to a solitary place of safety. At times I'd felt like a rabbit that has poked its nose out of the warren to bask in the warmth of the sunshine and nibble on the lush, juicy grass, but is startled by something and scrambles back to the dark, enclosed confines of the burrow.

I could sense Jade joining me in my meditation. She'd lit some josticks and sat back next to me, as I was enveloped by their exotic pungency. It was quiet and still now on the bus, just the slow, rhythmic in and out of our breathing. As we sat like this, I could feel her presence, tantalisingly close, as if our energies were entwining. I imagined her eyelids hovering closed, as lightly as a butterfly's wings, her lips gently pressed together, the skin on her face smooth and serene.

In that intense silence, I could hear her, drawing in the air through her nostrils, the same air that I was breathing. I imagined her chest gently rising, then falling, as she let it out with an almost inaudible sigh. Outside our little capsule, I became aware of distant noises: voices, animals, somewhere a tractor, but they were in a different universe, separate from Jade and I, as we sat in our intimate communion.

Finally, I felt her hands close over mine.

'Right Marko, now spread the cards out over the table. Keep those thoughts in your mind and pick out ten cards that draw you.'

I must have frowned, because she elaborated: 'The cards represent a symbolic relationship between the internal and the external. It's important that those energies are balanced and aligned, otherwise we get out of synch with ourselves and our place in the universe.

'The first step is to listen to our true selves and to open up to the spiritual energy that is all around us. When something inside you needs to change, or is ripe for development, everything that you need is right around you. That's why people come into our lives, just when we need them. Everybody here has a message for you, Marko, and you have a message for them. It's just a question of listening and hearing and staying aware. So, don't over-think this. Close your conscious mind for a minute and just pick the cards that feel right. And if you do that, they will be the right cards for you.'

I nodded and smiled. Then, placing the deck on the table, I splayed them out in a smooth arc and picked out ten cards. Jade took them from me, giving me a little wink, and placed the first card face up on the central square of cloth.

'Ah, the Six of Swords…' Jade murmured, putting her hand to her mouth. A distant look had come into her eyes, as she looked down at the card she had just turned over, as if she had gone into some sort of trance.

It was a picture of a young man standing upright in a boat that crosses a bay with turbulent water and stormy clouds on one side, but calm blue sea and sky on the other. In front of him, six swords stood in a line. His long-golden hair and rich-purple cape flailed behind him in the wind, but his gaze was fixed purposefully into the distance, towards land, where clusters of houses perched on the hillside.

My eyes darted between Jade and the card. Suddenly, I wasn't sure how to take this. I'd thought it was just a bit of larking around and a chance to flirt with Jade for a while, but I could tell now that she was taking this seriously and I was starting to feel uneasy, overtaken by a queasy feeling in the pit of my stomach, just like that time up on the diving board in Farnham.

I watched her closely, waiting until it seemed that she was back in the room with me. 'What does it mean?' I asked.

'Well, what do you think? What do you see?'

'Well, the guy's standing tall, proud, even. There's a faraway look in his eyes. He seems troubled, but resolute, like he's carrying the weight of the world on his shoulders, but is getting used to it. Maybe he's had to make a big decision?'

'And that's kind of where you are, isn't it, Marko? It's interesting that you've picked it as your first card. This is the card that describes your current position: inner and outer.'

I laughed. 'Well, I'm not sure I *picked* it. It was face down, I didn't know I was picking this particular card.'

'Oh, Marko. You picked it all right. It's what I told you about the internal and the external. You've listened to what was in your heart and allowed yourself to connect with the energy that's in these cards. When you do that, you'll always pick the cards that are right, because the internal and the external are coming into harmony. You're trying to switch your conscious mind on again. Let it go. Trust yourself and trust the cards.'

I nodded and she continued: 'The figure in the boat is Orestes, who was the son of Agamemnon and Clytemnestra in Greek mythology. In the myth, Clytemnestra kills Agamemnon, in revenge for his sacrifice of their daughter to the Gods at the start of the Trojan Wars. The Gods tell Orestes that he must kill his mother in order to honour his father, but he knows that if he does this, The Furies will curse him.

'He is damned whichever way he turns. The suit of Swords is all about the story of Orestes and each card represents a different moment on his journey. In the six, after much soul-searching, he has finally made up his mind. Making that decision is allowing him to emerge into a moment of calm resolve. It is a card about understanding your position in the universe, about coming to terms with the need for action and of finding the inner strength to do what needs to be done, to respond to all of the challenges that life's journey brings.

'It's not too different from your situation, is it Marko? Things have happened to you and you've had to respond: to dilemmas that didn't seem to be of your making. That bloke attacked you and you reacted in the only way you could. It was the right decision, because it was the one that you made.

'You've travelled through turbulent water, but now here you are in a moment of calm and serenity. You haven't fully dealt with the bigger issues yet, but you have started the journey. Only time will tell how that will pan out, but you should make the most of these moments of calm, because they will give you the strength and the courage and the wisdom to deal with the next challenges that face you.'

We sat quietly for a moment, just looking at this figure, standing proudly in the bow of the boat. Her words made sense; I felt just like Orestes. I wanted to know how things ended up for him. Did he really kill his mother? And if he did, how did he deal with the wrath of The Furies that he unleashed, with the inner torture of self-blame and that brutal sense of being alone in the world that would surely follow? Maybe those things were all the same.

Jade must have guessed what I was thinking.

'It all works out well for Orestes, in the end, but that's not the point. Sometimes the problems we face can feel so huge we become convinced that they will engulf us. But remember: out there is infinity. Anything that happens has happened before and will happen again: an infinite number of times and with an infinite number of different outcomes.

'Your path has crossed with Orestes' in this moment

because he has a message for you, but they will diverge again. The important thing is to understand and accept where you are in this moment and to open up your mind and spirit to everything that is around you. If you do that, then you will find the path and the outcome that is right for you.

'The next card is even more important, because it signifies what is blocking you from moving forward.'

With that, she turned the next card, placing it face-up on top of the first. Death. It was the most grotesque card: depicting a monstrous figure, a bit like Darth Vader, clad head to toe in a black robe and helmet. Behind him, on the far side of a river, the sun was setting on a beautiful land of green fields, but on this side of the river the land was desolate and barren. At his feet, were three nymphs who seemed to be beseeching him, reaching upwards with gifts, but he just stood there, towering disdainfully above them, a merciless fire burning in his eyes. There is no way out from here, he seemed to be saying to them. Their destiny is the terrible underworld of Hades and that will be their eternal resting place.

Jade had spotted that my fists had clenched and my feet were tapping under the table, but she just laughed.

'Everyone freaks when they choose this card, but there's no reason to. Death is the *final* card of the Major Arcana, but, really, there is no *final* card, because the Major Arcana represents the cycle of life, so it just keeps on turning. Everything in the Universe is going through a perpetual cycle of birth, growth, death and rebirth or renewal.

'Think about the leaves on a tree. In spring the first buds

appear, fresh and filled with the potential of youth. By summer they've reached their zenith, verdantly green and bursting with flowers and seeds, until they move on to their swansong display of autumnal colour. Now, we're at the start of winter and those leaves have pretty much all decayed and fallen. That represents Death, but it isn't the end. The tree isn't going to die, but the leaves must fall to allow the cycle to begin all over again.

'What this card means is that one phase of your life must end, in order that a new one can begin. What's really interesting is where you've chosen it, as your blocking card. That suggests that you haven't been able to move on with the next phase of your life journey because you are still clinging to what you should have allowed to pass.

'Only you know what that is, Marko. Maybe you've not been able to accept the loss of your family. Maybe it's something else. Whatever it is, you must let it go, in order to move forward, just like a tree lets last year's leaves go, so that the fresh buds of Spring can emerge.'

We went quiet again. Jade was looking at me, with a concerned look in her eyes. I guess she was worried about the emotion this was stirring up and what was going on in my mind. I was thinking about that moment up in the woods during the storm, when I was at my lowest ebb, and I heard my family speaking to me, as if they were coaxing me through.

I remembered how, the next morning, I felt like I had turned a corner and was ready to move on without them, or at least to accept that they weren't physically with me any more. Then, within an hour, I had met Jake and Jade and Freddie. I had let one thing go and, right on cue, something else came to take its place. But there were still so many outdated things that I was holding on to, like an old hoarder surrounding himself with useless junk: old attitudes, old fears, old insecurities and my old self-preservation tools of insularity, mistrust and denial.

Maybe it was time to leave these behind as well. Maybe I had to leave *everything* about Farnham behind. There was nothing there for me anymore.

We sat in silence for a few minutes while I turned these thoughts over and then I started pouring them out, even surprising myself. Jade sat quietly and listened, nodding her head.

After a while, she looked me calmly in the eye and said: 'It sounds like it's all of those things, Marko. Those are all things that you developed, to deal with a world that doesn't exist for you anymore. If you keep hiding behind them, then you're never going to move forward and develop your potential. You're just going to stagnate and keep looping around the same old circle, until the energy becomes so negative that you'll implode.

A new situation needs new ways of being. I can't tell you what they are, Marko, that's not what the Tarot is about. It's about opening yourself up, becoming aware of yourself and what's around you. If you do that, then new ways will emerge.'

Jade carried on turning cards over. Every card had a story attached to it that she somehow interpreted to apply to me. I wrote them all down, which is how I'm remembering it now, but it's the themes that have really stuck with me.

263

She told me that I was leaving behind the terror of my flight from Farnham, emerging into a space where I could learn new skills and develop new ideas and ways of thinking. More than anything, this was an opportunity to build my self-esteem and the courage that I would need. That was the rub: my cards for the future also showed conflict, as though this was the calm before the storm.

I had pictures of Jason and his Argonauts desperately fighting for their lives in his quest to recover the Golden Fleece: his birthright that had been stolen from him. Jade told me that these were all metaphorical battles, just as likely within myself as with anyone else, and that any journey through life presented challenges and difficulties which had to be overcome. I heard her and didn't contradict her, but they felt ominous, like seeing dark storm clouds on the horizon.

The card that troubled me most was the Five of Pentacles. It showed a man, hidden by a ragged old cloak, creeping out of the back gate of a city in the dead of night into a dark, hostile landscape. There was a furtive, frightened look about him as he scurried away, eyes darting over his shoulder to make sure he was not being followed.

It took me straight back to Farnham, to those terrible hours and days after my crime, convinced that everybody and everything was watching me, convinced that, at best, I was destined for a life of running, lurking in shadows, waiting for that dreaded tap on my shoulder.

Jade had a response again. 'This card represents your hopes and fears Marko. It's interesting, because it shows Daedalus, who has been forced to escape from the city, leaving everything behind. It's not surprising that you've picked this card to represent your hopes and fears, because it is similar in some ways to what has already happened to you. You hope that it won't happen to you again, but you fear that it might. You've got to acknowledge those feelings, Marko, recognise them, learn from them, so that you can fulfil those hopes and dispel the fears.'

I was quite shaken after my reading. Half of me wanted to dismiss it, as superstitious claptrap, but I couldn't shake off how much some of the themes resonated with me, chiming with those dark feelings that lurked shamefully in places where I'd never admitted anyone. Finally, it ended with a nicer card to represent my 'Final Outcome'. The Knight of Cups showed a young Knight, jauntily riding a pure white horse through an orchard in full blossom, beside a babbling, blue stream from which fish were leaping.

Jade laughed when she saw it. 'Wow, right out of Chaucer! This is Perseus, the worshipper of love and beauty and self-appointed guardian of high ideals. What he really worships, of course, is the feminine, starting with the mother. It suggests to me that feminine love will be important to you, important in helping you to emerge from this cycle that you're in and to realise your potential. Maybe the love of a woman will help to complete you, to soothe some of your anxieties and to help you to see yourself and the world in a more rounded way. The future can be bright for you, Marko!'

We finished the reading on that note and Jade reached out to embrace me again. I accepted it gratefully, closing my eyes and holding her closely. Within a couple of seconds, my erection sprang back and this time I could do nothing to hide it.

She pulled away from me, laughing again: 'Whoa there, tiger! You're gonna have to wait a little bit longer for that woman to love – the cards don't work quite that quickly!'

And with a big grin, she tweaked my cheek with her thumb and forefinger and waltzed off the bus, leaving me to clear the cards away.

A couple of nights after that Tarot reading with Jade, I played in my first AlienNation gig. It was at the Prince of Wales, up at the top of Ham Hill, no more than a couple of miles from my old hideout in the woods. Word of the gig had spread at the CND Demo, so we were hoping for a good crowd and the whole camp came along, even Abi, somehow bundling into the van with all our gear.

The big pre-gig joke was all about how to keep me incognito. Everyone came up with more and more ludicrous suggestions, like dressing me up in drag, but in the end I settled for my beanie hat, pulled down as low as I could, and a pair of Rick's black sunglasses that were right out of the *Blues Brothers*.

As we set off, Rick piped up from the back in his best Brooklyn accent: 'We got six miles to go, we got a full tank of gas, half a pack of cigarettes, it's dark…and Marko's wearing sunglasses!'

Pete carried on the joke: 'Hey, we gonna play both types of music tonight, Country *and* Western!'

The pub was already filling up when we got there. Our

gig was under a semi-permanent tarpaulin that they'd rigged up over a big patio adjoining the pub, big enough to fit a couple of hundred people at least I reckoned. Everyone other than me had played here before, so they all seemed to know people. I just lurked around at the back of the stage with Freddie, making sure everything was set up properly, plugging things in, making sure the mikes were working.

I put myself in the back corner, where it was darkest, with Frank in front of me on bass guitar and Freddie, Pete and Travis to my left, with their bongo drums. Front-middle were two spaces with mikes, emboldened by the lighting, enigmatically waiting for Jake and Jade who were still in the crowd talking animatedly. To their left Rick stood, his electric guitar slung over his hips, strumming then tuning to get the sound just right and signalling to a guy at the back on a sound desk.

We'd practiced the opening song a lot in the few days before the gig. Freddie, Pete and Travis got it all going with a steady little drum beat, just to let the crowd know that things were about to kick off. It wasn't even half full, but more people were coming in steadily, as they heard the drums starting. Jake and Jade were still chatting with people in the crowd, but that was their signal to come back on the stage.

There were a few cheers, from the guys at the front, who knew what was coming, as they clambered on and took their positions. Freddie, Pete and Travis kept their slow, bongo beat going for a while, until everyone was in place, then abruptly stopped. This prompted more cheers, as

Jake, Jade and Pete turned to face us at the back. They gave a synchronised nod and then the guys leapt into a frantic, thrashing drum beat. Rick waited for a few seconds, before pouncing in with a jangly guitar riff that jolted the hairs on the back of my neck. Then Jake launched into the lyrics of *I Fought the Law* by The Clash, growling out the words, with a punky swagger, just like Joe Strummer. He was in his element, I could tell.

In front of me, I could hear Frank chugging out the base line. The chords didn't sound much on their own, but it was keeping the whole thing together, stopping it from turning into a ragged mess.

There wasn't much I could add on my harp, so I just followed Rick on the lead guitar to add some depth. We ended it with Jake and Jade repeating the chorus over and over and the crowd was already chanting along, fists raised. Rick hit a last riff to finish it and Jake punched the air and shouted out: 'No fucking Old Bill allowed... All right?' and the crowd roared their approval.

He paused for a second to milk the applause then shouted out: 'These next two are for the Wicked Witch of Grantham,' and we launched into a pair of Dylan covers: *Maggie's Farm* followed hot on its heels by a rocked-up version of *Subterranean Homesick Blues*.

That was a great song for me and each time Jake had finished a breathless series of quick-fire lines, he thrust a hand out in my direction and I burst into a series of licks I'd devised, giving the link into the next verse. Then I just kept the same licks going in the background as we built up the sound.

I was really into it now. My adrenaline was pumping and I'd completely forgotten I was meant to be keeping a low profile. I probably shouldn't have worried in the first place though: with my beanie hat, the shades that Rick had leant me and the harp covering my mouth most of the night, it would have been a miracle if anyone had recognised me.

I looked over at Freddie after the first couple of songs and he had the biggest grin on his face. There was a good crowd in now and the landlord had bought us all a pint, which we supped between songs. We must have played for over two hours, with a half-hour break in the middle. We played all sorts: rock, blues, punk, folk, a couple of classic old rock and rollers, mostly covers, but a few songs that Rick had written, or that we'd made up jamming together.

I didn't know all of the songs yet, but I just followed along as best I could, following Rick and Frank's lead, keeping my harp in the background, but occasionally throwing out something a bit more punchy, when it felt right. This was what I'd practiced for, all those nights up in the flat in Farnham, playing along to songs on the radio, making up parts for my harp.

The whole thing blew me away: the pulsing energy of the music, that I could feel as much as hear; the clamorous crowd, swaying and chanting along as we fed off each other's energy; the heady cocktail of beer, tobacco, dope and sweat mixing and swirling around us; the flashing lights, intensifying the darkness, but cutting through the pall of smoke that drifted from the crowd, loitering below the canopy roof. I'd never known a night quite like this before.

The week before, they'd asked me to pick a new song for the set, to showcase my harp. I chose *Hoochie Coochie Man*, because Uncle Harry and I had jammed that together, the last time I saw him. The opening riffs are just perfect for the harp.

We'd practiced it a good few times since and we got it pretty good, I reckon. Rick and Frank nailed it on their guitars and Jake strutted around the stage, growling out the lyrics, as if he *was* the *Hoochie Coochie Man*. Jade's backing vocals gave it a whole new dimension, softening, enriching, lifting it to new levels – her yin to Jake's yang, as she describes it. We opened up the second half with it. There must have been a couple of hundred in by then and the place was jumping.

It was crowded on the stage with eight of us up there. We even had nine of us for a couple of songs, when Abi joined Jade with some backing vocals.

I was almost within touching distance of Jade, who was wearing the tightest black, leather trousers and it was impossible to wrench my eyes from her, as she wiggled and gyrated right in front of me. She looked seriously sexy, those leather trousers and a spangly top clinging to her like a second skin, body arching and writhing with the beat, dreadlocks flailing, face flushed and those green eyes flashing like neon in the lights.

I was so hypnotized by her, as she teased out the backing vocals to *Get it On* by T-Rex, that it was all I could do to remember to keep playing. Later, as she huskily purred the lead vocals to *Denis, Denis* by Blondie, she had the crowd in the palm of her hand as they sang along: 'I'm in love with you,' and they all meant it, every single one of them. But not as much as I did.

Halfway through she turned her back to the audience and, back arched, arms raised above her head, as if in a moment of pure ecstasy, she looked right into my eyes and sang:

'I got a crush on you.'

It was a fleeting moment, but it felt like an eternity, an eternity where everything was beautiful and anything and everything was possible. But it slipped through my fingers, as, sensing Jake watching, she flipped back in his direction to sing:

'I'm so in love with you.'

I'm not sure if anyone else even noticed, but my heart-beat went through the roof and it took the rest of the song to get my rhythm back.

Towards the end I saw some guys at the back shouting and gesticulating aggressively in our direction. I couldn't hear what they were shouting, but I got the gist. I knew their type. There are ignorant wankers like Steen every-where it seems.

Within seconds there was a load of pushing and shoving. It calmed for a minute, then abruptly flared into a full-on punch-up. I could see the fists flying, as a hole opened on the dance floor. We carried on playing as if nothing was happening, but it only lasted a minute. The guys who started it must have realised that they were out-numbered and scarpered before they got beaten up. We'd been playing Iggy Pop's *Passenger* and as we brought it to a close, Jake looked up and sneered:

'See yer later Nazi boys!' and the crowd roared their approval.

Maybe I'd been lulled into a false sense of security, because I hadn't sussed out, until then, that there were people round here who really didn't like us, who viewed us as dirty, feckless, scroungers and wanted to blame us for anything and everything. That realisation probably didn't hit me until later, because, right in that moment, all I was worried about was that it was going to properly kick off. I pictured a load of police turning up and I suddenly remembered my need to keep a low profile. My eyes darted over my shoulder, to remind myself where the back exit was, in case I needed to get out of there in a hurry.

To my relief, there was no more trouble and we had the crowd all on our side for the rest of the gig. We finished it off with a rocking, riotous version of *Gloria*, which had them leaping around, chanting along and shouting out for more. I was dripping with sweat by the end, my nerves jangling, but I couldn't stop smiling.

'That was amazing,' I kept repeating.

They all laughed, but I could tell everyone else was just as pumped up as me, even Abi, who'd only been up on stage with us for a couple of songs. The landlord paid us fifty quid too, which was enough for a fiver each and an ounce of Red Leb.

We were missing Rick on the return journey. He'd taken off with a woman, who he'd been eyeballing all night, leaving Pete to take his guitar, but the rest of us were buzzing in the van on the way back.

'He's a Hoochie Coochie Man,' they all sang at me as we drove.

I answered them back with a riff on the harp and they finished it off: 'Everybody knows he's here!'

We had another gig a week after that, in a pub in Ilminster. The atmosphere wasn't as good as at The Prince of Wales, but I felt I was contributing better and I even strummed some guitar on Rick's acoustic on a couple of songs, which built out our sound a bit.

The next day, the last Saturday in November, we all went over to Sherborne to do some busking and try to sell some of our jewellery, mobiles and clothes to the shops there. Abi's starting to look quite pregnant now and we thought that might help, so we sent her and Travis round the shops. The strategy clearly worked, because when they eventually came back, they'd pretty much sold the lot.

The rest of us stayed at the Market Square, me with my beanie hat and Rick's sunglasses again, cooking up quite a sound with three bongos, Rick and Frank with their guitars and my harp. We had a big circle two deep for a while and the coins were raining into the guitar cases. And for those who were shy, Jade went round between songs chatting up the punters and getting them to fill her tambourine.

We went to the pub afterwards for a celebratory beer. We thought we'd done pretty well, with the weight of the coins and even a few pound notes, and we weren't wrong: we'd made nearly a tenner each, plus enough to fill the van up with petrol, some more diesel for the generator and a load of fruit and veg from one of the farms on the way back.

I thought my money worries were over. I still had nearly fifty quid left, even after making two contributions to the kitty, and we had at least two more gigs lined up before Christmas and three more Saturdays to busk and sell more stuff.

I counted without the weather. The snow arrived on the first day of December and it kept falling for the best part of three days, until it reached my knees. When it wasn't snowing, the skies cleared and the ice seized control, squeezing everything in its grip: snow, skin and spirit alike. I've never known a winter like it. I reckon I'd have died if I'd tried to stay on my own up in the woods.

The thought sends shivers through me every time it comes into my mind. Even here it's been almost too much to bear, but at least we've all been in it together. We ran out of diesel pretty quick, so we had no lights or showers for a week, but we had loads of candles and wood stored up after the storm on the day I arrived, so we've managed to keep the Aga going. There were some nights where it felt too cold to even think about trudging the few yards through the snow to my ambulance and Freddie and I have stayed in the Magic Bus all night, keeping the Aga going, drinking tea, talking and dozing.

That cycle repeated itself for over three weeks and there was no chance of even getting the van out of the field. Both of the gigs we'd booked were cancelled and we couldn't get out busking. I went from being relaxed that my money was going to keep stretching out, to worrying about it constantly. What would I do if I couldn't pay my way here? Every time I've looked out at the snow and the ice, I've pictured myself up in the woods, on my own again, freezing and starving to death.

It's the coldest winter for fifty years, or so Old Barry kept telling us every time we saw him. The only good thing about the snow was that a couple of his guys couldn't get to the farm and he's had some urgent jobs that he couldn't do on his own, so I've stepped in to help him out for a few mornings.

He's got a load of sheep that he needed to get hay out to and we were wading knee deep in snow, lumping great bales of hay across the fields. That was the toughest work I've ever done: I was knackered after a few hours and my hands red raw from the hay and the snow. He wasn't exactly generous either: five quid for working a whole morning, plus a jug of milk and a few eggs thrown in. I needed the money though; without it I'd have run out by the end of the year.

Even right now, with tonight's party to look forward to, I can't stop worrying. As it stands, I've only got just enough to make my contribution to the kitty next Thursday. And then I'll be down to nothing.

The first people will be arriving for our party soon. As I sit by the unlit fire finishing my tea, my thoughts turn to how different everything and everyone here feels from that moment I walked in on at that first morning in November. Then, I was like the new kid at school: looking at everything for the first time, trying to build and create the right first impressions.

I remember being overawed by Jake in those first

moments and days. He seemed to know what I was thinking and feeling before I knew myself and I was powerless to resist. I didn't realise this at the time, of course, but now I can see that he does this all the time, with pretty much everyone other than Frank. Frank's too switched on to take any of his bullshit.

I wonder how Jade deals with it. Sometimes I can't figure out whether it was Jake's spell or Jade's that got me here. She only has to look at me for all the weight to drain from my body and when she speaks I'm transfixed, I just can't seem to help myself.

I can see that Freddie's a bit overawed by Jake and Jade too, but he doesn't seem to worry about it like I do. We've become good friends over these past few weeks, Freddie and I. When the three of them found me up in the woods I was so dazzled by Jake and Jade that I barely noticed him, but as I've got to know him he's revealed hidden depths and I like him all the more for it.

He's told me all about his relationship with his dad, who corralled him into studying Physics, expecting him to forge a career in engineering and about his older brother who couldn't do any wrong and was always used as an example to put him down. He told me about his time at university in Birmingham, including the crisis in his second year when he couldn't cope with the stress of the work and his parent's expectations and came close to a nervous breakdown and dropping out.

At his lowest point, he sat down with one of his professors who told him that he needed to live a more 'authentic' life, which was all about being true to himself and doing things for himself, rather than to meet other people's expectations. Once he'd grasped that, he started to turn things around and that summer, rather than going home to his parents, he travelled around the summer fayres, where he met Jake and Jade and Frank and all the others. He still struggles with too much pressure, but being here takes most of that away from him and allows him to just be who he wants to be.

I've told him all about my family as well and what happened after they died, all the way up to the stabbing and getting here. He just listened and nodded, never trying to tell me what I should, or shouldn't, do. It felt so good to have someone listening and understanding, but not judging.

Freddie's been teaching me how to play the bongo drums and I've been showing him how to play the harp. They're similar in some ways, in that there are a few basic techniques and then it's all about improvising and letting the melody, or the rhythm, take you where it will.

Freddie struggles a bit with the harp. He manages to get some good sounds, but he doesn't seem to have the puff to really keep it going and ends up coughing and spluttering.

'You need to cut down on the old wacky 'baccy!' I tell him, but he just laughs and skins up another joint. I always take one small draw to his three – I don't want to end up like him that's for sure.

I get on a little better with the bongos. I hadn't appreciated the different tones you could get from them: by using different parts of the skin; by alternating between the lighter tone of the small drum and the richer, deeper tone on the larger; by bouncing my fingers off the skin to give a cleaner, less muffled, sound or by using my spare hand to close off the echo.

Sometimes I borrow someone else's, so that we can play together and before long I was able to follow him on simple rhythms. That's great, really absorbing and really powerful, except Freddie always throws in a curve ball by suddenly lifting the tempo, or making the rhythm more complex. Then I lose the plot and we both crease up laughing.

I was worried when Freddie decided to go back home to his parents in St. Albans for Christmas, worried that he would end up staying there and that I'd never see him again, but he turned up again a couple of days ago, with a big grin on his face and a new calm about him, as if he'd laid a few ghosts to rest. I could have hugged him, I was so pleased to see him.

Over dinner that evening I asked him how he'd got on without the *wacky-baccy* for a week. It was fine he said, but then he told us about his first afternoon back home and he had everyone in stitches with his deadpan delivery. He'd taken a few hash cakes back with him, which his mum had found. She had no idea what they were, so, on his first afternoon back, he'd sat down for afternoon tea with his mum and dad and brother and they'd scoffed the lot.

'I've never seen my mum and dad laugh so much,' he told everyone. 'Mum had something burning in the oven and Dad was doing impressions of Corporal Jones from Dad's Army, strutting round the kitchen shouting "Don't

Panic. Don't Panic." I don't think the four of us have ever laughed so much, together at least. My brother looked at me and asked: "What *did* you put in those cakes Frederick?" I thought for a minute it was all going to go bad, but he's so fucking straight that I don't think he even suspected. "Eggs, flour, sultanas...and a pinch of spice" I told him and we all just laughed some more.'

It's been the in-joke in the camp ever since. Somehow we've turned his brother into Monte Python's Pontius Pilot, so that every time Freddie makes a cup of tea, we all shout out: 'What *did* you put in this tea, Fwederwick?' That one's going to run and run I reckon.

Jade went off for Christmas, as well, back to London to see her parents and her younger sister. Her family sound weird. It turns out that her dad's an MP and her mum's an artist. She barely saw her dad when she was growing up and her mum was usually unreachable, hidden away in her studio, or in some drug-infused dream. So, she and her little sister just seemed to do what they pleased, going off to parties, bringing boyfriends home, drinking and taking drugs, disappearing off to festivals for days at a time. Her parents just let her get on with it, believing that she could talk to them about anything and that she knew where to find them if she needed them.

She's cynical about her dad: 'The only thing he cares about is the fucking Party,' she told me. 'As long as I don't disgrace him and the Party, he doesn't care what I do.'

There's always an undercurrent with her though, as if whenever she says something, she really means something else. The nastier the things she says about her dad, the more I get the impression that she actually idolises him. It feels like the anger is really directed at herself: for being unworthy of his attentions, or incapable of getting them. It always surprises me when I start sensing that – it just never occurred to me that she could suffer from insecurity, or low self-esteem. Maybe everyone has a self-hatred compartment that they keep hidden away from the rest of the world, no matter how happy and confident and composed they appear on the surface.

Rick and Pete both headed away too. It looked for a while as though nobody would be going anywhere for Christmas, but the snow finally started to thaw in the nick of time. On Christmas Eve we were all out first thing clearing snow and finally we managed to get the van out and onto the lane. That was lucky, because it was also Giro Day and everyone bar me had to go into Yeovil to sign on. As soon as they'd cashed their cheques, Jade, Freddie, Rick and Pete went straight to the station and scattered off in their different directions.

It was a quiet, strange Christmas with just Jake, Frank, Abi, Travis and me. We roasted up a pheasant, which old Barry had given us, but none of us are Christians and Jake and Frank, in particular, were really cynical about Christmas.

'It's a capitalist con trick to exploit and distract the people,' said Jake.

I couldn't disagree; I hate those trite Christmas pop songs just as much as they do, but there was a small, hollow part of me, that remembered those Christmases we used to have as a family, when everything felt cosy and sparkling and exciting. To them, Christmas is just a capitalist conspiracy, to me it's always felt more like a personal conspiracy, an overblown fantasia rolled out every year just to rub in that I couldn't be a part of it.

We were a bunch of Scrooges, the five of us, huddled up around the Aga, smoking joints and drinking some foul tasting wines that Frank had concocted, one from elderberries, the other from apples and pears.

Rather than Christmas, our big celebration was the Winter Solstice on the twenty-first, when everyone was still around. There had been talk about heading up to Stonehenge for the sunset and sunrise, but there was no chance of getting there with all the snow, so we made our own festivities instead.

I'd never really paid much attention to the solstices before, but Jade put me straight on that. She told me how the winter solstice is the start of the solar year: a celebration of light and the rebirth of the sun that has been marked by pagans for thousands of years.

'Christmas was just a Roman invention to replace their ancient pagan Solstice celebrations,' she told me. 'Isn't it exquisitely ironic that a religious festival to mark the birth of Christ is gradually transitioning back to its roots as a mid-Winter feast?'

It's typical Jade to give a softer, more spiritual spin to Jake's aggressive cynicism.

On solstice night everyone stayed up all night, sat on the

281

Magic Bus from sunset to sunrise. We'd spent a couple of days preparing, making special foods and decorating the bus. The snow hampered us a bit, but we gathered up fir branches, holly and mistletoe and draped them all around. As the sun started to descend, we lit candles and hung some new mobiles that we'd made: pentangles of stained glass in deep reds and greens and purples.

The effect was intoxicating: the flickering light of the candles, absorbed, filtered and reflected through the stained glass; the scents of spiced foods, sap, candle oils, incense and hash and the shared spirit of nine outsiders in the world, waiting together for light to emerge from darkness. I bought into it, with a growing sense that I too could emerge from my own place of darkness.

We couldn't play records, because there was no diesel left for the generator, but it didn't seem to matter. We had plenty of food and drink and Rick or Frank strummed their guitars, or I played some harp. When the music stopped, we took it in turns to tell stories about ourselves.

I told them about some of the places I'd slept as I walked here. They liked the sound of the place in the wood by the side of the lake where I'd sat, a little fire flickering, watching the sun go down over the water and they all laughed when I told them about being woken one morning by the cows licking the dew off my sleeping bag.

As always Frank's stories were the best. Everyone listened as he talked about his journeys to and from India, leading on to anecdotes about how different religious communities celebrated their religious festivities.

I was hooked as he told us about arriving in the city of

Yazd in eastern Iran, or Persia as he prefers to call it, on the day of the spring equinox of 1967. He found himself invited into celebrations of New Year for the Zoroastrian religion and being plied with food and drink as an honoured guest.

Zoroastrianism is the oldest monotheistic religion in the world, but has almost disappeared now, retreating to parts of Iran, India and a few other countries. I pictured Frank there in that thriving community, as far from his roots as he'd ever been, probably quietly entrancing them with his stories, just as he does with us.

In the centre of the table was Frank's prized Turkish hookah pipe, or the hubbly bubbly as everyone else called it. It was another souvenir from those travels he was describing, but one that he only brought out on special occasions. Its burnished copper was smooth and cool to the touch, curving exotically like a minaret, absorbing and reflecting the light all around. The base had been filled with water and the little bowl at its crown filled with weed.

Freddie started to tell me about the mechanics of how the smoke was filtered through the water, thereby cooling, purifying and strengthening it, but I was more interested in how beautiful it was. Everyone took turns to have a draw on it, becoming an almost serene ritual. I took my turn, drawing deeply as I was instructed. Nothing happened for a moment and then suddenly my lungs were filled with the smoke and I was coughing and choking. That gave everyone a good laugh, of course, but my head was spinning too much to care.

Later that night when we lit it again, Jade took her turn

before me. She looked over in my direction and winked at me:

'Ready for a blowback, Marko?'

I must have looked startled because she said: 'Relax, open your mouth, then just breathe in as I breathe out...'

Then she inhaled deeply from the pipe, knelt with her legs either side of mine and, taking my cheeks in each hand, exhaled the smoke slowly into my mouth. I gripped the side of the chair, closed my eyes, and drew her breath down into my lungs. From there it mushroomed, swelling my head, then my eyes, my ears, my nose, my lips, my arms and fingers and my legs right down to my toes, as if my toenails were going to pop like champagne corks.

It was like I was drawing Jade herself inside me, as if our boundaries had blurred, and, for that single moment, she had possessed me. I imagined her spirit surging around my body, reaching into every little corner and crevice. I felt light enough to take off like a balloon into the sky, yet so heavy that I was anchored to the chair.

At some point she finished exhaling, squeezing my face and giving my lower lip a little nip with her teeth. I opened my eyes and, looking deep into hers, breathed slowly out, the clouds of smoke drifting between us, as though we were flying through the sky together, on a magic carpet through the Arabian Nights.

She smiled and then, from behind us, there were loud cheers and claps. 'He was a blowback virgin,' shouted Freddie, and everyone laughed with him.

For those seconds I'd forgotten that there was anyone there other than Jade and I. Then, jolted back to reality, I became aware that my head was spinning and my cock was so hard it was threatening to split my jeans. Jade grinned and reached out to grab a cushion, which she threw in my lap, before getting up and sashaying back to her seat, as if nothing much had happened.

It's getting on for nine o'clock, less than three hours before midnight, and there's a whole load of people here. I recognise a few faces from the gig up at the Prince of Wales, but I don't really know any of them. Our lot are scattered around: Jake and Jade standing with a big group on the edge of the fire, keeping them entertained with their usual double act; Rick strumming on his guitar with Pete and a small group of girls who are watching him intently; Frank stood in earnest conversation with Old Barry and a couple of other guys and Abi and Travis sat on the Magic Bus with another group of people.

Freddie and I are happy enough to perch to one side of the fire, on the edge of things. We took some mushrooms a while ago, brewing them up in a tea then eating the softened mushrooms at the bottom of the cup. It tasted a little bitter, but not too bad. Frank was dead against the idea, calling it 'ill-advised', when there were so many people I didn't know around and so much other stimulation. I thought about it for a while, but Freddie was doing it so I just thought *fuck it*, let's bring this bad old year to a close in style.

Anyway, Frank needn't have worried; it's been nearly an hour since we took them and bugger all has happened. It's probably because, to keep Frank happy, I only took half of

Freddie's dose. Also, I've not really had anything else, just a couple of glasses of cider earlier and a couple of puffs of spliff that came round.

We're not talking much, Freddie and I, we don't need to; we're just taking everything in, letting it wash over us. It's hot by the fire and I'm starting to sweat; my hands are clammy, but my back is like a block of ice. We should be on a spit, rotating like a doner kebab, to make sure we're cooked evenly all over.

I'm staring in at the flames, at the rich reds and yellows and oranges, as they dance to some rhythm I can't hear. I become aware that Freddie is peering at me strangely. I know that look. It's normally when he's spotted something really funny that no one else has cottoned on to.

There was one time, when we were all stoned and listening to music and he started mooing like a cow. We all wondered what the hell he was doing, but then, one by one, we all started hearing a horn under the baseline of the song that did sound just like a cow. Within a minute, we were all mooing. That was hysterical, one of those moments that keep coming back to me as I mull over the year that's passed. Now, I look quizzically at him, trying figure out what's going on in his mind.

Finally, I look over at him and ask: 'What *have* you put in that tea Fwederwick?'

That's enough to burst him and he's folded over giggling like a maniac. I'm a bit annoyed that his mushrooms seem to be working when mine aren't, but his laugh is infectious and it hooks me in, just like it always does. A few people are looking over in our direction, wondering what's going on, and that's enough to make it even funnier. It's our own little private joke, passed on telepathically.

Freddie leans over and splutters in my ear: 'Don't laugh – Frank wouldn't approve!'

That gets us going even more.

'Stop laughing, it's not funny,' Freddie keeps repeating and each time, it's even funnier than before, until I'm almost wetting myself.

We sit like this for, I don't know how long, giggling to each other and then to ourselves. Eventually I get up to take a pee. I wander over to the hedge on the other side of the Magic Bus, still chuckling under my breath. Freddie's so funny. All those expressions on everyone's faces are hilarious and they don't even know it.

A new thought is dawning on me: the more serious something seems, the funnier it actually is. In fact, at the root of everything has to be its polar opposite, because only from that can you appreciate something's true essence: light can't exist without darkness; safety can't be appreciated without danger and joy can only spring from knowing misery.

I stumble past everyone ruminating on these thoughts. It's dark behind the bus, away from the fire. I start to pee out into the darkness of the hedge. I stare intently down and, as I do, I notice that my urine has become a fluorescent yellow, arcing out into the darkness like a laser. I'm transfixed. It must be something I ate earlier. I start to wave my cock around, carving golden circles of light into the darkness. I pee and I pee and inspiration pours out of me; I could surely gild a masterpiece onto this great dark canvas.

I stand there for ages, until long after I've run dry, admiring the patterns I've created. I watch, awestruck, as the light drifts upwards, morphing into the most beautiful patterns, taking on a life of their own. After a while they start to harmonise with the stars in the sky, joining constellations together in new and wonderful ways.

It's like my harp joining a melody, adding to it and then becoming part of the whole sound; or a snowflake, unique in itself, drifting out of the sky, to join the myriad others on the frozen ground below. That's what life is all about, being unique and then becoming part of a whole, adding to it, improving it, in subtle but meaningful ways. I've got to tell Freddie about this; he'll be amazed too.

On the way back, I see Frank.

'Are you doing alright, Marko?' he asks.

'Yeah, I'm good.' I'm about to tell him about what I've just created, but instead a new thought hits me and I find myself saying: 'There's light in the darkness and there's darkness in the light. I've only just noticed that.'

He looks me in the eye, nodding his head slowly, then grasps my shoulder with one hand: 'Well said, Marko, there is indeed. Hang on to that thought. It's a good place to start.'

I walk back to re-join Freddie by the fire. My feet seem to have become really light now, as if I could float over the ground. Freddie's sat in the same place and is gazing deeply into the flames. I sit down and follow his gaze. *There's light in the darkness and there's darkness in the light*. How hadn't I noticed it before?

I wonder if Freddie's seen it as well. I want to ask him,

but instead I find myself staring deeper into the flames. It's amazing how much beauty there is in there. And there *is* darkness in the light. The brilliance of the light somehow intensifies the darkness. At the root of each flame is a darkness as deep as a Black Hole. I feel myself holding onto my seat. The darkness is so deep it could suck me in.

I feel a hand on my shoulder. I look up and it's Freddie. Something about him has changed. He's shining, that's it: his skin, the whites of his eyes, even his teeth, amplified by the darkness of his beard. But it's more than that, his whole being is shining, there's an aura of light surrounding him, I can feel it pouring out of him.

'It's so beautiful, isn't it?' he says.

I can't stop myself from grinning. It *is* beautiful. I'm so pleased that Freddie can see it and feel it too. I put my arm around him and we just sit there, the two of us, staring into the fire, sharing the radiance.

Pink Floyd's *Dark Side of the Moon* is playing. The vocals are rumbling from deep out of the embers, softly at first, rising in intensity, then calming to a mournful lament, before rising again in a new cycle. The guitars have become the flames, leaping upwards, each taking on a life of their own, radiating their own energy, dancing to their own tunes, yet somehow adding to the mosaic.

The rhythm crackles, spitting sparks high out into the night sky and I watch them flitting upwards, defying gravity, until they disappear, replaced by a new beat that seems to come from nowhere. Each time I move my eyes I see new patterns in the flames and in the music. A chorus of voices and a new intensity in the fire surges out. I want to stand up and stretch my arms out to let the light wash over me, but I don't need to, because its essence is flowing through me and I'm captivated by it.

Sitting here, I can feel every single instrument and know just which flame it's coming from. I've tuned into the piano and each key is a small flame that flickers gently at the back of the fire. A saxophone billows from one side – there it is, a serpentine flame rearing, lifting the sound in its coils, as if those sassy notes are the only things in existence. Then I'm drawn to some eerie synth sounds, which jerk erratically from unexpected places, discordant, but challenging. They fade and I'm taken again by the lead guitar that I've now seen emanates from the largest log on the fire. It glows constantly with a rich and steady flame, the epicentre from which everything else gets its energy.

I can feel myself unravelling the music, dissecting each flame, burrowing deeper and deeper, until I can feel its core. The beat of the music has become my heartbeat; the flicker of the flames has become the blood pulsing through my veins. We've become a Holy Trinity: the fire, the music and me, feeding from each other, understanding each other, blurring together until we can't tell where one starts and the other ends.

I become aware that Freddie's not next to me any more. The music has quietened and I notice a new, blue light that I hadn't seen before shimmering in the flames. I look up and I see Frank and Jake walking past me towards the road. Frank is growing in stature, towering above me as he passes. The light from the fire catches his face and, with a sense of wonderment I see that he's not Frank at all, he's Obi-Wan Kenobi.

There's a stern look on his face, a burning focus in his eyes, as he strides past. Everyone is watching them and, for the first time, I become aware that all of the guests at the party are actually aliens. I daren't look too closely, but from the corners of my eyes I can see that they are all different shapes and sizes and colours, some with more than one head, some with only one eye.

With a wave of relief, I note that none of them are paying me any attention. They are all looking towards the road and, slowly, I swivel on my log to see where Frank and Jake are going. Now I see it, two sets of flashing blue lights over the top of the hedge. At first glance they look like police cars, but I quickly see through the disguise: they are space ships, hovering in the flickering blue haze. At the gate to our field are two policemen. These aren't ordinary policemen though, they're dressed like Darth Vader and they've both got long black light sabres at their hips.

They're here for me. I know it in an instant. Word must have got around. Just inside the gate they meet Frank and Jake, who stop abruptly, holding their hands upwards in a calming motion.

They don't seem to have spotted me yet, but they will do, I've got no time to lose. I glance back over my shoulder at the other creatures. There must be a spy in their midst, but they're all still looking away from me towards the road. Freddie's nowhere to be seen, but I can't wait. I shuffle slowly along the bench, then softly slide away to the other side of the fire and round the back of the Magic Bus.

It's dark here, but I know the way. I crouch down and tiptoe along the hedgerow. It's towering above me now, its branches rearing like the barrel of a wave. I've got to be careful; I can feel eyes and tentacles in the branches. I get to the gap in the hedge, which has become a great archway. That's lucky: they haven't posted any guards. I creep through unnoticed. It leads through to Old Barry's farm. Everything's quiet here, other than some noises from the cowsheds. I cross the yard and climb the gate that leads out into Barry's fields. I'm being drawn somewhere, I just don't know where. I can feel a force welling inside me and I know that I need to trust it.

The open fields swell upwards towards the darkness of the woods. High above the canopy the moon is the slimmest of crescents. That's good, I will easily see any spaceships and I can hide in the shadows. They've chosen the wrong night to come looking for me.

I cross to the far corner of the field. There, on the edge of the woods, is my favourite tree, a towering beech with branches that reach out protectively. It's Treebeard, I realise. How hadn't I noticed that before? We don't need to speak; his eyes welcome me and I just know that he's on my side, that he won't give me away.

I press myself to his trunk, reassured by the cool smoothness and his silent strength. I can feel my heartbeat, amplified as it presses against him, pumping blood around my body. It's pumping fast, but it slows now as I tune into him.

In this moment I can sense him as he really is, his roots sinewing deep into the soil, anchoring him to this land, connecting with it in a way that humans never can. How proud and strong his trunk is, his branches stretching up into the heavens, bare at the moment, but ready for that moment when his buds will burst forth once again. He does nothing quickly, but his power is immense. All that time on my own up in these woodlands. I could feel the energy, but I didn't know what it was. Now I get it, finally. I'll have to tell Frank. I'm not sure how I'll describe it to him, but he'll get it.

I let my thoughts go where they will and sit calmly at the base of Treebeard's trunk. From here, I'm looking back towards the camp and my eyes have adjusted so that I will see anyone approaching. They will probably come with powerful searchlights, but I can't discount a surprise attack.

I can still hear the music drifting back up to me and make out the glow of the fire. As I watch, the air above the flames becomes more and more distorted, bubbling into ghost-like shapes. Yes, that's exactly what they are, spirits rearing up over the hedgerow, twisting their heads in all directions, searching me out. I laugh, because I know that they won't see me here. I'm protected here: cloaked in Tree-beard's aura. The flashing lights from the police ships have stopped. That means they will be coming soon – they're just working out their plan.

I don't know how long I've sat here for. I've been staring up at the sky and, for a while, I forgot that they're looking for me. The stars are so vivid tonight, as if they've inched closer to me, amplifying their brightness and their clarity. There are patterns in them that I've never seen before and suddenly I know that the answer to everything is right there in front of me: everything that's existed, or ever will exist, the past, the future and the present.

Except it's not in front of me, it's all around me, inside me, inside everyone and everything. I just haven't been looking in the right places. That's what Jade was telling me when she read my Tarot; I can see that now. The thought from earlier comes back to me: *there's light in the darkness and there's darkness in the light*. Every one of those stars is a raging ball of light that penetrates the darkness even from this range.

As I look, a spaceship races across the sky like a shooting star. I become aware that the ground is moving around me. My heart leaps, but nothing seems to have changed: the music is still playing down below, an owl is hooting in the trees behind me, but no signs of anyone hunting me.

It's me, I realise. I'm shaking. As I've sat here, looking at the stars, it's like I've levitated, leaving my body behind. But now I'm back and the cold has gripped me. Looking down I can see ice crystals growing on the grass. I want to stay here, but it's just so cold.

I've got to find somewhere warm, but I can't go back to the camp. They'll be waiting there for me, thinking I'll just walk back into their trap. Just how stupid do they think I am? Down below, I hear the sound of sheep and cows coming from Old Barry's barns. Of course, they're calling to me. I jump up and, thanking Treebeard for his protection, skirt quietly down the side of the field. I know Old Barry's outbuildings well now and I reckon the sheep are familiar enough with me, after all the times I've fed them, that they won't make too much noise.

It's a big barn where he keeps the sheep. There are probably more than a hundred of them in there. I lean on the steel gate peering in. Amazing: there's light in this darkness too. I thought it would be the whiteness of their fleeces, but it's not, it's their eyes. They were making a hell of a racket for a minute, but now they've all backed into the corner of the barn and are turned, as one, staring out at me in silence, their eyes shining like they're possessed.

For a moment I think of turning back. Maybe they have been possessed? The number of eyes seems to be multiplying, row after row of spotlights piercing into me. But then, drawn by the warmth, I find myself climbing the gate.

I slide sideways along the inside wall, the eyes following me. In the darkness, I find a load of hay and lower myself to the ground, wrapping myself tightly into it, trying to get the shivering to stop. The sheep seem to have accepted my presence now and a few of them have wondered over, nuzzling me, or pressing their rumps into me. Maybe I should be frightened, but instead, as I lie here, I find myself revelling in a sense of awe that they have taken me in. Outside, my own species are hunting me down, but here, inside this parallel universe, these creatures have recognised my life force and accepted me as one of their own.

I start counting them, but their dark, hazy shapes are swelling and multiplying. The walls of the barn are expanding in all directions until it knows no boundaries and as it does so, it fills with more and more of those eyes swirling above and around me, until, finally I start to drift into an enchanted sleep, bringing this crazy old year of 1981 to a close.

Chapter 14

Happy New Year

There was a new light when I woke the next morning. The sun streamed in through the opening to the barn, rinsing clean everything in its beam, then diffusing, reaching into the darkest recesses and filling it with the fresh hope of a new day and a new year.

In that moment everything seemed simple, obvious even. The effects of the mushrooms may have been wearing off, but something fundamental had changed. It was as if I'd been watching the world in black and white and had switched to glorious Technicolor. The distorted visions of last night had gone; replaced by a new brightness and clarity and a certainty that I could understand anything if I just observed it carefully enough.

Some of those visions from the previous night were pretty freaky. It had been hard to tell at times what was real and what was fantasy, but surely some of them were more than mere hallucinations? If reality is defined by perception, then the previous night's perceptions were no less real than any other. Perhaps, as Frank said, I had just been viewing and interpreting things through a part of my brain that I don't normally use. Or maybe by distorting the visual perception of what was going on around me, my brain had been allowing me to see its real essence. OK, the police weren't really storm troopers, Frank isn't really Obi-Wan Kenobi and my beech tree isn't really Treebeard, but there is something of their essence in each. I had seen something in each of them that really is there; I just hadn't noticed it before.

Whatever, I was left with one new awareness: that if something exists, then its polar opposite also exists, as do all the colours of the rainbow in between. It felt so liberating to finally understand this: that feeling despair is, in itself, evidence that joy also exists; that hatred can't exist without love, nor darkness without light.

I walked back to the camp with a feeling of lightness and euphoria that lasted for days. The dark delusions of the night before, that sabre-wielding storm troopers had been hunting me down, dissolved in this new light and sure enough I arrived to a camp that was calm, if slightly hangover.

As I walked back, the first person I saw was Travis.

'Hey, Marko. Happy New Year. Where did you get to last night? Abi and Frank were worried about you, but I reckoned you'd just had a better invitation with one of the women from the village!'

'Ha, no such luck, I just woke up with a few of Old Barry's prize sheep.'

'Hmm, sheep worrying – well don't worry you're secret's safe with me!'

We both laughed and that was about it. I'd almost forgotten that it was New Year's Day, but in that moment it felt appropriate that this was the start of something new.

Frank and I had a good chat later on. It seems that the police just turned up for a few minutes to see what was going on and to get us to turn the music down a bit. Nothing quite came out right, as I started telling him about my experiences of the night before, but he has a way of drawing me out and making everything that I say sound profound. As we talked about resolutions for the year ahead, I felt that calm resolve resettling.

'Don't just make hollow promises to yourself Marko, or set yourself up to fail. Your resolutions should be meaningful little balls that you get rolling, balls that build the momentum of your journey through life. You don't need to shout them from the rooftops; just feel them and they will become part of you.'

He closed his eyes as he said that, holding a lightly clenched fist to his heart. I knew just what he meant. I felt as though I had started on a new journey of awareness: of myself, of the world around me and of finding a place for myself to fit into it. I drank some more coffee and we sat quietly together, watching the others emerge one-by-one, all looking rough as hell after the night before.

I should have known that this would only be a calm interlude before the next storm, but I was too elevated by my new mood and my new certainties to allow any doubts into my mind. Over the next few days I saw everyone and everything in a subtly different way. In my early days here, I'd always felt tense, looking for threats in what people said and did, weighing things up over and over before I did, or said, anything. Now I found I was absorbing everything in a calmer way and I noticed that people were listening more respectfully to me when I spoke. Even Freddie noticed it. I saw him looking at me a couple of times, with a wistful little grin on his face.

There was a new richness to my harmonica playing too. The notes were becoming a little less raucous, more confident, like I was polishing off some of their rough edges. That allowed me to contribute more to our jamming sessions, which I was enjoying more and more, and we were hitting some great new sounds together, really getting on the same wavelength. We had another gig booked in at the Prince of Wales on the fifteenth – it was going to be the best yet, I just knew it.

My serene state of mind lasted for about a week. I didn't know it, in those early, halcyon days of the New Year, but events were soon to start another dangerous downward spiral for me.

It was the prosaic reality of money that pricked my bubble, or gradually deflated it, rather. On those first few days of the year, I wasn't even thinking about the fact that I only had five pounds left in my wallet. The air inside my bubble was so pure, that I felt untouchable, immune to malignant forces, filled with a calm certainty that any challenge could be surmounted.

We went busking to Sherborne on the first Saturday and, even though we didn't even make a fiver each, I still wasn't worried. I did a morning working with Barry and made another fiver, but suddenly it was the first Giro Day of the year and I realised I only had a little over fifteen pounds.

I had a chat with Frank the day before and he said he would talk with the others to see if the kitty could sub me. I had at least one morning a week lined up with Barry now and the gig at the Prince coming up, so they agreed, but it didn't stop Jake from making sarky comments. I felt myself being pushed back on the defensive again, like a tide turning.

Then things got worse. On Giro Day the snow started to come down, before everyone had even got back from signing-on in, and throughout the rest of the day and the next it came down thicker, whipped up by heavy winds. It settled, layer-upon-layer, drifting and blocking us in again, just like before Christmas.

On Saturday, the snow turned to icy rain, which froze instantly, forming dagger-like stalactites from the branches of the trees and a crusty cap over the snow. On Monday, when it finally cleared, we found the shower block inundated by a flood of icy cold water that gushed from a cracked pipe, and an unresponsive generator. Frank and Jake are both experienced mechanics, but couldn't get it going.

'It's fucking ancient, that's the problem, we're gonna need at least two new parts and some new copper piping,' Jake growled.

They disappeared for most of the rest of the next day and returned having spent nearly half the camp's cash reserves on the new parts. They got it working, eventually, but the pressure inside me was building. I did my morning with

Barry and repaid my loan to the kitty.

After the trauma of being snowed-in, and without power, for that week, Rick and Pete decided they'd had enough, announcing they were heading back to London after the gig at the Prince the following Friday. They were always a bit out on a limb those two, but they added something to the camp.

We gave them a good send-off. The gig *was* the best one we ever did: even more people turned up than the last time and the landlord was so happy he gave us a tenner each. The next night the camp was full with people from the village and surrounds who knew Rick and Pete and we were up late into the night drinking and smoking and playing music.

Their departure left a gaping hole. At the time I was most upset at losing them from the band: in fact, without Rick, we didn't really have a band. The camp was quieter and our jamming sessions never had the same intensity without Rick's guitar and Pete's extra bongo.

We had occasional visitors, including an old pal of Frank's who sometimes turned up with his guitar. That was good, but his style was quieter and slower than Rick's and it was never quite the same again. I didn't know it at the time, but that second gig at the Prince was the last one we ever did together.

But it was more than just the music; the whole mood in the camp changed once they'd gone. They'd always been more light-hearted than the others, Rick and Pete, and without them the atmosphere became more intense, more serious, and we started getting increasingly irritable with each other.

Frank always rose above it, but he was keeping to himself more and more, so I was spending less time with him. We weren't even going out foraging every morning anymore. When we did, we were left with the occasional mushroom and acorns (boiling them to leech the tannins, then baking, or grinding them into a powder for bread), or some early nettles and other herbs.

Abi's baby was due at the end of April, so she and Travis were also keeping themselves apart. They spent less and less time on the Magic Bus, particularly when the air was thick with smoke, although Travis would occasionally sneak on for a sly joint when Abi was resting.

But it was my relationship with Jake and Jade that I found most perplexing. One moment Jake acted like he was my best mate, the next he was belittling me, putting me down with patronising or sarcastic digs.

Jade's behaviour confused me even more. She only had to look in my direction to get my pulse racing, but she would oscillate from flirting with me, to mothering me, to blanking me.

If Jake was around, her behaviour towards me changed altogether, as if she was talking to him through me. It was always the same: she'd say something to me, then, almost before she'd finished speaking, look up to see Jake's reaction. If Jade ever paid me any attention when he was around, Jake would put me in my place pretty quickly, as if to re-establish his possession of her and my humble position in the pecking order.

Freddie thought I was being over-sensitive, which I probably was, but each interaction added to my unease. It was just as well that Freddie was there, because our friendship kept me level. He was always able to make light of things and to make me laugh.

That didn't stop me from worrying about money the whole time. Over the following weeks I bobbed up and down on a two-week cycle of worry, of whether I could get enough cash to pay my twenty quid into the kitty and what would happen if I couldn't. Each time, I seemed to be a few pounds short and that moment of asking to be subbed for a few days was like a ritual of humiliation.

Frank was always calm about it, but I could feel the tension building. I didn't spend anything myself and I stopped smoking dope, because it was nearly always someone's personal supply. It was frustrating knowing that I had money in my bank account back home, but the police would be sure to be watching that. Yeovil was certainly too close to home, but I started to think that if things got too desperate I could take a chance in Taunton next time we went there.

This was all nothing compared to the chain of events that started on Thursday, the 18th March. Even two days later, it feels like a day that will stick with me forever, right up there with 20th August (another Thursday) and, worst of all, 14th March 1974.

It all started quietly enough. It was a beautiful day, the best of the year so far. The sun was shining, everywhere daffodils raised their golden heads, the branches on the trees burst with new buds, new-born lambs danced and played in Old Barry's fields, the whole world felt ready for a fresh start. It's my nineteenth birthday tomorrow and there'd been talk about that and the Summer Fayres and Festivals that lay ahead and even the possibility that Rick and Pete might be returning.

The others had gone off to Yeovil to sign on and I was left, as usual, on my own at the camp. I always liked those calm moments. Sometimes I would go for a walk, up towards my old hideout, but mostly I'd spend the morning on the bus reading and listening to music and then start preparing a meal for everyone when they got back.

Sometimes the guys went to the pub after signing on and cashing their giros and then stop at a supermarket to stock up, so it wasn't unusual for them to be out until mid-afternoon, but as it got later and later without any sign of them appearing, I couldn't stop an ominous dread from growing. By the time it started to get dark, I was getting properly worried; they'd never been this late before. Finally they turned up, just after six, on foot. The van had blown up on the way back from Yeovil. They'd managed to push it into a farmer's yard and then walked back from there, each of them carrying a couple of bags of shopping. I'd never seem them looking so glum. Jake, in particular, was in a foul mood.

I got them all a brew on in double-speed and then cracked on with heating up the stew that I'd been preparing that afternoon. The food and the warmth of the Magic Bus lifted their spirits a little, but it was still a tense evening. Once we'd finished eating, and a couple of obligatory spliffs had been passed around, Frank brought the conversation back to what we were going to do about the van. That was usually the way: Frank the calm, wise head who likes to keep things orderly.

Thursday night was different. Jake used to be a car mechanic and he was taking the whole thing very personally. He kept scowling at me as he talked, as if the whole thing was my fault. I had a guilty enough conscience as it was. I was ten pounds light on the kitty and everyone knew it. I didn't need to be a mechanic to suss out that this was going to blow the kitty apart and without the van we were stuffed. I just kept my eyes down as I listened to him ranting on.

'I know a clapped out engine when I see it. The big end's blown. Did you hear the noise? Did you see the black smoke? Sure sign. It's an engine-out job, at the very least. My mate Taff's got an old van in his yard. The sub-frame's shot, but the engine should be sound. We can either swap 'em over, or cannibalise it for parts, but it's a big job and it's gonna cost us.'

I felt his eyes burning into me again as he spoke. He must have said it all before to the others, because they'd been together all afternoon. He was repeating it just to rub it in that I was in hock to the kitty.

'Well we've got to get the van back on the road, Jake,' Frank was saying. 'I know my way round an engine as well, so we can work on it together. What about Taff?'

'I'll go and speak with him again tomorrow. He should be able to winch it out tomorrow night when he's finished his dayshift. I'll have to head over and help him. Then we should be able to get it to the farm on the back of his truck on Saturday morning. That arse of a farmer wants our van out of there. Did you see the look on his face when we turned up? He didn't even want to let us in to use his fuckin' phone.'

'He thought he was going to catch something from us,' laughed Jade. 'I wanted to creep up behind and breathe on him. Make him squeal like one of his pigs!'

'Oh, Malcolm's not so bad, but you're right, he won't want our rusty old heap clogging up his yard. Anyway, let's keep calm about this; we can only deal with what's in front of us.'

Jake and Jade went out for a while, leaving a vacuum in their wake which nobody could fill for a while. Freddie suggested some beer, which we all jumped on. There was still plenty of home-brew: barely anyone went near it on New Year's Eve. I hadn't drunk much for a while and it was welcome, loosening my spirits, giving me something to do with my hands.

Jake and Jade were only gone for about twenty minutes and they were more chilled when they got back, as if they'd resolved something, got it off their chests. Jade was very quiet, but Jake was more animated, going straight into telling some story about his mate Taff at Glastonbury a couple of years ago. He was back to his entertaining best, drawing everyone under his scurrilous spell.

Unlike everyone else, I wasn't giving him my full attention. I'd glanced up and seen Jade looking at me. My heart skipped, like it always does, but there was something different in her eyes this time. I couldn't put my finger on it. I sensed something mischievous in them, but an undercurrent of sadness too, maybe even fear.

She held my gaze for a moment, before abruptly lowering her eyes. That was strange, because it's always me that averts my eyes first with Jade. Normally, it's as if she can see right inside me when our eyes meet and I'm overwhelmed by a sense of panic, as if I've been caught, shamefully exposed, in her spotlight. This time it was her who dropped here eyes and I smiled to myself, allowing myself to be buoyed by a cocky surge of self-belief. I tuned back into the conversation and even joined in.

'Did you see The Cure at Glastonbury?' I asked Jake.

He looked at me, his eyes and his voice laden with contempt: 'The Cure? Oh probably. But hey, you don't go to Glastonbury, or any other fayre, just to see one band. That's a bourgeois way of thinking. It's about the vibe, about the people, about being in the moment and being who you are. I thought you were getting that, Marko.'

I refused to be put down. 'Yeah, but I'd like to be in that moment when The Cure are right there, and they dive into those riffs in *A Forest* – that would be some vibe!'

I aped Robert Smith playing the guitar as I spoke and everyone, bar Jake, laughed. Out of the corner of my eye, I saw that Jade had a secretly admiring smile on her face and I took a quietly pleased swig of my beer.

Jake carried on with his story, as if he hadn't noticed anything, and the evening continued it's meandering, distracted course, skirting around the issues that were bubbling like storm clouds.

That night, with a few pints of beer inside me, and my head spinning with all the dope, I fell straight into a deep sleep. At some point in the night I woke abruptly, my senses immediately acute. Something was different. Something had changed. I searched for it in the oppressive blackness, but it was so dense that my eyes were useless. It was warm in the cocoon of my sleeping bag, but this amplified the icy air on my face. It was colder than normal. The door to my van had been open; I could feel the fresh movement in the air.

Then I became aware of something else. A presence. It was Jade; I knew it right there in that moment. I could sense her. She was in here with me. Surely she couldn't be? I lay motionless, not daring to move, every part of me vigilant, right down to the hairs on my body that stood on end as if seeking her out.

A tiny creak came from near the door and, with that almost imperceptible movement, her scent reached me, its rich, sweet, earthiness unique, unmistakable. I held my breath as her shadow moved slowly towards me, until there she was, in the flesh, hovering over me.

'Hello, you,' she whispered.

I could hear her smile. I made to reply, but she pressed her finger onto my lips. She was kneeling on the mattress, with one leg either side of me. Leaning in towards me, she continued whispering in my ear:

'I saw you looking at me in the Magic Bus earlier. I thought: I bet his thoughts aren't pure. We're going to have to do something about that.'

She'd found the zip to my sleeping bag and was slowly pulling it down.

'It's cold out here. Mind if I come in?'

I shook my head, but she was already sliding inside. I was lying there, almost shaking with breathless anticipation. Then I felt her long fingers find my face, stroking my beard, gently scratching the hairs on the back of my neck, then drawing me towards her.

In that dark silence, our mouths met. Her lips were soft. Just as I'd imagined. We kissed, tentatively at first, delicately, tenderly, but then our passions rose, our tongues entwining, writhing together and I was filled with her sweet, intoxicating wetness.

Jade gasped for air, throwing her head back and I found myself kissing her neck, breathing her in, my hand sliding under her top to feel the smoothness of her back and the soft swelling of her breasts. I was waiting for her to stop me, but she didn't. I had fantasised about this moment every day since I'd arrived. Now it was happening I was overwhelmed, spinning wildly out of control, bewildered, yet exhilarated.

'Oh, my God, we should have done this before,' I heard her mutter.

I was desperately hoping that this was going where it felt like it was going. I wanted it all to happen right now and I wanted it all to last forever.

Then she was rising up again, lifting me with her. In the darkness, I felt her rolling my T-shirt up and over my head. As she pressed me down to the mattress again, I caught her with the strap to my watch.

'Ouch! That can come off an' all.'

She unclipped it, laying it down by the side of the mattress. Almost in the same moment she was lifting her top and my face was buried in her breasts, kissing them, pressing her nipples between my lips, rolling the tip of my tongue over them. Her hands were sliding my jockeys down and I gasped, as she squeezed my cock in her hand. Then we were kissing again, our hands roaming, caressing and exploring places that had always felt forbidden, our bodies sliding and rubbing against each other, until finally she was kneeling above me.

Pressing my chest down, she grasped me in the other hand and slowly drew me inside her. I lay rigid, mouth agape, eyes bulging, as if I could somehow extract even more from this moment. I felt her, warm and moist, as she lowered herself onto me, squeezing me as she did with muscles I'd never known existed. I gripped the mattress with my hands, my head flailing to either side, but it was too late, I couldn't stop myself, I was barely inside her and I exploded.

In that moment, it felt like the most shameful thing that had ever happened to me. All I could do was blurt out my mortification:

'Oh my God. I'm sorry. I'm sorry.'

I felt like crying, but Jade just laughed, whispering in my ear:

'Hey, no need to be in such a hurry, Marko, we've got all night, right? I bet there's plenty more where that came from!'

I don't remember much more. We lay entwined for a while, giggling like children, whispering into each other's ears until, at some point, I fell into the deepest of sleeps, images of Jade filling my dreams, swooping and swirling around me, engulfing me in a surreal new world.

I woke the next morning and Jade was gone. For the briefest of moments, I thought it might have been a dream, but her imprint was everywhere. I picked one of her hairs from the pillow, holding it up into the light and twisting it between my thumb and forefinger, as if to reconvince myself that her presence had been a reality.

I breathed in deeply. Her scent still permeated everything: my sleeping bag, my pillow, my hair, my skin, her essence branded into me, so that everything seemed like it was still filtering through her.

Most of all, I could still feel and taste her. My lips were still swollen and fizzy and, if I closed my eyes, I could still feel her tongue in my mouth, our bodies rubbing together, that heavenly feeling of her skin against mine, the ecstatic intimacy of her wild eyes, her glistening skin and her voice, imploring and unrestrained.

Then, with a sickening jolt, I remembered that it had been a disaster. That I'd come before I was even fully inside her. I covered my head in the pillow, groaning, as if I could hide from the embarrassment. That was why she'd left. Because I was such a disappointment. She was probably laughing at my performance, even now. I'd had my chance and I'd blown it. How would I ever be able to face her again?

Slowly, I pulled myself upright. What time was it? My watch wasn't on my wrist. Then I remembered Jade sliding it off, as things had started to heat up. Blurrily, I reached out on the floor for it. A volt of panic shot through me.

Where was Dad's watch? I was sure she'd put it right there by my T-shirt.

I was fully awake now, rummaging around on the floor, lifting the mattress, checking the sides, the pockets of my rucksack. Where the fuck was it? I couldn't lose Dad's watch, I just couldn't. Then I calmed myself. There would be a simple explanation. Jade must have put it somewhere safe, or held onto it, in case I trod on it in the night.

Pressing aside this turmoil of emotion, I got myself dressed and went down to get a shower. I felt like a different person, as if something had changed in the night.

It was quiet in the camp. Frank must have been out walking already. Freddy was the only one who seemed to be around.

'Morning, mate.'

'Morning.' I paused, trying not to be too obvious. 'You seen Jade?'

'Um…I think she went off with Jake early. Something to do with the van, I guess.'

I nodded my head, a layer of unease settling queasily on me. A sixth sense was telling me something was wrong, but I couldn't do anything other than wait for it to reveal itself. Travis and Abi joined Freddie and I on the Magic Bus and the four of us sat there in silence drinking coffee. Frank came back from his walk at some point, but went straight to his van.

'What's the time, Freddie?' I asked.

'About ten minutes after you last asked,' he replied.

Some time late morning Jake and Jade arrived back, Jake striding briskly a yard or so ahead. I leapt up, as if scalded, jumped off the bus and jogged after them, vainly trying to appear casual.

'Hey, guys…'

Jade had her head down, avoiding my eye contact, but Jake turned and stopped with his hands on his hips, looking straight at me. I could sense the others behind me, getting off the Magic Bus.

'What's up, Marko? You got a problem?'

Suddenly I couldn't talk properly: 'I, um, I…'

'Well go on, spit it out.'

I looked past him. 'Uh, Jade, have you seen my watch?'

Jake started laughing. By then he was shouting out, playing to the audience, as if he was up on stage:

'Oh, he's worried about his watch! He spends the night fucking my girlfriend, he's in hock to the kitty, while we haven't even got enough money to fix our van, and he's worried about his precious watch! Well I tell you what Marko, we got fifty quid from the pawnbroker's for it and now we've probably got enough to get the engine sorted.'

I stood mute for several seconds, unable to take in the enormity of what he'd just said. The implications of his words were swirling around my head and, for a moment, I thought the ground was going to give away beneath me. They'd stolen Dad's watch. The watch that had been fixed to my wrist almost from the day he died: strong, reliable, constant, it's pulse against mine, connecting me with him, guiding me.

Jake started to turn to go. As if that was the end of it. As if I'd been dismissed. For a moment I thought I was going to cry, but then something snapped inside me, an explosion of rage surged and I was launching myself at him.

'You fucking bastard,' I screamed, as I slammed into him.

I took him by surprise, knocking him clean off his feet. Then I was on top of him, raining punches down, as he cowered, covering his face with his arms. I felt hands grabbing my collar and dragging me off, as my arms continued to flail in mid-air.

'You fucking bastard,' I continued screaming.

Jake was pulling himself to his feet, blood trickling from his nose and his lip where I'd hit him. Frank had run over and was standing sideways between us, both arms outstretched to keep us apart. Freddie and Travis were holding me, one by each arm. I'd stopped struggling. I was looking at Jade, who'd had her back turned through all of this, and was now walking quickly away towards their van.

Jake was now on his feet, dusting himself down, wiping the blood from his face onto his sleeve. He looked at me, with undisguised hatred:

'What a cunt! I should've left you up in the woods. Everything we've done for you and here you are still taking the piss.'

He reached into his pocket and pulled out a slip of paper, which he screwed up and threw at me. 'That's the pawnbrokers ticket. Do what the hell you like with it. Now, I suggest you fuck off, before I kick the shit out of you.'

With that, he turned and walked slowly after Jade. In his absence he left a stunned silence. I was starting to shake and I felt Freddie and Travis' hold on me loosen. Frank was still standing, frozen on his spot, watching Jake walk away. He turned to look at me, but for once I could tell he didn't know quite what to say or do.

I looked him in the eye and just nodded: 'It's OK.'

Then I picked up the slip and walked, with all the dignity I could muster, back to my van to get my stuff together. Within five minutes my pack was on and I was leaving the camp, head down and without a glance back.

I wasn't long away when I heard footsteps running after me. I could hear them, but I was so numb that I couldn't prepare myself: for who it would be, for what might happen or for how I would respond. I was gone beyond anything other than putting one foot in front of the other. I could have worked it out from the sound of the steps and the breathing. It was Freddie.

'Marko, I'm so sorry, I don't know what the hell's going on.' He was standing in front of me, white as a sheet, eyes bulging, breathing heavily. 'I'm so sorry, Marko. Here, take this.'

He had a bag in his hand, which he'd stuffed full with bread and cheese, a couple of apples and a half-eaten packet of biscuits. And his copy of Remarque.

'I'll want that back sometime,' he said, trying to smile. All I could do was nod, looking down at my boots, as if I'd just noticed a mark on them. Next, he was thrusting a ten-pound note into my hand: 'Here, take this.'

I couldn't look at him. I had to keep my focus, or I was going to lose it.

'Thanks, Freddie, but no,' I replied quietly, 'I can't take it. None of this is your fault.'

315

'Mate, take it, please. If it helps you to get your Dad's watch back then that would be great.' He was stuffing the note into my pocket. 'What'ya gonna do now?'

'I've no idea...'

'I hope it works out for you, mate, I really do. I'm gonna miss you.'

I caught his eyes briefly, they were yellow and watery, and then with a clap on each other's shoulders, I was gone.

Part V

RESOLUTION

Chapter 15

A new track

I'm sat on a bare steel bench on a platform at the train station. The concrete is cold and hard and unforgiving. I can feel its grasp reaching up into my feet, as if it's turning me into stone, inch by inch. A clock hanging from the roof is beating out the time: second by second, minute by minute, my life draining away. I'm too numb to care. My mind and my body seem to have decoupled and gone off down separate tracks: my body anchored to this spot; my mind scrambled, tumbling deeper and deeper into unfathomably dark depths.

I've grown reckless. People might be watching me, talking about me. I don't care. Furious thoughts swarm, but I can't work out where to direct them: at Jake, at Jade, or at myself for my stupidity at being sucked in by those thieving bastards.

When I stormed out of the camp this morning, I had no idea where I was going, other than I had to get to Yeovil and somehow get Dad's watch back. I marched quickly and the rhythm slowly started to calm my mind. From a seething frenzy, some order started to emerge and, over the next hour or so, as I got closer to town, I pieced together a plan. I would withdraw as much money as I could from the cash machine, buy back my dad's watch, then get on a train and head west. The only place that came into my head was Falmouth, where we used to go on family holidays. I only had the haziest of memories of it, but they were happy memories and at that moment, it was all I could find to cling to.

It didn't take long for my plan to fall apart. When I got to the bank, I slotted my card into the machine and requested a hundred pounds. It whirred for few seconds then flashed back at me:

Refer to Bank.'

I checked my balance, to confirm there was enough in there, then reduced my request in ten pound multiples, until finally it gave out fifty quid. From somewhere I remembered that this was my daily withdrawal limit. I thought briefly about going inside and asking the cashier for more money, but then I remembered the tenner that Freddie had given me. Thinking that sixty should be enough to get Dad's watch back and get a train ticket somewhere, I set off for the pawnshop with hope in my heart.

I counted without the owner: the slimiest bastard I've ever come across. He dripped nauseous condescension every time he opened his mouth, taking great delight in telling me that, *technically*, Jake had *sold* it, not *pawned* it, which meant that he was now the *owner* of the watch.

Pointing to it, for sale, in the display case he said: 'It's a bargain at eighty pounds, I'm sure you'll agree, sir.'

'But it's my watch.' I shouted. 'He stole it from me.'

He sighed, replying: 'Well, of course, if you can prove your ownership of the watch, sir…'

All I could do was stand there, mouth agape and starting to tremble, then shout louder: 'It's my watch, you can't do this.' I was gripping the counter by then, leaning in towards him.

He took a step back and laughed: 'Well, perhaps we should call the police, sir. And see what they have to say.'

I took out all the money I had, which was sixty pounds and some loose change, but he just laughed and reached for the phone. I wanted to grab him, or smash his display stand, snatch my watch and run. His yellow eyes locked with mine for a moment, as if he was daring me, then I turned and stomped out before I could do something else I would regret.

I don't know how long I've been here, but the seething frenzy of earlier has fermented into something even darker and more toxic. I'm staring down at the track: at the rusted rails, which forge off into the distance until they fuse into one, then disappear altogether; at the bowed wooden sleeper boards; at the gravelly mass of stones that sit, grey, purposeless and unforgiving.

I'd decided to head west, all the way to Falmouth, but now I'm here I don't want to go anywhere. I can't leave Dad's watch behind. At some lucid moment it occurred to me that I should wait a day, take out some more money, then go and buy back my watch, but I've gone beyond that now. What's the point? Everything's turned to shit again, just like it always does. I was a fucking idiot thinking it was going to change.

I keep seeing Jade's face. In the darkness of last night it felt like we were together, so close we were fusing into one. Now, I can see that the reality was altogether different. The image of her face in my mind turns from ecstasy to derision, contorting from a soft, soothing concern to an ugly cynicism that's jeering at me. She was just using me. Taking the piss. She was laughing at me all along and now I'm the butt of their joke. Jake and Jade. It was always them; with me as the pitiful outsider that could be taken for a ride when it suited them. How was I so naïve as not to see it?

Now I'm back to where I've always been, alone and miserable. Nobody cares about me. Nobody would miss me if I were gone. Why should they? I should have been in that car with my family. All this staggering on alone, clinging to Dad's watch and those few other things of theirs that I've kept; all it's doing is prolonging the pain. I should end it all. Right here. Right now.

I hear a noise building, away to my right. There's no train due, it must be a fast one. I swallow quickly and shuffle to the edge of the platform. The ground feels like it's losing its solidity, my legs subsiding. The track has become a vortex, reeling me in, churning my stomach, screwing my eyes out of focus. The noise of the train is building. A long blast of its horn rips the air. Nothing can stop it now.

I can feel the shuddering vibrations of the train on the

track. It matches the turmoil raging inside me. That great horn is blaring again, now with deadly urgency. There's nothing in the world but me and the platform and the train. I inch closer to the edge. I can't breathe. My fists are clenched like rocks. My eyes clamped shut. I'm starting to go, starting to pull the trigger on my life. I'm squeezing it, squeezing it, squeezing it. But I just can't squeeze it hard enough.

My mind and my body are locked in mortal combat. My mind is urging my body to leap, but my body is mutinous, my feet rooted to the spot. I squeeze the trigger tighter. I'm on the brink. The trigger starting to snap. My body is rocking forward, preparing for the final plunge, but something's stopping me, my body sways back again. Then a wall of air and noise hits me, turning everything inside out. Finally, my feet move, but rather than forward to oblivion, they've chosen backwards, to life.

I gasp. I'm standing a good yard away from the track now and I've started to shake. I look up and see the back of the train hurtling away from me like a smash-and-grab raider that's gone without its prize. I stand for a moment, unable to move. Then I hear a voice shouting at me.

'Oi. What yer doin' standing so close to the edge? Trying to get yourself killed or som'at?'

I turn away from the voice and walk back to the bench. My pack was still on my back. I don't know what just happened. Maybe the weight of the pack tipped the scales? I pull it off and fall onto the bench, hugging it to my knees.

'Oi. Did yer hear me?'

I heard him alright. Out of the corner of my eye I can see him too, half way up the platform, by the entrance; a short, grey bloke in a station guard's uniform. I turn my pack over on my knees and just stare straight ahead. I can still see him, out of the corner of my eye, standing, arms on his hips, staring in my direction, but eventually he turns, shaking his head, and shuffles back into his office.

I'm sitting here motionless. Should I be feeling relief? If I should, I don't. I just feel numb. If I feel anything, I feel like a loser, a good for nothing coward. If another train comes I could just dump my pack and sprint towards the track, until I've got the same momentum as the train and nothing can stop me, eyes closed, so I'll feel nothing until the platform disappears beneath my feet. I'm listening for the sound of another train, but I can also feel my fingers gripping onto the underside of the bench, refusing to let go. And I know that I'm going to bottle it again. I can't even top myself properly.

I haven't moved for ages. There are footsteps walking up the platform. They only register somewhere deep in my subconscious, because thoughts are still swirling round my head. Whoever it is has sat down on the bench next to me. Still I pay no attention. Still I stare out over the track, beyond the next platform, through the old brick wall, plastered with jagged, graffiti hieroglyphics, as if my stare can bore on into infinity until it reaches a perfect blankness.

Somewhere in my deep trance, a smell is reaching into me. It's wood smoke and tobacco, a sweet hint of marijuana, metal and grease, a faint undercurrent of mushrooms that reaches down and takes over. Together they start to reel me in and I find myself drawing back into my body. I feel a hand resting gently on my shoulder. I look up into the weathered face and grey eyes of Frank.

'Hello, Marko.'

'Frank!'

I have to look away; I can't hold his gaze. We sit in silence for what feels like an age. I don't know what to say. I don't know what to think. I don't even know what to feel. A stomach dropping jolt of embarrassment, that's what comes first, morphing quickly into shame; then a tangled uproar of relief and joy and fear and anger that all wants to pour out together. Then suspicion. What's he doing here?

'You're wondering what I'm doing here,' he says. 'I couldn't let you leave like that, Marko. You must be at a pretty low ebb right now and I take some of the responsibility for that. I should have seen what was building up. Instead, I turned a blind eye. We're all meant to be there for each other and I let you down. I'm sorry.'

I go to speak, but no words will come out. I still can't look at him. Frank lets the silence grow, until it softens, then continues.

'I suspected that you'd head for the pawnshop, so I went there first. A thoroughly unpleasant character, but I've met his sort before, easy enough to put in their place once you know how. So, we'll get your dad's watch back, Marko, don't you worry about that.'

He pauses and I can feel him looking at me.

'OK, Marko, you're hurting, I can see that, son. Have

you thought about what you're going to do?'

We sit in silence for a while. Another train rumbles past and I forget for a moment that I'd been building up the nerve to jump in front of it.

Finally, I find my voice. 'I was thinking about heading west...maybe to Cornwall.'

'Do you know anyone down there?'

'No. I just thought I could hide out down there for a while.'

Silence hangs in the air again. I can almost hear Frank thinking. I can feel how thin and pitiful my reply sounded.

'OK, Marko, I have a question for you. Think hard about this. How long do you think you can keep running and hiding? Is that the kind of life you want?'

I can't answer. Of course it's not. All I can do is to shake my head and hang it in my hands. That great hopelessness and helplessness is swelling up inside me again.

'It's OK, Marko. You're feeling betrayed and you're feeling trapped, neither of which is conducive to rational thought, but I have been thinking about it. First of all, none of this is your fault. You might not believe it right now, but you've shown a lot of resilience and courage. And I've been impressed by how you've blossomed since you came into the camp.

'You're a good lad, Marko, and I'm sorry it's all ended up like this, but the more I've thought about it this morning, the more I've realised that it was only a matter of time before something like this happened.

'Running and hiding is all very well, if it gives you the time and the space to finding a solution to your issues, but it cannot become the solution. That's what you're doing, Marko, you're turning running and hiding into the solution. First up in the woods, then with us, now somewhere else. Where's it going to end, hey? At some point you have to face up to this.'

Frank has paused and I can feel him looking at me, as if to weigh up the impact of his words. I feel like a sandcastle that's being washed away by the incoming tide of his logic; I'm clinging to the possibility of escape, even as a growing part of me knows that he's right.

'Believe it or not, Marko, I think that you have already started dealing with some of your issues. When you arrived at the Camp, you were the most closed book I'd ever come across. I suspect that you'd never opened up properly to anyone since you lost your family. And that's totally understandable.

'I'll let you into a little secret, Marko. I did something very similar myself. All those years traipsing around Asia were exactly what I've just warned you against: running away. It was the hardest thing I've ever had to do, returning to Scotland to face up to my demons, but it was something that I had to do.

'It's a shame that Jake and Jade let you down, because over the last few months you've won over everyone at the camp. You're not the kind of bloke who can survive for long as an island, Marko; nor should you be.'

I laugh at that and raise my head. Tears had started to come as he spoke, but I've controlled them now and I rub my eyes with the palms of my hands.

Frank is looking at me, squeezing my shoulder with one

hand:

'You OK?'

I nod.

'Good. Well, we need to come up with a plan. First off, how much cash have you got?'

'I've got sixty quid now. The cash machine won't give me any more until tomorrow.'

'That's OK. That'll be enough to get your dad's watch back.'

'But that bloke said he wanted eighty. He was going to call the police.'

Frank laughs. 'Och, you leave him to me, Marko. Lets go there first, hey, then we'll get a cuppa and work out what to do next.'

I feel almost dizzy with relief as we get up and walk out of the Station together. I don't even notice the station guard, but I guess that's who Frank nods at, as we leave the platform and back onto the street merging in with the cars and the normal folk going about their business.

An hour has passed and we're sat in a greasy spoon that Frank knew. It's hidden away down a back street and there's only two other people in here: an old couple sat at the front looking out of the window through holes they've smeared in the steam. We've got piping hot cups of tea in front of us, and a stale bun each served on plates that stick to the table.

Most importantly, I've got my Dad's watch back on my wrist again. I sat in here whilst Frank went off to the pawn-shop with my money. For a few minutes I was seized by an icy dread that this was an extension of an elaborate plot.

That Frank was, at this moment, on his way back to the camp with my money. That they would soon all be laughing at me again, as they tossed my sixty quid into their kitty.

I shouldn't have worried. Frank would never stoop that low. I don't know how he did it, but he returned with the watch and even a fiver's change. Now, with the hot tea inside me, I'm starting to pull myself together again.

Frank's asked me again about my plan. Despite what he said at the station I still can't bring myself to think about anything other than escaping and hiding and I find myself resurrecting my Cornish plan: building on it, embellishing it, justifying it.

'In Falmouth there's a thickly wooded headland on the edge of town. I remember it from when we went there on holiday once. I can hide out there for a while. It'll be the summer season soon and I could get a job in a bar or something, I could even busk, like we all did in Sherborne that time.'

Frank's looking at me as I speak. He lets me gabble on for a while, then holds up his hand to stop me.

'Marko, remember what I said earlier about running away and hiding. There are things in life that you have to face up to, that you can't hide from, that have to be resolved, or they'll become festering sores that will never heal. Are you going to run away from this forever? Or are you going to face up to it?'

As he talks, my legs have taken on a life of their own. They're jigging up and down, as if I have no control over them, and I'm gripping the table, staring down at my tea, unable to keep eye contact with him.

Frank grabs my chin and fixes me with his eyes. 'You know what that means, don't you, Marko?'

I nod my head. I can see just where he's going.

'You've got to go back to Farnham and confront this. Right?'

I nod my head again.

Chapter 16

Fronting up

I've been in this cell for hours now, without a word. My only way of knowing how much time has passed is the angle of the sun coming in from the little window in the top corner. The silhouette it creates has inched up the far wall like a sundial. I've become obsessed with its slow motion journey, betting myself that somebody will come for me before it reaches each new brick mark: but each one has passed in turn and soon it will disappear altogether.

It's my birthday tomorrow. Will I still be here? Suspended like a fly in a web, powerless to do anything but wait for the spider to come and finish me off. I'm not expecting a cake with candles, that's for sure. My mind has gone round and round in futile circles of hope and recrimination. One moment I'm certain that I've done the right thing, turning myself in, convincing myself that I'll be able to resolve everything with a simple explanation, the next I'm overtaken by a certainty that I'll be spending the rest of my life locked away. I find myself cursing Frank for persuading me to come back, but even more my own stupidity for giving in to it. Finally, I give in to a wearied acceptance that I've done what I've done and what will happen will happen.

I can never settle at that, of course, so sooner or later I start round the cycle again, back to rehearsing the story that I'll tell the police when they come, rebuilding my expectations, until my story caves in under its own preposterous implausibility. Then all I'm left with is to sit and watch the silhouette inch along the wall. Waiting and waiting for something, anything, to happen.

We spent last night with friends of Frank. They were strangely normal: living in a small house with a garden, carpets and curtains, a bowl filled with fruit on the table and a television in the corner of their front room. They weren't what I expected of Frank at all, but they were nice to me, not asking too many questions, and I was grateful for that. I contributed politely to the conversation, but inside I was churning like a death-row prisoner waiting for the sunrise.

I didn't know what to expect the next morning. We tried several times to call Uncle Harry, but each time there was no answer. He could be anywhere, probably still touring in America. Instead Frank insisted on coming with me to Farnham.

'You're not in the right frame of mind to be on your own right now, Marko,' he said. 'Your emotions will be all over the place and you need someone on your side.'

He wasn't wrong. Without him I'd probably have bottled it even before I got to the train station let alone the police station. We set off early and by lunchtime we were back in Farnham. Last August it took the best part of five days of blistering footslog to reach Montacute, scurrying and hiding like a hunted animal; yesterday I reversed all of those steps in less than three hours. Just when I wanted to slow events down, it felt like I was reliving those days of last summer in super-fast-forward.

I had a book to read, but there was no way I could focus on it. I just sat, hunched into my seat, staring out of the window. I could see my own ghost on every footpath, in every bit of woodland, on every hilltop. Running. Hiding. Craving invisibility, yet desperate to be seen: to be understood, to be accepted, to be forgiven.

Opposite, Frank sat quietly immersed in a double-volume of Proust. I was grateful to him for leaving me to my thoughts, but he was a reassuring presence sat there across the table, as though nothing could happen to me whilst he was there.

At Woking we had to change trains and I got a fifteen-minute reprieve. We'd eaten the packed lunches that Frank's friends had made us, so we got a cup of tea from the station café. I clung to those precious moments of stillness, moments when it didn't feel I was racing to my doom, but the train was there before I'd even finished my tea.

Once we were on that train, I knew there was no escape. I remembered the route as if I'd only done it the day before: Brookwood, Ash Vale, Aldershot and then the short stop to Farnham, not even enough time to hit top speed. The terraced houses of Aldershot barely seemed to end before Farnham appeared, the turrets of the castle rising, away to my right, above the trees of Farnham Park and, finally, that ninety-degree turn as we crossed the A31 and slid down into Farnham Station.

As we left the train, I had the sudden weird urge to show Frank around town, to accidentally bump into people that I used to know, so that I could say to them:

'This is my mate Frank.'

I wanted people to see that I had a friend; that I wasn't the weirdo loser that they'd always thought. And I wanted Frank to see where I was from, as if that would somehow impress him and make him think better of me.

I don't know what I'd been expecting, but Farnham greeted us with silent indifference. Leaves on the trees must have fallen, then regrown, lives must have been lived, things must have happened, but after all the tumult of my life over these past seven months, it felt like the town had barely breathed in and out again.

Ron's face jumped into my head. He must be there in his shop right now, probably forgotten all about me, probably got a new young assistant working for him. I stopped in my tracks for a moment, trying to take it all in.

Frank gripped me lightly by the arm. 'It's OK, Marko. This is going to feel really weird, but I think we should get on with it. Prevarication is only going to make it harder. Now, do you know the way to the police station?'

'Yeah, it's just along the river on the edge of town.'

'OK. Let's go straight there then, hey?'

There wasn't much chance for prevarication. The police station was only a five-minute walk; we didn't even need to cross the river into town. As we got closer Frank could see that I was starting to get agitated, so we stopped and sat on a bench by the river for a few minutes.

We sat quietly for a while and then he started talking. 'Remember, Marko, that reprobate and his goons attacked *you*. All you did was defend yourself. You took off because you were frightened, that's all. Remember to tell them that.

'Those coppers will try and rattle you, so when they ask you a question take a deep breath before answering. A simple tactic, but it's saved my skin many a time. It buys you a bit of time and taking in some oxygen stops you from panicking. Then look them in the eye and speak slowly and calmly. And if things start looking dodgy, then stop talking and ask for a lawyer. I'll be waiting for you, OK? And if I can get hold of your Uncle I will.'

He looked at me and I nodded my assent. Inside I was churning, but I took a deep breath, as he suggested, hoisted on my pack and we walked slowly towards the police station.

Everything happened really quickly after that. We came into a waiting area, with torn-plastic seats fixed around a wall and a glass hatch to one side. There was nobody else in there and an eerie silence stained the air. The scuff-marked walls were a grimy, off-white and dust and cobwebs hung everywhere, as if nobody ever bothered to clean the place. The only embellishments were a few stained and torn posters, with pictures of angry looking blokes, or frightened victims, staring out.

My first thought was that they needed to get Jade in here and hang some crystals, to clear out some of the stagnant energy that lurked malignantly in every corner. Then I corrected myself, remembering what she'd done to me, that she wasn't on my side any more, if she ever was. In that moment, the desolate hopelessness of my position hit me with a force that knocked the wind out of me and my legs almost went from under me.

Frank rescued me again, helping me off with my pack, then nodding his head towards the window, giving me an encouraging wink. I breathed in deeply and strode to the counter with as much dignity as I could muster. I pressed a bell and a pasty-faced copper who didn't look much older than me came to the counter. I knew that if I didn't do this quickly, I would bottle it, so I looked the poor guy in the eye and said, slowly and clearly:

'I'm here to hand myself in. I stabbed someone. It was self-defence, but I stabbed someone. So, I'm here to hand myself in.'

There was silence from behind the glass. I was going to say more, but realised that I would just be saying the same thing again. I can still see his face behind the glass. He kind of froze, mouth agape, his back arching away from me, as if I was going to stab him too. He quickly regained his composure, like he was replaying what they had taught him in the academy. Then he started asking for my details and writing them down, stony-faced, as if he were processing a parking ticket.

At some point he clearly didn't know what to do next, so he asked me to wait while he called out to a colleague. I probably wasn't meant to, but I overheard their whole conversation:

'Sarge. There's a bloke here says he's stabbed someone

and he's handing himself in. What should I do?'

'There's nobody here to deal with something like that right now, they're all at the football, or at home. Have you taken his details?'

'Yes, Sarge.'

'OK. We'll have to put him in a cell 'til we can get hold of a DS.'

At the mention of the word *cell*, a wave of panic hit me. Once again the instinct to run seized me, but it was too late for that, a side door was opening and two coppers, the young one and a grey haired bloke with a sergeant's stripe, were stood either side of me, blocking my exit.

'This way please, sir.'

The older one turned briefly to Frank and asked: 'Are you his father?'

Frank looked at him and replied: 'No. I'm his friend. I'd like a word please, as soon as you have the chance.'

I only caught a brief glimpse of Frank, nodding his head at me in encouragement, as they pressed me through the door, one of them on either arm. All that was really going through my head, in that moment, was how Frank had called himself *my friend*. Beyond that I just felt numb, as if I'd been anaesthetised and was being wheeled down into surgery, my life no longer in my own control.

I've replayed all this, and more, since I've been sat here in this cell. The silhouette from the barred window is now at the very top of the wall. At some point soon it will slide onto the ceiling, then fade and disappear altogether.

I've spent much of my life alone, but this is a different

type of isolation. Here, I've been stripped bare until I have nothing left but my thoughts. Thoughts that are determined to torture me. Thoughts from which there is nowhere to hide. I try to shut them out, replacing them with new ones, trying little games to distract them, but they disguise themselves, seeping through my charades or leaping out from unexpected places, forcing themselves back into my consciousness.

Normally in moments like this I would take out my harp and breathe into it, casting my feelings out into the air. Without my harp, it feels as though all my emotions are trapped inside me, with nowhere to go, with nothing to do except gnaw away at me.

I haven't got any of my other comfort blankets either. Those bastard coppers have taken them all. Dad's watch is missing from my wrist again, Mum's St Christopher no longer sits against my chest for me to pull out and hold. I can't take Dad's wallet out of my pocket to breathe in its leathery sweetness, or look at my family photo to remind myself that once I was part of something.

I haven't even got my penknife. Normally, I would pull out all the blades and clean them, getting rid of any grains of dirt, polishing the steel until I could see my face in it, and the act would distract me for a few minutes from whatever it was that was troubling me.

The light is fading now. A stark striplight spluttered on a few minutes ago, banishing the silhouette on the wall in an instant. I'm wondering whether they will allow me some of my stuff back when I'm in prison. They won't let me have my penknife, of course, but maybe I'll be allowed my harp, maybe I can keep Mum's St Christopher. I'll be allowed books I reckon. I'll ask Frank, or Freddie, to send me some, if I get the chance to speak to either of them again.

The noise level has gone up outside. Several blokes have been taken past, shouting insults and chanting football songs. Aldershot must be at home, I guess. There always used to be stories of squaddies and local skinheads causing trouble when bigger teams came down, but I kept well away from it so I never saw it first hand.

There've been five or six of them; the cells in Aldershot must be full. They shout and bang on the door for a while after they've been locked in before giving up and falling silent, but only until one of the others starts up and then they're all chanting along again in unison. In my mind I turn each of them into Steen: fists raised, eyes bulging, tendons standing out like ridges on their necks.

It's got me thinking about everything that's happened over these past seven months. I had no idea, that morning, when I set off to get my A-Level results, of the chain of events that was about to start. It feels like I've been swept along by all that's happened, that I barely had control over any of it, just desperately grabbing at branches like a drowning man in a swollen river.

I think about those early days of running and hiding. Whatever led me to *those* woods in *that* village? It feels so random when I look at it now, but choosing that place changed everything. What would have happened if I'd taken different turns, stopped sooner, or gone on longer? Would I still be sitting here right now? Those woods became my entire world and I couldn't envisage anything else outside of it, yet now I struggle to conjure it up at all.

I can still picture the camp. Closing my eyes, I imagine it before things started to go wrong, before Rick and Pete left, before the trouble with the van, before Jade and Jake ruined everything. I miss it terribly. Its absence hurts like a part of me has been torn out.

In my mind, we're all sat around a big fire after eating a good meal. Rick's strumming on his guitar and Freddie is rolling one of his epic joints. Jade is looking over at me with a knowing smile and little twinkle in her eye. Abi is sat with a gentle, far-away smile on her face: one hand rested on her belly, Travis holding her other. Someone calls out for me to play my harp and I hook up with Rick's guitar. Frank lays down a little rhythm on his bass. Jade starts to shake her tambourine, looking at me as she does, and soon the others are joining in on their bongos.

I'm lost in the music and the warmth for a while, forgetting where I am. Even the shouts from the other cells have subsided. Somewhere, in my subconscious, there's a clank of keys, but it only half-registers, then I hear a loud voice:

'Mark Oban?'

Leaping up, I see a man standing in the open doorway: polished black shoes, dark trousers, a dark jumper with studded epaulettes and closely cropped dark hair.

He ignores my reaction. 'This way, please.'

I follow him, blinking in the changed light, a little dizzy from jumping up so quickly after being crouched for so long. I'm in no hurry, but he's off down the corridor at a brisk march and I rush to keep up. Fists are banging against the other cell doors as we pass.

'Let us out, let us out, let us out,' they're all chanting.

I want to be out of here too, but I don't want to reach my destination. I've been in that cell for hours, but I still don't feel ready for what's about to happen. We go through a door, out of the cell area and into another corridor. We turn a corner and then he's knocking at a door. I hear a faint reply and then he's pushing the door open and nodding me in.

The room is stark, bare but for a large table with two chairs on either side. There's a large window to my right, but a blind has been pulled down so nobody can see in or out. On the far side of the table, a middle-aged bloke is lounging in one of the chairs. He's recently lit a cigarette, which he's drawn on heavily. As he sees me come in he slowly breathes out a long plume of smoke, then leans over and taps the ash into an ashtray.

He doesn't say anything, just points one hand, palm-up, indicating me to take one of the seats opposite. I look behind me. The guy in the uniform has remained in the room and is standing, upright and stiff, as if in antithesis to the guy at the table, with his back to the door. His stare is straight ahead, like a guardsman, no longer giving me any acknowledgement.

'Well go on, sit down then,' says the guy behind the desk.

I do as he says, taking him in as I do. He's almost as scruffy as me, with baggy ill-fitting jeans and a dirty, quilted jacket over a faded sweatshirt. It looks like it's got that old ELO image: the one that could either be a spaceship or a Wurlitzer jukebox. He takes another deep draw from his cigarette and leaves it in the ashtray. Now he picks up a file that was on the table in front of him and starts to look through the papers inside, as if he's looking at them for the first time. I get the impression that he's doing it for affect, just to put me on edge.

It's an obvious tactic, but it works. I'm even more on edge than I was when I walked in. I try to take Frank's advice and inhale deeply, focusing on sussing this guy out. He looks tired and crumpled, with tousled, sandy-coloured hair and a couple of days' stubble on his face. He takes another drag on his cigarette, turns over a couple more pages, then flops it back on the table, as if he's bored with it.

'So, you're the infamous Mark Oban?'

It came so abruptly, that I almost jumped. He fixes me with his eyes as he speaks. They're a bright blue, which suddenly gives him an air of intelligence and authority that I hadn't expected, but what really gets me is how penetrating they are. Even more than Jake's. It feels like they can reach right inside me and rip out whatever they want to find.

'Uh, yeah.'

'Speak up,' he says.

'Yes.' I repeat.

'Good. I'm Detective Sergeant Bowles.'

He lets the silence and the tension build before he speaks again. He looks down at the file again, before looking up at me.

'It says here that you stabbed someone.' He picks up the file again, as if he has to double-check it, then bores his eyes right into mine and asks: 'Is that right?'

I'm trying to remember Frank's advice, but panic is taking over.

'Well, yes,' I stammer, 'But it was self-defence, I...'

He stops me. 'It's OK, we'll come to all that. Let's take a step back. Can you tell me who you stabbed and when?'

His tone is calmer now, even reassuring, and I remember to pause and breathe before replying. I look him in the eye.

'It was last August...'

'Last August? And you're coming to see us now?'

I can see that the quick, accusing retort is meant to break my composure, so I pause before replying, as calmly as I can: 'It was self-defence. But afterwards I was so scared that I just ran. And the longer it went, the more difficult it was to come back. It was Frank who persuaded me that I had to come back and give myself up.'

'That's the guy you came in with, right?'

'Yeah.'

'OK. So, you've been on the run, hiding out, since August last year?'

'Yeah.'

'Huh. That's why we've got a Missing Person Bulletin out for you. Well, that's cleared one thing up.' He scribbles something down on his pad, then pauses for a minute, stroking his stubble, before looking up at me. 'So, who's this person that you stabbed then?'

'His name was Steen.' I have to think for a moment to remember his first name; nobody ever used it. 'Dominic Steen.'

He lets out a guffaw. 'Dominic Steen? You stabbed Dominic Steen?' He's looking at me in utter amazement.

There, I've said it. I can't take it back now. I've gone beyond the point of no return. Goosebumps have covered me from my toes to my ears. I feel like I've been sucked high, high, up into the air and I'm about to be dropped. All I can manage is to nod my head. Then stare at my shoes, waiting for the reaction, waiting for the formal arrest process to start. Will they come from behind me with handcuffs? Will they cart me back off to the cell?

He's laughing now, shaking his head. Finally he looks at me and says: 'Well, you could have stabbed him a bit harder. That wanker's been inside for three months now. He set light to a shop up in Aldershot, nearly killed a family of six. It was a miracle they all got out alive.'

I look up in shock. 'What? Steen's alive?'

He lets out another guffaw. 'Alive? I'm afraid so. But he's going to be doing stir in Wandsworth for ten years, at least, if I remember right. He had form thicker than this file and they threw the book at him.'

He leans back now, with his arms behind his head. 'We nicked him last Autumn if I remember right. Stupid bastard. There were two people who saw him and he had petrol all over his clothes. Oh yeah, and he cut his hand breaking the window.'

I'm staring at him open-mouthed as he's talking. I don't know what to say, or do.

He's laughing again, shaking his head. He's looking over at the policeman who's been standing behind me.

'Did you hear that, Constable? He's been on the run since last summer, because he thought he'd killed that wanker Dominic Steen.'

He stops himself, then gets serious and looks at me with a more kindly look on his face.

'OK, Mark. Here's where we are. You've told me that you stabbed Dominic Steen. He's alive and well and he never made any allegations of a stabbing, against you, or anyone else. We don't have any open cases for knife crimes. I checked that before you came in.

'What we do have, Mark, is an open Missing Person file. Your Uncle, Harry Oban, has been here more times than I can count. Your old boss too, Ron Greaves; he reported you missing last August. He came in with your girlfriend. What was her name? Oh yes, Melissa. You stood her up, apparently. We spoke to people at your college, your ex-foster carers, some people at the Social. We came up with nothing. You'd just got the most amazing A-Level results and then you vanished …into thin air.'

I can't speak. His words are overwhelming me and I can do nothing but sit there in stunned silence.

He laughs again. 'You had us all stumped, Mark, that's for sure. Now, here's what we're going to do. We're going to write up a little statement, saying how Steen attacked you and how, in defending yourself, you thought that you'd stabbed him. There's no evidence of any injury and no complaint against you, so you were obviously mistaken, and there's no case for you to answer. Then I'm going to pick up a Chinese for my family to make up for leaving them this afternoon.

'Oh, and we've got your pal Frank and your Uncle Harry waiting for you in Reception. I'm sure you've got some catching up to do.'

Epilogue

2020 Vision

It was a strangely subdued way for those seven turbulent months to end. A few casual words from a scruffy detective, who was part of my life for all of twenty minutes, who'd reluctantly broken away from his family weekend, and it was over.

Shock. That was my first response. Followed by relief and a surge of giddy elation, like a balloon released from its tether. Then came terror, a sudden dawning that I had no idea what to do with my newfound freedom. Finally a creeping nausea, somewhere between shame and embarrassment, that I'd spent seven months running and hiding from a phantom menace, flinging myself into pits of despair, enduring levels of hardship and danger that had nearly broken me. And all for what? For nothing.

There were other emotions mixed into that cocktail, of course. Excitement that Uncle Harry was waiting for me just a few yards away and that Frank was with him. I was hoping that they would get on, that they'd become friends, that the three of us would bond together so that I could be

346

part of something again that wasn't just me.

And then there was Melissa. I'd pretty much shut out her memory, but when the detective referred to her as *my girl-friend*, her image sprang back into my mind, for a few moments even soothing the pain inflicted by Jade.

I never saw Jade again. Or Jake. The last I heard they were caught up in the infamous Battle of the Beanfield. I remember seeing the reports on an evening news bulletin. I was convinced at the time that I saw them: Jake's head was covered in a blooded bandage and Jade was being dragged, kicking and screaming, by two truncheon-wielding policemen.

I spent a long time trying to work out what had happened that night Jade came to visit me in the van. Whose idea had it had been? What did Jade really think about me? Was anyone else involved in their plot? In the end I just gave up and let it go, letting it rest, like an unsolved crime case.

By the time of the Battle of the Beanfield, Frank had seen the writing on the wall and was off in Ireland some-where, living the traveller lifestyle amidst a more tolerant community. He lives alone and off the grid on the Welsh border now, in another old bus that he's converted.

I still see him occasionally. He's got it all set it up just the way he likes it, with log burners, solar panels and a small wind turbine for power. He grows vegetables in a small patch of land behind the bus, tomatoes and marijuana in a makeshift greenhouse, brews his own beer and makes jew-ellery that he sells when he needs the cash. He barters what he doesn't need for coffee beans from a local roast-house and there's always a dark, strong, sludgy cup of it in my hand within minutes of my arrival.

He was always self-contained, Frank, never really needed regular social interaction like the others did. I guess that's why he and Uncle Harry never got on quite as well as I thought they might. We had a good night after my release, with lots of beer and a meal in a curry house, but I'm pretty sure they never saw each other again.

Freddie's the only other one I kept in contact with. He spent one more summer touring the festivals, but then he lost the thrill of it. He ended up cutting his hair, trimming his beard and getting a job in a civil engineering company. He's been all over the world working on big projects, but the irony of the fact that he ended up as an Engineer, just like his father wanted, has never escaped him. At least he's done it his way and whenever I see him that little mischievous twinkle is still there in his eye. *'What did you put in that tea Fwederwick,'* will forever be the punchline that bonds us.

I lost contact altogether with the others. Abi and Travis had a baby girl in May and I heard they'd got a house together in Yeovil some time after that. Rick was in a half-decent Indie band that had one big album in the late-eighties, but I never saw him, or Pete, again.

In the days after my reprieve, I went to stay with Uncle Harry in Putney. Frank went back to Somerset the next morning, so then it was just the two of us in his little flat. It was strange being there. He was on tenterhooks around me, as if he was anxious that I might disappear again if he turned his back for a second.

I guess he must have blamed himself for everything that happened. With hindsight, it's easy to conclude that he never really fulfilled his responsibilities to me after my parents died, but I've never blamed him. He was the polar opposite of my dad, an itinerant blues guitarist to counterpose my grey-suited accountant father. He did his best and that's good enough for me.

True to form, he bought me a guitar for my nineteenth birthday: another great present that I still own. It sits in one corner of my study, alongside a second guitar that I got to mark my fortieth birthday. He must have been feeling flush after a successful US tour and an album that sold a few thousand copies. We spent hours over the next couple of weeks practicing together. In the evenings we went out to his local pub, The Half Moon. There were usually bands playing in their back room and they knew my Uncle so well that they usually just waived us in for free.

He introduced me to his band mates and I even did a few gigs with them in the back rooms of pubs around London. I wasn't up to their standard to play guitar, so I stood at the back and played some harp and joined in on the backing vocals. They were amazingly tight and professional and played to studiously adulating crowds, but for me it lacked the raucous intensity of AlienNation's gigs at the Prince of Wales.

After a few days I went back to Farnham to visit Ron. He was overjoyed to see me, treating me like a long-lost son. He even closed the shop for a couple of hours and took me out for a cup of tea and a sandwich. Then we went up to my old flat at the top, where he'd neatly packed all my possessions into a couple of cardboard boxes. It felt like a different life: those few months of freedom waiting for my exam results, waiting for something to happen, anything except what actually happened.

I could soon see that staying with Uncle Harry wasn't a long-term solution, so I started working on a plan for my future. With my A-Level results, I was able to get a place at Bristol University to study History and I moved there in the early summer of 1982, getting bar work to pay my rent until the first term started.

My life rose on an upward curve after that. Starting again at university in a new city was exactly the clean slate that I'd needed. It didn't feel like it at the time, but those seven months of 1981, into 1982, had helped me to purge all sorts of demons. In the darkest moments of that storm of Halloween 1981, I'd finally started coming to terms with my grieving for my lost family. The pain was still there, but it was the start of an acceptance. For the first time I'd found a way to express it, to make a space for them which was positive, a guiding light rather than a stick with which to beat myself.

My time at the camp in Norton may have ended with an explosion, but I still owe them all so much. They rescued me in every sense of the word. When they found me I was in a pitiful state, physically and emotionally. It was no wonder Freddie thought I looked like Gollum. I had been so alone and so down on myself that I'd become a ghost, hiding from, rather than participating in, the world. Left to fend for myself, I surely wouldn't have lasted much longer.

My relationships there resurrected me. They each taught me something, or helped me, in their own way. Even Jake. With their help and friendship, I pulled myself back from the brink, rebuilt my self-esteem and slowly started to believe in myself again.

So, when I went to Bristol I did so with a confidence that I could fit in, meet new people and participate fully in a new community. And that's exactly what I did. I threw myself into my studies and made friendships that endure to this day. I had a lucky break when Uncle Harry told me that my parents had left me money. It had been placed in a Trust and came to me when I turned twenty-one, allowing me to buy a flat in Bristol and commit to a PhD at the end of my first degree.

That was only the start of my good fortune, because it was on my PhD programme that I met Maddy: the love of my life. We were inseparable from almost the first moment we met. She had so much wisdom, so much compassion, the most beautiful person I have ever known and I couldn't believe that she could see beauty in me too.

From the earliest point of our relationship we were able to talk about anything and everything with a spirit of openness and mutual understanding, trust and respect, that I have never got close to before or since. There were no taboo subjects, no areas that were off-limits, no offence taken and even when we did argue, we were quick to make up and forgive.

Maddy had completed her first degree in Geology in London and came to Bristol for her PhD. The process of researching and writing up a thesis can be a long and lonely one and we helped each other through it with humour, gentle encouragement and joint field trips. At the start of our second year she moved into my flat. In 1990, with careful synchronicity, we submitted our Theses at the same time and, the week after receiving our doctorates, were married at a Bristol Registry Office.

We weren't in a hurry to settle into academic life, so instead of a short luxurious honeymoon we loaded a pair of backpacks and set off for an indefinite period that quickly turned into a year. They were probably the happiest days of my life, but when two lecture posts became available at Exeter we were ready for them.

The arrival of Charlie was the biggest blessing of all. There was never any doubt that our son would be called Charlie, after my lost brother. Maddy suggested it before I had even raised it, with her usual telepathic instinct. How I wish we could have made a brother or sister for him, but Maddy became ill, even before his second birthday.

Maddy bore her illness with the same grace that she bore everything. She never gave in to the cancer, but accepted it as a new part of her, like an uninvited guest, communicating with it, getting to know it and quietly hoping that one day it would depart. Twice we dared to hope that it had gone. Then, shortly after Charlie's thirteenth birthday, it returned with a vengeance.

By the Spring of 2013 she knew that she was dying. We sat and talked about it, just like we talked about everything. I tried to shy away from it initially, trying to persuade her, and myself, that she'd recover, but she wouldn't let me get away with that. She wasn't afraid of death. She was ready for it, just wanted to make sure that Charlie and I were too.

At the end of August she moved into a hospice. I'll keep in my mind forever the image of the three of us joining hands by her bedside. She looked us both in the eye and made us promise to look after each other and to make her proud. She'd lost all of her hair, her skin was pallid and pasty, but there was a serenity in her eyes that held us, telling us that she was ready and we should be as well. Two days later she was gone.

From that moment forwards my only concern was Charlie. I suppressed my own grief to try and protect him. Suppression: still my default emotional response mechanism. I understood intellectually, of course, that grief is something you can't force down. Like putting a cork in a volcano, it will just erupt from a different place, with greater force and causing more damage. But emotional honesty is always easier said than done.

I made sure that Charlie got the best help from professional counsellors. And he responded well. I gave him space for the tears and the tantrums, the rage that was often aimed at me. I felt like Uncle Harry at times, but I was never going to leave him alone. His teachers, and even his schoolmates, seemed to understand and cut him some slack. And slowly, slowly he emerged from the other side.

Unlike me. Over two years later, my anger exploded twice in quick succession, first with colleagues at the university and then with a pair of my students. I was lucky that the Dean knew Maddy and I so well. I could easily have been dismissed, but instead I was taken off teaching duties for a couple of terms to *focus on a research project*.

I sat here in my study for the best part of the next year and sank into a depression. A depression that only Charlie was able to lift. I went regularly to see my counsellor, but I was obstructive and evasive, dancing around his probing with deft dialectic diversions. Or I thought they were deft. He just indulged me patiently, waiting for me to me to be ready, or for me to leak a rare moment of emotional honesty. I was paying by the hour. Who was the fool there?

At the time I thought I was dealing with it all very well. I convinced myself that I was being strong for Charlie and that my maturity and wisdom was helping him through his issues. It's easy with hindsight to see how deeply in denial I really was and how much damage I was doing by suppressing everything.

It was the night of Charlie's 'A' Level results in 2017 that proved the turning point. He'd done so well, exceeding his expected grades, and his place at Durham was in the bag. I had every confidence in him, I'd seen how hard he'd worked, but it was still a tense moment watching him open the results. I loved seeing the expression on his face go from fearful to elated.

To mark the occasion we drove down to the coast for a good lunch, just the two of us. In the evening he went out with his schoolmates to celebrate. I'm delighted that he has so many good friends. Why wouldn't he? He's inherited Maddy's charisma and social graces.

Once he'd gone I made myself a light supper and sat in the garden with a glass of wine. It was a balmy evening, the sun warm on my face as it dipped over the trees. I stayed there until the sun had set, then retired to my study. I've never been able to go to bed when Charlie's still out, so I was ready for a long wait.

The warmth of the evening, the chill of the wine and, not least, my joy at Charlie's achievements filled me with a warm, contended glow and the cocoon of my study drew me in with its familiar smells and tones. I poured a glass of single malt whisky that I'd been saving: inhaling it, then sipping it, savouring its peaty smoothness.

Then I decided to roll a joint. The little wrap of marijuana was still there in my drawer from my last trip up to Herefordshire to see Frank. It was years since I'd rolled one and smoked it on my own, but it felt like an appropriate thing to do somehow. I've never managed to master the art of rolling, like Freddie or Frank, but I could still get it tight enough for the tobacco and the weed to burn smoothly.

As I sat, indulging myself, I contemplated just how proud I was of Charlie and how proud Maddy would have been too. I don't quite know how, but at some point that golden glow started to fade and storm clouds bubbled up from nowhere to darken my mood.

All Charlie's achievements: how fragile they suddenly seemed, as though a single puff of malevolent wind could shatter his nascent dreams. I found myself watching the clock with growing anxiety and, as I did, the second hand slowed to a crawl around the dial, as if forestalling some inevitable, impending doom.

I'd spent many a night waiting up for Charlie, but that

night the terror seized me by the throat and throttled. First came a sadness that Maddy wasn't there to share it, then a gnawing cynical voice reminding me that every time something good had happened in my life it had been snatched away. I remembered that it was thirty-six years to the day when *I* had disappeared: A-Level results day 1981. Symmetry and coincidence have always frightened me, but this one sucked the wind out of me.

As the clock inched past midnight I became convinced that something terrible was unfurling. Visions of catastrophe seized me: a car misjudging the bend at the bottom of the hill. I could see it on its roof, wheels still spinning, its twisted wreckage fused with the scarred limbs of a smouldering oak. My head filled with the acrid stench of rubber and oil, of earth and bark ploughed and scorched. I heard the joy of a moment shattered, then absorbed by the silence of the forest casually accepting the offering.

I could do nothing, but sit and wait and watch the clock. I picked up my guitar and strummed a few chords. I breathed out some notes on my harp, just like I used to hiding out in the woods in Montacute, but each time I looked up at the clock it had barely moved.

Paranoid delusions possessed me, intertwining Charlie with my own eighteen-year-old self, running and hiding from what turned out to be a phantom peril. If only I could have been there to give my younger self a few words of advice. How much trouble and heartache I could have saved myself with a few carefully chosen words. I had been so alone in the darkest moments. I didn't want the same for Charlie. I wanted to be there for him. To save him from all those dangers that lurked in the shadows, dangers for which he was, as yet, unequipped to deal.

The raw emotions of 1981 poured back into me, merging with my newer grief until, together, they consumed me. Charlie would be on his way to university soon and then I would be completely on my own again, knocking around in this big house in the middle of nowhere. I hate self-pity, but in that moment I had no self-defence. The floodwaters of my grief swelled up, from the dark depths into which I'd consigned them, and washed me away.

Charlie returned, of course he did. A couple more hours had passed. I heard the crunch of his tyres on the driveway and I tried vainly to pull myself together, but I saw a look of horror on his face as he came in through the door.

'Dad! Are you OK?'

'Yeah. Yeah. Of course. How was your evening?'

He wasn't so easily fooled. He pulled a chair over and came and sat with me. Then, seeing the whisky, he poured us both a glass. After a minute, he sniffed the air and looked at me in amazement:

'Hey, Dad. Have you been on the wacky baccy?'

I laughed, what else could I do.

We sat up until the sun was rising the next morning. We shared most of the rest of that bottle, even smoked a couple of joints together. It was probably the first man-to-man conversation that we'd ever had. It wouldn't be the last. Something in our relationship changed that night. Like him it had matured, enriching itself, becoming truer.

We talked about Maddy, his mother, my wife, about our memories of her and how sorely we missed her. He astonished me by telling me how worried he'd been that I wasn't coping with my grief. How remote I'd become. How bad-tempered. How difficult to be with. He'd even talked about it with his counsellor, asking him for advice on how he could best help me. All that effort, on pretending-away my grief, to be strong for Charlie and it turned out that it was *him* helping *me*. I had to laugh. He was definitely his mother's boy.

'Have I ever told you about my A-Level results day?' I asked him.

He knew that he was named after my lost brother, that was part of our family folklore, but I'd never told him about that before. He listened with rapt attention, expressing astonishment, asking questions, shaking his head in disbelief. At the end I told him how I wished that I could go back in time to give my younger self some advice, to help myself through some of those darker moments.

Charlie laughed: 'Dad. I think you did amazingly to deal with all of that. I bet you wouldn't get through it now. You had all that strength and energy and belief. And what happened then made you what you are now. Maybe you need to reconnect with some of that now? I won't be here to look after you forever, Dad!'

We both laughed at that last bit. Only he could get away with a remark like that. But it was the wisdom of his words that really got me. All this time I'd wanted to reach back to my younger self to help *him*, but maybe Charlie was right, maybe what I really needed was to bring my younger self to me, to draw on his youthful vigour and resilience, to tap into that youthful capacity to absorb the new, to adapt and to reinvent. It took my son to draw this to my attention.

I started to muse on how I could achieve that, but then Charlie gave me the answer to that as well.

'It's an amazing story, Dad. I think you should write it down. It would make a great novel.'

And that's what I spent much of the next two years doing. Charlie went off to Durham at the end of September. The day before he left we went down to the cemetery to lay some flowers on Maddy's grave. It was the fourth anniversary of her death. We're the same height now and we stood side by side, bowed our heads and then embraced.

'She'd have been proud of you, Charlie. And I'm proud too. You're going to love university life. I know it.'

He smiled. 'Thanks, Dad.'

I drove Charlie up to his new lodgings in Durham. His excitement at what lay ahead energised me too. I spent a few days on the drive back, calling in on some old friends, but as soon as I was back I started work on this novel.

I made many false starts. How do you remember the truth after such a long time has passed? Was I remembering it as it actually was, or as I would like it to have been? As an Historian, I know better then anyone that memory and time distort reality. From the moment an event happens we are changing it, adding new upgrades each time we revisit, like a solitary game of Chinese Whispers. Sometimes they are great leaps of fictional delusion, but more often than not they are subtle shifts almost too small to notice: little details omitted, moments shuffled together, external influences absorbed.

I'm used to dealing with stories from the past, but they are other people's stories. When I look at original source materials, I expect them to be different, even when they are describing the same event. I take pleasure in deciphering them, seeking to understand each source (their positions, their interests, their cognitive characteristics and biases and all the other factors that could have influenced and informed their perspective), so that collectively I can piece them together into a more coherent, credible reality, to improve our understanding of a moment in time.

Now, there I was, trying to do the same thing with myself, and with all of the others who were part of those seven months. At first I distrusted my own memories as unreliable, too entangled with who I am now, or at least with how I now perceive myself. I tried to focus instead on deduction from the undisputable hard facts, but that's an impossible task when you're dealing with yourself.

I had to keep reminding myself why I was doing this. It wasn't just about piecing together a dead piece of history, to be fact-checked and peer-reviewed before publication. This was about reconnecting with my younger self, to put myself back into his skin, so that I could once again see and hear, smell and touch, all those moments that I had experienced back in 1981 and 1982.

That was when I decided I had to write the story as if my eighteen year old self was living and breathing it as it happened. For that, it had to be in his voice, not mine.

I made a breakthrough when I found a load of my old diaries. Maddy used to laugh at my tendency to hoard, but now it was payback. I found the moth-eaten, mouldy notebook that I'd clung to in the woods near Montacute, its pages stuck together with thirty-six-year old Somerset mud. Those spidery, smudged scrawlings, just a few words for each day, reconnected me with those emotions with a visceral intensity that rocked me. They were like a highly concentrated juice; I just had to add some water and it all came swirling back to life, as if I'd never left.

Suddenly I was filling pages of notebooks with those memories and the walls of my study disappeared under diagrams, time charts and maps of the areas that I'd crossed. It's been a long road to get it all in order, with many turns that I'd forgotten and many stretches that I've had to reenvisage, or question my own memory.

In the summer of 2018 I returned to Farnham with a backpack and walked from there to Montacute, following the route I took from my old diary notes. Back in 1981 I did it in six days. It took my older self the best part of two weeks and by the end I was feeling every day of my age, blistered and aching and wrung out.

I hung around in Montacute for nearly a week afterwards, staying in a little B&B above a vintage toyshop. I was delighted to find that the woods where I'd hidden all those years ago had been inhabited by a group of environmentalists calling themselves Tinker's Bubble. They'd built themselves timber houses amidst the trees that looked somewhat sturdier than the bivouac that collapsed on me on Halloween 1981. And just like my old group, they'd brewed their own cider. I bought several bottles and sat drinking it as I wrote up my notes.

I've also spent time with Frank and with Freddie. I didn't want to lead them too much. I wanted their memories of what happened to come from them, to challenge mine, to inspire new ideas. They didn't disappoint. Freddie's account of Jade giving me a blowback had me creased up and Frank challenged my perceptions with his typical mix of understatement and rhetorical flourish.

As I wrote I immersed myself in this reconnection with myself: with my journey, with who I was and with who I am now. Outside the waters of the world were becoming ever more turbulent, but I largely dismissed them, paddling my way through my own backwaters. The aftermath of the Brexit vote, the madness of Donald Trump, the rise of a pandemic, were all just background noise to me.

I returned to teaching and all of my colleagues told me there was a new calmness to me. I reconnected with friends that I had neglected and they welcomed me back with a warmth that humbled me.

We even got our old folk band, The Cobbetts, playing again. I'd been the frontman, but I had lost the impetus when Maddy became ill again and it fizzled out. We were never that good, and we still weren't, but we resumed rehearsing with renewed vigour and started playing the odd gig again in local pubs, until the virus put a stop to it, with a new edge of comedic self-deprecation and socio-political commentary.

Half way through my writing I started wondering about what had happened to Melissa. I'd been intrigued ever since that detective described her as *my girlfriend*. Social media was a luxury my generation never had growing up, something that Charlie always finds hysterically funny, but now it's a lifeline to broken connections.

To my amazement I found her almost instantly. It was a coincidence that she was at Exeter from 1981 to 1984, but when I looked she was right there on the alumni network site. After completing an English degree, she had gone into publishing and was now an Editor at one of the big houses.

I sent her a connection request through Linked In and got a reply within hours: 'Wow – thought you'd disappeared in 1981! Would love to catch up. Must be a story there!!'

Melissa became more than just a missing piece in my story. She was one of the first to read what I'd written, gave me sage advice and introduced me to one of her favourite literary agents. I would probably never have got this published without her advice and connections.

But it was more than that. There was a deeper relationship developing, which excited and frightened me in equal measure. One evening I told her that I was still grieving for Maddy, probably always would be, that I didn't know when, if ever, I would be ready for another relationship. I half-expected her to slap me for being so presumptive, but she seemed to understand before I'd even made my little speech.

She has grown-up children and went through a painful divorce, which was a form of loss in its own right. Over this last year it feels as though we've been able to help each other with the process of healing and learning how to move forward. Well, certainly she has helped me, I hope that I've helped her is some small way too. We've become closer than I ever expected was possible with another women and, as I think about it now, I think that Maddy would have approved.

Saturday, the 6th of June, will be Charlie's twenty-first birthday. He should be here by Thursday evening and then his new girlfriend, Hannah, will be arriving the following night. We were planning a big celebration, but this damn virus has put paid to all that. We'd booked a country house hotel with a tented extension at the back. The Cobbetts were going to play a special set followed by another band with some of Charlie's friends. Even Uncle Harry was going to do a turn. Just shy of his eightieth birthday and he can still crank out the chords.

It's another sacrifice to this strange year, but I'm more worried about Charlie than myself. I'm quite self-contained here, but his Finals were cancelled, together with all those university events and celebrations that would have marked the end of that period of his life. At least he will come away with a good degree, but I do feel he's had to miss out on a lot.

After much thought, I decided to tell him about Melissa. It felt like a betrayal of Maddy, admitting to a new relationship, but he was overjoyed. I had planned to tentatively probe whether it would be an appropriate time to introduce her, but he beat me to it, insisting that he wanted to meet her. So, on Saturday, I've now planned a barbeque here for the four of us and we'll uncork some fizz to toast him. Later in the evening we've got something rigged up on Zoom, so that he can have a virtual party with all his friends.

Rather selfishly, I'm glad that I will get a day to spend alone with Charlie. I want to speak with him about his plans for the future. I think that he wants to follow Maddy and I into academia, which I am pleased about. Maddy left some money that she wanted me to use to set him up, as my parents did for me. So, I want to talk about buying a flat for him wherever he chooses to set up home.

I also want to tell him about the publishing contract for my novel that is now finalised. As he was involved from the conception of the idea, I want to give him the first copy. I think he will like that.

There is one more thing that I want to give him. It's something that has become part of me; something that has been there for me through all of the ups and downs of my life; something that has given me a connection to the past that was torn from me. Now, I want my father's watch to be a link to the future too. As I sit here, feeling its reassuring presence on my wrist, I feel myself swelling with pride at the thought that soon my son will be wearing it on his wrist.

The End

To find out more about *The Hidden Road*, including discussion on the themes raised and a music playlist, please visit www.andrewtamworth.com